"THEY COME!"
A VOICE SHOUTED.
"THEY ATTACK!"

Istvan raced to the battle. Sword poised behind his head he dashed in among the scrambling, leaping men, staring over his shield's rim at the enemy soldier who turned toward him, dripping blade raised high.

Then that red-smeared sword lashed down at his head; his shield blocked his sight as it thundered on his arm. His swiveling wrist wheeled his hilt in his palm as his blade flew above his falling shield to follow the other sword back, flying at the startled eyes beneath the helmet's rim.

The other shield lifted too late: Istvan felt his edge break through bone, felt the tug on the steel as the man died and the corpse fell. Wrenching the blade free, he ran on, into a wild storm where sharp-edged death swayed like wind-whipped boughs in a thicket of steel. Red rain spattered: men's voices wailed under the thunder of shields.

A GATHERING OF HEROES

PAUL EDWIN ZIMMER

ACE BOOKS, NEW YORK

This book is an Ace original
edition, and has never been
previously published.

A GATHERING OF HEROES

An Ace Book / published by arrangement with
the author

PRINTING HISTORY
Ace edition / September 1987

ISBN: 0-441-27421-8

Ace Books are published by The Berkley Publishing Group,
200 Madison Avenue, New York, NY 10016.
The name ''Ace'' and the ''A'' logo
are trademarks belonging to Charter Communications, Inc.
PRINTED IN THE UNITED STATES OF AMERICA

10 9 8 7 6 5 4 3 2 1

For MOM
and all
who love Elves and Dwarves and Heroes

CONTENTS

CHARACTERS

MORTALS:
Men:

Istvan DiVega: Captain of Seynyorean mercenaries, and Master of the Three Swords School; born near the foot of Hastur's Mountain, in Carcosa in Seynyor on the other side of the world. Veteran of many battles along the Dark Border, he is famed in song as "Istvan the Archer"—a name he hates. He bears a blade forged by the Hasturs.

Prince Tahion: Rightful King of Aldinor, and Lord of Aldinor's Living Forest. Though mortal, he bears the memory of all the Lords of the Forest, even back to the Age of Peace. Born in exile in the Elfwoods in Y'gora, he has kin among the elves, and studied magic at Elthar along with Arthfayel and Calmar. The Sword of the Kings of Aldinor was forged in Ages before the most ancient legends: tradition says it has been thrice broken and thrice reforged; each time with magic greater than the last.

Carroll Mac Lir: most famous of the heroes of Y'gora. He has battled the armies of Sarlow before, and has fought against Grom Beardless, and even against the invincible Svaran, and lived to tell the tale.

Ingulf Mac Fingold: Hua Eliron (called *Ingulf the Wanderer*, or *Ingulf the Mad*) is from the island of Trey Ithir in the Airarian Empire. He has been to the City of the Sea-Elves, where men do not go, and bears a sword from the

Land of the Ever-Living, as well as the deadly bladed flail of the outer islands. His father, Fingold, was swordmaster of the Clan Hua Eliron.

Anarod Mac Moran of Clan Eamon: famous warrior of Elantir, and woods-runner of Elthar, who left Elantir to dwell with Eilith of Clan Gileran, a cousin to Prince Tahion, in her home near the Elfwoods. He bears a sword forged by the Hasturs.

Arthfayel Mac Ronan: Adept of Elthar, and foster-brother to Anarod Mac Moran.

Calmar Mac Tahal of Clan Eamon: Healer and Adept of Elthar; an old friend of Tahion and Arthfayel, who had thought him long dead.

Fithil Mac Murgad of the Curranach: swordmaster of Clan MacAran, from the island of Tongorem, part of the Airarian Empire. His favored weapon is the war-scythe of the Curranach.

Starn: chief of Clan MacMalkom.

Flann MacMalkom: Starn's bodyguard.

Fergus Mac Trenar: King's Champion of Elantir.

Garahis of Ordan: a knight of Cairanor.

Finloq Mac Alangal: woods-runner and wizard trained in Elthar, a son of Clan Gileran, though some say he is a Changeling. The elves often call him "Finloq Mac B'an."

Dair Mac Eykin: forest-runner of Elthar; bearer of a Hastur-blade.

Aillil Mac Aillil: a forest-runner.

Karik Mac Ulatoc: a stranger from islands far to the east.

Cormac Mac Angdir: harper, warrior, and wizard.

Conn Mac Bran: world-ranging adventurer, plotting to seize the throne of Airaria.

Larthon Mac Kehar: slayer of trolls, an Airarian companion of Conn.

Layareh Mac Lohar: (called Layareh the Proud) of Clan Ua Kellyn, swordmaster of the Bleeding Wind School, from the islands east of Y'gora (part of the Airarian Empire), exiled with Conn.

Hrivown: a knight of Cotarjon allied with Conn.

Peridir: a knight of Cotarjon allied with Conn

Lamon of Atliprecan: a knight of Cotarjon allied with Conn.

Gurthir: an adventurer from Ualtime and one of Conn's followers.

Yolaru of the Ua Cadell: chief of the Clan that lives in the forest below Rath Tintallain.

Alphth the Changeling: a mortal boy raised among Elves.

Dwarves:

Cruadorn: smith of Rath Tintallain.

King Aurothror: Dwarf-Lord of Rath Tintallain, co-equal ruler with Arderillon.

Prince Tyrin of Dunsloc: Ruler of a great dwarf city far in the south, deep in the Forest of Demons.

Ogar Hammerhand: warrior in the guard of Prince Tyrin.

Thubar: warrior in the guard of Prince Tyrin.

IMMORTALS:

Kandol Shadowslayer, the Hastur-Lord: eldest living Hastur, born in Nardis before its fall, five thousand years ago; famed in song for destroying the Web of Shadows created by Nargil in Bircrandbar, during the great war in which the Land of Galdor was laid waste.

Aldamir Hastur: most skilled of the younger Hasturs in reading the fan-shaped roads of the future.

Tuarim Mac Elathan: the greatest of the heroes of the elves. His deeds in the company of Hero-King Fendol have been sung for five thousand years: through the centuries his power and skill have grown. He destroyed the last vampires in Y'gora centuries ago; he wounded the great dragon Komanthodel and slew his mate. But he has not been among mortal men for centuries.

Ardcrillon Crystalweaver: Lord of the Elves of Rath Tintallain.

Artholon Mac Ioldan: his brother
Arduiad Mac Artholon: his son, a famed elf archer.
Brithlain: the daughter of Artholon.
Tarithwen: the mother of Ardcrillon and Artholon.

Ethellin the Wise: leader of the Sea-Elves

Dorialith: a Sea-Elf, said to know more of mortals than any of his people save Ethellin the Wise. Friend to Ingulf.

Falmoran: a Sea-Elf, a great lord and sea captain from the Land of the Ever-Living.

Liogar and Z'jar: part of the Mystery of the Hyades; silver swallows from another Universe who fly on starlight through the Hyadean Gate to the aid of the Children of Hastur. Also known as the Birds of Morvinion.

Among the Foes they must face are—

Svaran: commander of the armies of Sarlow, whose invulnerable armour is tempered to resist even a Hastur-blade.

Grom Beardless: skilled and deadly swordsman, a captain of the soldiers of Sarlow.

Vor Half-Troll: head and shoulders taller than other men, one of the most feared captains of the armies of Sarlow.

Komanthodel: the last Great Dragon on Y'gora—until his brood has grown. He has not been seen outside his cave for centuries, but his children hunt the land for miles around.

The Tromdoel: one of the Great Dyoles from Beyond the World.

The Island Continent of **Ygora**

CHAPTER ONE

The Call

The forest-scented wind hinted at magic as it blew across the water of the bay. Above his head, Istvan DiVega heard the sharp slap of canvas, and the shouting of the seamen as they scrambled in the rigging, but his eyes were held by the storied shore, and his mind by memories of tales told him in youth.

Behind him, unbroken ocean reached the horizon where the twin suns sank toward his distant home, halfway 'round the world. Their light gilded the great bay before him, gleaming on crystal towers rising from the thick green trees, and painting little houses mystic hues. It had been more than fifteen years since he had last walked the streets of ancient Elthar, or spoken with those eldest of all Immortals who dwell there. Deeply as he longed to be home in Carcosa far away, after all these months of fighting on the far eastern shores of the island continent of Y'gora, still Istvan found himself wishing that the ship could stop longer here . . .

There was a soft whisper of displaced air at his back. Swordsman's reflexes brought him around, hand flying to hilt: he heard men gasp on the deck. But his hand dropped away from his sword as he saw the blue robe on the red-haired man who had appeared out of the air behind him, and recognised the broad face and blue eyes of Aldamir Hastur.

1

Istvan DiVega was Carcosan born and bred: his bow, though formal, bore no hint of the deference another might have shown to one of the Guardians of the World, for to the proud nobles of Seynyor, the House of Hastur is but one of the great families of *the Land of the Lords*.

"My Lord Aldamir," he murmured, and smiled at the gasps of the Nydoreans as the Hastur mirrored his bow, the greeting of one Seynyorean nobleman to another.

"My Lord Istvan," Aldamir replied. "I understand your company has finished its term of service with the Airarian Empire? That you are now free for hire?"

"A Hastur need never speak of hire to a DiVega," Istvan said stiffly, rebuke in his voice. "Where shall we march? When? It will take us—" he paused, thinking, sorting with his mind the gear below decks—"three hours perhaps, and we will be ready. Command us."

"It is not the company whose services we need," the Immortal said "but your own." Istvan blinked in surprise, and ran fingers through grizzled black hair. Aldamir smiled. "It is your sword-arm we need, and not an army." Pride rose through Istvan's confusion: trumpets played in his heart. "No army could fight its way to where we ask you to go: your road is a path for a few. Have you ever heard of—"his voice dropped to a whisper— *"Rath Tintallain?"* Istvan shook his head; Y'gora was filled with similar names.

"It is an elf fortress, built above a city of the dwarves, and there elf and dwarf together guard for the Hasturs a secret of which I will not speak. But on all the paths of the Future, now, we see an attack, and great danger and destruction should Rath Tintallain fall. Will you go?"

Glancing quickly around, Istvan saw Nydorean sailors openly staring, while his countrymen pretended, with amused tolerance, that the appearance of an Immortal upon their ship was an everyday affair, not worthy of curiosity or notice.

"I—of course I will go," said Istvan. "But I do not understand how my single sword can aid you. And why should a city warded by elves—and by your kin—need the aid of any mortal man?"

"Not even the Hasturs can see the true future," said Aldamir, "nor know which of the many branchings we do see it may take. Our meeting today I have seen on many branchings, and always the future is more hopeful upon those roads that lead from it. And you will not be alone. But remember that the sword you bear was wrought by Earnur Hastur, and some call the arm that wields it one of the most skilled in the world.''

"Aha!'' Istvan exclaimed. "I knew it! You've got me mixed up with my cousin Raquel!'' Aldamir laughed.

"Not so! Your cousin Raquel is in Heyleu, counting up the money from his last campaign and considering an invitation from his old friend Birthran, swordmaster of the House of Ore, to visit at the Court of Kadar. No, my lord, there is no mistake.

"A party of picked warriors will gather tonight: if you would join them, you need but ride before midnight to the Inn of the Silver Axe, at the crossroads by Nockarv.''

"Should I not take Alar D'Ascoli with me?'' Istvan asked. "He is trained both as wizard and warrior, while my only skill is the sword.''

"Of wizards, Lord DiVega, there will be no lack,'' said Aldamir. "But time grows short. It is a long ride to Nockarv hill. You may go or stay, but you must decide soon, to be there by midnight. Fare well!''

The Immortal vanished as suddenly as he had come, and Istvan faced empty air that rippled like the air above a fire.

He was aware of the curious eyes of the Nydoreans, and of furtive glances from his own men. The twin suns had reached the sea, and were sinking in a splendour of peacock light. Alar D'Ascoli came slowly toward him, curiosity raging in dark eyes.

"Take command,'' Istvan told him, "and when you get home, see that every man is properly paid. It seems I am to stay in Y'gora for a time.'' D'Ascoli's eyebrows rose.

"What is it about?''

"If I knew that,'' Istvan snorted, "I might have the sense to go home and forget it all!''

It was full dark by the time the boat put him ashore, and then he had to arrange for a horse. A flight of little moons soared up ahead of him as he picked out his road and urged the horse to a steady trot through the streets of Elthar.

Midnight, Aldamir had said. As he left the docks behind, the houses grew wider apart, nestled among groves of trees. That made him homesick for Carcosa. Bright archways opened in the ground, doorways down into the dwarf city. On either hand, the guarding towers flamed atop the great black hills that cradled the city between them.

The trees thickened as he left the mortal sector behind; the trees themselves were citizens of Elthar, with rights protected by the Elf-Folk. Leaves rustled in the wind, and faint music and laughter sounded in the trees. A bright-eyed, delicate face glanced briefly from the branches above the road. Elf-lights glimmered among the leaves.

Earth reared up in a sudden wall before him, while the road dived into a well-lit tunnel, iron gates ajar. Dwarf soldiers in gleaming mail leaned on broad axes. Their eyes moved over him quickly; they saw the Hastur-blade at his side, and nodded. He left Elthar behind, and rode east on the broad road that led to the mountain land of Tumbalia, at the edge of the Forest of Demons.

Tiny moons hurtled between the stars: shadows around him shifted and changed. His horse was nervous and his sword-hand tense, although he knew it was seldom any Night-Thing dared come so close to Elthar. This was elvish country, and their eyes would be upon him.

He pondered Aldamir's words. It was true, perhaps, that he had some talent for coming through battles alive, and he did bear a Hastur-blade.

But it still did not make sense. He had grown up at the feet of the Mountains of the Clouds, where Hastur's fortress of Carcosa rises amid eternal snow, and he knew well the power of its Immortal dwellers. The thought of the Hasturs asking anyone's aid was not comforting.

The big moon, Domri, rose like a huge white mountain from the horizon, and by its wan light he saw the slopes of Nockarv hill a pallid green. It was still an hour or more before midnight. He rode toward the window lights that clustered in the hill's shadow.

He came to the crossroads, and trotted across the broad highway that stretched across the long miles from Cairanor and the Dwarf Kingdom, south beyond Elantir. He had never ridden that way, although he had ridden north on that road, to the realm of the Two Kings in Galinor. He had been little more than a boy, then, serving with Cousin Raquel in old Belos Robardin's company. The Two Kings had hired them to drive back an invasion from Sarlow . . .

So long ago! He reined his horse before the gigantic, earth-brown inn, its peaked and gabled roof like a range of triangular mountains against the moon-filled sky. Four smaller buildings stood dark, but the windows before him blazed with light.

Domri climbed free of the horizon, floating like some gigantic pearl, dwarfing lesser moons to mere sparks. The sight took Istvan back to his childhood in a surge of emotion: the big moon had not been visible from the continent since his youth, and would not rise there again for more than twenty years. He might well be long dead by then.

Two harried-looking small boys with excited, grimy faces, were dashing about outside the door, trying to tend what seemed a herd of horses: more than a dozen were still tied under the painted silver axe, though the boys led them to the stables by twos and threes.

Dismounting, Istvan wrapped his reins around the hitching post, and then, after a moment's thought, pulled his shield and the heavy bag that held helmet and tight-rolled mail-shirt from the saddle. He tossed a coin glittering through torchlight into a grubby urchin's hand. Stepping up the stairs to face the richly carved old brown door, he heard behind him high boys' voices.

"Where's *he* from? Never saw no one like that!"

"From over the Western Sea. A Seynyorean he is, from Hastur's Mountain!" Awe in the voice reminded Istvan that here *he* was the wonder, from the world's other side.

The curlicues and spirals and legendary heroes on the story-carved oak door swung back from his touch, opening on a booming noise of men's voices and laughter, and a glare of firelight.

The room throbbed with light from a huge hearth, piled high with flaming logs. Pillars and panels of brown polished wood glowed warm wine-red: tiny fluttering candles were like stars around the room. As Istvan stepped through the portal, the many-voiced roaring fell to murmuring, and he felt dozens of keen eyes turned upon him, searching him from head to toe.

"DiVega!" a voice shouted, and Istvan saw a big-boned blond man waving at him from one of the tables. The voice was familiar, but he could not place the man, dressed in a brown shirt and a kilt of smoky blue tartan, bare-legged in the usual Y'goran way.

Noisy voices rose again as he felt gazes turned away. He set out for the table where the man had stood, dodging out of the path of a bustling servant woman with a roast and four beer mugs balanced on a tray. A massive man, broad-shouldered, black-bearded, in a tunic of purple and blue checks, moved out of his path between the tables with cat-like grace, surprising in so huge a man.

Now individual voices rose out of the crowd.

". . . summer, the daughter of Falmoran, and she was as sweet as the piping of Ciallglind, and her eyes were as . . ."

". . . cut his way out, they say, and fled into the forest. So now Conn Mac Bran is in exile, and some say that he is in Cotarjon, and plotting with Athprecan's younger brother—they do say that one fancies himself quite the kingmaker." Cups rattled loudly.

". . . and struck it off. 'My curse upon you!' says the head . . ."

". . . under the ground, and a good vein it was, too. But the posts must be set in carefully, or the roof will go . . ."

". . . safe, but Grom Beardless came down from Sarlow with a horde of his butchers, and a skull-headed, shriveled sorcerer to aid them, and slaughtered men, women, children, and dragged off as slaves those left alive."

"Aye. Vor Half-Troll would have done the same at Ardaraq, had Carroll and Anarod not chanced to be there. It was Anarod who drove back the . . ."

". . . if his song cannot move her, then I am forever lost and alone in the evil world, and mocked by . . ."

". . . near a jest. Tormac himself laughed as he died. You never saw a merrier fight. And even his own kin did not like that stingy little tyrant, Tormac Beag Mac Cuon. Yet the Piper Athev made a lament for him some call the saddest music ever made by mortal man . . ."

"Even old Komanthodel stirs, they say, and the young dragons roam each . . ."

". . . the black one from the hills . . ."

Istvan rounded a table of dwarves. The man who had hailed him was sitting alone, and he saw in surprise that it was Tahion, Prince of the House of Halladin, Lord of the

Living Forest across the sea, exiled heir of the ancient Kings of Aldinor.

At the prince's side was the blade his father had taken into exile, the enchanted, two-handed Sword of Kings: he wore kilt and shirt in Y'goran style, and Istvan remembered that Tahion's mother had come from here, a woman of the Clan Gilleran, who live at the edge of the Elfwoods.

"Well met!" Tahion rose, and his grip was firm on Istvan's arm. "I did not know you were in this part of the world at all. Serving the Empire during raiding season?" Istvan nodded. Tahion's smile widened. "Now, it would be an odd chance that could bring us both here tonight, unless . . ."

"Then the Hasturs summoned you as well?"

"The Hasturs?" Tahion's eyes widened. "Why—no, it was Dorialith of the Sea-Elves who sent word to me, through my kin in the Elfwoods, to meet him here." Istvan was startled: few men at any time had dealings with the Elves of the Sea. "And when I came—" he waved a hand at the crowd around them, "I recognise half the famous names of Y'gora, and then you walk in, A strange clientele. So! It was the Hasturs called you here?"

Istvan nodded, and tugged thoughtfully at his dark, greying beard.

"Aldamir Hastur appeared on our ship—we'd put in at Elthar for provisions and some last bit of cargo—and asked me if I would go to aid in the defense of—" Istvan paused, trying to remember the name, "Rath—Rathtallin or—Rathtainlinn—something like that."

"So," said Tahion, thoughtful. "I think in truth you may know more of this matter than I. Yes, the elves who bore Dorialith's message said that some great danger marches on Rath Tintallain. What all this may mean I cannot guess, unless one of the greater terrors from the Dark World has broken through once more; perhaps one of the Great Dyoles, or the *Sabuath*."

"Not the *Sabuath*, at least!" A deep, resonant voice broke in, and looking up, they saw a lean man, black-bearded, hawk-faced, standing by their table, a polished staff in his hand. "All that live know when *that* one enters the world, and sleepers wake screaming for a thousand miles around." A dark cloak was around him, over a tartan robe with a pattern of grey, black and gold. "And I am surprised at you,

Tahion Mac Raquinon, that you should have forgotten that. Do you remember me? We studied together at Elthar.''

"I do indeed, Arthfayel Mac Ronan, though it has been long and long," said Tahion. Istvan, noting the threads of silver in Arthfayel's beard, wondered at that, for the man was plainly older than Tahion, perhaps as old as Istvan himself. "Join us." The wizard pulled out a chair and sat.

"I cry your pardon for breaking so rudely into your speech," he said then, turning to Istvan. "I heard you, my lord, addressed as DiVega. Are you not Istvan the Archer?''

"No," Istvan lied, cursing the poet who had coined that hated name. "You must be thinking of someone else." Prince Tahion quickly hid a smile behind his hand.

"What do you know of all this, brother Arthfayel?" Tahion gestured at the room around them.

"That both the Elf-Folk and the Clan of Hastur gather warriors for the defense of Rath Tintallain. That you knew already: by looking among the company here, you see that only the pick of the Champions of the World have been summoned. As to why?" He stroked his beard and his eyes were somber. "You, Tahion, will surely have noticed there is some mystery about Rath Tintallain. Rarely will the Immortals speak of it, and their speech is well-guarded. I have been there—once, long ago. It is deep in the Forest of Demons, and not far from the borders of Sarlow. But there are other cities, both of elves and dwarves, that are as near.

"A mist of illusion guards it, and cloaks—a very strange feeling. A tension. And a sense of—evil. Have you ever heard the legend of—Osadkah?" Tahion looked up, startled. "Other tales there are, too, of evils so great the Hasturs could neither slay them nor drive them from the world.''

"I have always doubted that tale," said Tahion. "It is like the tale of Anthir and his Stone: it goes against all I have learned of magic.''

"I dare not claim it is true—one must ask a Hastur for that—but the tale goes that Osadkah was sealed by spells into a mound. It is my belief that Rath Tintallain is built atop such a mound, to guard it, and I believe that the servants of the Dark Lords now seek to free—what is buried there—from its prison.''

"But wait, now," objected Tahion. "Rath Tintallain is a

city of dwarves, as well as elves. Is not a great part of it underground?''

"Indeed," Arthfayel nodded solemnly. "The mines of the little people stretch under the earth for miles around. You are asking how the dwarves dare tunnel with such a thing in the earth? I have pondered that myself. But the dwarf city is very old: my belief is that it was there before, and that the Hastur-kin imprisoned the creature in some chamber of the mines, and . . ."

"I'm sorry, Master," a woman's voice broke in, "but the dwarves have drunk the last of the beer, and the roast is gone, too!" Looking up, they saw a harried-looking woman with iron-grey hair, balancing a tray of empty mugs in her hands. "Would you like whiskey, perhaps?" Tahion nodded. "And your friends—" A voice bellowed somewhere in the back of the hall, and she started. "Ah, they're calling me. I'll be back as soon as I can. What a night!" She bustled off.

The door slammed loudly, and they all started. Two men had come in, wearing bright plaids of red and blue. Tumbalian hillmen, Istvan guessed: small round shields were on their backs, broad bladed swords at their sides; each wore a belt bristling with daggers, and bore three javelins—two light, long-bladed and wooden-shafted, the third a sharpened iron stake: the terrible iron javelin that is the distinctive weapon of the Y'goran warrior.

Silver gleamed at the throat and belt of the smaller, dark-haired man, and on the jutting hilts of all his weapons. A silver brooch, richly worked and set with moonstones, pinned his plaid at the shoulder: his shirt was fine white linen, and the feathers of a chief rose from his cap.

His companion was a red-bearded giant, towering over the other, even stooping; his shirt was rough-woven saffron-cloth, his belt plain leather, and the hilts of all his weapons unadorned.

Tahion and Arthfayel looked at each other.

"It is a bard's repertoire of hero-names tonight," said Arthfayel.

"Who are they?" Istvan asked.

"The dark man with the silver trim is Starn, chief of Clan MacMalkom of Benbiel. He has led his Clan in many a fight: at the battle of Quol Ardavin, he slew sixteen men with his own hand. It was he killed Duvnal VicMahan, a man skilled as any here, who might well have been called, had blood-feud never risen between the Clans of Mahan and Malkom.

"A good man of his hands, Starn MacMalkom, but the man with him is a better: his bodyguard, Flann MacMalkom. He has stood at Starn's back in every battle, and for every man his chief has killed, Flann has slain two. When the sorcerers of Sarlow raised the demon-host against the Tumbalian hills a few years gone, Flann wrought great deeds with the enchanted blade that the elves gave him; and it was he alone who sought out and slew the dragon-bird, S'thagura, who ate a hundred men in one day. Not a champion in Y'gora has more songs about his deeds, saving only Carroll Mac Lir: the songs of the harpers ring with his name."

"Except for Tahion," said Istvan, "I know no one here. And what songs from Y'gora cross the ocean usually tell of things long past, so I know little of living heroes. Tell me, who is that at the next table? The islander there, with his war-flail? And the other, with the scythe?" He gestured at the gaunt, big-boned redhead, who wore the long tartan robe of an islander from east of Airaria. Across his table lay the bladed war-flail, which Istvan had seen used in battle: a tricky weapon, that only an expert might use safely, with a long flattened iron bar attached to a longer handle by a length of chain, part of the bar filed to a chisel-edge.

"That is Ingulf, Son of Fingold," said Arthfayel, "of the Clan Hua-Eliron from Tray Ithir in the Eastern Isles. Some call him 'the Wanderer,' but others call him Ingulf the Mad. He is a strange one: they say he served in the Emperor's army for some years, but came west and wandered about the Three Kingdoms. Some say he has been to the City of the Sea-Elves, where men do not go, and that it was there that he got the enchanted sword that he calls *Frostfire*. It was he, with Carroll Mac Lir, who led that wild raid into Sarlow which freed so many men and women from slavery. The other islander is Fithil of the Curranach, Swordmaster of the Clan MacAran, from the Isle of Tongorem. Some say he is the best swordsman of the Isles."

The man he indicated was blond: his eyes pale blue on each side of a nose hooked and lean, that stood out like a beak from the thin face. His red-and-blue checked robe was held shut by a broad leather belt with ornate buckle. The handle of the scythe stood up by his chair.

"Being from the continent yourself," said Arthfayel, "you may not know how deadly the war-scythe of the Curranach may be—"

"I've seen it used in Airaria," said Istvan.

"Ah, have you indeed?" White teeth flashed in the black beard. "During this last Raiding Season, no doubt. I hear tell of a grim battle there against Norian Raiders, and of great deeds done by your kinsman, Istvan the Archer."

Istvan looked away, wordless, but Tahion's voice cut in. "There is another islander here," he said, gesturing toward the shadows near the back of the hall, "whose face is not known to me, nor is his plaid familiar. Do you know him?" As Arthfayel turned to see, Istvan shot Tahion a silent look of gratitude.

The third islander sat alone in a far, dark corner of the room, away from the fire, and with no candles near. He was a short, heavy-set man, black-haired, with skin as brown as ale, and the dark checks of his tartan robe were set aslant, in strange diamond shapes. He seemed ill at ease, gripping a short spear or staff in his brown fist, and casting wary glances around him.

Arthfayel's brow crinkled, and he turned back with a puzzled shake of his head.

"He must be from far away indeed, from the Duvgall Islands, or beyond. His sword is straight, or I might guess his Clan some kin to the McDymio. But I do not know the plaid. It is not the MacRu nor the MacArik, but those are the only Clans from that far away I have seen."

"Is there no rumour of any such traveler in Elthar?"

"None, unless it be that brawler, Karik Mac Ulatoc," Arthfayel snorted. "*He* is not one the Elf-Lords are likely to summon!" He rubbed roughly at his beard. "I wonder, now—?"

"But who is that, at the table beyond?" Istvan asked quickly, waving a hand at the black-bearded man he had passed on his way to the table.

"Yon black-bearded bull of a man? That is Fergus Mac Trenar, the Champion of the King of Elantir. Ruro Halfbreed, famed wizard-smith of the dwarves, wrought that glittering sword of heroes, *Aibracan,* that Fergus had from his father, and with which he has again and again stood off invaders from the Forest of Demons. His defence of the Ford of

Avabor will be sung while the world lasts. Only he and Carroll Mac Lir survived the battle of Girt Fullav.''

"And the group of forest-runners, there beyond?"

Arthfayel turned to look: there were five of them, naked but for kilts in varying patterns of green and brown. Bundles of javelins lay by their chairs, and small, dark shields. One wore a Hastur-blade, like Istvan's own, the rest, short stabbing swords. One had a bow and a quiver of arrows, and all had long knives and short-handled throwing axes.

"Ah, I keep hoping that my foster-brother Anarod will be here," said Arthfayel, turning back. "The tall, lean one, with the catfish moustache and his brown hair tied up atop his head, is Ronan Mac Carbar. There was a monster like a great worm lived in a mountain tarn at Galenor's border: slaying it was a notable deed. That ugly, gnarled, red-bearded, hairy man, with shoulders broad as any dwarf's on him, that is Dair Mac Eykin. He bears a Hastur-blade, and has studied at Elthar. Men say he can walk through a thicket of dried leaves and make no sound. The slender, dark-haired boy next to him is Finloq Mac Alangal. It is said that he is half-elf, or perhaps a Changeling, and an elf indeed: certain it is he is still beardless, though long grown to a man's years."

"He is as good as an elf in the woods, surely," said Tahion. "He is of my kindred of Clan Gileran, and also an Adept of Elthar."

"Aye, and he has lived near elvish country all his life," said Arthfayel. He shook his head. "It still troubles me that Anarod should not be here. Though indeed, he lives now nearer to Rath Tintallain than to this place. Ah, well. That little dark-bearded man next to Finloq is Ailil Mac Ailil, and a good friend and a dangerous enemy he is. He has been a good friend to Anarod: the two of them together went into the dread valley of Baelgor to rescue the stolen daughter of Lindaetur. I think it may be his brother Cahir who is next to him, but it could be Colin Mac Fiacron, they are all—"

"Here I am at last!" It was the grey-haired woman, but this time she bore no cups. "I fear the whiskey's gone, too. There is a little wine, still, and . . ."

"Wine then," said Istvan, laying a gold piece on the table. "What food have you left?"

"We are plucking chickens, to be roasted and stewed, and there are hams, I think—"

"We may have to leave before there is time for anything to cook," said Tahion. "Midnight is near upon us, best have something quick. Have you cheese, perhaps?"

"And a loaf of bread," said Arthfayel, "if any is left."

"There may not be," said the woman. "A pitcher of wine, then, for the three of you? And a wheel of cheese, and bread if there is any. I'll be back." She took the gold piece, bit it, and dashed off.

"Ah, now, where were we?" Arthfayel said, leaning back in his chair. "Had I spoken of Cahir Mac Ailil and Colin Mac Fiacron?"

"Who is the big blond man, there at the next table?" asked Istvan. Arthfayel looked, and his teeth flashed in his beard.

"Ah! I was wondering when you would ask about him! They say you Seynyoreans are accustomed to heroes, yet were your famous kinsmen Istvan and Raquel DiVega here, and all the great heroes of your continent, Birthran of Kadar, Ironfist Arac, or Tugar of Thorban, they could not outshine the glory of that one! Look well, Seynyorean, for you are never likely to see a greater hero than Carroll, the son of Lir.

"Bards sing of him that his sword is like blue lightning unleashed upon the wall of shields." Arthfayel almost chanted the words. "Too many to tell, the deeds of Carroll Mac Lir." But he looked as though he were about to try.

"And what of the dark man at the table with him?" Istvan asked quickly.

"The one with the harp, you mean? Ah, that is only Cormac Mac Angdir, the harper. He will be the envy of every bard in Y'gora. For he is a good man of his hands, as well as an Adept of Elthar; a hero of many deeds who deserves a place at this gathering. And surely that will give him matter for song such as few harpers ever have."

Poets! There was no escaping them, Istvan thought. There was always one around somewhere, to pester you with questions and get all the answers wrong, and weave your name into their songs with the most outrageous lies . . .

"Luck is with you tonight!" The grey-haired woman appeared out of the crowd, and set down a hot, steaming loaf of bread. "No butter, though, but here's your cheese—half a wheel—and the wine."

She set the things on the table and vanished into the crowd once more. Arthfayel cut himself a generous slice from the loaf, and reached for the cheese. Tahion poured wine for Istvan and then Arthfayel, and finally for himself.

"It was Cormac who made the song," Arthfayel said after a moment, "telling how Carroll Mac Lir escaped from the slave-pits in Sarlow." He smiled and Istvan guessed he was about to sing.

"Who is the young man in the armour there, at the table with the dwarves?" Istvan gestured, and Arthfayel craned his neck to look.

"Garahis of Ordan," Arthfayel said. "A knight of Cairanor. He is young, but his life has been spent in battle along Cairanor's northern border. When dark things from the forest swarmed into the Border Kingdom, three years ago, he rode with scarce a hundred men to the aid of Monacard." He seemed about to say more, but Istvan forestalled him.

"What of the dwarves? Are they heroes, too, or are they here on some other business?"

Arthfayel blinked at him. Tahion covered a smile. Arthfayel opened his mouth to speak, then stopped, listening.

All around them the murmur of speech died.

CHAPTER TWO

Secret Paths of the Elves

At first, in the sudden stillness, they heard only the crackle of the fire and the crying of the wind.

Yet Istvan felt a sudden prickle on his skin, and a lifting of his heart.

Music began, weirdly sweet: music such as no mortal man can play. Unbearable longing was in that music, and an unquenchable joy that somehow mingled with infinite, heart-breaking sorrow.

The heavy oaken door was suddenly and soundlessly open. Istvan blinked tears from his eyes, and stared. A figure stood outlined in crystal moonlight.

At first Istvan took him for a man, black-haired and beardless, slender yet tall. But as he stepped into the light of the room, Istvan saw the fine, fragile bones of the face, and the wide, ageless, glittering eyes, and knew him for an elf—big-boned for one of his kind, his shoulders broad even for a man.

"It cannot be!" Tahion gasped. "Surely that is—" there was awe in his voice— "Unless my eyes deceive me, that is Tuarim Mac Elathan, who rode with Fendol: Tuarim Mac Elathan, the greatest of the heroes of the elves!" Istvan stared, while his spine pricked and thrilled: Legend stood in that door.

Five thousand years had passed since Fendol, Hero-King of Galdor, had brought a great fleet over the ocean to the aid of beleaguered Elthar. The very land he had ruled was barren desert now: generations of poets had mangled the tales of his deeds. Ruling houses of a dozen kingdoms pointed proudly to his name in their genealogies.

But Tuarim Mac Elathan still walked the earth—stood now in the doorway with wind blowing his dark hair and huge eyes gleaming like jewels . . .

In the doorway behind him, two others appeared: long beards covered their chests, but the faces above them were lineless, delicate, like children's faces, or young girls'. And the sight of one took Istvan back twenty years.

"That is Ethellin the Wise behind him!" he gasped.

"And Dorialith of the Sea-Elves," said Tahion.

Now voices joined the music, rising in song. Higher and higher the voices rose and wove, while men in the inn sat like stone.

Suddenly, the song ended on a note like high-pitched, maniacal laughter, and every man in the room started.

Then the voice of Tuarim Mac Elathan rang all around them, not deep, like a man's voice, but high and clear as a bell.

"I greet you, dwarves and men! I am Tuarim Mac Elathan, and I ride to war!" Istvan heard gasps all around him: few had guessed who had come among them. "My kin, and the sons of Hastur, have sought you out; they tell me that the greatest living warriors are gathered here. I ride now to Rath Tintallain, ringed by dark powers: goblins and demons from the forest, as well as warriors of Sarlow, and the sorcerers they serve."

Istvan felt his blood soar and sing in his veins—and deep within him, angry independence burned. The elf's voice was playing upon their emotions, and there was no need!

He heard his own voice, as harsh as a bullfrog's after the melodious chiming of the elf.

"We know all that! but what is so precious about Rath Tintallain that you assemble such a company as this to defend it?"

Tuarim's wide eyes blinked in surprise, and elves and men stared. But it was Ethellin the Wise who answered.

"Your question, Lord DiVega, deserves an answer. This much I will say: whether Rath Tintallain stands or falls will shape the fate of the World. But what it is that is guarded at Rath Tintallain, and why mortal warriors are needed for its defense—these are secrets I dare not tell—even to Istvan the Archer; even in such company as this."

Men muttered all around as the Sea-Elf named him, and Istvan became acutely aware of the eyes upon him—and most of all Arthfayel's.

"Well, if we are to trust you, let us trust you, then," he mumbled, and was about to say something about free will and spells, when Tahion's voice broke in.

"It has been long since you have been among mortal men, Son of Flathan, and you have been forgetting much in all those years. Remember that you speak for mortal ears, and forget not the doom of Ranahan!" Tuarim's huge silver eyes rested on Tahion. Istvan wondered who Ranahan had been—but it was plain that the elf knew.

"It is the truth." Tuarim's voice was still inhumanly beautiful—but the edge of compulsion was gone "My thanks for the warning. You are Raquinon's son, are you not? Your father. . . ?"

"Dead these many years."

"I feared so." Long lashes swept down over the wide eyes. "He was a good man. So." Tuarim straightened again, and the closed eyes flashed open, shining like stars in the firelight. "So! We must ride! An age indeed has it been since I was riding with a company of mortal men!" Clear laughter bubbled out of his mouth. "Glad will I be to know the names of those with whom I ride. Istvan DiVega has been named to me, and Tahion Mac Raquinon I remember from his youth. Not long ago a bard was telling that Mardil O'Corrie was the greatest of mortal heroes living. Is he here?"

"He died more than fifty years ago," Tahion said, quietly. Tuarim was silent.

"Ingulf the Wanderer is here," said the Sea-Elf whom Tahion had named as Dorialith. His voice was deeper than was common among the elves, and in the firelight he could have been taken for an old, frail man, had not the wind that blew through the open door shaken his beard like a maiden's hair. "I hear he has done great deeds upon the paths of the World with the sword that we gave him. Carroll Mac Lir and Flann Mac Malkom are here, and Finloq Mac B'an, and. . ."

"And Cormac the Harper!" Cormac himself came pushing between the tables, his harp clasped to his breast. "If it is knowledge of heroes you want, is it not a harper you should ask?"

Istvan groaned. *Poets!* He wanted to go to bed. Morosely, he stuffed his mouth with cheese.

"Time passes." Dorialith's voice cut through the harper's. "We must depart. There are thirty or more here to name, counting these dwarf-folk. There will be time on the road, and more within the fortress, to learn the names and deeds of our companions."

"That is so," said Tuarim sadly, to Istvan's great relief. "Come, harper! You shall ride by me, and tell me the name and fame of our comrades. But it is many a mile to Rath Tintallain, and hard riding it will be for mortals! We must be there before three days have passed, or we shall be cut off!"

Arthfayel whistled, and Tahion sat up straight, blinking. Istvan heard exclamations from all around the room.

"What is it?" he whispered. "How far away is this place?"

"Hundreds of miles," said Arthfayel. "Nearly a month's journey, as men reckon distance."

Outside the door, the sweet music had begun again. Then, just inside the threshold, two blue-clad figures appeared. Copper hair gleamed in the firelight.

Istvan blinked in surprise, recognising Kandol Hastur-Lord, the oldest living Hastur. Rarely did any mortal who dwelt outside Carcosa see him: his presence here was itself proof of the importance of this matter.

"Kandol!" shouted Tuarim Mac Elathan. "Kandol Shadow-slayer!" With a chime of wild laughter he bounded across the room and caught the Eldest of the Lords of the World in an exuberant embrace. "Is it riding with us you are?" Next to the Hastur-Lord, he seemed fragile.

"No." A smile spread across the calm, ageless face of the Hastur-Lord. "No, I travel by swifter means. But when danger closes on the fort of Rath Tintallain, you will see me there, old friend."

"We shall be glad of that," Tuarim said.

"Well, it is good someone is glad," said Kandol, somberly. "There will be much to mourn ere all is over," Tuarim nodded. "There always is."

"My Lord Istvan," a low voice murmured, and Istvan looked up to see Kandol's companion beside the table. It took him a moment to recognize the Hastur, then rising, he bowed in the Carcosan fashion.

"My Lord Ringion." Was there a twinkle in the Hastur's eyes? Ringion spoke to Tahion and Arthfayel, and went from table to table, greeting each of the assembled champions by name.

"Some day it must end," Kandol was saying, his voice somber. "Either we shall hurl them back to their own place, and imprison them, as Hastur did in the beginning—or else they will overcome us at last, and eat all living things, and darken the stars themselves."

"Even that would not be the end, for us," said Ethellin the Wise. "There are worlds beyond this, which must still be guarded if Carcosa falls." Kandol nodded.

Dorialith stepped to the door and looked outside. In a moment he turned back, lamplight gleaming silver on his long pale beard. His voice rang loudly through the room.

"All now is ready." Men began to gather their weapons and move toward the door. Istvan gulped down the rest of his wine, and cut himself a large piece of cheese. Arthfayel and Tahion divided the rest, and Tahion cut the loaf into thirds. Istvan slung his shield on his back and the bag of mail over one shoulder, and moved away from the table thinking of the unfinished wine he had paid for . . .

"Tell me, Karik Mac Ulatoc," Ringion Hastur said loudly, "who was it bade *you* to this gathering?"

The brown-skinned islander in the strangely slanted tartan stopped short, only a few feet in front of Istvan: brown knuckles whitened on the wooden shaft of the strange weapon he carried.

"I—I was with Fithil of the Curranach when—when one of—your kin came to—summon him. I heard—" the islander's stammer hinted at a voice normally deep, but shrill now. "—They said you needed warriors . . ."

"Indeed, Karik," Ringion Hastur said, "you are brave enough, to be sure. But your weapons are all of plain steel or bronze or wood, and little use against the enemies we face. And you are young yet, and have not gained the skill or the experience of the others. Do not let your pride weave a shroud for you."

Black eyes blazed as the islander straightened. Istvan studied the strange weapon—a kind of spear, perhaps, since one end did sport a kind of spike of bronze, and back-curved hooking blades on the shaft below.

"I'm as good a man as any here!" Karik cried, his voice shrill. The black eyes glared around wildly. "Who do I have to fight to prove my skill?" His eyes fixed on Istvan. "You?"

The bronze spike leaped at Istvan's eyes.

For a moment Istvan thought he had merely dodged. Then the end of the spear fell, neatly sheared through, to clatter to the floor, and he felt his sword's weight in his hand.

Control! he thought, angry at himself.

The brown man stood frozen, staring at the shortened stick in his hand. Istvan stepped back, blade poised and ready.

"I—I am sorry," Istvan heard himself say. "I—I did not mean to—"

With a shout of rage, the islander threw down the useless piece of wood, and reached for his sword-hilt. There was a sudden blur, and Tuarim Mac Elathan gripped Karik's arm.

"Hold!" The elf's voice rang with compelling music. Istvan's spine shivered. "There is no need for anyone to fight. We have no wish to turn away any who would help. You are welcome to come with us. But do not fight with your comrades in war! There will be foes enough for all!"

The islander's breath hissed out in a long gasp. He seemed dazed, black eyes staring. Istvan sheathed his blade, and, dropping to one knee, lifted the bronze-tipped wood from the floor and offered it to the brown man. "You should be able to repair this," he said. "We will be riding through a forest." Karik took the half from Istvan's hand without a word: a curious smile played about his mouth. His eyes stared into empty air.

The music grew louder, more insistent.

"Come!" Tuarim's voice wove into the fairy music. "It is time to ride!"

The music enfolded them, and they were moving, dancing through the door. Karik Mac Ulatoc moved like a man caught up in a dream.

Istvan found himself suddenly outside. Stars gleamed bright against a clear deep velvet sky, and tiny moons wandered between them. Domri hung gigantic above the hills, its pale light glowing mystically on the snowy coats of graceful, deer-dainty horses.

Saddles were on them, but no bridles. Istvan caught his breath. He had heard strange tales of such horses: tales that they could run forever, tireless, at speeds no mortal horse could match. Some said that they could run over water or fly through the air, but that he had never believed. Some said that they were elves shape-changed, not horses at all; others said they were an immortal breed the elves had brought from their own world. And many said such tales were only legend, and no such creatures existed at all.

The sight had stopped him, but now the music plucked at his nerves, hurrying him toward the horses. He shook his head, trying to fight the compulsion he could feel so thick around him.

Why were the elves driving them thus? Why could they not let a man's will alone?

Stubbornly, he held his feet to a slow walk. A man jolted into him, another swerved and danced 'round him at the last second. His heart beat fast, and he could feel his nerves twitching as they tried to set his feet to dancing, leaping with the whirling music of blending pipes and horns, and shrilling strings . . .

His feet took two dancing steps he had not willed.

"Istvan!" Tahion's voice cried above the music. "They mean no harm! But haste is needed now! Do not fight them!"

Speed, Istvan thought, and let the music take him. He saw Tahion balanced on the back of rearing white glory. The horse's hooves came down, it neighed, and became a blur, a streak in the moonlight.

He was the last now, well behind the others. Ahead he saw men and dwarves moving, dancing to their horses, feet all pounding to the music's rhythm, weaving in and out, leaping like brown leaves onto the horses' backs . . . The best-drilled company of Kadarin cavalry could never mount and ride so quickly.

A milk-white horse rushed toward him, mane and tail flowing like sea froth. The music carried him straight into its path. Fear flared, but he let his body trust the elves, and a wave of music launched him into the air and set him in the saddle. His hands found a grip in the fine silk of its mane. It neighed three times, shaking itself; and then the ground was rolling away under its hooves.

There was sudden wind in his face, rich with the smell of grass and leaves. His heart still pounding with the music's pulse, he gripped the saddle tightly with his thighs, carefully fitted his feet into the stirrups, and, twisting, slid the saddle-bags from his shoulders down to the horse's rump.

The sky was better to watch than the blurred ground: never had he seen it pass so quickly under a horse's hooves. He looked up at the glittering stars. A bright, tiny moon had wandered between the bull's head and shoulders, and the stars around were dimmed by its light.

Other horses were dim white shapes: the music slowly fading behind. He became aware of the uncanny smoothness of the creature's gait.

Trees reared up and before he had time to think, they were in among them. His fingers tightened in the long mane, expecting at any moment to be struck from the saddle by some low branch. Gleaming horses appeared and vanished in moonbeam and tree shadow. He heard the shrill pulsing cry of tree frogs, and the sleepy plaint of a disturbed bird.

Suddenly, in the moonlight he saw what seemed a solid wall of underbrush: the elf-horse's race toward it never slowed. He had only time to close his eyes and let go the mane to fling his arms before his face.

Rustling filled his ears: strange smells rode on a warm wind. Hesitantly, he opened his eyes, cautiously peeled his hands from his face. Darkness around him: tiny patches of dim light flickered, flew past and were gone.

He closed his eyes again and fell forward against the horse's neck, listening to that mysterious leafy rustle, and smelling the sweet horse smell as he tangled his hands in its mane.

There was no sound but the whisper of leaves and the scraping of branches, and the occasional crash of a startled animal. He kept listening for something else, but a long time passed before he realized with a chill, that the sound he strained to hear, but did not, was the sound of hooves.

How long that dark ride went on he never knew; it seemed endless ages he lay pressed against the horse's neck, listening to leaves. But at last the feel of the breeze changed: the leafy murmur faded, and he opened his eyes on a blaze of moon and star.

A white elf-horse flashed past, a slender figure clinging to the saddleless, smooth back. Others appeared, gleaming against the dark ground, weaving among scattered trees and huge, shapeless boulders. Men crouched warily in their saddles, looking uncertainly around. But among them elves rode bareback, in wild mood. One sprang up and stood swaying on his steed's bare back, while high voices laughed and jested all around. A sleepy bird, disturbed, called softly from a tree.

A deeper voice laughed at Istvan's side. Turning, he found Prince Tahion riding with him, his horse matching Istvan's stride for stride.

"Ah, now, this will be a merry ride! It is Oranfior Mac Robind about to play! He is one of the great pipers of the elves; the best, they say, of any born in this world. Some say that even among the Eldest, only Ciallglind and Riarbind surpass his skill. He comes to the Elfwoods sometimes, and I have seen wild beasts dance when he plays, and have heard him pipe men's souls into dreams that would teach wisdom to fools. I think Tuarim wishes to cheer the harper."

Among the rushing horses ahead, Istvan saw tall drone pipes jutting above a rider's shoulder, and as Tahion's voice stilled, a deep note roared. Out of it rose the sweet high trill of the chanter, a rapid string of darting notes, in a wildly warbling air.

The standing elf began to dance, bare feet flashing sure atop the horse's moving back. A fiery joy in Istvan's veins made him suddenly twenty years younger, and as he saw other elves spring up to dance on their horse's backs, a mad desire began to grow to stand and dance himself . . .

Tahion's horse darted away in a frantic blur of speed and suddenly was racing alongside the piper's horse, while astonished elves turned to stare.

Istvan's desire to dance faded as suddenly as it had come, and he gripped his horse's mane tightly as he fitted his feet back into the stirrups.

They came suddenly into vivid moonlight, Domri and Lirdan bright overhead, and scores of lesser moons clustered about them. A level, treeless plain stretched ahead, and elvish voices rose, mingling sweetly with a sudden cascade of melody from the bagpipes. Wind plucked at them as their horses' speed increased; it whirled Starn MacMalkom's cap from his head, and a dancing elf caught it out of the air and waved it gaily at the astonished chieftain.

The ground rolled away in a blur: trees marched to meet them out of the night, and vanished as they came abreast.

Hours passed, and still they rode. Twice they dashed into the rustling darkness of dense thickets, and emerged blinking on the other side without branch or leaf having touched them. Countless moons raced past Domri and Lirdan in the sky.

At last, dawn paled the sky and gilded the eastern moons. They galloped up a steep slope, and Istvan saw ahead a sharp-edged ridge, black against the gold and pink light. Starn and Flann MacMalkom shouted to each other in wonder, for this was their own homeland: the western chain of the Tumbalian hills, nearly ten days ride from Elthar on a mortal horse.

As they topped the ridge, one sun peeped over the eastern chain of hills, across the long, deep valley. Then it vanished again as they dashed down the thickly wooded slope into the shadow of the far mountains.

Cocks crowed around them, and they could see farms in clearings in the forest and hints of folk beginning to stir. But Istvan doubted that any man saw them pass.

The sense of youth and strength which the music had brought had faded when Oranfior had laid aside his pipes. Istvan's bones ached as they crossed the valley. Both suns glared in his eyes as they raced up the eastern slopes. The horses slowed as they climbed, but Istvan gasped at the treacherous steeps up which they scrambled at a speed still greater than a good horse running on the level.

It had been a strange, lonely ride. Only Tahion had spoken to him, of all his companions, and for the most part the men had been wide-scattered among the elves.

At the top of the slope the horses drew together into a long line, as they wove along a narrow trail between outcroppings of rock. Suddenly, they came out among the barren, wind-swept crags, and looked down upon an endless sea of treetops that washed against the slopes below.

Here began the Forest of Demons, running on and on to fill the heart of Y'gora, stretching two thousand miles or more to the mountains that guard the borders of Ualfime.

Under that green roof lived elves and wild men, and, here

and there, vast cavern cities of the dwarves. But these were few and far between, and other dwellers were not so friendly: the black, shapeless demons from Outside who gave the forest its name, and the trolls and goblins who served them. Somewhere in the leafy distances before them lay the strangely guarded lost city of the Hasturs, only partly in this world, and the dragon-haunted waste where the spawn of ancient Komanthodel hunt 'round the cave where their monstrous parent slumbers, near the southern marches of Sarlow, whose rulers serve, not the Hasturs, but the Dark Lords from Beyond the World.

But most of the Dark Things were underground now, hiding from the light.

Istvan shut his eyes and gripped the horse's mane tightly as it darted down the steep, wooded slopes. Soon the twin suns vanished behind a thick roof of leaves, and a pale gold-emerald glow stained the elf-steeds' coats. Their hooves barely stirred the dead leaves as they raced between the trees.

Starn MacMalkom, Lord of Benbiel
Marched with his men to war . .

Cormac the Harper began to sing as he rode beside Tuarim.

He had a fine, sweet voice, no doubt, as such things were usually reckoned, but after the beautiful, chiming voices of the elves, who sang even in speech, Cormac sounded harsh and off-key. Istvan had little patience for the lying tales minstrels told of men's deeds in any case, and was glad when his horse dropped back far enough that he need not listen as the minstrel sang song after song about the men with whom he rode. No doubt, Istvan thought glumly, some lying story about "Istvan the Archer" as well.

Eventually the minstrel's throat gave out, much to Istvan's relief. But the ride was beginning to tell on him, and he began to wonder how much longer they would have to ride, and if the elves ever planned to let them sleep. His legs cramped in the stirrups, and he began to worry about saddle-blisters. He pitied the men—and it was most of them—who were riding in kilts.

Pain does not hurt, he told himself, *only fear hurts.* He freed one foot from its stirrup and stretched it.

Between the trees, he glimpsed other men doing the same.

Weights pulled down his sticky eyelids. He had learned long ago to sleep in the saddle, but that was on a slow-moving horse, not on something that sped through thick woods in a tangled blur . . .

Suddenly, there were two elves behind him, one riding on each side, and a soft, crooning music surrounded him. Yet he saw no instruments. Was it their voices? His eyelids drifted down. He could not think. But the slow song sang of sleep, of Elf-Kings on bright horses, riding through enchanted forests, of dreams of women too delicate and too beautiful to be human . . . .

CHAPTER THREE

Elf-Shock

Istvan woke. The horse had stopped. Blinking in the full light of both suns, he saw before him a green mound swelling up to a dome. Around him, men, dwarves and elves dismounted.

He clambered stiffly down from his saddle, still struggling to disentangle his mind from the maze of dreams. The elf-horse nickered, and suddenly blurred away into the trees. He took a single, useless step, then stood staring after it, thinking of the little cheese that had been left in his saddlebag.

"Man! I'd near forgot what feet were for!" a deep voice boomed nearby. Turning, Istvan saw Fergus Mac Trenar stamping his feet as though to be sure the ground was real. "What, Flann? How did you get here? Did they put *two* horses under you? Surely they did not let you break the back of one poor, lone beast?"

Flann only grunted, stretched his massive limbs, and the red beard twitched with a grin.

"You're no so light yourself, Fergus!" laughed Starn MacMalkom, straightening his plaid. "I mind well when I pulled you from that bog. I was sure you'd taken root!" Men around them laughed, and it was plain the young chief spoke of some well-known tale.

"Ah, Starn, lad!" Teeth flashed in Fergus' black beard,

27

and he turned twinkling eyes on the Tumbalian as though noticing him for the first time. "I see you got your hat back, feathers and all. Wasn't the bird dead yet?"

"Indeed," a new voice rose above the roar of laughter, a kingly voice, rich, deep, and melodious, "we all saw the birdeen fly straight up to the elf's hand! The wee feathers lifted it up—" Carroll Mac Lir came striding through the crowding heroes, hands fluttering in pantomime, "—and away it flew! So now we know why Starn is so famed a war-leader: in battle, his hat sings to cheer his men!"

Louder grew the laughter. Istvan joined, yet even as he laughed he felt alone, alien. These men knew each other well, it seemed, and their teasing followed long-established patterns. He was out of place and knew no one. He looked around for Tahion and saw him a little way off, kneeling with Arthfayel beside something in the grass, with Fithil and Ingulf standing above them.

The banter continued behind him as he walked away.

Karik Mac Ulatoc lay sprawled on the ground; Arthfayel was massaging his temples, while Tahion stared into his eyes, speaking softly. The other islanders leaned on their curious weapons, their eyes somber.

Karik's brown face was still, blank eyes staring. As Istvan approached, Tahion nodded at the other wizard, and Arthfayel's long fingers dropped away from the dark man's temples.

". . . come out now, come out into the sunlight," Tahion was saying. "Wake now! Be freed from dream!"

The black eyes blinked, and life came into them. The eyebrows wrinkled in a puzzled frown, and Karik stirred and sat up slowly like a man sluggish with long sleeping.

"Where are the kings—and their ladies?" He shook his head in confusion. "And the glittering palace of jewels? The white-armed queens in their beauty; the unicorn riders—" He hid his face in his hands and rubbed at his eyes.

"What is it?" a strange voice whispered. "Elf-shock?" Looking around, Istvan saw that it was one of the forest-runners, the gnarled, red-bearded man. Tahion pressed a finger to his lips for silence, and nodded sharply. The woodsman nodded back, and prowled soundlessly away.

Everyone knows what is happening but me, Istvan thought.

The islander took his hands from his face and looked around in confusion. "I—have I been dreaming? What has happened to me? I—I was—I was about to—'' His eyes focused on Istvan and he heaved himself to his knees. "I was about to fight—*you*!''

Before Istvan could think of any words, Arthfayel caught the islander's shoulder.

"Easy!" the wizard said. "That is Istvan the Archer.''

"I don't care who—'' He stopped, mouth hanging open, and Istvan saw pallor under the dusky skin as the black eyes widened. Karik shut his mouth and swallowed.

"I'm not afraid of him!''

"And why not?'' It was Fithil of the Curranach who spoke, from where he leaned on his great war-scythe. "I am.'' Karik's head swiveled toward him in disbelief. Fithil smiled. "And if I am not ashamed to admit it, Karik Mac Ulatoc, it is a very madness of pride on your part. Tell me, did you see his sword move when he sliced up your—stick?'' Karik started, and looked down at the pieces of wood still gripped tightly in his fist.

"If you did,'' said Fithil, "it's better eyes you have than I.''

Slowly, Karik's fist unclenched. The cut wood fell to the ground, and suddenly the islander fell back into Arthfayel's arms, shivering uncontrollably. Tahion waved back Istvan's instinctive step to help.

"What is *wrong* with me?'' Karik gasped, panic in his voice. "And where *am* I?''

"You are at the Elfmound of Neadvolac, on the road to Rath Tintallain,'' Tahion said in a quiet voice, "and you ride in the company of the greatest heroes in Y'gora. But you have ridden more than three hundred miles in a single night, and a glamour has been upon you, so that you would not delay us by fighting, and under it you have felt neither hunger nor thirst, nor the weariness of your own body. Rest now, and you will soon be well.''

As the islander lay back and closed his eyes, Istvan started, hand leaping to his hilt, as a silent figure moved past him—an elf clad in a green tunic, carrying an earthenware pitcher and a small wooden bowl.

Looking around, he saw elves everywhere. He could not tell where they had come from, with their wide eyes and frail, children's faces, unless they had sprung from the earth or dropped from the sky. He looked at the green mound above them, but there was no sign of an opening upon the green slope.

An elf in a plaid of green and brown offered him a bowl of nuts already cracked. As he filled his hand, he glanced over is shoulder, to see Arthfayel supporting Karik Mac Ulatoc with one arm while he held a wooden cup to the islander's lips.

But Tahion was on his feet and striding purposefully toward Tuarim Mac Elathan, wrath in his eyes.

Quietly, Istvan followed, accepting along the way a wooden bowl filled with the mixed juices of several fruits.

"I am surprised at you, Tuarim Mac Elathan!" Tahion's voice was low, but filled with rage. "I can see that many of your companions are wild elves, who know no better, but you have been among men before!"

"Not for more than a hundred years," said the elf, silver eyes troubled. "But surely I do them no harm? I have forgotten much, I own it, but . . ."

"You will kill these men," said Tahion. "You will drive them past the edge of their endurance, lulling weariness with glamourie, and when the spell is taken off they will fall down dead! And any that live to reach Rath Tintallain will be withered scarecrows, too weak to lift a sword!"

"What, then, must I do?" The golden voice was muted. "Already, my kinfolk tell me, the forces from Sarlow move toward the citadel; and we are still so far away! But it is my task to bring these men there alive. Tell me, then, what must I do?"

"Let them sleep, first," said Tahion. "On the ground here, not in the saddle! Let them stop and rest at times, and let their bodies work by themselves, and not by magic! Surely among your companions there must be some who are used to men? Let them guide. And try to hold down the glamour in your voice and in your eyes!"

"It will not be safe to ride in the night much further," said Tuarim, his eyes troubled. "I will let them sleep for a time—"

"A few hours, at least," said Tahion.

"Let them sleep, then, and do you come and talk with me."

Istvan's sleep was deep and dreamless for the most part, stirred only by rare, fleeting glimpses of eldritch beauty.

Food waited when they woke, late in the day, with the

green Elfmound above them like a mother's breast. Men and dwarves ate and felt strengthened, even Karik Mac Ulatoc, while birds sang in the trees. But there seemed to be only a handful of elves, in moss-colored garments, who brought the men food. Istvan could not be sure whether these had been with them during the night's ride, or if they were out of the Elfmound. But neither Tuarim nor the Sea-Elves were anywhere to be seen. Neither were Tahion and Ingulf the Wanderer, though Istvan hunted for them through the crowding champions At last a dwarf named Thubar said he had seen them atop the knoll, with one of the elves.

"By the tall pine there," said the dwarf pointing. Istvan rose, brushing crumbs from his fingers. The dwarf, too, stood, his head barely on a level with Istvan's elbow. He gestured again with his broad hand. "There's an elf going there now—" He stopped, and looked around him. "Is that not strange? Do you see any of the elves still with us?" From his greater height, Istvan looked around. All the elves who had brought their food seemed to have vanished. "Something strange is about to happen. Prince Tyrin!" Thubar waved to a younger, gold-bearded dwarf who sat nearby talking with Garahis of Ordan.

Looking up, Istvan saw Tahion walk out of the trees, with the gaunt, red-haired islander behind. Istvan strode off to meet them, dimly aware that the two dwarves and the Cairanorian knight were following.

Tahion smiled.

"Ah, my sombre friend!" he said with a laugh, as Istvan came up. "I might have known *you* would wonder where I was, and worry, too."

"Well," said Istvan, "who else will explain all this to me—and you *did* promise me an explanation back at the inn. And I will be more than surprised if you try to tell me we are in no danger here!"

"Using your eyes and ears again, I see," said Tahion with an approving nod. "Yes, there is danger, and because of that, you will get your explanation in a moment. Come with me now." He began to walk on toward the others—but stopped, with the dwarf, Thubar, planted in his path, head thrown back to glare up from under bushy eyebrows.

"Tell us first, Tahion Mac Raquinon, why have the elves left?" The dwarf's voice was even deeper than Fergus Mac

Trenar's, deep as a lion's roar. Tahion dropped to one knee, so his face was on a level with the dwarf's.

"Because I asked them to leave," he said. "Some ride ahead on the road, to reach Rath Tintallain before us. Others will join us after I have spoken to the men here."

"And why is that?" Thubar demanded, bristling. Tahion laughed.

"Can you not guess? If not, follow me and learn." He rose, and the dwarf, frowning, stepped aside.

"I can guess, Thubar, if you cannot," Prince Tyrin said, his voice not so deep as Thubar's, though deeper than most men's. "Your zeal does you credit, but you are too suspicious."

Tahion turned to Sir Garahis, who had followed Prince Tyrin and listened, mystified. "If you would sound that horn I see at your belt, good knight, it would help greatly."

Before them, men and dwarves were rising and stretching after their meal; some polished weapons, some laughed and joked. Cormac the Harper was playing some rapid, difficult tune, his face tight with concentration. Fergus Mac Trenar and Carroll Mac Lir were sparring with shields and scabbarded swords, and shouting raucous comments at Starn and Flann, who were wrestling nearby.

Garahis lifted from his side a gracefully curving trumpet wrought of silver and gold: its pure tone sliced through chattering voices and silenced them, lifting men to their feet. Swords flashed, and suddenly all were moving, striding grim-faced toward Tahion. Istvan, who had led men for nearly thirty years, felt a sudden chill.

This was a company of men unmatched—not only in each man's skill and prowess, but in some common factor of training or temperament that made them act together as one.

There were no foolish questions: even Karik Mac Ulatoc waited in silence for Tahion to speak.

"Listen, men!" cried Tahion. A faint quiver in his voice told Istvan that Tahion, too, had only now realised how deadly a force this select troop was. "Swords are not needed now: no foe is upon us. And yet we are in danger—danger of which some of us know, but not all."

Swords slid back into their sheaths, yet the eyes of the heroes were watchful. Istvan heard birds sing in woods beyond, and leaves stir in the wind, but no other sound.

"We all know the danger we face from the Dark Things,"

said Tahion, "but that is not the danger we face here. Many of us—most of us, indeed—have lived as neighbours to the elves all our lives, and know them as friends of men and allies of Hastur. And we love them for their beauty and their wisdom.

"And in this lies danger. Not willingly or wittingly would the elves harm us. Yet the Elf-Folk are not subject to the weaknesses of mortal men: they do not tire, they do not age, they need no sleep as we know it. And they live by magic, surrounded by it. Elves that live near men learn to control their power, that mortals may take no hurt. But at Rath Tintallain we will be among wild elves, who know little of men."

Istvan saw that Carroll Mac Lir and the five woods-runners seemed only half listening now.

"It would never occur to them their magic might hurt us—it does not hurt them! They are like children with too much power: magic and illusion are their toys and their tools, with which they guard themselves and feed themselves, and make the world about them beautiful."

Ingulf the Wanderer broke in, his hoarse voice bitter as a raven's croak, and filled with pain.

"Listen to him! Do not let your hearts be trapped by the beauty of the elves and elvish things! Listen to him; I have cause to know the truth he speaks! I spent a night in the Sea-Elves' city, but a month went by while I was there!" He hesitated, as though to say more, then his head sank to his chest, and he stared at the ground. Tahion nodded.

"Yes, they can make time pass unnoticed, so that a man might age and die without thinking more than a day had passed. Or starve without knowing he was hungry. From mistaken kindness—or even as a game—they could cast an illusion on a man that could lure his mind to wander lost forever in a dream. They would mean no harm: they weave such dreams for one another as easily and innocently as children play—and escape from them as easily as children end a game when their mothers call. Then, too, they have spells against weariness and pain—"

"I would think we would need those," said Starn MacMalkom.

"Is it so?" said Tahion. "Think, man! A spell that can make a wounded man think himself whole, so that he would bleed to death without realizing he was hurt? There is a story of a woman under an elf-spell who danced until her toes wore away.''

''I was told of a man who danced until he died,'' said Ingulf.

''What was the doom of Ranahan, that you spoke of to Tuarim?'' Istvan asked. But it was Cormac the Harper who answered.

''Why, that is a very old song, older even than Fendol's day, and few sing it at all. I have only a few words—the chorus, I think—

> *Where do you come from, Ranahan?*
> *How long in this world will you stay?*
> *I am Ranahan, a mortal man.*
> *And it's quickly my life slips away . . .*

''They say the tale comes down from the days when the Elf-Folk first came to this world, the first elves who answered the call of the sons of Hastur in the Age of Terror, long ago.''

''They speak the truth,'' said Tahion. ''Tuarim Mac Elathan has the song; when we are safely in Rath Tintallain, ask, and surely he will sing it for you. But we have no time, now. A careless word from the Elf-host's lord drove Ranahan witless, and brought him in time to his death. He was the first in this World, but he was not the last.'' Istvan saw a curious smile twist Ingulf's face, and suddenly he remembered Arthfayel saying that some called him ''Ingulf the Mad.''

''It is easy to tell you 'be wary,' harder to tell you how,'' Tahion said. ''Arthfayel and I, and Finloq and Cormac, are Adepts of Elthar, and know how to guard ourselves. The forest-runners of Elthar, too, have learned somewhat of these dangers. To the rest of you, I can only say: beware of too much beauty. Beware of elvish music, and do not look into their eyes. I would warn you against their food, but there will be no other. Do not wander alone among the elves—that will be hard, I know. If anything seems strange or doubtful—and most of all if a troubled mind is filled too suddenly with joy—come to me. Or to Finloq or Arthfayel. I have lived alone among the elves for many years, and know their magic well. But the great danger is that you will not know that a spell is upon you, so it is on me to watch you all. Do not make it hard for me. Let me know if you go off alone, or with other men who stand in the same danger, and watch your comrades well.''

"Come, Tahion!" Carroll Mac Lir's voice rolled out. "To warn them is well, but there is no need to frighten them to death! Wild elves can be dangerous, true enough; yet there will be elves that have lived near men before, and other mortal wizards, and the Children of Hastur themselves to ward us! They know the dangers of elf-shock!" His voice rippled with melodious laughter.

Above birdsong and the breeze, air hissed loudly from the lungs of near a dozen men, men not accustomed to fear. Yet Istvan saw a grimness in the eyes of the heroes that had not been there before.

Karik Mac Ulatoc still looked puzzled and uncertain, and seemed about to speak, but Carroll's regal voice cut off whatever he would have said.

"And are we going to Rath Tintallain, or will it come to us? Are we to ride? And where are the elves hiding?"

"All around us," Tahion smiled "We ride when I am sure we have rested enough for another long stint in the saddle. And that," he said, looking about, "would seem to be now." No one answered: Istvan felt the ache in his hips and thighs, and dreaded a second ride, but said nothing. Tahion laughed. "What! No sluggards in this troop, no shirkers? A refreshing change! Be it so, then. Sir Garahis, the use of your horn would be a kindness now."

The young man looked up. Istvan guessed suddenly that this boy—he was hardly more—had grown up on tales about his new comrades. Without a word, he took the horn from his belt, and, instead of sounding it, handed it to Tahion. Surprise flickered a moment in the prince's eyes, then he took the trumpet with a grave bow. Sunlight jeweled its metal as he lifted it.

"Dwarf-work?" Tahion asked. Garahis nodded shyly. "I thought so," said Tahion, and set it to his lips.

A sudden clear cascade of notes sang from the horn's bell, thrilling along the nerves between ear and heart: Cormac stared, and under the long, golden call, drums pulsed in the ground.

Through screening leaves burst white and mystic horses,

daylight glowing on snowy coats, flowing tails and manes wind-whipped. Their brightness blurred the eye.

This time, no music lifted men into the saddles: hooves sounding on sod, the bright steeds trotted up and stood to be mounted like any horse. Dwarves lifted each other up, or scrambled onto tree stumps. The bare-legged Y'goran's took time to lay their plaids across the saddles, to give some protection to their already sore thighs.

Istvan swung up over his horse's back, and in a moment that wild ride began again, trees flashing past in full daylight now, as the elf-steeds threaded their uncanny way through the wood. Cloud-white horses with elves on their backs darted shining between trees to join them.

A wall of solid brush reared up ahead. Istvan cringed and closed his eyes as his mount plunged straight into a solid mass of green. In a moment his ears were filled with that mysterious leafy murmur he remembered from the night.

The sound of hooves had grown louder for a time, but now it faded, became a scarcely-heard faint patter. Cautiously, he opened his eyes onto dim green dusk. Above him and on either side, braided branches wove in solid walls, but ahead branches parted, bending as though lifted by invisible hands. As he passed, they fell back into place behind him. He flinched back, expecting at any moment a stinging cut across the face, but neither leaf nor branch touched him.

And under him, the soft sound of hooves faded to silence.

For a long time he watched the lithe branches writhe and twist out of his path with terrible speed, like an endless series of opening gates; then at last he hid his face in the horse's mane and held onto its neck, shuddering.

Time passed. Suddenly, he sensed a change in the air about him, in the light falling on his skin. He looked up. A blaze of light fell blinding from a long, leaf-fringed ribbon of blue sky that crossed his path. As he straightened, sudden fear choked him as he saw, beneath it, a broad stretch of dark water, flowing between thick, gnarled trees.

Before he could shout or draw breath for a shout, they were at the river's brink, and between his thighs he felt the horse's muscles bunch convulsively: suddenly the water was underneath them as his mount sprang out over the wide river.

Startled shouts sounded all around, and he glimpsed white shapes soaring above the murky water.

Then his horse's hooves were scrambling up the muddy bank, and it was galloping—no faster than a mortal horse—through open woods. A quick glance over his shoulder showed the rippling breadth of the river beneath a scattering of tiny, scudding, cloud-white blurs; and, beyond, trees shrinking on the distant shore. Other horses flashed through the forest nearby.

Fear knotted his fists in the silky mane: he would have reined in, had there been reins. But only Tahion, among all the men and dwarves, seemed to have any control over his mount; all the rest were swept along, helplessly.

The wild wind of the horse's speed increased: its hooves turned to a white blur and vanished. Sudden leaves blocked his vision: as his eyes closed instinctively, they stirred. He heard the rustle as woven branches parted before his horse; then the murmuring dusk of the thicket was about him.

The twin suns moved across the sky. Three more times they emerged from the dimness of thickets to ride through open woodlands: twice more they leaped rivers. Countless tiny streams vanished behind almost before they were seen.

Twice they halted, and men and dwarves dismounted, stretched their legs, and ate. The shining twins dipped ever nearer the horizon.

The forest stretched endlessly around them. They saw no signs of men and few enough of beasts. They were riding through an area of low hills covered with great pines and hemlocks, when suddenly the horses slowed and, spiraling into a great clearing, stopped.

"Listen!" cried Turaim Mac Elathan, raising his arm as the men and dwarves, thinking this but another rest, began to laugh and talk among themselves. Istvan saw that all the elves were tensed, listening—and Tahion as well. Yet he could hear nothing but the ancient sorrow of wind in the treetops. Tuarim straightened.

"That was a message from Rath Tintallain," he said.

"*What* was a message?" Starn MacMalkom asked. Prince Tahion laughed.

"You forget, son of Elathan, that mortals cannot hear as you do." He turned to the men around him. "A whisper passed through the trees, and of course you could not hear it! But elves often send messages so, through the minds of the trees, for those who can hear. And the tale the forest bears is of dark forces gathering, of demons and goblins on the road before us, of armies moving out of Sarlow, and of dragons. Old Komanthodel has been seen outside his cave for the first time in centuries, and his spawn gather there.''

"We dare not stop!'' Tuarim Mac Elathan cried, his wide eyes burning and his face pale. "Already we are likely to be cut off! You heard. Yet each mile we cover will make it more dangerous to ride at night!''

"We have good scouts, and better fighting men than most,'' Tahion answered. "If we must, we can fight our way through—if we still have strength to lift our swords! We will stop at Shi Culsavaq, as agreed, and then, when men and dwarves are rested, ride on into the night. I myself will scout for you!'' Elves around him burst into laughter.

"Now, *that* is a new thing!'' Tuarim said. "Never has a mortal scouted for me before. And yet—'' he paused, and looked long at Tahion. "And yet the Wood of Aldinor has always been the greatest wonder of this World, and of the powers of its rulers I have heard strange tales in plenty. I will accept that offer, then. But now we *must* ride!''

And on that word, Istvan felt his horse stir, and suddenly it was turning away, and all the elf-steeds were darting from the clearing in a long line, one after another.

Trees rushed past. Behind, the twin suns dropped toward distant mountains. Istvan felt the weariness of the ride grinding down upon him, and longed for the rest Tahion had spoken of. He wondered how much further it could be. Already the suns were so low that lances of light streamed beside the horses, piercing thick foliage to paint faded leaves with flame. The light grew red as the twin suns dropped, and still the trees flashed past. He saw ahead nothing but trees.

Until, at last, the horses swept out of the wood, into a wide green meadow; beyond it, grass sloped up into a sudden dome—an Elfmound. At its top, tall chestnuts towered over dark, gnarled apple trees. The breeze was scented with apple blossom, though spring was long past, and Istvan stared at ripe red spheres dangling from the boughs. It was not time for apples!

Fleet elf-steeds swirled through the meadow in a spiral, stopping all together at the ground's first swell. Istvan slid down from his beast's back, hearing a sound like a faint tinkling of bells.

All around him, men stretched and yawned and stamped, and their voices, exuberant after the long ride, drowned all other sounds in jesting and laughter. Fergus Mac Trenar jostled Flann MacMalkom, and the two began to wrestle.

That was worth watching, Istvan decided. They both stood braced as though rooted to the earth, strong legs straining as each gripped the other's shoulders. Istvan sensed terrible strength warring up and down the two sets of knotted, swollen arms. Even Ironfist Arac, he thought, would work up a sweat against either of these men.

Flann, red-maned and heavy-boned, was the taller of the two, but Fergus' arms swelled like knotted tree-roots, and his shoulders were broader.

Fergus hurled himself backward, trying with a sudden twist to pull the taller man off balance, but Flann stepped calmly forward with his long legs, and Fergus, turning, braced himself against the red-bearded man's weight.

The twin suns vanished behind endless leaves: rainbow colour spread across the sky. Twice Fergus twisted in Flann's hands. Twice Flann's long stride took up the slack. Ghostly moons loomed in the darkening east: the fading rainbow net in the west deepened to somber red.

The black-bearded man was tiring now. again he twisted, trying for a hold, but Flann, startlingly quick, hurled his full weight on the shorter man. Fergus' knees buckled and straightened, heaving back the bear's weight that pressed him down. Flann's hands blurred, locked on the other man's wrists. A sudden wrench forced Fergus to his knees.

Flann let go with a booming laugh.

"Is it a fine rest you're having, Fergus?" He shook his weary, knotted arms. "We are to ride on again tonight, I hear. When we do, they will have to put beds instead of saddles on our two horses, so well rested will we be!"

The last white horses vanished in the forest as Istvan looked up. West, the sky's angry red lip was fading: above, the blue deepened into velvet where diamond stars sat twinkling, and moons rolled between like pearls.

Tuarim and Tahion strode together into the midst of the men.

"Rest now, friends!" Tuarim's voice was soft, haunting music. "Rest and eat, and sleep a little while. Your sleep, indeed, must be short: before midnight you must rise and ride. My folk shall ride before and all about you, to find a safe path through the terrors of the night." His beautiful, inhuman voice faded, and Tahion's deeper human voice spoke.

"The elves here shall wake you, and see you on your way. Fear nothing: the folk of Shi Culsavaq have many dealings with men. I ride with the elves. Rest well."

A fine rest they would have here on the bare hillside, Istvan thought, hugging his cloak more tightly about him. The chill was settling into the marrow of his bones. A fitful wind moaned in the treetops, and tiny bells jangled. An owl hooted. Istvan's eyelids drooped.

A sudden burst of music and laughter flicked his eyes open on wonder: a great door had opened in the grassy mound's side, and from it came light and music and a rushing band of elves.

Silver lights cast a bright shimmer about them as they ran to the heroes, darting about them in a wild and complex dance, food and drink in their hands.

Istvan's ears were filled with the rushing torrent of music. Faces and eyes of amazing beauty looked into his, vanished, leaving his hands filled with food: apples and berries and nuts, and bread made of flour ground from nuts. The sweet milk that filled the clay bowl in his hand surely came from neither cow nor goat.

In a moon-white blur of hoofbeats, the elven steeds swept by, and Istvan knew that Tahion was gone, out scouting with Tuarim Mac Elathan. Despite Tahion's parting words, he feared the beauty around him—the music and dance seemed to drive out thought.

But if spell there was, he was too tired now to resist, and when he had eaten, he let laughing elves lead him by the hand to a bed laid under a bower of boughs, and allowed them to spread warm blankets over him, while wild music wove him dreams.

CHAPTER FOUR

The Silver Swallows

Tahion rode on through the night with Tuarim Mac Elathan. His mind reached out from his weary body, touching the minds of the creatures of the forest—bird and beast and tree. He ignored tiny flutters of individual fear, watching for the telltale mass panic that would show the Dark Ones near.

Rabbits ran through moonlight. A hunting owl soared, soft feathers bearing him soundlessly between dusk-hidden trees, while Tahion glanced quickly through his eyes. An ancient oak enjoyed a gust of wind that tossed its limbs about.

Then a wide-antlered stag leading his does through the forest tossed up his head, snorting as a gust of wind brought a scent burning and dreadful to his nostrils. Trees screamed in the darkness as cold death brushed against them, withering leaf and limb where it touched.

The deer leaped into full flight, and all about them rabbits and birds were scattering. The trees, rooted, could only stand and scream.

Tahion called soundlessly to the elves. Tuarim's voice spoke in his mind: *We hunt! Lead us in.*

Tahion touched the mind of his horse, and sensed elves all about him on their cloud-white steeds, turning, wheeling, matching their pace to his.

41

A wolf pack fled precipitously from their new-found trail as a whiff of the demon-scent came to their nostrils. The owl saw the rabbits scattering through moonlight, drifted in ghost-like for an easy kill—then hesitated, as other movements in the grass caught his eyes. Then he, too, wheeled and flapped away swiftly.

Tahion saw another horse lift mist-white out of the brush, and then Tuarim's horse was beside his, soundlessly matching stride for stride.

Ghost-white horses came flitting out of the black tangles of the forest, leaping over the bodies of tiny fleeing things. The deer ran past, and the wolves, scattering in panic from advancing death behind.

Black fire moaned among screaming trees.

Hunting elves swooped like white moths out of the night, and on their swords and arrows need-fire glittered. Bright gold the Sword of Kings glowed in Tahion's hand, and the sword of Tuarim Mac Elathan, *Itelindé* that had flamed beside Fendol's blade, was drawn, blazing with silver light.

Transparent blackness writhed away as arrows tipped with magic flame arced through the dark.

Elf-horses circled, surrounding the demon. It avoided the glowing arrows with a speed even the elf-horses could barely have matched; and suddenly it was rushing upon them like wind-driven wildfire.

The Sword of Kings and *Itelindé* rose flaming to meet it.

Radiance filled the frail black film. A shrill screech grated their ears, and the demon flared, faded, and was gone. A sudden burst of overpowering stench made even the elf-horses snort, and Tahion gagged.

Then the night was clean about them. Tuarim Mac Elathan laughed.

Istvan drifted in strange visions of unicorns and flowers and music, and vague and wonderful beauties: suddenly he came awake, fully refreshed and alert. A slight figure darted silently from his side to vanish in the shadows.

He sat up, feeling by habit for his sword, and looking quickly about. All around him the other heroes were rising, and the white horses were trotting down from the trees atop the hill.

He cast off the soft blankets, wondering a little at their

feel—they were of no cloth he had ever touched or smelled before—and rose, shivering slightly in the chill.

The bed on which he had slept was a thick, springy mat of living grass.

Bright moons raced among the stars, silver lights swung from the trees. The door of the mound was closed.

There seemed to be only a few elves about, but these were so soft-footed, and vanished and appeared so quickly, that there might have been thousands in the surrounding woods and he would not have known. One appeared beside him as his horse came trotting up, and courteously helped him into his saddle.

Four elves were mounted and riding with them; when all the heroes and dwarves were mounted, two of these were the first to leave the clearing, and horse after horse followed them, running like deer.

When Istvan's own steed darted off in his turn, the Seynyorean found himself riding next to Carroll Mac Lir. After a moment, Istvan turned to ask the question that had formed in his mind.

"I thought Tahion said that we need fear no spells from these elves? That did not seem like a natural sleep!" The big man looked at him in surprise, and then moonlight showed teeth flashing in a smile.

"So you can talk after all!" said the Y'goran. "I was beginning to wonder! But that was not what Tahion said. He said that they were used to men. And so they are. And so we had nothing to fear from their spells. They put a light sleep-spell on us, aye, and broke it again at the proper time. And I have no doubt they shaped our dreams for us, too. Simple, harmless magic, to keep us from lying awake and missing sleep, and to see to it that we all woke up at once.

"Now a wild elf, seeing that you needed sleep, might put a sleep-spell on you, and then forget to take it off—or he might decide that tired as you were, you needed to sleep for a month, or a year—or even a lifetime. More likely, he would put a spell on you to keep you from needing sleep or feeling weariness—and then when the spell wore off you might drop down dead from exhaustion. Around wild elves you never say, 'I wish I could sleep for a week,' or 'I wish I could dance forever.' They do not tire and they do not age, and they have no way of knowing either how brief or how frail our lives are. They have as many curious legends about us as we have about them.''

Trees were passing in a blur, the horses drawing further apart. As Carroll finished speaking, his steed bore him away. The big man turned in the saddle, waved, and shouted something, too far away for Istvan to make out words.

From somewhere ahead came the deep, rumbling bellow of an angry troll.

Istvan's Hastur-blade flew free. The barest hint of need-fire glowed in the depths of the steel.

On sped the horse, through shadow and moonlight, while the roars of the troll grew louder, and the sword's flame brighter.

Suddenly, Istvan saw it—a vast, manlike shape with glowing eyes, standing in the midst of a huge moonlit clearing. And as he watched through blurred trees, a cloud-white horse darted through the clearing, glowing in the light of the several moons.

The troll hurled itself into a blundering charge, but the elf-steed eluded it with ease, and then another darted into the clearing, and with a roar of baffled rage the monster turned and bore down on the second horse—but like a blur in the moonlight, the fleet steed was gone.

A clump of brush hid the creature for a moment, then the clearing opened out and Istvan's sword blazed in his hand as the huge red-eyed shape rushed roaring; then the horse was across the clearing and the troll had turned in vain pursuit of another ghostly horse.

On sped the elf-steed between night-hidden trees at a speed its rider could not guess. Spears of moonlight pierced the forest: silver columns glimpsed as his mount rushed past. It seemed a wind blew in his face, but he knew that it was but the speed at which his steed ran. The moonbeams' flicker hurt his eyes.

Hours passed in a giddying whirl of moonbeams. Then the elf-horse slowed, and Istvan saw Ethellin the Wise standing beside the path.

Patches of white in the darkness became men on fog-white steeds that wove through the wood to crowd around the frail figure of the Sea-Elf. They stopped so suddenly that Istvan's throat pinched with fear that Ethellin would be trampled.

Men, elves and dwarves were packed together where the

horses had stopped in ordered ranks. No cavalry in the world, thought Istvan, could have closed ranks more perfectly.

There was silence in his ears where wind had been. Then, from the darkness of the wood, tiny sounds of leaves told him that the creatures of the forest were about their nightly business.

But then it seemed to Istvan that there was something not quite right about the sounds. Before he could decide what it was, the voice of Ethellin the Wise, gentle and sweet as a distant horn-call, drowned both sound and thought.

"There is a demon in the woods ahead, and since we cannot depend on our speed to escape it, we must be prepared to fight. It will not be wanting to attack so large a group as this, but if we went past it at a run it would doubtless be able to take a straggler or two." As he spoke, there was a sudden flare of light as thirty swords, blazing with need-fire, flashed from their scabbards almost as one. The elf smiled.

"Tuarim is watching it now, with Dorialith and your friend Prince Tahion. But we shall go on slowly for a time. It is a strong demon; if we have to fight we will no doubt win, but I fear some of us would die in the process."

Some of the men whistled, and Istvan stroked his beard thoughtfully. The Sea-Elves were reputed to be near as powerful as the Hasturs, and certainly Ethellin the Wise was among the greatest of them. A demon that he feared to attack must be a potent one, indeed!

Suddenly, he realised what was so odd about the sounds from the forest. All those thousands of tiny pattering feet were going the same way, running past the company of heroes, away from the terror in the woods ahead.

Ethellin turned and his horse turned with him and began to walk softly at his side. Seeing this, Istvan slid down from his own mount's back and walked, his Hastur-blade glittering in his hand. Since the elf-horse had no reins, he could not lead him in the ordinary way, but he was sure that it would follow, and it did.

His legs were stiff and sore, but stretching them was a relief. An ordinary horse would have had to be walked many times on such a ride as this. It had made him feel guilty.

The need-fire of their blades cast a circle of light around them. At first there was shocked scurrying of tiny feet at their approach, as frightened creatures fled from the unexpected light. After a time, this died away, and they walked in uncanny silence.

Lights flashed through the trees ahead, and watching, Istvan saw mist-white horses grow, and soon Tuarim Mac Elathan and his companions rode to meet them. The swords of the elves burned with blue-white flame, but the Sword of Kings that Tahion bore glowed pale green like sunlight through a leaf.

Tuarim Mac Elathan's merry laughter shattered the silence.

"Sure and I thought it was dawn!" he said. "Or perhaps that a moon or two had decided to try the forest instead of the sky!" He sobered and nodded grimly at them. "It's been many a year since I've seen a gathering of such blades as these."

Dorialith slid from his horse and walked, one hand on its neck, beside Ethellin, but Tuarim Mac Elathan stayed mounted. The Sea-Elves' swords shone like ice, a crystal glitter unlike the other blades.

Beyond the circle of their swords' silver light, dense shadows shrouded the wood. Men's feet moving over leaves made a constant low rustling. But that was the only sound Istvan could hear; neither beast nor bird stirred in the bushes. All had fled the fear that hunted there.

The path broadened ahead, and starlight filtered through the thinned branches. Istvan was glad to see the stars. Tahion and Arthfayel were walking their horses beside his, and a little behind them Starn and Flann, and the islander, Ingulf, whose sword glowed with the same crystal light as those of the Sea-Elves. Istvan remembered what he had heard from Arthfayel: *Frostfire*, the sword was named, and like frost indeed was the cold glitter that lit the night about it.

The dwarves walked behind, stumping along on their short legs, with young Garahis of Ordan in their midst.

A faint, sickening odour fouled the air. Tahion's blade glowed bright gold, and Istvan felt that same crawling on his nerves that he had felt before on the Dark Border, when shadows out of the Dark World had come hunting men.

There was a sudden shimmer in the starlight above them, and a swallow swooped into their path, a swallow that seemed woven of moonlight and starbeams. Istvan blinked at it. Could it be a real bird?

And Tuarim Mac Elathan was staring up at it, open-mouthed, with wonder in his eyes—

"Liogar!" he breathed. "Liogar? Z'jar?"

It perched on a high branch that hung in the starlight, and looked at them from glittering eyes. Its beak opened, and from it came a sweet, melodic trilling of shimmering, liquid song—which shaped itself into unmistakable words; though whether they formed in the ears or in the mind alone, Istvan could not tell.

"Greetings, Son of Elathan, and greetings ye lords of the Sea-Elves. Greetings, elves and men."

"Greetings, Liogar," said Ethellin the Wise. "So the Hyadean Gate is open."

"The Gate is open, and they at Carcosa told us there was need."

Some vague memory of childhood tales that he had long disregarded and forgotten were stirring in the back of Istvan's mind. *Liogar . . .*

"It has been a hundred years and more since your star last shone through the Gateway," said Tuarim.

"Not so long on our side," said the trilling voice. A second swallow appeared, and swooped down to sit beside the first.

The whole company had stopped to stare at the swallows while they talked, but now there came a faint muttering from the rear that Istvan could not catch, but the elves laughed.

"That is so," said Tuarim Mac Elathan, and his horse began to move.

The swallows left the branch and whirled through the air about him, circling his head, while the Sea-Elves walked beside him, their horses following silently.

Istvan followed the elves, his mind still struggling with elusive memories. Suddenly Tahion's voice burst out from beside him.

"The demon is following us! keep close, and walk warily! Do not stray away from your companions!" He held up the Sword of Kings, its blade now blazing brilliant blue.

"Can you help us against the demon?" asked Ethellin the Wise, and the swallow's sweet, trilling voice answered.

"Not so long as it remains under the trees—not without setting this whole forest ablaze. If it comes into starlight, we will do what we can."

Suddenly, the swallows were gone. Istvan stared at the spaces they had filled, but even as his mind groped for some explanation, Tahion's voice rang out again.

"Listen to the trees!" The elves ahead stopped and turned, and Istvan saw their eyes phosphorescent in the dimness.

"More demons are coming!" cried Tahion. "There are two more ahead of us, coming this way! Common forest demons, I think. It has summoned them! A third is coming on our right. Hear the Rooted People shrieking as it rushes by! They mean to surround us!"

Istvan looked down at the flaming blade of his sword, and looked away again, half-blinded. All about him blades were blazing, burning with need-fire.

The company shrank together, surrounded by the light of their own swords.

In the shadows to the right, a deeper blackness moved. A thin shrilling, utterly unlike the voice of any natural beast, sent shivers down Istvan's spine: his nose filled with a revolting, unnatural smell.

Any mortal horse would have gone mad with terror by now, but the elf-horses were uncannily still.

And through the strip of clear sky above the trail, two silver swallows swooped.

Ahead of them, fleshless blackness came screaming through the trees, and from off to the left came a sound like muffled thunder. The blue gleam of Tahion's blade turned blinding white, and the mingled light of swords drove through the tangled net of branches to strike and stop on writhing walls of oily blackness.

Demons hesitated before the blaze of so much need-fire. But from the left came a single croaking sound, and from out of the trees oozed a wall of liquid blackness. Flaming swords rose to meet it . . .

Istvan saw the writhing darkness at his right in *front* of the trees, and lunged. Cold chilled his hand as the Hastur-blade drove into the transparent darkness . . .

A shrill scream, and the darkness was gone.

Tendrils of blackness leaped from the left, darting toward the men behind the flaming blades. There was a sharp tinkling sound, like glass breaking, and one of the glowing swords was suddenly dimmed.

The swallows vanished from the sky above. A beam of

light stabbed down, piercing the darkness from which the tendrils came.

The earth shook under them. Sudden wind nearly swept them from their feet. A crackling roar was swallowed by the wind.

Demon voices rose in agonized wailing that faded in the distance and was gone.

Where the blackness had lain, a huge hole gaped in the forest floor.

Above it, the silver swallows soared, jubilant, triumphant!

Dair Mac Eykin stood staring at the hilt of his broken Hastur-blade. About a foot of faintly gleaming metal jutted from his hand. On the ground at his feet lay blackened splinters. Istvan squeezed the hilt of his own blade protectively.

Dair raised a face white with shock under the copper wires of his beard. "I guarded it away," he said. "The blackness faded like a cloud, but . . ." He dropped his eyes to the hilt in his hand.

Dorialith of the Sea-Elves was beside him, and put his arm around his shoulders. "Bring the pieces, lad, and the smiths of Rath Tintallain shall reforge the sword stronger than it was before."

He turned to the others. "A strong demon, indeed! I think it would have shattered any single blade here—or even four or five at once—and it was wise enough to fear to attack us all. We are fortunate that the Birds of Morvinion were here to aid us, and banish the creature for us. We owe you thanks, Z'jar and Liogar!"

The silver swallows dived out of the starlight, and their trilling voices answered him. *"This is the task for which we came to your Universe. But if you would have our company on the road before you, mount and ride, for dawn shall soon turn from under us this side of the world, and bear us to other lands. Yet we shall see you when night comes again."*

The elf-horse laid its head on Istvan's shoulder. Istvan blinked and then turned and mounted. Had there been some signal from the elves he had not caught? Or did his horse understand speech? Or was it, indeed, that the speech of the birds was spoken to the mind and not the ears, so that horses could understand it as well as men?

All around him men were mounting—the elves had all

leaped into their saddles as Istvan had turned. Istvan sheathed his sword, his head spinning with questions.

"We owe thanks, also, to Istvan the Archer!" Carroll Mac Lir's voice boomed out. Istvan winced at the name, as always.

Then the horses were moving again, and the wind in his ears shut out Carroll's voice as the big man went on, explaining what Istvan had done. Trees and bushes rushed by with a blur, but the white swallows hung in the air, effortlessly keeping pace. When tree branches hung shadows across the path, the swallows bobbed up in a little flash of silver light, to skim above the branches and then dart down again. Istvan wondered that any bird could keep pace with them at this speed—and then remembered that Z'jar and Liogar were not really birds.

But what *were* they, and why did they choose to take the shape of birds? Brows knotting, he tried to remember that old story from his childhood. For a second, one line from a song stood clear—*"Liogar cloaked in a sun's bright flame"*—he shook his head. That did not seem right. Starlight, perhaps, or moonlight, but . . .

White horses raced through the moonlight, the swallows flashing above. With Immortals from legend to guide him, he rode to the aid of the mysterious city of Rath Tintallain.

CHAPTER FIVE

The Secret Gates

Ghost-white elf-steeds galloped toward the dawn; golden moons rode above the trees. Tahion rested, his horse surging under him. When they reached the journey's end, he could sleep.

At least, when the dawn came, demons and trolls must hide from the sunlight.

One of the swallows vanished in a blur, and Tahion knew it had materialised in Rath Tintallain with news of their coming. The other darted down to Dorialith, circling about the Sea-Elf's head

A moment later the Sea-Elf's horse loomed up next to Tahion, and he heard Dorialith's voice through the wind in his ears.

"Liogar is telling me," the long-bearded elf said—and once again Tahion wondered how he told Liogar from Z'jar—"that there are men and goblins in the woods about Rath Tintallain. We will not reach the main gate without a fight, and we will have fighting enough once we are inside. But if we go craftily, we should be able to reach one of the hidden gates to the dwarf city. Ogar Hammerhand will be able to lead us to it, and if you ride with Ogar you might bring us there with the least trouble."

51

Through starlight and shadow the elf-horses ran. Trees rushed past. Bright-gold dawn moons hung before them in the east. The swallows, white, glowing, darted through the sky.

Once, demon-wailing came from the path ahead; a swallow blurred to a light, and vanished. A slender shaft of brilliance glowed above the trees. The demon's voice rose in a wild shriek, thinned and faded. The beam of light was gone, and there were two swallows in the air above.

The sky paled ahead. And the shocking-sweet, trilling whisper of the swallows sang through all their brains.

"Farewell, friends. We have come now to the very edge of the world. Now we must leave you. Watch for us tomorrow, when night falls!"

And with that, the gleaming swallow-shapes shot straight up into the air, shrinking rapidly to tiny twin stars, and were gone.

The sky paled. Golden moons faded. Birds woke and shook the branches of the trees, while their voices rose, twittering, calling. The twin suns climbed through the treetops.

And as sunlight came pouring over the edge of the world, it leaped in flame from the topmost towers of Rath Tintallain that thrust up from the trees.

Tahion stood by his horse, looking out through a screen of leaves over an endless green carpet made of treetops, that swept to the top of the far-off hill where glittering spires clustered like a crystal crown tipped with blood.

Even across the valley, Tahion could sense the magic that throbbed about it.

Squawking ducks lifted with beating wings from the sleepy little river hid among the trees. Arrows flew among them: one fell.

Through the eyes of a well-hidden squirrel, Tahion watched the hunters then moved on. Demons had sunk into the ground with the coming of dawn, and trolls had hidden themselves hastily in deep caves; but Rath Tintallain was still guarded. Men from Sarlow, sorcerers in black cloth and soldiers in mail, camped before the gates. Savage, half-human Irioch from the Sarlow border prowled through the woods. In the darkest thickets they could find, goblins hid from sunlight, watching about them with huge, nocturnal eyes.

Most were one variety or another of the common rat-goblin, found in shallow networks of burrows all through the Forest of Demons; their spindly bodies, bullet heads, and long, sticklike arms and legs covered with dirty fur—grey, black or brown.

But there were also a few of the rare, deep-cave goblins, smaller than the others, hairless and ink-black, with nearly human features under great bat ears, and bodies nearer to human proportion—scaled, long-tailed hobgoblins that the Dark Ones were said to have bred from the tiny lizards that hide under rocks, and pallid, sluglike goblins from the southern caves.

They hid in the darkest thickets, frightening out small creatures who had hidden there from foragers for the army of Sarlow. Few natural beasts were left: Tahion could not get as clear a picture as he would have liked. But the trees near an elvish dwelling are more aware than others.

As Tahion's mind swept through the valley, he became aware of some disturbance from beyond, a wave of terror that spread through the trees from the direction of Sarlow. Something moved there, moved in sunlight . . .

Ogai Hammerhand shaded his eyes under his broad palm. He was still mounted. Dismounted, his head would have barely reached Tahion's elbow, though in the saddle he was as tall as any.

"Well?" the dwarf asked. "Are we to go on today at all?" His voice was thick and gruff, his beard dark, with coppery tints. Tahion did not answer, but turned instead to Dorialith.

"Something is coming up from the north-east," he said. "Something that does not fear the light of the suns."

"Then we'd best move quickly," said the Sea-Elf, stroking his long beard. "We do not want to be caught outside the walls."

Tahion studied the valley once more, his mind seeking out each group of men and goblins, noting landmarks as he charted a course between them.

"We ride," said Tahion, scrambling to his horse's back, and touching the creature's mind with his own.

The horses rushed down the hillside, a silent avalanche out of the wood. They overtook birds on the wing and as they raced down the slope shifted among themselves, until men with no woodcraft rode in the middle. Suddenly they were running on level ground, and men could see greensward between great pillars of trees that held up a roof of layered leaves.

Tahion led them a twisting, turning course, avoiding men and goblins. The elf-horses, silent as ghosts, followed as though bound by invisible strings. There were foes to the left and foes to the right who never saw them pass.

They stopped all together, like a flock of birds settling in a tree.

"Now you must guide us, dwarf," Tahion said as Ogar Hammerhand's horse drew up beside his. "A group of the enemy is over there," he pointed, "just over that knoll. There are goblins in that thicket."

The dwarf looked thoughtfully around, and then up at the hill where the towers of Rath Tintallain glittered. He swung his short legs and pounded his heels against the elf-steed's snow-white flanks. Dorialith looked pained. The horse moved forward, slowly.

Tahion's mind haunted the forest, looking through the eyes of birds, sensing through the dim awareness of the trees . . .

A choked death scream, suddenly cut off, came from the left. An Irioch scout had blundered in among the elves there. His cry brought others, who rushed into a swarm of elf-arrows.

"Hurry!" said Tahion. The dwarf scowled, and pointed through the trees.

"There," he said. "Get to that rock."

All around them they heard crashing brush and shouting men.

The elf-horses leaped forward, a blur of flashing white. They pulled up in front of a rough slope of gnarled grey rock. The dwarf slid down from the saddle and waddled quickly toward it on his short legs.

A frightened bird leaped up from a bush, and through its eyes Tahion saw scarecrow shapes in a dense thicket. He shouted a warning, and his horse blurred ahead of the dwarf.

Ogar Hammerhand pulled free the sword slung on his back. Tahion leaped from the saddle, and the Sword of Kings flashed in the sun, while pallid need-fire flickered along its edge. Dorialith's steed came swooping in.

Out of the bushes burst hordes of scrawny, long-limbed

creatures with dull grey-black skins and burning red eyes, waving short, curved iron blades. Little taller than the dwarf, they scuttled toward Tahion, and swarmed shrieking around him. The Sword of Kings swung in a sparkling wheel, and pointed heads flew from narrow shoulders.

Others rushed past toward Ogar, but the dwarf stepped to meet them on short sturdy legs, sword drawn back over his shoulder with hands locked on the hilt. As they charged it came lashing out like a scythe, cleaving through bone as through air, and their bodies made a breastwork before him. War cries changed to screams.

A blur of white, and Dorialith was among them, his blade a flickering of icy flame as he struck from his saddle. White horses came weaving through the trees. Goblins fled screaming.

The dwarf ran to the rock. He groped a moment over rugged, weathered stone, then thrust his hand into a narrow opening.

Soundlessly, a part of the stone began to move.

Cracks appeared, and the outline of a wide archway became visible. A huge slab was rolling into the hillside, the top falling back more deeply than the bottom.

"Quickly now!" shouted Dorialith "We must not let the goblins find the gate!"

"They'll find it anyway!" growled the dwarf. "Or they'll tunnel into the passage behind, through the stone."

Elf-horses gathered like wisps of fog at twilight. Men and elves slid from their backs; elves and forest-runners darted with drawn blades into the thickets where the goblins had fled. Wails and crashing brush were heard: they glided noiselessly back, tarry blood dripping from their steel. Men pulled saddlebags and gear from horses' backs.

The stone rolled. Ogar Hammerhand leaped up onto its receding surface and ran toward the sinking end.

A deep voice spoke from the stone.

Tahion stared into the archway. With a rasp of rock, the tilting door settled into the floor of the opening. Mail-rings jingled, and short, broad figures bounded up, scrambling surefooted over rough stone. Down in the tunnel behind them, a dim light glowed.

Deep dwarvish voices rumbled; gnarled figures swarmed into sunlight. Sparkling mail burned his eyes with pinpricks of brightness. Glossy helms glimmered wetly above heavy, thick-furred brows and bristling beards. Great double-bitted axes were gripped in broad hands.

An elf whistled a birdcall, and Tahion's mind flew to the sound, blending with the senses of trees, listening with the ears of a frightened cricket . . .

Booted feet smashed through grass. Leather creaked, iron rings jangled and clashed.

"The soldiers of Sarlow are coming," he said. "Many are their feet, and they run swiftly."

"Inside!" came the deep voice of the dwarf who stood foremost among the warriors by the archway.

Dorialith's voice rose, and suddenly the elf-horses were whirling, rearing, tossing their creamy manes. In a blur of speed they bounded into the forest, like patches of fog driven by wind, and straight toward the approaching soldiery.

"They will have a marvel to report," laughed the Sea-Elf. "Swift, now, into the tunnel!"

Istvan DiVega, shield on his arm, saddlebags draped over his shoulder, stared after the vanishing elf-steeds. To what far country would they go?

The towers of Rath Tintallain reared glittering above the trees. Shimmering magic hung about them, a wild thrill in the blood, a tremor in the heart's deep core: he felt it, like a strain of music played along his nerves, and distrusted it, just as he had distrusted the elf-music in the inn.

Elves were hurrying through the arch, hastening to obey Dorialith's word, but men and dwarves were hanging back, looking up the hill from which, now, the sounds of approaching foemen could be heard.

"Inside!" the dwarf leader roared again. "Fools! Will you waste *all* our lives to prove your courage? Do *you* know the paths to the hidden gates? *Go!*"

Shame-faced dwarves turned and scrambled over the stone of the sunken door, and Tahion and Carroll turned with them, leading reluctant heroes stooping under the arch. Each man lagged, jostling, struggling to be last.

Behind came shouting and the crash of steel. Over his shoulder, Istvan saw double-bladed dwarf-axes wheel in the sun, as tall men, sparkling in a glare of mail, burst through the leaves.

Istvan stumbled off rough rock, and felt his foot slide on smooth, slick stone. Men jostled and muttered all around him. They could stand erect now. A deep voice shouted in the dim-lit cave.

"Close the gates!" They heard the grinding of stone on stone. Rising dark rock locked away the sunlight and the fighting outside. Istvan's sun-glared eyes peered through spark-scarred darkness at rock that rang with muffled shouts and chimes.

"Fear not for those who fight outside," echoes boomed behind him. "They know well these woods. They will but fight their way to another gate, leaving none living who can tell where this door lies. But come! The Lords of Rath Tintallain await you." Torchlight flared at the other side of the crowd; Istvan barely glimpsed the golden beard and fire-jeweled mail of the dwarf who held it.

Echoes rustled with the sound of feet as they followed, stooping in the low-roofed tunnel. Close to his head, Istvan saw glinting specks in the grey stone. Yet the floor was black, polished, and smooth. Above the sound of their feet, a faint, rhythmic chiming pulsed far away, and grew steadily louder.

They passed the mouths of tunnels still marked with the scars of the pick, and tunnels whose polished walls were inlaid with bright mosaics. The rhythmic chiming, ever louder, grew into the sound of distant hammers battering. Jeweled lights glowed in the walls. Their guide put out the torch. They passed through chambers walled with rose marble, and chambers walled with jade, and down squared corridors of planed plain stone, while ever stronger grew the sound of hammering.

Lone dwarves came scurrying by on errands. Stone rang echoing with the deafening sound of metal on anvils clamouring. Groups of dwarves bustled past. Istvan smelled dry smoky iron in the warming air.

Heat and noise swelled before them. They saw more dwarves. The air began to sting their eyes: the belling of the forge hurt their ears.

Soon dwarves thronged the corridors, staring from under bushy brows as they drew aside to let the strangers pass.

A cool breeze blew through hot, smoke-tangled air. They hurried forward, suddenly aware of running sweat and tears.

The breeze poured down a marble stair, sweeping furnace heat away, comforting their faces as they climbed. Behind them, the deafening racket lessened. Then they were blinking at the sudden glare of the twin suns: tan and white and green blurred around them.

After a moment, Istvan could see that the white was the bright stone of towers and walls, the green was leaves and grass, and the tan was the skin of half-naked men and women who wore the green tartan of one of the wild forest clans.

Wild men stared, curious, yet wary, at the weary travelers. Under their feet, stone and earth throbbed with the din of dwarf-hammers. Istvan drew a deep breath of flower scents. On the edge of his nerves he felt something ancient, rich and wild: thrilling anticipation ran through him.

Sweet eldritch music healed his ears. All about him Rath Tintallain shimmered in glory. Already their guide was trotting on his short legs down winding paths between flowering shrubs, elves and dwarves at his heels. Soft music that seemed to come from the air itself moved Istvan's feet, playing on nerves and heartstrings, to bear him dancing down the path between singing flowers, whose small, winged spirits soared dancing out, to whirl with all life in the garden toward its secret center, the source from which poured a throbbing flow of power . . .

"Will they never let us be?" It was the harsh voice of Ingulf the Wanderer, shrill with passion. Istvan, stopping, saw the scarecrow figure flail the air with knotted fists at the end of long, bony arms. *"Why will they not leave us alone!"*

Yet Tahion made no outcry, nor Arthfayel, and the music seemed to be doing no harm. Forcing himself to relax, Istvan let the music sweep him along the winding paths.

A dazzling mystery of white stone towers rose before them. Two rich thrones stood atop stairs at one tall tower's door. In one, a bearded dwarf sat, glittering with jewels, and a gold band binding the blond mane of his hair; yet every eye was drawn to the other throne, for there sat the heart of the wonder and spell that had drawn them across the garden.

Keen eyes, grey as the sea, glowed on them from a face soft and lineless as a child's face, eyes that had seen sights not known to mortal men, and Istvan knew he looked upon one mighty among the elves, one of those great ones, maybe, who had come to the aid of Hastur's sons in ancient days, in the Age of Terror, when Kandol Shadowslayer and Tuarim Mac Elathan were alike unborn.

A jeweled fillet of silver bound his raven hair, and his robes rippled white and silver-grey in the glory that wrapped him 'round. A smile came to his lips, and joy leaped in each man's heart.

"Tuarim, lad!" the Elf-Lord called, his voice sweet and wild as a blackbird's call. "It has been long indeed, since—"

"No more!" A hoarse crow's croaking shattered the music of the Elf-Lord's voice, and a gaunt scarecrow drove elves aside like a whirlwind. "I'll bear no more! I demand justice from the Lords of Rath Tintallain!"

Ingulf the Wanderer stood glaring before the double throne, his face twisted with passion. Men, elves and dwarves gaped at him: the eldritch music stopped.

"Madman!" Carroll Mac Lir's voice rang with disgust. "Ingulf, come to yourself, now!" Istvan heard men mutter all around him, and the gangling figure seemed very alone. "Mad as a hare," Carroll said. "Who but Crazy Ingulf would dare rage so?"

Istvan stepped to Ingulf's side.

"I dare," he said, his calm voice ringing clear. "I, Istvan DiVega of Carcosa, and mad or sane, I demand an accounting for spells placed on us, in the name of my noble kin, the Hasturs of Carcosa."

A startled look shot from under Ingulf's tousled red hair. Tahion stepped to Ingulf's side, followed by Arthfayel and Karik Mac Ulatoc.

"Indeed, Ardcrillon Mac Ioldan," said Tahion, "I myself accuse your spells! You bewitch when there is no need."

"Never have I felt such strong spells, or so many," said Arthfayel.

"Already on this journey I have had to treat one man for elf-shock," said Tahion. "Do they not face dangers enough, without elf-magic to drive them from their wits? Surely you mean no harm, and I know this last spell was but to keep us from losing our way—but of the next spell, and the next? Surely—"

"Why?" Ingulf shrieked. "Why would you do this to us?" I feel your illusions, thick all around us, blinding us! Why?"

"To protect you against that which we guard!" answered

the Elf-Lord. "You fear *we* will drive them mad? Very well,
then! Reach out, mortal wizard, stretch out your nerves, as I
lay down this magic that you fear. Feel what we strive to
shield you from!"

Glory faded and was gone. Colours dimmed: music stilled.

Under Istvan's feet, stone still shuddered with the clamour
of hammers on the anvils of the dwarves, but now its rhythm
was no longer woven with the song of birds into strange elven
music. Birdsong was once more only birdsong. The air smelled
only of the scent of flowers, and the light about them was
only sunlight, no more. The twin suns climbed toward noon,
and Istvan felt the weariness of the long ride suddenly in
every bone.

Above them, red-capped towers rose like white trees.

Arthfayel's face twisted, and he gasped. Tahion shuddered.
And even Istvan could feel *something,* a faint gnawing of
unease at the ends of his nerves.

But he had felt far worse before, across the sea, standing
guard on the Dark Border of the Shadowed Mountains, on the
continent.

It did not seem enough. He tried to remember his boyhood
training in Carcosa, and reached out. There was evil, right
enough—and still, blended with it, a singing in the veins . . .

Sunlit evil, a canker in a rose, cold in the heart of a flame,
striving, aching . . .

"Will they not go mad, having to live with *that*?" the
Elf-Lord cried.

"Elves might go mad, maybe," said Tahion. "Men will
not."

The Dwarf-Lord, his kingly presence no longer drowned in
the other's power, stirred on his throne, and spoke.

"I have told you before, Ardcrillon, that my people never
shudder and suffer as you elves do. That is why the Hasturs
left *us* to watch this thing. It seems that men, too, can bear
it."

"Men can bear it better than they may our magic," said
Ethellin the Wise.

"But *we* may go mad," said another of the elves.

"And it will grow worse as the Night-Things gather about
us," the Elf-Lord said.

Suddenly the hammers underground were stilled: the silence was as sharp as a shout. Elf-lord and Dwarf-Lord

stiffened on their thrones. Istvan felt tension rippling through the crowding elves.

Tahion, too, must have sensed it, but he gave no sign.

"You must protect yourselves, indeed," he said, carefully. "But men do not feel what you feel, and do not suffer as you suffer. There is no need for you to wrap illusion—"

He stopped as a running dwarf pushed through the crowd, and bowed, gasping, before the Dwarf-Lord's throne.

"Goblins are tunneling in the West Maze!" the messenger panted. "Already they have broken into the Chamber of Garnet, and can be heard through the walls of the Old Coal Mine. We have sealed the tunnel to the Chamber of Garnet, and warriors stand watch in the mines. The forges are stilled that we may better listen to their digging. Command us, Lord—is it your will that we seal off the mines as well? Or—"

"No!" The Lord of the Dwarves leaped down from his throne, and stood firm as stone on his short legs. "No! They must pay for entry: let them learn the cost! My axe!" From behind the throne ran one bearing a great, double-bitted dwarf-axe nearly as tall as himself. "Arm yourselves, People of the Rock! When they break through, they shall find us waiting!"

"And our swords, also," said Carroll Mac Lir. "Command us!"

The Dwarf-Lord stared up, and burst into deep, booming laughter. "Nay," he gasped between chuckles, red-cheeked with mirth above his bristling beard. "Nay, my large friend. You are too tall for the tunnels where we must fight! We thank you, but for now you will serve us better resting from your journey: you are weary with long riding, and need sleep and food. There will be fighting enough for all when night comes, doubt not! Cruadorn!" The dwarf who had led them here sprang forth, bowing. "Lead our allies to the chambers prepared for them." Turning back to the heroes, he bowed gravely. "Rest well, my friends, and sleep if you can, for night will bring the worst danger. Sleep well!"

His broad hand closed on the haft of his axe, and he strode off proudly in the midst of his folk.

The Lord of the Elves of Rath Tintallain rose from his throne.

"Sad indeed it is, that you should have cause to complain

of your welcome here,'' he said, ''and most bitterly I regret troubling you. Yet, surely you know that no harm was meant! Rest then, mortal men, and sleep until the night. But you, my kinsmen, come swiftly with me now!''

In a blur of light and laughter, the elven-folk were gone; behind the two thrones the great door opened and closed, and men were blinking at empty thrones on empty steps, and the blank white-crystal wall looming beyond.

CHAPTER SIX

The Mystery of the Hyades

They stared at the shut door. Above, they saw two towers branch like crystal tree trunks, and a third beyond them.

Glancing over his shoulder, Istvan saw that they were alone now, neither elf nor dwarf in sight, but for Cruadorn.

"Come!" said the dwarf. "I will take you to the others."

"Others?" Ingulf asked.

"The other heroes, of course!" Laughing, the dwarf strode away on sturdy short legs down a path of crushed shale that ran between rosebushes. Turning to follow, Istvan glimpsed between trees a low wall that ran out from the ends of the fortress wall, and beyond it a dizzying blur of distant treetops.

The rose-scented wind that blew about them was a rough, chill, hilltop wind that carried a screeching of angry birds.

When the enchantment had been on him, the song of birds had blended into the music of the elves, and all had seemed peaceful; now he knew the noise of birds disturbed by strangers.

Under their feet, the dwarves were marching to war, and goblins tunneled their way into the mines. And somewhere, that dark menace he had only half-sensed slept at the heart of Rath Tintallain.

Yet though the mist of magic and mystery was gone, beauty still remained. Pale-blue blossoms on flowering vines

63

wreathed tree branches like smoke. Beyond the rose bushes were apple trees, some bright with blossom, others heavy with fruit.

Hard gravel crunched under Istvan's feet: weariness weighted his limbs. The long ride had been hard on him. Perhaps he was getting old. After all, his son Rafayel, the ungrateful brat, was a man full-grown now, off adventuring on his own. But then, so wild a ride would surely have tired even a younger man.

"What has become of that Sea-Elf who said my sword could be reforged?" Dair Mac Eykin grumbled behind him. "It was very well for you to offer our swords to the Dwarf-Lord, Carroll—you have one! But what use am I in a fight, with a broken sword?"

"If it is a sword you want forged," said Cruadorn, "why would you ask an elf? Let me have the pieces of your blade and I will forge you a sword that will cut an anvil in half, without dulling the edge or nicking it." The dwarf halted. "Here, give me the pieces now, and I can work during the night and have the new blade for you in the morning." Istvan stepped aside to let Dair pass, and the woods-runner, joining the dwarf, handed him the pieces.

Cruadorn's breath hissed in a gasp, as he weighed them in his hands.

"This is a Hastur-blade!" He frowned. "I have heard strange tales of Hastur-blades. Well, we shall see."

They went on again. There were no more rose bushes beside the path: beech leaves and hazel leaves whispered in the wind above low, friendly apple boughs. Through the streets ahead came glimpses of wide, grey stone.

"So, is this what the place really looks like?" Starn MacMalkom asked, staring 'round. The dwarf laughed.

"Hard to say! We see it seldom! Old Ardcrillon and the rest are always playing their tricks up here!"

The grey wall grew closer, and through the leaves Istvan saw a vast, red-brown roof, and realised it was all one gigantic building, as large as the fortress behind them.

"Ingulf," said Carroll Mac Lir's voice, "I think, perhaps, I owe you apologies." But there was no penitence in the proud voice. Ingulf snorted.

"You think so, do you? Well, Carroll, when you've thought about it enough that you know for sure, do you be letting me know!'' Yet the lean islander's voice was calmer now and he laughed. ''Myself, I know well that I should be thanking Tahion Mac Raquinon and—Ishvawn—UaVeaga and—and I fear I've forgotten your name, my friend. . . ?''

''Why, that is Arthfayel Mac Ronan!'' Cormac the Harper's rich voice burst in. ''Have you never heard how he turned the Dark Host aside from Gloccamora? Or how he drove the demon out of Tollnagow?'' Istvan smiled to himself. *Poets!*

Before them now, a clear path appeared that ran straight to a door in the great grey building. But to Istvan's surprise, the dwarf passed it by, and took instead the path that circled the building, with the wall on their right. It was a round building like a stubby tower, with a broad red-brown cone for a roof, huge as a hill.

''But could you make any sense out of that elf's babble?'' Ingulf asked. ''What was he so frightened of? I felt nothing when he took off his spells!''

''Some great evil is buried in the heart of Rath Tintallain,'' the wizard said somberly. ''You'll remember, Tahion, what I told you at Nockarv.'' Tahion nodded.

''It must be a great evil, indeed,'' said Tahion, ''to be fenced about with such strong spells. In truth, it is not so much the evil itself, I think, as the conflict of power about it, that drives the elves half mad, so that they wrap themselves— and us—in so thick a mantle of illusion. Not even on the Dark Border have I felt such strong spells in conflict. It made my head ache. It must be far worse for the elves.''

They stepped out of tree-shadow and stood blinking in bright sunlight at a broad, green, sloping lawn, and breathing a rich smell of growing herbs. On their right loomed the weathered stone of the curved grey wall of the round building.

A swallow twisted in the air and darted away. Startled, Istvan looked at it closely, but this was a flesh-and-blood bird, blue wings flashing in bright sunlight, above a pale, butter-coloured breast.

''Tahion?'' he said, his memory stirred. ''Were—those—'' he waved his hand at the skimming, swooping bird, ''those swallow-things we met on the road also illusions of the elves, or—or what were they?''

''Not of the elves, no,'' said Tahion slowly. ''They were— well, not real birds, no—they take that shape for the eyes of men—but they are allies of Hastur, who come from outside the Universe entirely. It is a part of the Mystery of the Hyades.''

"What are you talking about *now*?" groaned Ingulf.

"Well," said Arthfayel, laughing, "I will tell you all *I* know, and then we can all be mystified together. When I studied at Elthar, they taught me that the stars of the Hunter and the Bull are at once in two Worlds, and shine not only here but on that World from which Hastur first brought the ancestors of men; and that those stars form a Gateway into that other Universe. Every so often, the movement of the stars allows the light of one star in that Otherworld to shine through the Gateway. And where the light of that star shines, there those two mighty powers, which those who must use tongues to speak name Liogar and Z'jar, may manifest themselves, forging out of starlight such shapes as you have seen.

"But as to what they are—who can say? The Hasturs call them the Star Children; the elves, the Birds of Morvinion. At Elthar, men and elves who think themselves wise have long argued what that might mean. Some say that the heat and pressure at the heart of a sun—and the stars are suns—is so great that it must produce mind, and that Z'jar and Liogar are emanations of the mind of that star. Others say that they are the creations of some unknown race of wizards in that other Universe, creatures forged of energy, like Arbahir, Tintinarë, or ancient Nurgil who served Thale the false Hastur. Still others claim that they are primordial spirits, kin, perhaps, to Hastur and Awan A'Tawith, bound to their star as punishment for some ancient, inconceivable crime. Who knows? *I* do not!''

About them on the lawn were scattered bands of ragged forest-folk: tangle-haired women, washing clothes in a fountain that leaped and sparkled in the light, stared shyly at the heroes as they passed. Savage hunters glared at them, sullen and suspicious.

"Long ago," said Tahion slowly, like a man struggling to remember some vague dream, "Z'jar told me—told my ancestor, King Onetatsi—that it was because swallows were so beautiful that he and his brother took that shape for the eyes of men—also because a larger shape would be hard to form from the starlight. And—" he straightened, eyes wide with sudden wonder, "and—Hastur himself told—told Halladin, the first of my line, that the Dark Lords would have devoured that other Universe as well, had not the Brothers—so he called them—had not the Brothers defended it.''

"It is said at Elthar that they help the Hasturs defend the Hyadean Gate,'' mused Arthfayel.

Ahead, the open lawn ended; cold wind blew through open metal gates where their path pierced a thick thorn hedge. Beyond, aspen, poplar and white birch mingled with rowen, thorn and oak; leaves rustled and roared overhead. Between the boles, Istvan glimpsed the furtive figures of more of the wild tribesmen, slinking away among the trees.

"And Hastur told King Showenhone, two hundred years after,'' Tahion went on, his eyes still bright with wonder, "that the Brothers fly as far as light can reach through space, and watch all that happens in that Otherworld, though they rarely interfere or manifest themselves. He said they suffer neither harm nor fear of harm, for they cannot die unless their star is destroyed, and thus, only the Dark Lords are a threat to them.''

"Wait, now!'' Fergus Mac Trenar boomed from behind them. "Will you be telling us that the Dark Things have the power to destroy a star—a *sun*?''

"The power of the Eight Dark Lords in concert,'' said Tahion, "is far beyond my reckoning, or my knowledge. But they teach in both Elthar and Carcosa that Hastur found here a ruined Universe, where many stars had already been destroyed. But such questions you must ask of the Hasturs, and not of us poor mortal wizards!''

Wind-lashed leaves rustled and surged, and a wall of brown stone appeared through them. Then, on their left, the trees were gone, and they saw, above a low, brown breastwork, the treetops of the Forest of Demons spread out like a carpet of moss far below.

Before them, the breastwork reared up into a house that grew out of the wall, its squared corners of dwarf-worked blocks of stone fitted so tightly that it was smooth to the eye—whatever mortar used, invisible. A red roof angled down from the wall's top. Their path ran straight to a fine wooden door.

"Here we are,'' said Cruadorn. "Welcome, heroes, to our hall: I hope you find it a fit home for you! Here your comrades wait.'' He threw open the door, and they filed in after him.

Steps below them led to a sunken floor laced with lines of light from narrow arrow-slits in the cliff's face at their left; from the right, light poured through wider arches. Leaf-shadows stirred on the floor.

Men looked up at them, hands on swords. From behind a table near the foot of the stairs, a great brute of a man laid down the bone he had been gnawing, his smouldering blue eyes glaring suspiciously from under a shock of black hair bound by a slim silver band: he was as still as a cat about to spring. Thirty or more warriors thronged the hall beyond, all poised and still.

"I will leave you now with your kin," said Cruadorn, weighing the two shards of Dair Mac Eykin's broken Hastur-blade in his hands. "I have a sword to forge."

"Wait!" said Cormac the Harper. "Has any news come to you about the band of dwarves who went out when we came in?" The dwarf shook his head.

"Not yet."

"Well then," said the Harper, "it would be very kind of you to find out, and tell it me. And if you could, bring word also of the fighting in the mines."

"I will," said the dwarf. He turned to leave. Below, the silent, deadly men had dropped their hands from their swords, and low murmurs came from the back of the room. A slender, elegantly clad man with silky yellow hair whispered something to the black-maned brute at the table, which brought a gust of hearty laughter from a grim, scarred face.

"Well, now!" Carroll Mac Lir's voice boomed. "*That* is better!" He strode forward to stand at the head of the stairs. "You at least know *me*, Conn MacBran! So you need not sit glaring at us as though you thought we were spies from Sarlow!" Again, the giant at the table laughed.

"True, Carroll," his deep, powerful voice called back, "but not all *my* foes are from Sarlow!"

"*Arthfayel!*" a voice shouted from the back of the room, and the crowd split to make way for a lean, ragged, red-topped man.

"Anarod!" shouted Arthfayel. "Brother!" He ran down the stairs. Now laughter and conversation sounded on the floor below.

"Quite a little army," Tahion murmured to Istvan. "Small, but select. Conn you've surely heard of—he was over the sea fighting for Kobol and Thernhelm a few years back. They say he comes from one of the wild head-hunting tribes south of Ualfeim."

"They say that," said Cormac the Harper, joining them, "and they say there is no man better to lead in war against the forest barbarians—since he is one himself. It is said he was a galley slave in Sarlow, and wrought a bloody vengeance on his captors even before he drifted into the civlised world, and has since acquired sword-skill in every land. He was made a general by the Airarian Emperor not long since, but was caught conspiring to seize the crown, and now there is a price on his head."

"From their dress, I would guess most of these to be from Ualfeim or Cotarjon," said Tahion. "Do you know any of them, Cormac?"

At the stairs' foot, Arthfayel embraced the red-haired man. Cormac looked out over the crowd

"Very few," he said. "The sun-haired, frail fellow there by Conn, I think, is Lamon of Athprecan, the youngest brother of Lord Athprecan in Cotarjon, and he, too, has been an outlaw in his day. He is a clever man, but unlucky, I fear. And there beyond them, the tawny-haired man with a moustache like a catfish—that is Larthon, slayer of trolls. See how his shield is dented and battered? There are good songs about him. And Anarod Mac Moran, of course, Arthfayel's foster-brother. He comes from the Three Kingdoms originally, Elantir, I believe, but he married a woman of Clan Gileran and has been dwelling in the woods with her people."

"He is the one who descended into the Caverns of the Veneduaith, is he not?" Tahion asked, as they went down the stairs.

"He is," said the Harper. "That was a famous deed! And the islander, there—"

But a cry from Anarod silenced him.

"Dead! Eilith is dead, and our little son motherless!" The voice was shrill with grief: shock replaced joy on Arthfayel's face. "Evil *Urushe* came in the night, and the fire was at our little house as we woke. I snatched up my sword, and she the babe, and we ran outside, with them all around us, and smoke from the house, and I struck and I slew in the smoke.

"I heard her scream, and the baby crying, and I saw her lying in her blood with a spear through her, and the baby crying in her arms. Then, in the smoke, something dark and small snatched up my son and ran with him, and I followed through smoke and darkness by the sound of his crying, until I caught the goblin who had taken him, and then I killed and I killed . . .

"Then I wandered, my little son hungry in my arms, until the elves found me."

"And where is little Liam now?" Arthfayel asked gently.

"He is here. There is an elf-woman nurses him—I have no milk for him. I will die soon, too, I think."

"Anarod . . ."

"Will you take the baby, Arthfayel, when I am dead? Or must I leave him among the elves?"

"Anarod, man, do not talk so! You must live to be a father to him now. Of course I would care for him, Brother, but it will be better for you to raise him yourself. When he is weaned, you can reclaim him from the elves, and then . . ."

"I shall not live till he is weaned," said Anarod, shaking his head. "Man, I saw what they'd done to her! When I came back. They'd played with her body. They ate—they—" Huge, calloused hands hid the anguished face, and great sobs broke the voice. Arthfayel glared at the men who had stopped to listen; they drew away, guiltily. This was no tale for strangers to hear.

Istvan saw Tahion's face grim, and remembered that the dead girl had been of Clan Gileran—the clan of Tahion's mother.

"Did you know her?" he asked gently. Tahion nodded.

"My cousin's child. I remember her as a little girl. I have not seen her for—years. I had been meaning to ride down and meet this famous western warrior she had wed." His face twisted. "Well, I—" He fell, silent, brooding, and Istvan sought vainly for some comforting word.

All around them men spoke, greeting one another. Suddenly, out of the battle, Istvan heard his own name. Turning, he saw a tall, lean-featured blond man in an islander's tartan robe, who walked with a strange grace; a walk that said plainly to Istvan that this man was a master of the "Bleeding Wind" Sword Style.

"Is it not Istvan the Archer?" the islander said. Istvan

stiffened at the hated name. "Do you not remember me? We were both at the battle near Innijvalga, where the Emperor's fleet smashed both the Norian raiders and the fleet of Svaran of Sarlow that had come to their aid." That long-nosed face was familiar and, after a moment, Istvan remembered it.

"Layareh," he said, pronouncing the name with care, recalling that men called him *Layareh the Proud*. "Yes, I remember you. So you, too, are here." The islander nodded.

"Of course. Ah, Ingulf, it has been years, indeed. And Fithil, I am glad to see you again. But what are *you* doing here, Karik Mac Ulatoc?"

The brown man started, and hesitated, but Ingulf spoke for him.

"You need not look over your nose so, Layareh. Tuarim Mac Elathan himself bade him come."

The pale, blue eyes, cold as death, widened in mock surprise, and a false smile curved the thin lips.

"Is it so indeed? Ah, surely, 'tis what they say, 'a wonder by daylight,' is it not?" He turned and strode away, leaving Karik Mac Ulatoc glaring after him, and strode over to Conn Mac Bran. The barbarian glowered suspiciously at the three islanders.

"They say Layareh the Proud went into exile with Conn Mac Bran," said Cormac, low-voiced. "He is one of the greatest of the swordsmen of the Isles. But see how Conn glares! He is remembering the price the Emperor has put on his head."

"Let us hope foes come against us quickly," Tahion replied in a whisper, "before the politics of Airaria, or some feud between the clans, set us all at each other's throats. I see men here in the tartans of the Ua Haldir and Ua Killym, and I know there has been bloodshed between those Clans for centuries uncounted; and I know that there are more foolish hatreds and feuds in Y'gora than I can ever remember."

Cormac nodded. But at that moment another figure came through the crowd. It looked more like an elf than a man. Istvan stared a moment, uncertain. In Y'gora, many men had elf-blood . . .

"You should remember me, Tahion Mac Raquinon," the newcomer's voice was a high, chiming tenor, like bells of silver. "I am Alphth, the Changeling; Ardcrillon Stoneweaver has asked me to help care for you mortal men, since—since I am one myself.'' He smiled. Tahion laughed.

''I remember you indeed. Does this caring for us mortals involve such matters as food or beds?''

''Indeed!'' Alphth laughed. ''You look as though you need such. Follow me!''

They wove through the crowd. At the back of the room, a table held dishes of apples and bowls of beechnuts and hazelnuts. Nearby, a sink was piled high with dirty dishes, and the table was littered with bones, crumbs, shells and apple cores.

''You are not, alas, first at the feast,'' Alphth observed wryly. ''The wine is gone, also. Would you like water or milk?''

''Milk will be a pleasant change,'' said Tahion. Istvan nodded agreement, and Alphth filled two horns from an earthen pitcher. Tahion started as he sipped it.

''I had thought it would be deer's milk,'' he said, surprised. ''My thanks to the giver! We are highly favoured!''

''She will be pleased,'' said Alphth. Istvan sipped sweetness that was headier than wine, that seemed to burn the weariness from his bones—a wild sweetness, that stilled the gnawing of his hunger.

They ate hazelnuts and beechnuts and bright apples rich with juice: a dwarf bustled in with sausages and mushrooms. Istvan felt comfortable and sleepy, his weariness no longer pain.

''You mentioned beds, did you not?'' he said at last. The Changeling laughed.

''Indeed,'' he said, ''beds for all.'' It was a far better bed than Istvan had expected, soft down in fine linen, and he had soon settled into a soft sleep, heedless of the men snoring all about him.

CHAPTER SEVEN

At the Gates of the Singing Fountain

Prince Tahion was the first to wake, as sunset reddened brown stone walls and lit up piled dishes. On soundless feet he stole between snoring herocs, and slipped into stillness outside, under a roofless blue sky where high-sailing caravels of cloud were dyed pink and gold by twin suns poised at the edge of the world. Crystal towers glowed rose and violet above the trees.

All about him, Tahion, Lord of the Living Forest, Initiate of Aldenrah and Adept of Elthar, could feel the subtle mysteries of the trees: ponderous, wordless thoughts like solemn music. Potent trees of guarding magic, oak, ash, and thorn, were planted all along the wall and below, at the cliff's foot. The native power that they drew up from the earth had been fanned to bright flame by the elves: they throbbed with glowing power, the vigor of their sap tingling in his blood.

The twin suns slid behind distant hills, and against the broad band of rainbow light they left, small dark dots appeared: flocks of waterfowl, wings rowing on the wind toward some nearby lake or stream. But as they neared Rath Tintallain they swerved away in fear.

Sudden, sweet music sounded near the base of the towers, and Tahion knew that elves danced among the trees. Another mortal would have thought it but sport; Tahion knew that it is by song and gesture, dance and verse, that the elf-kin weave the spells through which they are fed and clothed and sheltered by the life of the wood.

He felt deer drift, ghostlike, between the trees: a lordly stag and his does. An elf-woman met them singing, and, slipping a cord around one doe's hind legs, began to milk her.

Rowan trees throbbed with the fires of life: power prickled from the thorn. Scattered birch and aspen, poplar and alder, all added their unique energies to the fence of living power formed by the pattern that the elves had planted.

Carefully pricking his thumb, Tahion let fall a drop of blood, a gift to the earth, and his mind spread out through root and leaf and branch . . .

He felt through earth the gathering war: battle in the deep dwarf mines, goblins tunneling, and demon shadows stirring in the stone. Radiance protected the dwarf tunnels, but outside them deadly shadows prowled. Goblins scrambled from dense thickets, armed men crashed over dead leaves.

Far to the north and east, trees screamed as cold death crawled through them.

One of the beating hearts in the building behind had wakened: he felt it come to the door, feet soft on the stone. Tahion did not turn until he heard a sudden rasp of steel. Even as trained reflexes brought him around, his senses recognised Istvan DiVega, and knew that the older man was making up for the practice lost on the long ride.

The Seynyorean's blade flashed with need-fire as it glided through one of the training dances of the Three Swords School—the exercise that DiVega normally did each dawn. Tahion watched, joying in the grace of the older man's movements and the power that flowed through DiVega's body —an unconscious power of which DiVega himself was no more aware than were the trees about him.

The elf-woman bound and milked the does, one by one. Elves sang to the trees. The armies of the dark gathered: goblins scuttled through brush. Bird and beast fled. Stars pricked out in the sky as the last light of sunset faded. Swarms of moons drifted between the stars; the head of the Bull lifted above the hills.

And on the wings of starlight came the silver swallows, their silent voices singing in the minds of men and elves:

Danger! Arm yourselves, elves and men! The ground between the trees is thick with the foe, and demons rise from the earth! Beware!

Sleeping heroes woke: feet sounded in the hall; metal clashed. Istvan DiVega stepped to the wall. Tahion joined him, and drew the Sword of Kings: golden light glowed in the steel.

Carroll Mac Lir and Conn Mac Bran bounded from the door, and behind them poured the heroes of Y'gora. Need-fire from their swords lit the parapet like bright moonlight. Elves came rushing through the trees.

Below, Tahion sensed trees throbbing with power. Goblins cringed back though it could not harm flesh and blood. Soldiers from Sarlow tramped stolidly through the barrier, mail-rings jangling.

Withering trees screamed as demons rushed through the forest like black fire.

"Hastur preserve us!" DiVega swore. "Look at them!"

Life flared up in the rowan trees as the black fires neared the fort. Demons recoiled from the living flames. But Tahion knew that the trees could not hold them back for long.

A blue-robed figure appeared upon the wall.

One of the silver swallows blurred into an intense beam of condensed starlight, which stabbed between the trees into a writhing mass of darkness. Tahion could feel the starbeam drilling into the cold, black fire, felt the fabric of space tear. Power erupted: a shrill screech echoed in their ears.

Flame sprouted: the demon crackled and vanished in light. The swallows soared, triumphant!

Five flaming figures appeared at the cliff's foot, need-fire streaming from their hands. Black fire blossomed red, and shrill demon voices wailed.

The demons were gone; burned or fled. Flaming figures vanished as spears flew toward them. Five blue-robed figures appeared upon the wall.

Kandol Hastur-Lord turned inward, and stepped down: other Hasturs followed as a flight of arrows soared through the air where they had stood.

But Tahion, startled, saw their faces drawn with pain.

Elves were gathered all around now, more every moment coming through the trees: savage warriors of the Ua Cadell gathered in a sullen knot. The flame from the swords of heroes and elves lit the wall as bright as day.

"Kandol!" Tuarim Mac Elathan cried. "So, you have come at last!"

"We are here, old friend," said the Hastur-Lord, nodding— but his voice was faint with weariness and strain. Tahion's fine senses quivered with the pain and weakness of the Hasturs; he could see now the muddied colours of the auras around them, flickering and wavering, as though some force tore at them, draining their power . . .

His senses focused, then drifted, seeking. The power that tore so at the Hasturs came from underground: that same surging crash of clashing good and evil that the elves guarded against, the mystery that lay somewhere at the heart of Rath Tintallain.

Tuarim stepped to the wall, and looked down.

"Not a demon in sight," said he. "And we've seen no dragons yet. Men and goblins must needs climb the wall. This may not be so desperate as we believed."

"We have but met the first challenge, old friend," said Kandol somberly, "but more will come. Many powers move against Rath Tintallain."

"Something very deadly moves in the north," Tahion said, watching the Hastur-Lord's face. Kandol turned to him, and then back to the wall. Awkwardly, the Hastur-Lord climbed up onto the stone. Quickly glancing around, Tahion saw Arthfayel and Finloq and other Adepts of Elthar staring.

Arrows came hissing up from the ground, but they curved away from Kandol's body as though deflected by an invisible wall. Kandol stood staring into the north, and then, turning, shouted aloud.

"Come, my kinsmen!" Kandol shouted. "The *Tromdoel* is coming. Let us go to meet it. There is little more for us to do here! Beware of arrows as you leave!"

Tahion met Arthfayel's eyes. This was unheard of. The children of Hastur could speak from mind to mind: why should the Hastur-Lord need to use his voice to speak to his kin?

Could it be the Shadow of the Ancients? Yet that would have affected him as well, and he had never heard of the Shadow of the Ancients in Y'gora before . . .

Kandol Hastur vanished, and the other five Hasturs, who

had been scattered among the elves, all came walking to the wall and, climbing upon it, balanced there a moment, then vanished. All the wizards exchanged glances. What power was this, that could so affect the Lords of the World?

Istvan, too, wondered: he was Carcosan born and bred, and knew there was no reason for the Hasturs to walk or talk like mortal men. He frowned as he looked down the long cliff face, and saw torches coming out of the trees, glittering on the mail-shirts of tall men.

"Look there, Carroll!" Ingulf the Wanderer's voice rang. "See! Grom Beardless survived the wound you gave him!"

Carroll cursed. Other men stiffened.

"Grom Beardless!" snarled Conn Mac Bran. "He'll be Grom Headless if I catch him!" He spat.

Other voices muttered. Istvan looked down, and Ingulf, understanding, pointed. A line of steel-clad men with great, wheel-like shields were drawn up near the cliff's foot, and a little ahead of the line one had turned up a handsome, boyish face, smooth-jawed, and Istvan saw a swordsman's grace in the way the man moved.

More men were coming out of the trees. One towered above his fellows by more than a head. And near him was a black shape like a statue.

"Vor Half-Troll is here, too!" exclaimed Ingulf. "And that butcher, Svaran!"

Heroes gathered at the wall. Carroll Mac Lir heaved high his heavy iron javelin, and drove it down with a snarled curse.

Grom Beardless leaped aside; the pointed iron bar buried itself where he had stood, less than a third of its length quivering above the ground.

Fergus Mac Trenar's iron javelin flew to better effect, smashing through one of the huge wooden shields to spike the man behind it to the ground. And now others of the heroes hurled the terrible iron stakes down the cliff face.

Arrows leaped up, and the heroes drew back, swatting arrows with their swords. Elves sprang to the wall, drawing deep bows. Another elf came with spare bows and quivers, passing them out among the heroes.

" 'Tis poor light for shooting," Anarod grumbled, seizing

a bow. Istvan hesitated, filled with loathing, then reluctantly reached to take one. Angrily he strung it, then snatched a quiver with his other hand. Awkwardly jerking out an arrow with the hand that held the bow, he sprang to the wall, sliding his arm through the quiver's strap and letting it hang as he fitted the arrow to the string. Anarod's bow was already drawn back: he loosed and the arrow flew, to quiver at the edge of one of the great round shields.

Istvan pressed his body into the bow, his angry mind remembering a scarred face from his youth. *Coward,* he remembered: the string strummed and his arrow hummed down, and pressed above Anarod's to vanish behind the shield.

The shield swayed, dipped, and then fell forward with the man on top. An arrow broke under the face: by luck he had struck the eye.

Murderer, Istvan thought. Already he was fumbling for another arrow. All around him bowstrings thrummed in a steady, musical monotone.

He sprang up on top of the wall, nocking the shaft. An arrow drove at him, and he brushed it aside with his bow, as though it were a sword thrust. This was better! He need feel no shame if his enemies could kill him as well . . .

His eyes quickly hunted out the archer: he felt the bow stretch in his hand. Arrow and string strummed free from his fingers; he reached for another. The archer fell and lay still. Istvan's fingers closed on feathers, but they slipped from his grasp: the quiver was in the wrong place. He tossed the bow into his other hand, and drew out the arrow with his left. He had always been able to shoot equally well with either hand, another unwanted talent . . .

An archer below had his bow raised, and his shaft came skimming up as Istvan loosed. He tensed to dodge or guard. . .

Another arrow met the rising arrow in midair, and split it.

Even as Istvan drew a deep breath of relief at his luck, two other arrows met and skittered aside.

He jerked out another arrow and nocked it, even as he watched shafts meet in the air below. His eye picked out an archer, and his bow felled him, even while his mind stared at battling arrows.

"Well shot, mortal! And skilled with either hand, too!" The voice was the high, chiming tenor of an elf, and a quick glance to the side showed Istvan the speaker balancing casually on the wall beside him, his hands a blur as he nocked and drew and loosed with a speed a man could barely see, and no man could match, his bowstring strumming and humming.

Mechanically, Istvan nocked another arrow, aimed and killed. But in the time it took him to draw his bow, the elf's close-spaced arrows had scythed down nearly a dozen men.

"Not for a hundred years have I met a mortal who shot as well as you, not since Diornach the Changeling, and I am not sure you may not be better than he was." As the elf spoke, shaft after shaft flew from his bow. All along the wall men and elves were shooting, and under that rain of arrows the steel-clad men of Sarlow were falling back into the trees, shields and mail-shirts bristling. Istvan lowered his bow. This was only slaughter now, the kind of long-range butchery he hated—the kind that had won him his first fame.

In a moment there were no targets left, as the last of the enemy vanished under the trees. One figure stood, all in black armour like a statue: arrows shattered on the steel.

The music of bowstrings died away, except for the one elf who stood on the wall beside Istvan, his hands still blurred, his string still humming as he hurled shaft after shaft into the mass of leaves below. *Useless,* Istvan thought, but then he heard the screams from under the trees, and realised that the uncanny vision of the elf archer was allowing him to find men through the leaves, and then place his arrows through tiny gaps between leaf and branch that a mortal man could never have seen.

Shivering, he jumped down from the wall and, sick with disgust, hurled bow and quiver to the ground.

"Are you not he that men call Istvan the Archer?" the elf asked. Istvan shuddered; his hands clenched.

"Some call me that," he whispered, his throat dry and harsh, "but never my friends."

The elf stopped shooting at last, and leaped lightly from the walk. "Well, then, I must learn to call you something else!" said the elf, with a smile guileless and joyful as a child's. "It pleases me to meet so skilled a bowman, and—" His smile slowly faded, as it met no reflection in Istvan's face. After a moment, the elf bowed gravely. "I meant no offence, yet I see I have offended you. Forgive me."

He walked away, and a part of Istvan cried out for the

smile he had seen; but he stared at the thrown bow with
loathing, and shook as with an ague. How many men had that
Immortal killed? How many men had died, cowering under
the trees, unable even to see slim death slip between the
branches?

He had hoped his skill had gone: he had not touched a bow
in years.

"Man!" Cormac the Harper's voice sounded in his ear.
"Do you not know who that was? Arduiad Mac Artholon, the
greatest bowman of the elves! I heard him speak to you, there
on the wall, telling you how well you shot! Ah, what a
song!"

Istvan clenched his hand to keep it from his sword's hilt, to
keep the blade from the bard's throat. Another song about
Istvan the Archer! He could never be free of it! But he could
kill this one song now with a simple movement of his arm. . .

There was already too much blood on his hands.

Arduiad, the son of Artholon. Oh yes, he knew that name.
Songs of the elf-archer's deeds went back more than a thousand years. In truth, it had been some of those songs that had
first sent his hand to a bow as a small boy.

Rage and shame filled him.

But what need had brought such famous warriors as Arduiad
Mac Artholon and Tuarim Mac Elathan here, to say nothing
of the mortal heroes? What was so precious in Rath Tintallain,
or so feared, that such ancient elvish heroes, as well as the
most famous of mortal men, must be gathered to its defence?

He saw Tahion wince, and then heard from the wood
below the sound of axes. He knew that Tahion felt the axe
bite, heard the trees scream . . .

Such great heroes, and they scarcely seemed needed. The
best human archer was no match for an elf: the Hasturs and
the swallows from the stars could beat back demons; dwarves
could fight in tunnels where a man could not stand. What
need was there here for him?

"Are we to fight at all?" grumbled Carroll Mac Lir,
echoing Istvan's thoughts. "I am sure Cormac will be glad to
see all this, but for the rest of us, it hardly seems worth
coming all this way to stand and watch a battle."

"The attack was barely begun," said Tuarim Mac Elathan.
"Later, there will be fighting enough."

"Indeed, they make siege ladders now," said Arduiad,

leaning on his great bow. "Can you not hear them?" Axes rang louder and faster in the wood below.

They were suddenly drowned in the sound of drums. Wild yells came from inside the wall. A fierce glow blazed among the trees, and looking inward Istvan saw a great bonfire, and about it the savage warriors of the Ua Cadell, dancing and shaking their weapons to the throbbing of the drums.

"I should call it a long ladder that would come up this cliff," said Ingulf.

"I've carried assaults on higher walls than these," snorted Conn Mac Bran scornfully.

"There have been ladders at this wall before," said Tuarim. "And when enough of those trees have fallen, you will see goblins swarming up like ants at a honey pot."

From behind, drums throbbed. Wild men danced.

Conn Mac Bran's teeth flashed in the firelight.

"Ah!" he said. "That is better than standing here watching. Bah! Let us go out one of these secret gates, and come back with a few of their heads. If I had the head of Grom Beardless, I would be glad to dance!"

"Are you a fool?" snapped Carroll. "There is a very big army out in those woods!"

"I am tired of sitting, also!" shouted Anarod. "I want to kill a few of those filthy, woman-eating, vicious, murdering . . ." His voice became shrill with hate.

"You will kill some soon," said Tahion, his voice pained. "They will be coming."

With a deep, throbbing moan, a bagpipe filled, and its music wove itself into the pulse of the drums. Turning, Istvan saw in surprise Starn MacMalcom, firelight flashing from the silver of his trappings while his fingers flickered on the chanter, playing by the fire where the Ua Cadell danced.

Elves gathered to listen. Flann MacMalkom stood watching his chief, naked worship in his eyes.

A dwarf came trotting through the trees.

"Ah, Cruadorn!" cried Dair Mac Eykin. "There you are! Have you my sword?"

"Ach, 'tis not ready yet!" the dwarf exclaimed. "The fire's not hot enough."

"How goes the fighting in the mines?" Cormac called. "And have you news of—"

"I have no time!" cried the dwarf. "Listen and you shall hear! Tuarim!" The elf turned. "There is trouble upon us, and we need your aid!"

"What is this?" asked Tuarim, springing to the dwarf's side in a blur.

"The fighting in the mines goes badly, and we are hardpressed. But this morning Cadvan, son of Guorvan, went forth with forty warriors to guard the gate by which our mortal friends entered, and keep safe that gate's secret. We had word this afternoon that they reached the Gate of the Singing Fountain, and were resting there. But now Naf, son of Amron, has come, badly wounded, bringing news that goblins have tunneled into the hallway behind the gate, and have trapped them there.

"But King Aurothror and his warriors are caught in a bitter battle in the mines, for hordes of goblins have swarmed through many tunnels and Aurothror can spare little of his force. Hetun, son of Aurothror, has gone, and with him Prince Tyrin and his followers, and after them twenty more, under Kilith son of Kimon. Aurothror has sent me to beg you for aid."

"Enough!" said Tuarim. His voice rose in a shout. "Listen, men and elves! I go to aid the dwarves! Who goes with me?"

"I come!" cried Anarod, echoed by Conn. "I am with you!" cried Ingulf, and then a chorus of voices joined.

"I remain!" Tahion said, as the shouting died. "Soon goblins will be swarming up this wall, as the magic that holds them back falls with the trees. Go, Tuarim, but some must stay here."

"I stand with you," said Arduiad. Fithil of the Curranach said nothing, but his sharp scythe gleamed on his shoulder as he stepped to Tahion's side.

"Good! I always hated crowds," exclaimed Lamon, the dapper knight from Cotarjon. "There's not much room in those tunnels!"

"Come!" cried Tuarim, and he and the dwarf turned away, Anarod close on their heels. Starn MacMalkom's pipes played on, unheeding.

"We will be back before they are halfway up the wall!" shouted Arthfayel, as he followed Anarod. Istvan hesitated, then, with a backward look at Tahion, joined Arthfayel and the others. It would be sword-work, rather than bow-work, in the dwarf tunnels, and he would be of more use there.

"Sure, Grom Headless will be glad to see you, Conn," exclaimed Lamon gaily. "It will be a joy to watch so sweet a reunion!" but the barbarian only growled in reply as he strode shoulder to shoulder with Carroll Mac Lir.

Istvan looked for faces he knew among the men around him. Most of them seemed to be Easterners: several were dressed like mainland Airarians; he guessed them to be the men who had followed Conn into exile. Layareh the Proud marched at their head, with Lamon. Sir Garahis of Ordan was here, with Arthfayel and Cormac. He recognised Fergus Mac Trenar, and Ingulf with his terrible flail. A glance behind him showed the set, grim face of Karik Mac Ulatoc.

Over grass and under trees they hastened, and suddenly Tuarim and the dwarf seemed to sink into the earth. Anarod followed, then Conn and Carroll, and then Istvan saw them all pouring down a stairway that spiraled down into the stone, lit only by the light of their swords.

Then his turn came, and he found himself surrounded by the windy echoes of drumming feet. Through the hollow clamour came other vague, stormy sounds, like rain on a metal roof, mingled with muttering thunder and shrill whistling shrieks that grew louder as they went down and down.

"At last!" a deep voice crashed, moaning and quavering weirdly in the echoing hollow. "Pass on! Kiluth and the others are just ahead!"

Metal echoes clashed and clamoured in their ears. Two armoured dwarves dragged open a metal gate. Tuarim and Cruadorn dashed through, the rest following. Beyond a short corridor was another stair, and again they sank into echoes: the hollow booming of voices and the sharp clang of weapons, mingled with squealing like hordes of giant rats.

The stairwell rang with whispering, scurrying sounds. Suddenly the dark below them filled with glowing crescents, as the light of their swords was thrown back by dozens of huge, sickle-shaped eyes.

Then a shrill, many-voiced shriek was all about them, deafening echoes torturing their ears. A downpour of fleeing feet was like an avalanche: through the clamour, Tuarim's inhumanly beautiful voice chimed in some war-cry whose words were lost in echoes, and then they were all racing in pursuit.

An arch of bluish light outlined the fleeing, twisted figures before them, and louder grew the echoes of the clamour of battle: metal weapons hammering, loud goblin squeals, and the deep shouts of dwarves like thunder in the stone.

Istvan thought he glimpsed a human figure, outlined against the light, but it vanished too quickly into the blackness for him to be sure.

They dashed through the arch: beyond, blue light glittered on the water of a fountain that splashed and splintered dancing from tiny plates of glass.

Beside the fountain, swords and axes hewed. A wedge of dwarves fought in red-stained armour. Istvan recognised Ogar Hammerhand, laying about him with his great, two-handed sword, and near him Thubar and Prince Tyrin.

Beyond them, across the hall, great gates stood open to the night, and near them, backs to wall, armoured dwarves stood, axes whirling.

And all the floor was hidden by a packed mass of goblins.

Black, deep-cave goblins clustered at the foot of the stairs, yammering and struggling their way into a mass of brown-furred rat-goblins.

At the sight of them, Anarod shrieked and leaped down the stairs. Cruadorn raised his axe, shouting some strange, dwarvish war cry.

But before either reached the spears and swords that waited at the stair's foot, Tuarim Mac Elathan had vaulted ahead of them, and his flaming blade vanished in a flickering blur.

Goblin blood flew and goblin bodies fell, sliced through by a blade made invisible by speed, a blade that clove flesh and bone and armour as easily as air. A red path opened before them as they scrambled down the stair.

Goblins screamed and scattered, and tried to come around behind, only to meet Anarod's sword or Cruadorn's axe. Ingulf's great bladed flail swept out, and left piled broken bodies behind.

But never had Istvan seen greater slaughter than was wrought by the single sword of Tuarim as he strode through the goblin ranks, his blade a blur, a flicker of lightning, that struck down goblins by threes and fours, whirling in circling strokes that never slowed or faltered.

Istvan heard a sudden cry, and saw Karik Mac Ulatoc pitch forward, striking down at long, clawed hands that gripped his ankle. Two goblins had thrown themselves at the islander's feet, and a spear rose above him.

Istvan's blade skimmed in air, slashing the spear-shaft and darting back into the brown-furred throat as the iron head fell. Ripping free, the sword slashed through one of the skinny, scaley hands at Karik's ankle. The islander scrambled to his feet, laying about him with his plain steel sword and the headless spear shaft he still carried.

From the other side, Fergus Mac Trenar drove in, the bright sword *Aibracan* flashing about him speckled with fire: red flames, and blue and white; and the blood of goblins smoking as it burned from the blade.

And now with stabbing spears and hissing swords the creatures pressed in and Istvan realised that this was to be a grimmer fight than he had expected. His bright sword whistled about him, darting and skimming in his hand.

He cursed himself for a fool: shieldless and clad in cloth he had come to this battle; now the Hastur-blade must be shield as well as weapon.

Istvan's metal-braced boots protected his calves, but the bare-legged Y'gorans were in constant danger. Swords grated on bones; screams and hammering rang from the rocky cave around them, deafening echoes of the clamour of battle.

A deep-voiced cheer from the dwarves welcomed them as Tuarim Mac Elathan burst through the encircling goblins, and the rat-folk squealed and fled. Tuarim's shield gleamed without a dent: no foe had lived to strike a blow.

"To the gates!" shouted Prince Tyrin, and another dwarf near him echoed the cry.

"To the gates! Once we join with Cadvan we can drive these rat-things out!"

Goblins scurried back, squealing, as mailed dwarves surged away from the fountain and formed into a line. Tuarim leaped over the dwarves' heads, and as he landed in front of them, his sword again vanished in a flicker of death.

"What a song this will make!" Cormac exulted.

But Anarod ran past the edge of the dwarves' line, and with a wild shriek hurled himself into the packed goblins, his sword lashing in a frenzy.

"Anarod! Brother!" Arthfayel shouted, running after him.

He had not yet drawn his sword, but goblins who sought to bar his way toppled before some invisible force, as though blown over by a mighty wind.

With a curse, Istvan leaped to follow the wizard, Karik and Ingulf at his heels. Already goblins were flooding into the gap Arthfayel had made, cutting the two off from their comrades.

Bristling spears blocked Istvan's way, as goblins swarmed to meet him. His hilt stung the palms of his two hands as he warded them away. Then Ingulf's great flail smashed a sudden swath in the dirty-furred ranks.

Arthfayel had reached Anarod's side, and his staff flared with need-fire. Anarod, berserk, drove ever deeper into enemy ranks, his sword whirling, his shield battered and chewed by goblin blades.

Istvan's point caught a moment in a goblin's ribs. A spear stabbed at his side. A long wooden staff swept it away, and Karik Mac Ulatoc leaped past, his lightless sword slashing.

A hoarse shout came from the gates. Tall figures came looming out of the night, and the blue light sparkled on rings of mail. Goblins made way for the men of Sarlow.

Conn Mac Bran and the men with him had moved out from behind the dwarves, and were fighting in a grim unit. A wild shout broke from them at the sight of their old foes.

All this Istvan saw in a quick glimpse over goblin heads, as they pressed around him, dirty spear points stabbing and rusty blades raised.

Now Anarod and Arthfayel were only a little ways off. Istvan and Karik fought back to back, as goblins, scattering from between the lines of men, swarmed around them. Arthfayel still had not drawn his sword: need-fire played about him, and goblins cringed away. Twice Istvan saw a goblin spear rebound as though from an invisible wall around the wizard, and several times he saw goblins hurled from their feet by some unseen force; they rose unhurt, but scuttled away, fearing to fight more. Nearby, Ingulf's deadly flail heaped bodies high.

Stone walls shouted with the anger of the fighters, and rang with the pealing of steel. Istvan's arms and shoulders ached with strain as he hurled the sword from side to side, sweeping away stabbing spears, slashing shafts, cleaving skulls and clipping off heads, guarding cuts from heavy blades. His ears ached with echoes.

The lines of men neared, and the shaggy hordes scattered from between them. Suddenly, the dwarves by the gate charged into the Sarlow left: an axe whirling at knee level sent a legless man pitching to the floor like a felled tree.

Tuarim Mac Elathan sprang over the fleeing goblins, and his invisible blade clove one of the huge wooden shields like a lightning stroke.

The two lines met with a crash that echoes turned to deafening thunder. Pieces of shields and armour flew as both lines dissolved in a maelstrom of fighting, man against man. Unblooded enemy swords glittered in the blue light, rising and falling.

In a moment, the goblins around him were fleeing as the battle of men rolled back to engulf them. One of the mainland Airarians, reeling, backed toward Istvan, his shield clamouring, and blood pouring through a rent in his armour. A sword lashed over the edge of the shield, and he fell, bleeding. A blond-bearded man in the armour of Sarlow leaped over the body and ran at Istvan, his huge wooden shield hiding him from his eyes to his knees.

Istvan heaved his sword high above his head, barely in time to keep it from being swept aside by the shield.

Then the red-stained sword was whirling at his face, and Istvan lashed his own blade down atop it, driving it down onto the shield rim, and danced back as the shield surged at him like a moving wall.

Such huge shields must be thin to be light enough to move at all, he realised. It lifted, and he knew the enemy sword was coming around to cut low at his undefended ribs.

With all his strength, he lashed out in a cut he knew the enemy's shield would catch, depending on the strength and sharpness of his Hastur-wrought blade. It shocked through the metal rim and tore through thin wood, ripping away nearly a quarter of the shield.

The falling part of the shield hindered the blond man's sword-arm, and then as Istvan's blade reached the bottom of its arc, he hurled himself point first against the other, his shoulder slamming into the shield, while his point, driving past the sliced wood, plunged through the mail-rings over his enemy's chest.

As he ripped the sword free, he saw three of the Easterners

falling back, battered by the blows of a single man. One went down, and a black-bearded figure burst through, blade whirling.

"You!" Ingulf's voice screamed from nearby, and he sprang at the black-bearded man, the terrible flail swooping out.

A deft movement of the shield sent the flail sliding harmlessly off, and Ingulf himself reeling off balance as the sword whistled at his unprotected back . . .

It fell on the shield of Carroll Mac Lir, as he cast his shield-arm protectively around Ingulf. But the islander toppled him back, and while he reeled, the black-bearded warrior sprang away and his edge came wheeling at Istvan's head.

It skittered along the Hastur-blade, and Istvan tried to stab at the wrist, and then the wooden circle slammed against him, hurling him staggering back. A goblin squealed behind him and slashed at his leg—he jerked aside barely in time.

"Vildern, you filthy dog!" Carroll Mac Lir shouted, rushing at the black-bearded man, and then the two of them were battering and hammering each other's shield, and the swirling madness of battle swept them away behind other fighters.

Istvan lashed at the goblins around him, and they scurried away. They seemed to have no more heart for battle; he saw many of them rushing to a rough hole in the wall and squeezing through.

Nearby he saw Conn Mac Bran crash through the press, laying about him in savage fury; Lamon of Cotarjon beside him, cool and unruffled, his face calm and almost amused, fighting with a dancer's grace and skill.

A flash of light turned Istvan's eyes away. He glimpsed Anarod's sword lashing, saw Arthfayel raise the wooden staff to block, saw steel twist and glance an inch from the wood. The wizard's open, empty hand shot out toward the enemy's chin, and the man from Sarlow was catapulted back, flying through the air to crash into a mass of men, knocking several to the floor.

A spinning, whirling figure broke suddenly from a knot of Easterners: Istvan saw Layareh the Proud hurled senseless by a blow from the flat of a shield, blood pouring from his nose, and at the same moment another of the Easterners went down, cut thigh bleeding. A mail-clad figure leaped from between them.

"Grom Beardless!" Conn Mac Bran bellowed.

The rugged, boyish face came up: Istvan was startled by

the likeness between the two. But Grom's blue eyes were cold, cold . . .

Conn Mac Bran sprang like a wounded tiger, his blood-drenched sword flying in a wicked arc. Grom Beardless turned his shield to brush the blow aside, and chopped straight down into the barbarian's shoulder, cleaving through mail-links to smash deep into the chest. The headhunter swayed in a cloud of blood, but before the other could pull his sword free, Lamon had lunged for the exposed armpit.

The blade sank into the thin wood of the shield as a supple twist of the body rolled the shield above the iron helm, then the freed blade whipped back, and the elegant, slender man sprawled in blood.

A cry went up from the Easterners, but Grom Beardless rushed on, never still, leaving piled bodies in his wake.

Garahis of Ordan reared before him and the heavy blades thundered on shields; then the armoured Cairanorean staggered back, dazed, his helm dented, and sat down on the floor.

And Grom Beardless whirled away, seeking new foes, and dashed straight at Istvan, his shoulder bracing the huge shield.

The steel of his sword licked out low, to force Istvan to guard, but the Seynyorean sprang instead toward the shield, out of the arc of the blow, cutting down inside the wood . . .

The wooden wall smashed against his shoulder, throwing him back, and he felt his point jerked through empty air. He braced himself, trying to control the shield with his own arm and shoulder, to force it down enough for a cut . . .

There was too much weight on the other side. He was hurled back, and the bloody blade lashed at his head, forcing him to bring his sword into guard . . .

He felt his steel driven down, and the flat of his own blade cracked against his head: light flared white in the center of his skull; his eyes were blinded; wood smashed against his face, and he was flying, spinning, falling . . .

Stone met him. The air was driven from aching ribs; he lay in pain-filled, silent darkness. . . .

Dim sounds around him—shouting, belling, squealing. As they grew louder, Istvan blinked his eyes and tried to move. Dim forms loomed through a thick mist. His head hammered and throbbed. His hands clenched . . .

His hands were empty! His sword was gone! Blinking, he saw a form above him, and others that bobbed in and out of vision. Steel clanged on steel, clanked on wood.

His vision cleared. A tartan robe stood over him, and beneath it bare legs were pillars on each side of his body, and shoulders and back under the cloth bunched and surged as its wearer bobbed and twisted. Dark hair flew. Hands and elbows were moving, and in one hand was a blur of bloody steel, and in the other something long and dark whirled and clacked as spears came stabbing in. And all around goblins darted in and out of sight, their wide, crescent eyes burning and yellow fangs snapping as they chittered with rage.

As the mist cleared from his head, he saw Karik Mac Ulatoc standing over him, beating away the goblin spears and swords with his own sword and staff. Istvan tried to sit up, his hand groping for his sword, but a wave of dizziness caught him when his head was barely clear of the floor. Weakness made his arms heavy.

Suddenly, a steel-clad figure loomed, and a long, red-smeared steel strip wheeled out. Karik's blade crashed to meet it, and broke off short in the islander's hand.

Again Istvan heaved himself up, got to his elbow despite the dizziness, looking for his Hastur-blade. He saw the gleam of its need-fire, not far away, and launched himself at it. His fingers locked around the hilt, and he rolled up, head throbbing.

He saw Karik throw the useless hilt at the face of the armoured man, but the broad wooden disc met it, and the steel sword sheared through the shaft that Karik threw up into its path. Karik staggered back, the point barely missing him, and then brought up the two pieces of cut wood, ready to fight. Istvan forced himself up to his knees in front of Karik, raising his point against the armoured man, and saw above the shield rim the cold blue eyes of Grom Beardless . . .

A high, shrill voice, like a trumpet call, and Grom turned as Tuarim Mac Elathan and Carroll Mac Lir came rushing out of the dimness, shoulder to shoulder, shield to shield. Grom Beardless tensed to spring, then leaned back as the top half of his huge shield was sheared away by a flicker of flame. Grom's blade lashed down, denting the shield of Tuarim Mac Elathan, and then the sword point flew off his blade, and Grom threw himself backward in a wild somersault, vanishing behind the wall of shields.

They fell back, back to the gate, and Istvan saw that there were now but a few left. Corpses littered the floor. Goblins, too, were surging toward the gate. Vertigo and pain swirled in Istvan's head, and the floor came up and sent him into darkness once again.

CHAPTER EIGHT

Up on the Wall

"Listen!" Ailil Mac Ailil exclaimed. "Can you not hear? The Hounds of Sarlow are out!"

Tahion listened with the rest. Now that Starn MacMalkom's piping and the wild men's drums had stopped for the moment, he could hear faint and far on the wind the distant howling of wolves.

"I hear them," said Dair Mac Eykin. "But they'll not be coming up this wall!" He laughed.

"But they may be coming through the tunnels, if our friends cannot stop up that gate," said Fithil of the Curranach, grimly. "And werewolves at their head! But Tahion, here, will be able to warn us—will you not?"

Tahion, barely listening, only grunted in answer. The living face of Hastur looked down the long corridors of eons stored in his mind, where ancestral memories whispered verses from the Song of Ranahan. He knew that if he had stood in his own land, his mind and heart one with the Heart of the Forest, he could have remembered it all.

. . . yet these shadows of ghostly memory helped him to shield himself from the pain of dying trees below, as axes cut them away from the earth, and sharp steel trimmed leafy limbs . . .

"I should be down at that gate with Anarod," Ailil muttered, as though to himself. "He needs his friends with him now. I should have gone with him."

"Indeed, that you should not!" exclaimed Colin Mac Fiacron. "Anarod should have stayed with us, rather! But he seeks death, and he is like to find it in those tunnels. That kind of fighting is not for us! It is not like fighting in the woods. Let him find death on his own, if he wishes it, and not drag us down with him!"

"Fighting in tunnels is no more strange than behind a wall," Dair Mac Eykin grumbled. "And I without a sword!"

"At least there are trees here," Finloq said. "There will be room for our kind of fighting if we were forced back."

"If they ever come at all," said Colin.

But they were coming: Tahion could feel them, unclean and alien, clinging to the stone far down the cliff, gathering. If he listened, he could hear the soft scrape of flesh on stone, and the scrabbling of goblin claws, far below. He could feel them like a sickness, pressing past the dying trees, pushing up against the cliff, and could dimly sense behind them the mounting tension of another mind, driving them, like a rising tide . . .

"Flann tells me that Tuarim and many of the men went off somewhere. What is happening?" Starn MacMalkom had come up, his bagpipes under his arm, his giant bodyguard hovering behind him like a nursemaid. "Where did they all go?"

"There is fighting at one of the dwarf-gates," said Ronan Mac Carbar, stroking his long mustache. "And they say there will be enemies at this wall soon, and we waiting for them. When we are old men, perhaps, and too weak to draw our swords, we may be needed."

"Have you no ears?" said Finloq. "Can you not hear goblin claws on the rock?" He leaned out over the cliff, and others joined him.

In the darkness, they saw the stone black with bodies. Fiery sparks glared up at them.

Metal scraped on stone as Fithil of the Curranach laid his war-scythe's blade across the wall. He positioned his feet carefully, then with a smooth motion, right foot and scythe went back together, the scythe-blade rasping on rock. Then it was behind him, and those nearby scattered to give him room. He smiled at them.

"Aye," he said, "keep well away from my right side, else your feet may shield my foes. I do not like to maim my friends." His hips twisted: the blade hissed inches above the rock, to rest where he had first laid it down. "How soon will they be here?"

"A few moments," said Tahion. He could feel them, like a tide of sickness mounting the cliff. "There will be men here, too. The ladders are almost finished." He felt men's pulses leap, and sensed elves moving in trees nearby. Behind him, he felt the throbbing, painful mystery at the heart of Rath Tintallain. "Here they come."

Fithil stepped back, sweeping the great scythe behind him. Tahion raised the Sword of Kings.

Claws scrabbled on stone. Eyes like great moons lifted in a long line above the rim of the wall.

Fithil's scythe hissed: a dozen pairs of eyes flew free and fell spinning, eye over fiery eye, into the night below. A deafening choral screech tortured Tahion's ears. The Sword of Kings looped out, cleaving unclean flesh and bone.

Savage shouts met the screaming, as the warriors of the Ua Cadell came running from their fire, whooping, waving weapons.

Need-fire flashed from the Sword of Kings as it lashed back and forth, felling one twisted shape after another. But more scrambled up on the parapet, dirty spears and rusty blades ready.

On his right, Tahion saw the parapet bare, where Fithil's deadly scythe swept in steady strokes. But on his left, swarming goblins hurled themselves onto the swords of the heroes, and madness flamed in the great eyes. Elves and savage tribesmen rushed to join the fighting, but Tahion could feel goblins in thousands pouring from the forest, hurling themselves onto the cliff face. Again he sensed the malign will that drove them.

Fending off a spear thrust cost him a cut, and six more goblins reached the top. Off to his left, swords rose and fell: he glimpsed Dair Mac Aykin laying about him with a short elf-axe; glimpsed goblins on the ground, rusty blades slick with new blood. One of the Ua Cadell staggered against him and fell, blood pooling beneath him. Goblin bodies fell inside the wall, piling up at his feet.

Tahion's blade circled and spun, but still they came, an endless, flame-eyed host. Blood covered the wall and the ground, and the heaped dead drove him back as cut corpses took foot room.

He could sense a wave of hate, driving the enemy onto men's swords. Stung by some maddening spur of spells, the howling goblins by legions fell in blood-drenched rows on the ground.

All along the parapet, the fighting raged in a tangled scramble of tossing blades. Screaming drowned the clamouring of steel.

It was *one* scream, from a thousand throats, a constant, pulsing wail. Tahion's ears ached with it, as eyes swarmed over the wall and over heaped-up bodies. The weight of his flaming blade strained at his shoulders as he lashed it back and forth in swift two-handed cuts, cleaving goblin bodies and turning goblin spears.

All along the wall, men and elves were falling back. Only Fithil of the Curranach stood his ground, sharp scythe sweeping clear a length of bloody wall, hurling furry bodies down the cliff.

Step by step, Tahion was driven back, his sword rising and falling, wingbeat-swift. Eyes poured toward him, the shrill monotonous shriek deafened him. Then, behind Fithil, Tahion saw waving brown blades.

With a shout he rushed to the islander's aid, but Dair Mac Eykin was there before him, his thrown hatchet flying in a blood-stained swirl to dash out the brains of a thrusting goblin. Bounding like a panther over enemy heads, the forest-runner followed his axe, long knife drawn and dripping. Stabbing and slashing left and right, Dair made space for himself, and jerked the short elf-axe from the cloven skull.

The endless goblin keening drowned Tahion's shout of encouragement, as well as Dair's attempts to warn the islander, fighting at the wall, of how near danger was.

Yet something warned Fithil: he glanced over his shoulder, then, wheeling, scythed down a bloody swath, and fought his way to his rescuer's aid.

Back to back they battled against endless hordes, while Tahion, the long flame of his sword lashing, cut a path toward them; above goblin heads, he could see Ailil and the forest-runners doing the same.

Then, even through that endless, deafening, many-throated wail, Tahion somehow heard or felt the moan of slowly dying trees, and knew that the green wood of the siege ladder touched the stone of the wall.

Spears and swords drove at him. His bright blade battered them aside. Sudden wind brushed his cheek, and then goblins were falling in piles all around him, feathered arrows blossoming in ratlike fur.

The arrows almost touched him as they passed. A quick look showed Arduiad Mac Artholon, his hands hidden by speed, with arrows streaming from his blurred bow as he mowed a path through the goblin ranks to where Dair and Fithil fought.

In a moment the two were falling safely back, while Ailil and the others ran over goblin corpses to join them.

Tahion, too, had a clear path—but he could feel the weight of armoured men on dying wood, and turned instead into the thick-packed ranks that poured over the wall, cutting straight into the heart of the wave of eyes, toward the pain of the tree. . .

Mail-rings shimmered in moonlight.

Rust-red blades were brushed aside by the spinning Sword of Kings. He kicked his way through heaped-up corpses, goblin stench fouling each breath. Over the heads of the swarming, stunted horde, Tahion saw an armoured shape climb up onto the wall.

A wheel of golden flame, the Sword of Kings heaved hacked goblins from his path. His arms and shoulders ached from hewing flesh and bone, as the will that drove them hurled berserk waves against his sword.

The moonlit mail of the soldiers of Sarlow spread out as more clambered over the wall. Pulling shields from their backs, they ringed the ladder's head.

Tahion plunged through the deafening scream, sword rising and falling. Wave after wave of hate-filled eyes, with fanged mouths gaping in unending screams, rose against him; wave after wave, his flaming blade hewed down.

Then a Sarlowaq shield was rushing like a wall, a steel strip above it throwing back his sword's light. Keen and swift, the Sword of Kings clove light wood with a lashing stroke, shearing off a shred of the shield's thin disc.

He stepped in the direction his pommel pointed, and falling steel sprang from his sword. Body and blade whirled together, and Tahion felt his edge wing cleanly over the chopped-out gap in the shield to sink through steel rings into flesh. Pulling it free, he sprang past into the ring of men.

The soldier at the ladder's head still had his shield on his back, but his sword was drawn, and he sprang to meet Tahion with a two-handed cut. Tahion stepped into the cut, jerking his hilt up sharply, hurling his weight against the other sword as it skittered down his own; as he felt it slide off his blade, he stepped, freed blade flying in a spinning slash that sliced steel like wool.

Other men were closing in, and hordes of tiny, shaggy bodies. Weariness weighted his limbs as he lifted the sword again . . .

A soldier staggered back, groping at an arrow in his eye. Tahion felt the wind of arrows fill the air about him, and sprang up on the wall. He reached for the ladder, and a sword stabbed up from the rungs below. He leaned aside and chopped down with his flaming blade, cleaving the helm. The falling body tore men screaming from the rungs below. Tahion reached out, gripped the ladder's end . . .

Agony flooded him, the pain of dying wood . . .

Sorrow and horror convulsed into rage that knotted frenzied fingers around wood. He could hear men scream even above the constant goblin shrilling.

The ladder pitched sideways, and struck the cliff face, scraping away the clustering goblins that swarmed there. Tahion swayed on the edge, looking down the long drop, clutching the stone . . .

The whole world seemed to shift, as if the cliff had lifted and was turning. Weakness washed over him, and pain . . .

With his last strength, he pushed himself back, away from the yawning fall . . .

He fell inside the wall, gasping and strengthless. His head struck stone. The goblin scream was all around him, it was inside him: it tore at his lungs and his throat; it raged in his head like a needle in his brain, the hate, the pain, the hate, the throbbing, burning hate . . .

He felt rock under shoulders and back. Dimly, he sensed

his body lying, somewhere, limp as a rag—vague, distant, not important.

It could not matter, surely. It could not help him in this sea of pain and hate and endless wailing. Hopeless, bodiless, he floated in darkness above the limp flesh . . .

Yet some obscure impulse set him fumbling in aching darkness, groping for his drowsy flesh.

His blood surged and pounded. A shrill screech pierced his aching head.

But there was a light in the darkness. He pushed himself up, and saw the Sword of Kings glowing near his hand.

He reached for it, and as his fingers curled around the hilt, his head cleared.

Not far away, he saw goblins falling in a pile as arrows lashed back and forth across their ranks. Still they kept on, charging the invisible line where death met them, carried on a wave of hatred . . .

The same hatred, the same will, was bent upon him, stabbing into his brain . . .

The hatred. He was still too weak to rise. He reached into the Sword of Kings, seeking strength.

Inside metal crystals, holes trembled in space. Flame flooded them: sparks leaped. Long metal threads hummed with power; need-fire flowed through metal nerves, into his own nerves, through hand and arm to the spine, to blossom in his brain. Sweet fire sang like wine in his veins: like sunlight on ice, its warmth and strength melted cold numbness and despair. The world grew sharp and solid.

He pushed himself up and leaned on the wall, looking out into the night. Out of the dark, the enemy's will beat upon him . . .

He called out for help, and although no voice could be heard above the goblin chorus, Arduiad Mac Artholon heard, and came leaping over the heads of the goblins.

Tahion tightened his grip on the Sword of Kings, drawing on its warmth, and power to fight flowered in his brain. He sighted back along the line of power, and found in the darkness the will that sent it, a dim shape under the trees . . .

His mind reached out, and through the trees sensed the hooded shape that gripped in one hand a black crystal staff that radiated freezing cold . . .

As Arduiad came up, Tahion pointed, less with his arm

than with his mind, and Arduiad raised his heavy bow. An
arrow glowed on his string. The elf stood poised, taking
careful aim into the darkness.

The arrow flew. A second followed it.

The goblins' screaming changed pitch, became shriller,
hoarser . . .

Ended.

Tahion's ears ached with sudden absence. Now he could
hear steel clattering and men shouting, and a wild hint of
strange music.

The goblins screamed again—but now it was a jumble of
screams from several throats, and suddenly the goblins scattered and ran, throwing down weapons, fighting one another
in their rush to get away.

And above the scattered goblin shrieks, Tahion could still
hear that strange, surging music—exultant, terrible! For a
moment he could not tell its source, nor tell whether it was
bugles, or bells, or pipes.

Then words formed in the notes, and he knew. The elves
were singing as they fought.

> *Drink Blood, ye Growing Things;*
> *The Falling Rain is Red!*

A handful of mail-clad men, shields bristling with arrows,
tried vainly to stem the rout and rally their ratlike allies, but
goblins rushed past them unheeding, scrambling over the wall
and scampering headlong down the sheer cliff. Many slipped
and fell, to lie as smashed skeletons upon the ground.

And on the heels of the squealing, panicked hordes came
men and elves, and the mailed soldiers of Sarlow sprang to
meet them, swords whirring in the night.

Tahion gripped his bright sword and stepped away from
the wall, then swayed, the world reeling about him crazily.
His knees folded. A sudden blur of motion caught his wrist,
and then Arduiad was under his outstretched arm, staggering
with his weight.

Blinking, he glimpsed Ronan Mac Carbar's face, vanishing
behind his shield as a sword crashed down. Ronan's flaming
blade flew out from above his shield rim, and the wooden
shield thundered with the blow.

> *Drink Blood, ye Grasses;*
> *Drink Blood, ye Bushes;*
> *Drink Blood, ye Growing things;*
> *The Falling Dew is Red!*

The battle song of the elves soared, triumphant, terrible. All around him Tahion saw men fighting, long swords whistling and whirring above shields, while goblins poured past in a nightmare flood. Beyond Ronan, he saw Flann MacMalkom, towering above the others about him, split an enemy shield with a single, terrible blow, hurling the mailed man reeling. Fithil's great scythe flashed, and a legless man went sprawling into a mass of fleeing goblins. For a moment the goblins swirled and scuffled about the screams of their fallen ally— then dashed on, mouths bloody, hands filled with red-dripping meat.

The Falling Rain is Red!

Ronan's blade clashed against chiming mail—the enemy's arrow-studded shield lay in splinters on the ground. The Sarlowaq staggered back, red blood bursting from rent mail; but as the forest-runner stepped toward his fallen foe he suddenly reeled back, staring at the goblin spear that had driven in under his shield.

He slashed at the goblin, but it darted away, mingling with streams of its kin that poured in a torrent over the wall. Ronan fell, and at once a wave of goblins poured over him. Starn MacMalkom leaped into the midst of them, his bright blade flying, scattering goblin heads, and then Ailil Mac Ailil sprang to his side, face twisted with grief, and the two fought together back-to-back above the fallen man, piling up the dead until the snarling goblins abandoned their prey and ran to the cliff.

Ailil fell on his knees at his friend's side, and the other forest-runners gathered about them amid the heaped goblin dead.

The rush to the wall became frenzied: in a moment, the last goblin had scrambled over the cliff, leaving only tangled corpses lying in deep, blood-stained drifts, and the proud, high, mingled voices of the elves singing above them.

Warriors' lives are pouring from their veins;
Warrior's pain is falling as red rain.
Warrior's toil pours life into the soil;
All death brings life to Earth!

Drink Blood, ye Grasses . . .

The shouting of men and the clattering of steel went on until Flann MacMalkom struck down the last of Sarlow's soldiers, and stood panting above him, while the war song of the elves slowed to a dirge.

Tahion, still leaning on Arduiad's shoulder, felt the elf's health and strength flow into him, thrumming like song. All key centers stirred, drumming with sweet power.

The elf still staggered under his weight, but Immortal life-force throbbed through the frail frame, renewing numbed nerves as it poured into the mortal's body.

Tahion's exhaustion fled from the elf's healing, subtle strength, although he still leaned on Arduiad's shoulder.

Unbreathing, bleeding, making no sound,
The dead lie upon the ground

The high, eerie voices of the elves wove their lament as they wandered through the piled goblin dead, seeking wounded men. Dimly, Tahion sensed danger: too many of these were wild elves, whose healing might harm weak mortals . . .

. . . Their widows are crying:
Death in the morning or evening of day
Brings sorrow and yearning.
But there's no returning
Of life to the Loved One that's taken away!

The lament soared sadly to an end, and stopped. But into the aching silence that followed came another sound—a muffled wailing of deep voices that seemed to come out of the earth.

Tahion wondered for a moment if it might be Aurothror's host returning, then realised that these were not the voices of dwarves, but of men. A single voice rose above the others, and words emerged in a plaintive chant.

A tempest you strode through the forest of spears:
Your hand was as strong as the storm!
My grief! That our lord into exile rode:
No more shall his sword terror spread through the foe!

The voice was familiar. Then, through the trees, he saw a head and shoulders rise out of the ground, and knew that the men who had followed Tuarim had returned. Then he recognised the voice of Layareh the Proud.

No more shall the deer flee his dart!
No more from the fear of Conn MacBran
Shall Airaria's Emperor tremble on his throne!

My grief! You have died in a land unknown!
Lost all our pride and our hope and our joy!
Lost now our cause that has taken our blood,
And driven us, Outlaws, from our own land.
We gave all for the love of Conn Mac Bran!
Now shall the Sovereign King of Kings
Laugh from the safety of his high throne!

The long line of men came up out of the ground. Layareh the Proud led them, tears streaming down his face. Wet were the faces of all the Easterners who had followed Conn, as they bore his blood-stained body among them. Cormac the Harper walked among the Easterners, and Tahion could see his fingers moving on the strings, but not a note could be heard above the keening chorus.

Now upon Grom Beardless be my curse!
You've stolen my peerless master's life!
Bloody death waits for you by my hand!
Doomed is the slayer of Conn Mac Bran!
Now let us heap up high our lost one's praise!
Now will be weeping for our slain king!
In him to keep life I'd have given my own!

Yet more than one bloody body was being carried up those steps. Tahion stirred and, lifting his weight from Arduiad's shoulder, began to walk toward the line of men.

After three steps, he staggered. His legs were still weak

and his head swam; diving into his body, he saw that some of the elf's healing, though not all, had been illusion.

As he stood swaying, the keening voices of the men were suddenly drowned in a wild shrieking of women's voices.

Women of the Ua Cadell, seeking their men beside the wall, had found the dead. They threw goblin bodies aside, and pulled their men to their breasts, bathing their wounds with their tears.

Tahion looked at the keening women: they washed their long locks in the red wounds. Swords had cut the flesh of men: blades killed in war. He wanted to go to them, to comfort them, but his legs were shaking and he had to lean against a tree.

Through the tree, he drew strength from the earth. The sad women wept, but he turned away from them, toward the heroes. The flames of their blades were hidden, gloom was about them. Behind the mourning Easterners came others: Tahion saw Carroll Mac Lir striding, grim-faced and stern; but behind him Ingulf and Fithil laughed, and Fergus Mac Trenar jested while Garahis of Ordan clung to his arm, face pale and helm badly dented, yet still able to smile.

His heart lurched as he saw Istvan DiVega, prone on the shoulders of dwarves, with Karik Mac Ulatoc and Arthfayel hovering near, and Anarod striding morosely behind. Then his weakened senses felt the beating of DiVega's heart, and he knew there was still life in him.

Many were wounded, Tahion saw, and now elves came, slipping from the trees, seeking out the wounded men. Tahion could sense webs of enchantment weaving there, and forced himself to move. There was danger here . . .

Tahion saw Ethellin the Wise, walking between piles of the dead, and called to him. The Sea-Elf came, his white hair shining in the light of the moons.

"Is it not dangerous," Tahion said, as Ethellin reached him, "for wild elves to be healing the wounded?" The Sea-Elf's bright eyes met his gravely.

"It is, indeed," said Ethellin, and laid his palm on Tahion's forehead. "Arduiad!" he exclaimed. "It is better than this that I had hoped from you!" Tahion felt health and strength pouring into him from the elf—in truth this time, without illusion. "Come!" said Ethellin. "Between us, we shall right their spells!"

"Follow me," Tahion said. Ethellin followed. Golden moons rose: night was ending. DiVega lay like stone, but Tahion saw him still breathing.

"So, there has been fighting here also!" said Arthfayel, looking around him at the piled goblin dead. "You have all been busy!" Anarod, his face fierce and bitter, kicked at the piled goblin bodies.

Suddenly, out of starlight, the silver swallows formed and swooped above, sweet voices thin and shrill as the stars faded above them, and streaming sunlight swept the sky.

Beware! We have failed! The Tromdoel *comes!*

Distant voices haunted the dim mist where Istvan floated, lost, groping through pain-filled, throbbing dark . . .

Until, at last, the pain stirred, rippled like water. A spark seized him, pulling him toward the sound of voices, and he listened desperately, trying to hear . . .

". . . have proved yourself the man indeed, Karik!" That voice was too deep. No man's voice could be that deep, as deep as the roar of the sea. "It is a sad thing that your sword snapped off so. Now you must have a new sword, a sword worthy of you."

"Indeed!" This voice was high, chiming: the voice of an elf. The voice of Tuarim Mac Elathan! "No more plain steel for you, Karik! It is a hero's sword you must have, a magic sword, an elf-sword!"

Tuarim Mac Elathan? This must be a dream, surely; perhaps he was even home in Carcosa, and in a few moments he would hear Silvia's voice . . .

"He drinks healing well." It was not Silvia's voice, but it came from close beside him. Istvan's eyes snapped open, and he found himself looking into the star-bright gaze of Ethellin the Wise.

His mind flew back twenty years and across broad seas, to another continent, with the Dark Border blotting out the eastern sky—and Ethellin the Wise wading up out of the western ocean at the head of a mighty host, with need-fire playing all about them . . .

"See? He wakes! No spells on him at all, only stunned from having his head broken."

". . . break as easily as glass!" the deep voice roared as Ethellin's gentler voice stopped. "Great swords were forged in long-ago days, aye, but no elf-smith lives in this World now who can shape such blades!''

"There was no one but Tuarim or myself," said Arthfayel's voice from nearby, "to put healing or magic on him at all—well, Cormac, I suppose, but he is no great healer. But there has not been time. I had barely begun to feel his wounds when you came.''

". . . power in a blade," Tuarim's voice sang from behind Arthfayel's, "and no dwarf-smith since Ruro Halfbreed has tried to learn." Istvan pushed himself up, saw Tuarim standing, facing a dwarf, and recognised Cruadorn.

"And who could teach me?" Cruadorn demanded, his deep voice a roar of passion. But Tahion's voice, somewhere nearer, drowned out his words, though the deep tone rumbled underneath.

"There are plenty of elves playing at being healers now! And we will have many men wandering in dreams if we sit here long!''

" 'Tis right you have," Ethellin said. "Come, Arthfayel, help him to his feet and into his bed, and then join us again. I fear we will need you.''

Arthfayel had been kneeling at his other side all along, Istvan saw, while Tahion had stood over them. Now Tahion turned away, and strode quickly toward a crowd of babbling men. Ethellin followed. Istvan put his hands on the grass and tried to push himself up: earth and sky tilted crazily. Arthfayel's strong arm was under his shoulder, lifting him; his head pounded.

"I—I'll be able to walk in a moment," he protested. "I'm not badly hurt.''

"Indeed not!" said Arthfayel, staggering under his weight. "But you must sleep some time, surely, and what better time than now?''

"Here, Arthfayel, let me help," said a voice Istvan did not recognise, and another arm caught him from the other side and steadied him. Istvan glimpsed through whirling dimness a pale face under a thatch of shaggy black hair, and a tiny tuft of beard on a strong chin.

"My thanks," said Arthfayel, "but who—Calmar! Is that you? I had thought you dead these many years! In that massacre at Srunarsog!''

"Ah, that is one of many things I have lived through in

these long years,'' laughed Calmar. ''But it is a long road to Elthar from Ualfime's back country, and small wonder you had no news of me.'' The high chiming of Tuarim Mac Elathan rose into the end of his sentence.

''. . . is true, the great elf-smiths of this Universe are gone, but in Elvenhome, beyond the World . . .''

''But—where were you last night?'' Arthfayel exclaimed. ''Why have I not seen you before? I had no notion you were here!''

''Ah, it's a fair crush of men here, is it not?'' said Calmar. ''I had not seen you, either. But if you can manage this man now, I should be helping Tahion.''

''And so should I!'' said Arthfayel. ''Ho, Fergus! Can you make yourself useful now?'' A nearby figure turned, and the broad-shouldered champion loomed before them. ''We have more wounded to tend. Can you help our Seynyorean friend to his bed? Or is that too much work for you?''

''Work? Me? Why, is it Flann you want me to lift?'' Fergus looked closely at Istvan. ''No? Why then, there's no other man—or horse—that's any trouble at all! And glad I am to help!'' He moved, stepped with a swordsman's sudden grace, and Istvan's arm was around his shoulders.

''I can walk!'' Istvan snapped pettishly, his head whirling. ''I'm not that badly hurt!''

''Ah, indeed!'' said Fergus. ''And is all that blood in your hair a new fashion at court in Seynyor, then?'' Startled, Istvan raised his free hand to his hair and found it caked and sticky. Subdued, he allowed the big man to lead him along, while the bickering voices of dwarf and elf faded behind and were lost among babbling voices of men.

Sir Garahis was conscious but dazed. Tahion finally persuaded him to lie down, and then reached into the young man's skull with his mind, shifting his senses to avoid the throbbing ache while he felt the young man's brain.

''*Help is coming,*'' Ethellin thought. ''*Dorialith is here and—who is that with you? You will be no help, Falmoran!*''

''*I will but watch,*'' a mental voice throbbed, rich with power. ''*I wish to learn more of these mortal men.*''

Inside the young man's brain, Tahion could feel the leaking capillaries and the oozing blood in bruised tissue. He felt along the inside of the skull: if the bone were sound, the bruises would be easy to heal. It seemed sound enough, but this was not his skill, and he could not be certain, especially with that constant throbbing from under the ground that made him think of some great, dark creature beating its wings against a cage of blinding fire. It was worse than a toothache.

Silently, he called to Ethellin, and felt the elf's mind join his own, groping along the smooth inside of the skull. The Sea-Elf found no break, no splintering. Together, they guided brain and body, milking healing balms into the blood.

Back behind his own eyes, Tahion saw the twin suns well clear of the horizon, and felt fatigue in his own body. The throbbing ache of the thing under the ground tore at him, but he forced himself to ignore it and helped Garahis to his feet. There were many others who were much more badly wounded than the young Cairanorean knight.

Cruadorn had brought bandages and thread and other supplies. The dwarves had skilled healers—but their hands were full from the fighting in the mines. Wearily, Tahion looked around. Nearby, Arthfayel bent over a prone and bleeding man, and argued with Alphth. The Changeling knew little of his own kind as yet. such injury a long-lived elf's uncanny strength could heal on its own. Men were more fragile.

Nearby, another man was sewing up the slashed arm of one of the Easterners. His face was familiar, but Tahion could not place him, until the man looked up from his stitching and grinned. Tahion recognised that grin.

"Calmar!" His mind flew back through the years to student days in Elthar, and the long nights that he and Calmar had spent in the esoteric discussions that wizards-in-training always have: on the true nature of the *Urlar*; why the Elf-Lords came to the aid of Hastur; or on such obscure legends as the tales of avatars of Hastur, or of the Anthir-Stone, which fused the warring essences of both white magic and black, or of fabled towers sealed in the Norian Ice where men still slept from the days before the Dark Lords had come.

"I wondered if you'd recognise me after all these years," said Calmar. He made a last stitch, knotted and cut the thread, and rose.

Tahion looked wearily around. A little way off he saw one of the Easterners, a young man, seated on the ground, with an expression of peaceful rapture on his face, while blood welled through the rings of his rent hauberk.

Choking back rage, Tahion strode to the young man's side, his mind tasting the spell, tracking it.

At the touch of his mind, a frowning young elf stepped forward. Tahion had met him on the ride: his name, Tahion remembered, was Carasir.

"I have taken away his pain," said Carasir, "but the blood does not stop! Why will he not stop himself from bleeding?"

"He cannot," said Tahion, forcing gentleness into his voice. "An elf's own power will heal him if you take away his pain and tell him he is whole. A human needs more." Sighing, he turned to the injured man.

The elf-spell's bright images beckoned and called as he slid into the man's mind, but he went resolutely past them, to the disregarded flesh, to the splintered collarbone and bleeding lungs . . .

"*Help me, Calmar!*" he gasped, back in his own body. His voice was barely a whisper, his own lungs contracting from the contact, but Calmar heard the mental shout the lungs could not give. He came, as Tahion began grimly to strip the unresisting body of the mail-shirt whose weight kept the wound open, while his own vitality flowed to replace that leeched by the loss of blood.

Calmar's mind joined his, and four hands worked together, using Calmar's skill to staunch the bleeding, to move and set the bone, to smear healing balm and sew the sundered skin. Calmar, over the years, had made far more use of his healing skills; on the fringes of consciousness, Tahion glimpsed uncomfortably furtive hints of more blood than he had ever seen.

Fitting the bone together, they shaped healing power through marrow, welding the cells. But branching rivers of blood that should have clenched from shock were still swollen, pouring blood into the lungs. Like an innocent child that breaks fragile bones as it tries to comfort an injured bird, Carasir had locked away the sources of the body's own healing powers.

Trusting his hands to Calmar's care, Tahion's mind crept questing into the brain, seeking the keys that would release the flood of drugs into the blood.

Tahion tried to keep his mind on the jellies of the physical brain, on the living cells he sought—but the illusions reached for him, caressing, beckoning, summoning, glowing through the brain, drawing him in, flowering around him . . .

The unicorns glowed white against the green. Tahion knew he must be near his goal, but the healing fountains, and the very roots of fear and pain, were locked away behind the fairest and most perilous visions.

No fear or pain could enter *here*, under the rainbow's guarding arch. Sweet flowers scented air filled with soothing music.

Far above him, in the infinite deeps of the mind, Tahion could see the man's attention fixed on deeds of dream, and adoring women's watching eyes. But Tahion's path lay downward, past childhood fancies all new-sprouted from their graves: past talking toys and dancing flowers, and wild games played by rabbits and lambs.

Far above, a winged horse swooped and whirled in the blue sky, its rider performing for the eyes of unclad women.

Ahead, Tahion sensed the fountains that he sought, and hastened toward them. But now dreams rose thick around him: honey filled his mouth, soft hands stroked him, sweet voices sang of sleepy joy, almost making him forget his mission.

Carasir! he shouted, shaking off the hampering joys, shrieking until the mind trembled about him as he tried to reach the elf who had made this vision. *You must let fear work!*

Dimly, he felt Carasir stir in the distance.

Fear not, the elf's sweet voice thundered out of the sky. *I have asked the aid of one older and wiser and greater than I. She comes!*

And the clustering joys about Tahion echoed, *She comes!*

Anger stirred in Tahion then, rousing him from the near-sleep that had come on him, and he forged the anger to the shape of a sword in his hand, and taking upon himself the form of a warrior out of Sarlow, he cut his way toward the fountains.

He slaughtered lambs and stomped on rabbits, and slashed the tapestried wings of giant butterflies—but the beautiful, unclad women he could only bring himself to strike with the flat of his sword. And all the mind shuddered about him, and ahead he saw the fountains stir and he hurled himself at them, to drive the blade of his anger in to wake their fears fully, to pour their healing waters into the blood . . .

But now a new joy came pouring: first it flowed white around his ankles and up to his knees, and a scent of sweet warm milk was in his nostrils, and then a warm wave washed over him and swept him from his feet, and all those other joys were swept away, and suddenly *Her* love was about him, wrapping him in ecstasy.

He could feel his purpose and his will drowning in that wondrous sweetness: he struggled to return to his body, and reached out, calling to Calmar for aid. He felt the touch of Calmar's mind . . .

And suddenly Calmar's soul was there with his, floating helpless on a tide of love and joy. And only Calmar's wild, panicked struggles kept Tahion from drifting into a mindless, passive dream of infancy, so sweet it was to lie tasting that wildfire joy . . .

But, at the fringes of Calmar's mind, terror took the form of a great ship sinking, its decks already awash with red when the sea lifted over them, and in that image was concentrated such memories of anguish and horror that the pain snapped Tahion out of his passive lassitude like a blow. Behind were dim images of the slave-pits of Sarlow, and fearsome demon-feasts . . .

Waves rose about them, lifting them, swirling them about, and another force strode into the milky flood, like a giant that wades into the sea.

Tarithwen! the voice of Ethellin the Wise thundered about them. *What is it you would do?* An arm like a tower of stone swept out to seize them, and they clung to it, shivering in ecstatic spasms.

I heal! answered a trilling voice that sang with all the sweetest music of creation: birdsong and water-sound, infinitely loving. "*Will not the life of my body heal? Will not the milk from my breasts heal?*"

And a form shaped itself out of the milky ocean, rising up from the white waves, lifted up to stand upon them as upon land.

Tahion shivered with desire and awe.

Her flesh glowed with pearl light: milk dripped from the tip of one rose-nippled breast. The other was hidden by a tiny head, a baby's head, he thought at first, nursing—then suddenly realised that nursing figure was not a babe, but a man, tiny in her arms—the man in whose mind he was, the wounded man he strove to save . . .

And her face was the face of his best beloved . . . perhaps of every man's best beloved . . .

"*Airellen!*" a voice wailed.

"*By the Hand of Nuadan!*" Dorialith's voice was like stones thrown into the tide. "*Stop, Tarithwen! The man will become a suckling babe indeed! Look! Where is his memory? It drowns in your milk, Tarithwen!*"

A storm swayed waves of milk: ripped Tahion's grasp from Ethellin's arm. He floundered, seeking a new anchor.

Suddenly, he sensed through the layers of illusion the faint piercing pain from underground.

"*Tarithwen, stop!*" cried Ethellin. "*Mute your power! You are enchanting every mortal man near us! You will drive them all mad!*"

Tahion dived into the milky depth, seeking that dimly felt pain of clashing power—dived through swirling music and surging ecstasies . . .

He drove spread fingers into the earth, and the pain of throbbing power surged through him.

He knelt, blinking, in sunlight. Calmar lay still at his side. And before him, cradling the wounded man to her breast, was one whose face was hidden by her long, dark hair. The body that burned through her robe was more slender and fragile than a mortal woman's body: like a slender girl barely out of childhood—yet milk poured from her breast . . .

"Airellen!" that wild voice shouted again, shrill as a gull's cry, and he recognised the voice of Ingulf the Wanderer.

And in his mind then rang another voice, that rich voice he had heard but once before—but he heard it only in his mind, no air stirring in his ears . . .

"*This, then, is Ingulf?*"

"*It is, Falmoran,*" the voice of Dorialith answered, equally soundless. "*And you may see yourself the state he is in. He does not see Tarithwen at all, but thinks it Airellen there.*" Tahion looked up, confused, and saw one standing by Dorialith, inhumanly tall and slender with a long, dark beard flowing down his pearl-grey robe.

But Tahion could feel the elf-woman's witcheries all around him, caressing, enticing.

"*I will think on this,*" answered Falmoran's silent voice. "*I must study his kind more deeply, before I can judge fairly.*"

All around him, Tahion felt men caught up in Tarithwen's enchantment, and even with the secret pain of Rath Tintallain throbbing through bone and nerve, he could feel her power grow, feel it reach to enfold him again. Beside him, Calmar stirred and groaned, and then settled into unconsciousness. His features were still tight with panic, but as Tahion watched, they began to relax. Arthfayel lay silent, and the Changeling lay with a face like a sleeping babe's.

"*Tarithwen!*" Ethellin said, his silent voice tired. "*You must listen to me. Mute your power.*"

And Tahion, crouching there with that aching, terrible power surging up through his fingers from the ground, echoed his words, lashing out with the pain that surged from under the earth—

"*TARITHWEN! STOP!*"

Elvish voices screamed on every side.

He saw Tarithwen reel back, arms flung across her face, nighted webs of hair tossing around her. Dorialith and Falmoran staggered against each other, and Ethellin the Wise fell to his knees. The wounded man fell from Tarithwen's breast.

Tahion felt his skull pounding. While he had spoken he had felt his words throbbing with pain, beating in his skull like hammers.

At his side, Calmar rolled over and sat up. His face was white.

"It *is* here!" he muttered, as though to himself. "And it is real! But—who used it?"

Tahion cradled his head in his arms. His pulse speeded and slowed, like a child beating a drum: his stomach fluttered as waves of pain crashed in his skull. He could hear Tarithwen sobbing.

Was it I who did this? he wondered. The world was spinning with pain. He heard men's voices muttering, and lifting his head to squint through the glare of sunlight, saw the dim figures of men lifting the stricken elves.

"Grandmother!" It was a young girl's voice: a maiden tall and slender, who seemed to burn with beauty. A green gown was on her. Long, dark hair fell down her back. "What was it? Fear was on me, like cold horror in my heart!"

Tahion let his aching head drop wearily again. The sunlight glared, yet it seemed like night. Someone was lifting him, and a voice was talking, but his head hurt too much to listen. He let himself go, drifting into unconsciousness.

CHAPTER NINE

The Vision of Darkness and Light

Istvan woke with an aching head, but he had had worse before. He could see daylight outside.

He sat up carefully. His head throbbed, but not badly, and there was no dizziness. It was better, he decided.

The hurt to his pride was another matter. A fine showing he had made! A DiVega of Carcosa; a student of the Three Swords School, and this barbarian swordsman, Grom Beardless, had made him look like a fool. And a dead fool, nearly!

Sleeping bodies sprawled all around the room. Yet he heard voices—men, rather than elves or dwarves. That was good. He wondered who was on watch—who, for that matter, had set the watch.

Tuarim Mac Elathan, he supposed. The elf-hero seemed to be in command, if anyone was . . .

If anyone was?

His eyes widened as his mind surged all the way awake. So far in this elite army, only Tuarim had dared assert command—Tuarim, and to some degree Conn Mac Bran and Tahion. His eyes sought and found Tahion among the sleepers. And Conn was dead . . .

Could *this* be why the Hasturs had brought him here? He was certainly no better swordsman than any of these others.

114

Yet he had commanded his own company in battle for many years now, and more than once commanded a group of companies, and once a whole foreign army. He might well have more experience in command than any here . . .

Or, again, he might not. Was it not mere vain folly to aspire to command such an army? Was it perhaps a fool's desire for glory, to have songs sung about him as commander of the defence of Rath Tintallain?

His brow wrinkled with disgust. Songs of "Istvan the Archer," no doubt.

He laughed. Would the Hasturs permit any songs at all to name this place, considering the secrecy that seemed to surround it? He pictured Cormac's face, and his lips pressed his teeth in a wolf's grin.

But why *had* he been brought here? As just another swordsman, no better than any of the others but—he hoped—not too much worse? Or did he have some talent the others lacked?

Why were *any* of them here? What were they defending? At least he now had some inkling of why mortal men were needed, since he had seen Kandol Hastur-Lord forced to open his mouth to speak with his kin. Whatever was here sapped the powers of the Hasturs and drove the elves mad: such a weapon could hardly be allowed to fall into the hands of the Dark Things.

But would anyone here accept his command? It was one thing to take orders from a companion of Fendol, but he was merely a foreign warrior, no more famed than the others . . .

He was on his feet, moving toward the door. He hesitated, then stepped back to his bunk and pulled his saddlebags from under it.

He would not again find himself in a battle clad in plain cloth and shieldless! He tugged the twelve-pound steel and leather shield free from the pack and tossed it to the bed, then the bag that held his tight-rolled mail-shirt. Next time, Grom Beardless would not find him such easy prey!

The voices outside grew louder with anger, and he stiffened, suddenly remembering the deadly feuds between the scattered clans of Y'gora, the senseless hatreds that went back thousands of years. He, at least, was free from all that: he had no enemies here, and even in Seynyor the once-deadly feud between the Vegas and DiVegas had fallen to a jest . . .

The rolled-up mail fell jingling. He unrolled the tight-packed metal, found the bottom, and pushed his arms through, then ducked his head.

Strands of his hair caught as he let its weight fall on his shoulders. He shook himself to settle the weight, then buckled his sword belt over it. He thought of the few, still starched ruffs in his pack, but put the thought aside. If he did find himself in command, some such touch of finery could be useful, but there was no point to it now.

The angry voices died away. Only a single voice was speaking outside now, a high, hoarse voice, and as he opened the door he recognised the voice of Ingulf the Mad.

". . . leaving me trapped in an evil world, and each time that it seems there might be some touch of happiness, some reason to live after all, then some curse of malign fate twists the world awry again and mocks me. And so Dorialith's songs are my only hope, for if the Daughter of Falmoran does not repent, then I am lost forever, and there is nothing for me in this evil world."

"Enough, Ingulf!" Layareh the Proud sneered. "I must admit you know why you are here, but none of the rest of us are love-struck loons like you. Why should we die for—"

"Ingulf!" a deep bull-voice bellowed. "Sheathe that blade! And you, Layareh, keep your tongue off the lad, or—we need no fighting among ourselves."

Istvan leaped down the stairs. Men were gathered all around. Fergus Mac Trenar stood between Ingulf's glittering blade, *Frostfire*, and Layareh the Proud, who stood tensed with his hand cupped over his hilt in a gesture Istvan recognised.

Softly, almost casually, he stepped toward the islander's back, his own hand floating by his hilt.

"And who are you giving orders to, Fergus?" said Layareh. "I came here for Conn Mac Bran, to follow *his* orders, and now that he is dead, I take orders from no man!"

"Aye," snarled another Easterner. "The King of Elantir does not rule here! You have no right to set yourself up over us!"

"At least the king I serve is the rightful king, and no usurper!" Fergus snarled. "I have never—"

"*Silence!*" Istvan roared, in his best parade-ground voice, concentrating all his experience of command into the right tone. "We do not need to fight among ourselves—you yourself said that, Fergus, so step away. And you, Layareh, if you try a 'Looping Wind' cut, you will lose your thumb." Layareh, startled, glanced over his shoulder at Istvan, and the position of his hand changed; but Istvan's voice, perfectly level, went on calmly, implacably. "And if you change to the 'Five Winds' draw, I can still cut the tendon in your wrist before your point is clear of the scabbard."

"Istvan the Archer!" Layareh groaned. "Are you, also, against me?"

"I am against Grom Beardless and his masters," said Istvan, "who will doubtless be overjoyed to learn we have all killed each other."

Layareh's head drooped, and his shoulders rounded. His hand fell away from his sword.

"You are right," he said. "Yes, I do have a reason for staying here! But when Grom Beardless is dead—then I will ask of the Hasturs and of the Lords of Rath Tintallain an accounting for the death of my master, and the wasting of my life!"

Istvan looked quickly at the others. Fergus looked at him with respect and approval, but Ingulf's face was still twisted, though he had sheathed his sword, and suddenly turning his back he strode to the wall and stood looking down the cliff, shoulders heaving with violent breathing.

Now there was time to look at the others around them. The other Easterner, a short, red-faced, black-bearded man in mail-shirt and helm, was frowning.

The men who had gathered during the quarrel were turning away, to go back to interrupted tasks. He saw Flann MacMalkom heaving at a pile of goblin corpses, stacking them in his arms like firewood, turning and striding off. Turning to look after him, Istvan saw a cloud of dense smoke, and became suddenly aware of a faint smell of tainted smoke. Fergus, Starn, and Karik joined him, with smaller loads. Four of the forest-runners were standing in a group, talking in low tones. Layareh joined them.

Istvan looked at the cloud of dirty smoke, and wondered if the goblins' burnt bones would blight the soil, or whether the fire would burn away the taint of the dark magic that had warped and twisted them. Legend said their ancestors had been men once, long and long ago . . .

They were flesh and blood, certainly, yet his Hastur-blade blazed with need-fire when they were near, which meant that somehow the dark fire that destroyed life had been linked into their living flesh, as light and darkness were said to be linked in the legendary Stone of Anthir . . .

"Look there!" Ingulf shouted from the wall. "Come and look, and tell me what it is that comes!"

Istvan whirled and sprinted for the wall. Starn and Fergus and the four forest-runners also rushed to crowd around the islander. Ingulf pointed over the parapet, across the green carpet of treetops below.

Far away in the distance, fire seemed to leap and crawl about the base of a domed black hill that loomed above the trees, far to the south and east. The fire crawled over the hill's surface. Need-fire, Istvan thought. The Hasturs must be there.

He watched the fire writhe across the dark for some time before he realised that the black dome was moving.

Beyond it, he saw a valley fringed with sickly yellow, a blight-edged road through the forest.

Lines and flickers of fire darted over the blackness, as need-fire flamed between the Hastur-Towers on the Dark Border when the Dark Things attack.

"Some creature out of the Dark World," Istvan said. "One of the Great Dyoles, perhaps." Suddenly, he remembered the warning cry that the silver swallows had trilled at dawn. "The *Tromdoel,* it must be."

They stared at it: a great black teardrop, mountain-huge, that crawled slowly toward them.

"Well, Flann," said Fergus lightly, after a moment. "You know well that at times like this, it is on your strength that we all depend. Do you plan to pick it up and throw it in a hole, or will you just step on it?" The red-bearded giant turned and smiled down at Fergus with one of his slow smiles.

"I'll not be letting you get out of your share of the work that easy," Flann said. "If I have to lift it, I'll be asking you to pick up the other end." He scratched his beard, and gazed across the green miles. "And it looks to be more work than I care to tackle before I eat. But as slow as it's moving, we should be able to wait for dinner."

It did seem to move slowly, Istvan thought thankfully.

"The Hasturs will take care of it," he said, more cheerfully than he felt. "They always do on the Border." *Almost always,* he thought. He had many times seen the Great Dyoles crossing the Border with the Armies of Uoght, scattering all before them. He was used to watching the Hasturs battle the greater Dark Things, while he held his men in readiness to fight the lesser.

But he knew that the Great Dyoles often took days to drive back into the Dark World; those Dyoles powerful enough to be given a name, as this one was, were worst of all. Only Uoght and the *Sabuath,* and the Eight Dark Lords themselves, were mightier.

"Dair Mac Eykin, is that you?" a deep voice rumbled from behind. Cruadorn's voice, Istvan thought. The forest-runner turned.

"Indeed it is—" he stopped. "Cruadorn? What happened to your face? Your beard—why, man—your eyebrows are gone!"

Turning, Istvan saw the dwarf's face bald as an egg and covered with soot, skin blistered, all hair singed away. And in his hand he held a glowing sword.

"Here is your blade, Dair Mac Eykin, and I wish you well of it!" the dwarf growled. "May it bring you better luck than it has me, and be worth all my trouble!"

"My thanks!" Dair said. Stepping forward, he took the blade, and looked on it in wonder. It was broader than before, though the hilt and guard were the same. "Well, a good job it is surely, and you may be proud—"

"No pride for me in this!" said Cruadorn. "All day I strove to melt the steel, or soften it, at least, that it could weld. At the greatest heat in our hottest forge the pieces barely glowed, and when I laid them one over the other to try to hammer them together, my hammer could barely dent them. They would not anneal: for all the heat, the temper was hard as before.

"At last I shook the blade in anger, and swore by Hastur's name, 'How can such metal ever be worked?' And behind me a voice said, 'In a far, far hotter fire than this.'

"I turned, and one of the Hastur-kin was behind me. 'Blow up your fire, child of earth,' he said smiling, 'and I will help you anneal and weld the pieces.'

"We laboured at the bellows, blowing up the fire until we cringed from the heat, while the Hastur searched through the slag about our foundry. I saw him changing the slag in his hands, and at last he came walking, with a handful of powdered metal, up to the forge until its flame wrapped around him, while we shrank back.

" 'Now stand back, children of earth—hide yourselves and cover your eyes!' And, so saying, he cast the powdered metal into the fire.

"It was as though the sun had come into the room: forge-hardened as we were, we fled that heat, fled into the corridor beyond. But I, trusting in my darkened forge goggles, peered around the edge of the door.

"White-hot light burned my eyes, and my hair shriveled and burned. But I saw the Hastur in the heart of the fire, wrapt in flame, and the two pieces of the sword flew to his hands.

"I had looked for him to hammer them one on the other, as I had planned. Instead, the steel stretched itself out into long, glowing wires.

"Then those white-hot threads, hanging in the air as though upon an invisible loom, looped and knotted around each other, and the two strands braided together and came twisting back until they were woven into a thick rope of steel.

"My eyesight blurred; dark patches hid the flames. Yet before I turned away, I saw the woven steel float to the half-melted anvil, and the head of my hammer—for the haft was burnt away—rising and falling by itself. Then at last I drew my head back into the cool dark of the corridor, and closed my aching eyes.

"Painful green light throbbed behind my eyelids, and the forge goggles burned the palms of my hands. I could hear the hammer pounding, and then the Hastur called us. The heat began to die away. We proud, singed smiths crept back into our smithy. Friends led me, for I could no longer see.

"Then I felt fingers touch my temples, and a voice said, 'That was foolish, son of Kvarlov. You could have lost the sight of your eyes forever.' And I felt strange warmth flow through my eyes, and slowly my sight cleared.

"The glowing steel still lay on the anvil, and the head of my ruined hammer still rose and fell by itself. But the forge's light was red once more.

"Then the hammering stopped, and the hammerhead fell to the floor. 'The steel is annealed, the pieces welded,' the Hastur said. 'Now use your utmost skill!' The glowing steel rose from the anvil and floated to the flame. Coals piled around it.

" 'But when the blade is shaped, do not use water for the quenching,' he said. A second Hastur appeared in the room, and in the air before him floated a jar coated with ice. 'Instead, take this, but touch not the vessel, nor that within it, with your bare hands. Pour it with your longest tongs, and stand well back from the quenching trough.'

"Then he vanished—both Hasturs vanished, leaving an ice-cold jar in the forge's heat, and the smithy half ruined. One of my kin brought me a new hammer, and I laboured then to shape the steel as you see."

"I—sorry I am that my blade has brought such care to you," Dair Mac Eykin said. "And I know not how I can ever repay—?"

"Our lives will be payment enough: fight well with your blade, and protect our city! But indeed, a king's treasury would scarce suffice to buy such a sword. Two diamonds were worn away in the sharpening—for only adamant can mark such steel! There is a low spot now in the center of the anvil: so great was the heat of the blade that the iron softened beneath it as I hammered. And the tools nearest the forge were melted, and many forge tools ruined. Ah, it is a costly blade! Fear not!" The dwarf laughed, shaking his burnt head. "You shall pay us well, in the blood of our foes!"

Others joined the dwarf's deep, booming laugh. Istvan turned away, and looked out somberly across the treetops at the mountainous dome of fire-covered darkness that crawled slowly toward them.

Even a Hastur-blade was no use against that.

But there was some other unease that gnawed at him, he realised. As though hidden eyes were watching him, considering, weighing . . .

Well, there were eyes enough, certainly. He turned back. None of the men seemed to be looking at him. They all seemed to be watching the dwarf. His skin crawled. But any of them could have been looking at him. It was a foolish notion, surely. Just nerves, he supposed . . .

"Are we to eat at all?" said Flann. "I want my breakfast! Are you coming, Fergus?"

"Coming," Fergus said. "We had all best eat while we may."

"Some of us should stay on watch, while the rest eat," Istvan said. "I will stay. Karik, Dair, Layareh, stay with me, and we will eat when the others are done."

"Is it Istvan the Archer that is trying to give me orders now?" said Layareh, his sword-hand cupped at his side. "Tell me, who has put you in command here?"

"It is time someone took command," said Fergus, frowning. "I would as soon follow Istvan the Archer as anyone."

"I, also," said Starn MacMalkom unexpectedly. "He at least has no feud with any man here."

"Why should it matter!" snapped Ingulf, pettishly. "It is all foolishness, and men no better than sea birds that quarrel over a barren rock, or rutting stags fighting for a green patch of turf. Yet this man did not fear to take up our cause against the Elf-Lords, and I will trust him for that alone."

All eyes were on Istvan now. Yet he had stood before groups of men before without this feeling. There were other eyes on him. He was sure of it now. Were the Hasturs watching him?

"Why should we let this foreigner set himself over us?" the red-faced Easterner snarled. "For myself, now that Conn is dead, I am content to follow Layareh Ua Kellym."

"Well, now." Layareh bared his teeth at Istvan, a mirthless grin, and Istvan, recognising the greed in his eyes and the subtle tension in his sword-hand, braced himself for the duel he knew was coming. "Perhaps it is I who should be giving the orders. Or will you fight me, to see who is the leader?"

"I did not come here to fight you," said Istvan, his hand relaxed, ready to fly to his sword hilt, while his eyes measured the other's stance, noted the muscles that were tensing. "We have both fought in Airaria, so you know a little about me. But have you fought in Kathor, or Norbath, or Tarencia, or Darna? Have you ever stood at the Dark Border, facing the Legions of Dragon-Headed Uoght? I have experience that you lack. So far, we have all served Tuarim Mac Elathan, but without him we are wasting time squabbling, when we should be dividing ourselves into watches, that some may sleep while others stand guard."

He saw shifting muscle patterns in Layareh's body, and his wrist and finger muscles poised, ready to fly to his hilt. But it was working, he saw. Layareh hesitated. Istvan controlled his breathing carefully, waiting for some sign of attack. Layareh frowned.

"Sure you cannot expect they will attack by daylight?" he sneered.

"Why not?" Istvan answered, and forced his wrist to relax again. He could see Layareh's doubt growing. Perhaps he could avoid this fight. "The soldiers of Sarlow are men. They do not fear daylight. If they attack by day, and the goblins and werewolves by night, sooner or later lack of sleep will do their work for them. I do not think them so stupid that such an obvious strategy will not occur to them." His eyes held those of Layareh, and his hand was poised to draw and strike, as Layareh's hand was poised, but he thought perhaps that the fight might stop now.

Both men started as a new voice spoke.

"Only a man would think of that." It was the voice of Tuarim Mac Elathan, and it spoke from the midst of crowding men.

Whirling, Istvan saw Ingulf and Fergus turning to look at the elf who stood between them. Starn and Flann MacMalkom edged away. Had he sprung from the air, like a Hastur? Or had he simply been standing there all this time?

A quick glance up at the head of the stairs showed that the quarreling voices had awakened those who had been asleep inside. Tahion was leaning, pale and weary, against the door jamb, and Arthfayel and another man, black-haired, whom Istvan could not place. Fithil and Cormac and others filled the stairs. Istvan frowned. This brief time of sleep was too precious to be thrown away for such a foolish quarrel . . .

"I had forgotten," said Tuarim, striding from between Starn and Flann, "how strong is the hold sleep has upon your people. Long ages have passed since I have fought beside mortal men, and I have forgotten much—too much, I see, to lead you well. You need a leader of your own kind—more than one, in truth. Prince Tahion has served well, but he needs sleep, as you all do.

"But now tell me, Layareh Mac Lohar, and you, too, Ingulf and Fergus, what it is that has raised strife among us, come so near to causing death and cruel wounds?"

"Why is my master dead?" cried Layareh. "We should have been preparing to capture Brannark, and seize the throne! Why should Conn come *here*? A few months, and Conn would have ruled all Airaria—but your summons came, and he rushed off to die in this stupid little fortress—for nothing! What can be gained here? What is Rath Tintallain to me or mine?"

The voice that answered was the voice of Ethellin the Wise.

"If Rath Tintallain falls, it will not matter who sits on the throne of Airaria." Istvan started, and his eyes sought the Sea-Elf among the men, and found him. He blinked, and forced himself to look again. Had there not been two others?

"Conn knew that he might die here," said Tuarim, "but he knew, also, that if the Lords of Sarlow, or the dragon Komanthodel, gain the power that we guard, then Brannark would not be safe, nor all the power of the Airarian Empire sufficient. It is sad that such a man should die, but all men die in time—"

"But *you* do not die!" Layareh shouted. "And you do not care if *we* do! Others beside Conn have died here—many of my comrades, and these forest-runners have lost one of their companions. Why should we die for you?"

Istvan forced his eyes back to the dark-robed shapes at Ethellin's side, that his eyes had glided past, barely noticing. His eyes blurred, and began to ache. He forced himself to look into each hood in turn. Was that Dorialith? He could not recognise the other. His eyes throbbed until he turned them away.

"You Immortals guard well your lives!" Layareh shouted. "We die, you say, when our time comes, but if our time comes sooner, because you have plucked us out of our lives to fight for you, you feel no guilt! You destroy our lives, you ruin our dreams and our hopes, you take from us our—"

His voice stopped in the middle of a word, and Istvan saw his eyes caught, staring at something beyond.

And from the direction in which he stared, Istvan felt a warmth and a prickling flow over his nerves . . .

All eyes turned to follow Layareh's gaze, and *her* beauty stunned them all.

She was taller than the men who stood around her: a woman of wonder with the eyes of a queen, and the glory of those eyes made day seem like moonlight.

Above the eyes, the petal-smooth skin of her shining brow was white as apple blossom against the night-black frame of her hair that fell as a cloak about her.

And as Istvan stood, rooted like the other men with awe, he saw red lips writhe in the exquisite face, and trembled at the soft, singing tones of her voice.

"Do you think yourself, foolish man, apart from all life? You would blame us, because your empty games of power have come to nothing, and your leader has died a few decades too soon? You say we destroy your dreams and your hopes, yet what know you of *our* dreams?"

"Be gentle, Tarithwen," said the voice of Ethellin the Wise, faintly, as though far away.

"If we did not care, why should we be here? See now what *we* have given up for *your* sake!"

And before any voice could protest, the twin suns vanished, and the vision was upon them.

Istvan saw a land more green than any in the World. Jewel-coloured birds sang in the feathery leaves of trees that shone with supernal light, and the singing of the birds wove with the singing of the happy people of that land, under a single sun.

Undying flowers perfumed the winds, and in the dawn the flowers sang for joy. Health and youth flowed in the flaming waters of that land and wonder lay over all.

"To this land came the elves, after ages of sorrow and struggle that you short-lived folk cannot imagine," her sweet voice sang. "There, in joy, I might yet dwell—had Hastur's barriers not failed, and the Dark Things not returned."

And suddenly a new vision swept upon them, too vast to comprehend. But it seemed to Istvan that Worlds and Universes blossomed endlessly out of a single source, linked and throbbing.

And some Universes glowed with fire, and others with dark force. Istvan sensed a precarious balance between the throbbing powers . . .

And suddenly that balance was broken!

A flaw appeared in that pattern of linked light and darkness; a black stain spread where the darkness leaked into the light . . .

Forces that should never have met, never have touched, were locked into sudden, fatal opposition, a growing cancer that marred the pattern and made the foundations of Universe after Universe tremble . . .

Too vast that vision: Istvan blinked in confusion. What had he seen?

For a moment he saw sunlight again, and the slim stalk of Tarithwen's body, surrounded by ranks of kneeling men, and felt cold stone under his own knee.

Then that vanished: once more he saw the Living Land, with fires of life flaring through grass and tree, through bird and folk. Only now he looked upon the wave-lashed strand of the sea: on jeweled sands white ships took shape under elves' skilled hands. They were launched on the sea, and rose and fell on the waves.

Songs of power wove and thrilled: invisible forces moved. Again a vision, a place where worlds linked like the petals of a flower. A gate opened there to elvish magic: the crystal ships sailed through, and once again invisible powers wove a mighty gate . . .

White ships sailed into the twin suns' light. The Elf-Host landed. Then there was battle against ravening hordes of monstrous, nightmare shapes. Ageless Immortals died in war.

"We know," sang Tarithwen's voice, "that you grieve, you mortals, when your kin and your loved ones die. And it is a great wonder to us that any of your short-lived kind should ever dare to love at all, knowing that parting and sorrow must come upon you.

"But can you even dream of the grief when an Immortal dies? Can you imagine the sorrow when a death is the first among your people for more than a thousand years?" As she sang, Istvan saw those deaths, and knew that he looked back into legends—back to the battles that had ended the Age of Terror, thousands of years before Fendol, long before the birth of Kandol Hastur-Lord or Tuarim Mac Elathan. And yet he was sure that the visions that he saw were memories of true happenings of those days.

"Yet we remained," Tarithwen's voice went on, sweetly compelling, "remained to die, and to bear children who will defend this death-filled world, which is not ours. And others of our kin still come from the Living Land, aiding the Hastur Clan in war, and bringing us magic from our homeland.

"So you need not reproach us with your sacrifices, or blame us for your sorrows. For however great they be, we have shared them, with sorrow and sacrifices of our own."

Her voice ended; the vision faded. Istvan found himself kneeling along with all the other men.

But when his eyes found the spot where that woman of wonder had stood, she was gone.

CHAPTER TEN

Elf-Spells

For long moments no man spoke, nor moved.

Istvan knew that the stunned awe he saw on other men's faces must be on his own as well. He struggled, kneeling in silence, to understand the vision. Its end he knew from legend: the help of the Elf-Host had enabled the grandsons of Hastur to drive from the Universe the Eight Dark Lords, as well as the *Sabuath* and the Great Dyoles, the most terrible of their servants, and to rear once more the weakened barriers between the Worlds.

But it was the earlier part of the vision, with the Light and Dark Universes pressed together like the legendary Stone of Anthir, that troubled him and eluded his grasp. He sat, staring: beyond the masses of kneeling men, the great, vaulted roof reared above the trees, and beyond that, the crystal elf towers, shining in sunlight. Veins of bright pink glowed in the walls.

Cruadorn scrambled to his feet, shaking his burnt head angrily.

"Is there never an end to your family's witcheries, Tuarim?" grumbled the dwarf. "Why can I not go about my own business in my own people's city without having the flowers turn to butterflies, or bushes grow in the walks, and the trees all turn to stones—or I find myself thrown suddenly into someone's memories? A fine way to treat your neighbours!"

"Tuarim?" It was the voice of Cormac the Harper, from the steps by the door. "Who is that—woman?"

"That was my grandmother," said Tuarim, looking up. "Tarithwen, the wife of Ioldan. My mother's mother."

"And also," said Cruadorn, still indignant, "the mother of Ardcrillon Crystalweaver, who calls himself Lord of Rath Tintallain, and holds himself co-ruler with Aurothror! But it is Tarithwen who rules—or, at least, she rules Ardcrillon!"

The edge in the dwarf's voice cut through the calm in which Istvan had contemplated the patterned Universes, and, suddenly aware that he had been trapped in an illusion, he sprang to his feet angrily. Other men, too, were stirring. Soon the others were on their feet—all but Ingulf, who knelt with his face buried in his hands as though he wept.

Glancing at him curiously, Istvan felt his vision blur, his eyes start to slip away. Blinking, he stubbornly forced his eyes back to the islander. Three vague shapes stood over Ingulf; it hurt Istvan's eyes to look at them.

Blinking again, he saw that the three grey-robed Sea-Elves stood there. He allowed his aching eyes to slide away.

A hand touched his shoulder.

"Is it well with you?" asked Arthfayel. "Or—are you feeling perhaps—*too* well? Is there ground under your feet?" Istvan shook his head, and laughed.

"Do you mean, am I free from that mystical—dream? I think I am!" He laughed. "I *hope* I am! Are *you* real?" Arthfayel laughed.

"I think I am! I *hope* I am!" he mimicked. "Indeed, from the great, raging hunger that is on me, I would call it likely!" He clapped Istvan on the shoulder and walked on with the dark-haired man, whose name Istvan remembered hearing the night before, but could not recall now . . .

The two wizards stepped to the parapet, where Arthfayel stood staring out across the treetops at the looming dome, while the other yawned and stretched, hands reaching up until the wrists crossed, then falling again.

"Ah, Karik," Istvan heard Cruadorn's deep voice boom below. "Is there a sword for you yet?" Istvan turned back toward them, away from the two wizards. The stranger's arms were rising again, almost as though he signaled someone as he yawned. Istvan found himself yawning. Sleep! They all needed it.

"No sword have I," said Karik, dolefully. "If in this battle I am to be fighting with sticks and with a knife, I shall not loudly praise your hospitality!" The dwarf laughed.

"Come!" he said. "I will make you a sword, sharp and very—wait!" The dwarf turned again. "Tuarim! Where is that Sea-Elf you told me of?"

Tuarim answered with a nod and a wave of his hand, and Ethellin the Wise came walking from where Istvan had seen the three standing around Ingulf, followed by Dorialith and by that strange elf whose features Istvan now saw for the first time: a face rougher and darker of skin than the others, above a beard brown as sealskin that fell to his waist. And all of the moods of the grey-green sea seemed to surge in his great, wise eyes.

"Crudadorn Mac Kvarlov am I," said the dwarf, bowing low. "Are you not Ethellin the Wise?"

"Ethellin of Findias I am, indeed—" the silver head dipped, "and this is my kinsman Dorialith, and the great mariner Falmoran, who captains one of the ships that sail from World to World. How may we serve you, son of Kvarlov?"

"It is not for myself, indeed," said Cruadorn, "but for Karik Mac Ulatoc, here, whose sword was broken in battle. I offered to forge him another, but Tuarim says that it is a magic sword that he needs, an elf-sword!

"Now, it is true that we dwarves have lost the art of keeping the fire in our swords, to flame against demons and other Night-Things. Though the steel we make is very strong, and will cut through troll's flesh, it remains but steel, with no magic in it. Yet it is stronger than any the elves can forge in these days . . ."

Istvan had been listening with keen interest, but suddenly swordsman's reflexes brought him around as his trained eyes warned of danger in the stance of Layareh the Proud, suddenly crouched, fingers tense and too near his hilt . . .

But it was not against Istvan that Layareh tensed to draw, but another he had chanced to meet face-to-face in the crowd.

"*Do I not know you?*" The islander's voice was deadly, velvet soft. "I remember that face." And that memory chilled the eyes beneath his frown and tensed the fingers that could send the sword flying lightning-swift out of the scabbard . . .

" 'Twas not I," said the stranger, eyeing Layareh as he might have eyed a viper coiled to strike.

"This is Calmar," said Arthfayel, stepping to the other's side, "one of the Adepts of Elthar summoned by the Hasturs. He was my fellow student at Elthar, along with Tahion."

Layareh's eyebrows knotted, and he stood, frowning, hand still poised to strike.

". . . Elf-smiths of this world are long dead." Istvan heard Cruadorn's voice, filling the silence that had fallen on all nearby. "But Tuarim says that some still know that skill in the Land of Living, and that at times they sail to this World, and dwell in the city of the Sea-Elves, so I was wondering . . ."

"Is it so?" said Layareth at last, his brows slowly unknotting, and Istvan breathed again, seeing the tension in hands and bent knees ease. "Ah, it's mistaken I am then, surely. But there is one in Sarlow whose face is much like yours. Your pardon."

He bowed and turned away. Calmar watched him go with guarded eyes. Istvan relaxed, pent breath jetting in a sigh. Layareh, Ingulf, Anarod—so many men here, ready to burst into fires that could consume them all. But he must speak with Tuarim . . .

". . . not long ago," the high voice of Ethellin the Wise chimed behind him, "perhaps a century or so back. But I have not been there since."

"No," came the voice of Dorialith. "No, he sailed home to the Land of the Ever-Living."

"Then," Cruadorn's voice rumbled, "there is no smith living now in this world who could teach the old techniques?"

"Do not be certain," a new voice chimed in. "Though I am no smith, I myself am a friend of Govanan, and the time I was in Tir-nan-Og, I would be now and again visiting at the forge of Govanan, and many a time have I helped him with his spells."

Istvan saw that it was the stranger, Falmoran, who spoke. Just beyond the Sea-Elves, he saw Tuarim Mac Elathan, and strode toward him while Falmoran continued . . .

"If you have the craft of the hammer, mine is the knowledge of the forge-magic—of the crystal in the flame, of linking light into patterns of power, of the dance of atoms. But have you the metals to carry the power? For magic swords cannot be forged from one metal alone, but must be woven of many strands of different metals, all interwoven, so that . . ."

But Istvan had no interest in the secrets of the master smiths, and now he stood before Tuarim Mac Elathan, racking his brains for the words to convince a hero out of the elder ages of the World that a mere mortal was more fit than he to order the defence. He opened his mouth, fumbling for words . . .

"It is right you have," Tuarim said, smiling at him. "Long years you have watched the Dark Border, and it is you who have the knowledge of mortal men." Istvan gaped at him.

"But has not Tahion Mac Raquinon also commanded battles along the Dark Border, like his fathers before him? And he understands the wizardry of elves and men. So it is he who will lead you short-lived folk, but doubtless he will be glad to have you as second-in-command. Come, let us speak with him now." He raised his head and looked about like an eagle, hunting through the crowding men.

Turning with him, Istvan felt his breath suddenly catch in his mouth, as rainbow colour rippled wildly through the crystal of the towers beyond the trees. He stared, dimly hearing Falmoran's voice . . .

". . . poisonous cousin, from the same ore? And silver you have, no doubt; but have you the alchemy to refine the slag, again and again, until you find the true and magical silver? Have you the burning metal that is mined from salt . . ."

Istvan gasped at the waves of colour that washed through the crystal. Tuarim glanced at him, saw him staring.

"Ardcrillon weaves sunlight," Tuarim said. "Soon the *Tromdoel* will be upon us, and we will need all our power. So he gathers sunlight spells in the crystal walls, and weaves them into need-fire. Ah, there is Tahion yonder!" He gestured, and Istvan glimpsed the blond head above the crowd. Tuarim strode away.

"Is it mad you are?" Cruadorn's voice roared behind him as he followed the elf. "That cannot be worked! Your blade will burst and the metal burn!"

"It must be sealed in silver, and kept from the air," the quieter voice of Falmaran answered. "This is the secret of the master smiths, for the power flows through the channels formed when . . ." Loud laughter from Fergus drowned the elf's voice. Nearby, Ingulf sobbed, his face buried in his hands. Harp-strings rang. Istvan looked up and saw Cormac seated on the steps, his harp in his lap, fingers wandering on the strings . . .

Ingulf screamed.

"Will I never be free?" the islander shouted, lunging to his feet, shaking his fists in the air. His contorted face was wet with tears. "Had I been an evil man—even if I had been a bad black dog—there would be no need to torture me so! Though I am Ingulf, though I was a fool, I am a true man! It was she who would be beautiful!" His voice became shriller, a squealing, whining howl.

"Though she is a seal now, let me be! It is she who would be a seal! Let me be! Why do you hate me so?" Tahion and Carroll came pushing through the crowd. Tuarim gazed down at Ingulf with wise, sad eyes.

"It is you, Airellen, who is beautiful! But you elves, with your evil harping and music that destroys my brain, you trap me in this evil world!" He glared around wildly, shaking his fist. Cormac's harping stopped, and the harper stared down at Ingulf.

"Ingulf, man!" Carroll said. "Calm yourself, now! Do not be . . ."

"What hope is there for me?" the gaunt islander shrieked. "I could be at peace at the bottom of the ocean now, if their harping had not drawn me back!" His shoulders drooped; his head sank to his chest. "That was all that I heard in the Sea-Elves' city, their music, their accursed harping, plucking at my soul and driving me here and there at their whim. It was a toy I was, and it is a toy I am, driven this way and that by invisible things! What evil could I have done that would draw such a curse on me?"

He sank to his knees once more, and covered his face with his hands.

"I am tired of this sorrow," he moaned, swaying back and forth. "There is no hope for me. The one that I love is a seal in the islands of the north, and I have become a ghost to her: she will neither see nor hear me; she will not speak or touch my hand! I am lost, I am trapped, I am cursed! Why should I live? Why did you drag me back out of the sea, oh seals? I could have peace now, in the water! Let me go! Why should they torment me so? I can never find her! She is a seal now—far in the wild ocean . . ."

Istvan was sure that the expression of sick pity on Carroll's face was mirrored on his own; Tahion was frowning thoughtfully and biting his lip.

Anarod pushed through the crowd, and his face was a twisted mask.

"*Be still!*" he shouted, and kicked the islander hard in the ribs. "I am sick of your wailing!" Ingulf rolled up to his feet, hand groping for his hilt. "Your girl may be a seal," Anarod went on, "but mine is *dead*! Dead and savaged and torn apart by Night-Things!"

Firefrost flew free from its sheath. But Anarod did not move.

"Go on, Loon, kill me!" he hissed, as Istvan and Carroll moved to get between them. "Help me to join her!"

Ingulf froze, bright blade raised. Pain-filled eyes met and locked. Tahion laid a comforting hand on his shoulder, but before anyone could speak, a loud shriek was suddenly cut off.

"They come!" a voice shouted from the wall. "They attack!"

Istvan wheeled, saw a reeling figure clutch at his throat: sunlight glinted off soaring arrows. Suddenly, running elves were everywhere. Tuarim darted away, a blur of speed as he sprang to the wall, *Italindé* flaming in his hand.

Ingulf snatched up his flail from the ground as he ran, his teeth flashing between twitching, twisted lips. Anarod followed, his own face contorted, his eyes wild.

Near the wall, Istvan saw Layareh the Proud lounging casually, sword still sheathed at his hip. Then, just beyond him, sunlight glinted on a steel-capped head as it rose above the wall, and Layareh's blade was sudden lightning flying from the sheath: the head leaped up, trailing red, and fell from sight.

But now other heads appeared. Heroes ran to the wall: Istvan raced to join them, but stopped, swerved, and made for the door of their quarters.

Inside, Cormac was carefully laying down his harp. Istvan snatched shield and helm from the bed. Wounded men groaned and stirred: one mumbled a question Istvan could not quite catch. Slipping his arm through the straps of his shield, Istvan followed the harper through the door. Cormac had taken a small buckler on his hand, and now pulled out a short stabbing sword whose edges glowed with need-fire.

Outside, shields thundered. Swords thrashed above the swaying backs of men and elves: between their bodies, Istvan glimpsed a glint of mail.

He saw one of the forest-runners reel back bleeding, staggering against the Easterner next to him. A sword whirled, and both men went down with a flood of red around them. Sunlight rippled on the ring-mail of the man who sprang over the falling bodies. More mail glinted behind.

Istvan raced to the battle: he heard shields roaring under blows, and the wails of wounded men. Sword poised behind his head, he dashed in among the scrambling, leaping men, staring over his shield's rim at the enemy soldier who turned toward him, dripping blade raised high.

Then that red-smeared sword lashed down at this head: his shield blocked his sight as it thundered on his arm. His swiveling wrist wheeled his hilt in his palm as his blade flew above his falling shield to follow the other sword back, flying at the startled eyes beneath the helmet's rim.

The other shield lifted too late. Istvan felt his edge break through bone, felt the tug on the steel as the man died and the corpse fell. Wrenching the blade free, he ran on, into a wild storm where sharp-edged death swayed like wind-whipped boughs in a thicket of steel. Red rain spattered; men's voices wailed under the thunder of shields.

All around him, men were prancing back from the row of lashing swords behind huge round shields lapped in a moving wall. With a shout, Istvan hurled himself against the advancing phalanx, and then his steel shield was belling on his arm, his eyes and mind filled with the tiny openings through which he must strike.

He became aware of someone fighting on his left, but could not turn to see. Then Starn and Flann rushed in on his right, and now others. Istvan stabbed over a shield, ripped the blade free and slashed across the top of another.

Splinters flew from the huge wood shields: great chunks hewn away. The soldiers behind glowed in mail turned red by the light of fading day. But beyond the waving enemy blades, something slowly rose into sight—black, looming, crowned with crawling fire.

Elves flitted weirdly past, moving too quickly to be seen; one darted in as a sword rose and planted a spear through mail under the arm, and was away again before the sword could fall.

The shield-wall was caving in before them; they stood upon the bodies of the dead, bright blades flying. As man after man went down before him, Istvan caught momentary glimpses of the battle. The dwarf Cruadorn had snatched up a shield, and his other hand swung his heavy smith's hammer, shattering shields and breaking bones.

He saw Ingulf's flail wheel above a shield that caught its haft, crush the helm behind, then whirl down under shields, raking across men's shins, snapping bones like twigs, and a whole section of the shield wall fell, as screaming men toppled on top of the shields that pulled them down. Anarod and Tahion leaped into the gap.

Stone shook underfoot. A horn shrieked.

"Back!" a voice shouted. "Get back down the cliff while you can! The *Grusthole* is coming. Retreat, you fools!"

The man Istvan fought bolted for the ladders. The shield-wall dissolved, and with wild shouts the defenders leaped after them.

In the chaotic swirl of running fight, Istvan saw Anarod hurled from his feet, his sword flying from his hand. As the Seynyorean turned, hopelessly, toward the fallen man, he saw longing on the face looking up at the falling blade . . .

. . . turned to sudden rage as Fergus, closer, leaped in, his shield hurling the enemy back while *Aibreacan* looped through mail.

Istvan stopped. Anarod glared at his rescuer.

The soldiers were going over the cliff, scrambling down the long siege ladders.

But beyond, less than a mile away, as high as the cliff, shaking the earth as it crawled, loomed the black shell of magic that covered the *Tromdoel*.

CHAPTER ELEVEN

The Fortress of Beautiful Fire

But even as Istvan stared at the great black dome, a voice brought him around.

"The towers!" Starn shouted. "What has happened to the towers?" He was pointing back into the fortress behind them. Istvan turned to look and every hair on the back of his neck prickled.

The crystal towers had turned black—so black they seemed but holes in sunlight. The air around them glowed and shimmered, wavering with dark specks. Istvan felt ice pouring down his spine. Had the *Tromdoel* done this?

"Fear not!" the calm voice of Tuarim Mac Elathan chimed. "It is nearly sunset, and the *Tromdoel* is close upon us. Ardcrillon and Artholon thus seek to suck up as much sunlight as they may before the suns set, and draw in, therefore, *all* the light that touches the tower. But that is a spell that cannot be held long—see! Already it ends."

And indeed, as he spoke, the darkness vanished, and suddenly the towers blazed bright blood-red, like tree trunks carved of ruby.

A single high tone sounded from the tower.

"I must go!" said Tuarim. "Ardcrillon prepares the defence!" And like a bird falling into sudden flight from a

137

branch, he blurred and was away, a flitting shadow running almost too fast to see. A dozen other shadows gathered as he ran, vanishing into the shrubbery.

"So they will run off now," Ingulf said. "Perhaps we should all be running, too! Can anything stop that? It's big enough to crush this hill. The ground is shaking—or is that me?"

"If we have any hope at all," said Arthfayel stiffly, "it is in the magic that the elves have gone to make! So keep your tongue off them, Ingulf Mac Fingold! I know how little reason you have to trust the elves, but they are our only hope now!"

But Istvan was not so sure. Looking across the slowly shrinking stretch of forest that separated the advancing blackness from the cliff on which he stood, he could see tiny, flaming figures that appeared and vanished, with need-fire spraying from their hands. The fires swarmed futilely over the surface of the dark dome. Istvan frowned. What was it that the elves thought they could do against a power that brushed the Hasturs aside like flies?

As suddenly as he had gone, Tuarim dashed in among them again. "Are wounded men still inside there?" he asked Tahion.

"There are!" said Tahion, and the elf, whirling, cried out on a long singing note, and suddenly elves ran swarming toward the door.

In a moment they emerged, bearing the wounded men on stretchers, four elves to each.

"Where are they taking them?" Tahion demanded.

"To the old dwarf-hall, there, at the heart of the fort," Tuarim answered, waving a hand at the dome-roofed building above the trees. "They will be safer there. We may not be able to stop the *Tromdoel* here, but whatever happens, they will be safe there."

Tahion frowned, but before he could speak, Tuarim was gone again, a blur of motion.

Istvan felt the stone of the crag tremble underfoot as the *Tromdoel* neared: the ground groaned under its weight. Behind it, its track stretched like a deep valley, with the trees at its rim withered and dying. Its menace and terror beat on them like a cold wind.

In the ravaged strip of land below, Istvan saw the soldiers of Sarlow scurrying to break camp, gathering up weapons and packing their gear as the mountain of doom ground slowly down upon them.

It loomed above the trees, higher than the wall. Istvan shuddered. As it grew closer, he could see the other shape inside the blackness. He forced himself to look away. He had heard that the sight of the Great Dyoles could drive a man mad.

The shell of blackness that surrounded it was a bit of the Dark World, shielding it from the Universe of Light: a filter that changed all light or other energy that touched it into another kind of force, the energy that the *Tromdoel* ate.

If that shell were breached, the thing would be hurled, seared and wounded, back to its own Universe. But unless and until some power could break that barrier, it ate the very power that was thrown against it and grew ever stronger.

Sudden music came from the air.

Startled, they fell silent, listening, and heard in the distance elvish voices singing. Istvan turned to listen. The voices came from the glowing towers, whose crystal now shone with a pearly light shot with lines of rose. But as the voices went on, his keen ears caught a strange shifting, as though the singers moved away from each other, spreading apart . . .

After a moment he was certain two groups of elves sang as they moved away from the tower, in opposite directions, each echoing the other—

No, not echoing, he realised, as he began to pick out words. Each seemed to sing half a line and the other group completed it.

"*Bitter Nut!*" one group sang, and "*Berries Red!*" the other answered. Istvan frowned, listening. The voices were still faint.

"*Evergreen!*" voices sang on the right, and "*Mighty Root!*" answered the voices to the left; then, "*Thornyleaf!*" sounded off to the right.

He frowned and shook his head, unable to make out the answer to that one.

"*Holly Tree!*" the voices chanted on the right.

"Why do they sing at such a time?" grumbled Ingulf, drowning the reply.

"*Snowy Bark!*" chanted distant voices.

"They do not sing for the joy of it!" Arthfayel snapped. "They make a spell! Now be still!"

"*Shining Birch!*" The voices were nearer now, and suddenly Istvan realised that the two groups must be circling the wall—but in opposing directions.

"*Fir and Furze!*" sang voices on the right. "*Oak and Ash!*" answered the left. "*Holly! Birch!*" came the reply.

"*Lighting Links!*" sang the left, but "*Sunlight Drinks!*" answered the right.

"*Earth and Sky!*" came from the left: "*Poured from High!*" the right.

"*Light of Storm!*" one group sang. "*Light of Suns!*" the other.

"*Lighting Flash!*" they sang. "*Flames of Dawn!*" the answer.

"*Crashing Flame!*" they sang: "*Eyes of Fire!*"

"*Fire in Rain!*"	"*Rising Higher!*"
"*Power in Clouds!*"	"*Above the Sky!*"
"*Fire in Water!*"	"*Bake Earth Dry!*"

Closer came the voices, and now through the leaves came glints of fire—candles, or torches—on both right and left.

"*Towering Clouds!*"	"*Warming Light!*"
"*Powerful Clouds!*"	"*Golden Bright!*"
"*Press the Air!*"	"*Pour through Air!*"
"*House of Dark Cloud!*"	"*House of Dawn!*"

Istvan turned as the voices came level with the men, and looking down the wall to left and right, he saw elves come running 'round the corners of the wall from both sides. Their arms were laden with bundles of wood.

"*House of Lightning!*"	"*House of Noon!*"
"*Flame of Lightning!*"	"*Flame of Sunset!*"
"*Fire From Heaven!*"	"*Burns on High!*"

Men stumbled back from the wall to let the singing elves pass. Istvan gasped, for he saw that, despite their burdens, they were not only running, but dancing—weaving in a complex pattern that brought each elf in turn to the wall to lay down a bundle of rods.

And nearly as Istvan could tell, each bundle was spaced

exactly the same distance from the others, laid out in that wild rush with orderly precision.

The two groups raced toward each other, swift as birds, still singing—and behind them, flames were springing up. At the rear of each group ran an elf with a torch, setting each bundle aflame as he passed.

Suddenly the old wound in Istvan's shoulder throbbed angrily.

> *"Fire from Water!"*   *"Fire from the Sky!"*
> *"Fire from the Sky!"*   *"Falls to Earth!"*
> *"Falls to Earth!"*   *"Lights the Earth!"*

Now, directly in front of the great black mound, the two groups met—and now they danced indeed, weaving past each other at a speed that blurred mortal eyes. And still placing wood bundles on the wall . . .

> *"Light from the Clouds!"*   *"Light from the Sun!"*
> *"Light of the Storm!"*   *"Light of the Day!"*
> *"Fire made of Light!"*   *"Fire from the Sky!"*

Istvan saw that the bundles of each group differed: they seemed made of different woods, and those of one side were bound with yellow cords, the other with blue and red . . .

And now each group was laying its bundles down in the precise spaces left between the bundles of the other . . .

> *"Lightning Fire!"*   *"Sunlight Flame!"*
> *"Thunder's Flame!"*   *"Day's Bright Fire!"*
> *"House of Dark Cloud!"*   *"House of Dawn!"*

From each side came an elf with a torch; they met, running. Their free hands linked as they swung round each other, torches unerringly dipping to light the last bundles, and the singing soared up in chorus—

> *"Fire of the Storm!"*   *"Fire of the Sun!"*

And they ran on, each lighting unlit bundles between those the other had lit.

> *"Sun and Storm!"*   *"Storm and Sun!"*

"Gather Together!"   *"Burn as One!"*
"Fire made of Light!"   *"Drawn from the Sky!"*
"Sunlight and Lightning!" *"Ring us 'Round!"*
"Storm and Sun!"   *"Sun and Storm!"*
"Ring us with Power!"   *"Against all Harm!"*
"Power of Light!"   *"Surrounding Life!"*
"Circle of Light!"   *"Circle of Life!"*

"So that is thè spell that is going to stop—that mountain out there?" asked Anarod cynically.

"I—" Karik Mac Ulatoc spoke hesitantly, "I know that the Dark Things fear fire, but—I—"

"These are not common fires," the voice of Alphth the Changeling broke in. "One fire was kindled by Ardcrillon from the rays of the twin suns, focused by the crystals of his tower. The other was brought from a lightning-struck oak on the hills of Darogesh, and has been preserved against such need as this. There is mighty magic in such fires. The storm fire was brought out widdershins, as the storm winds circle, and the other laid out sunwise."

"And the different kinds of wood in the bundles," said Arthfayel, "are woods that are by tradition linked with either the sun or the storm."

"Good enough for an ordinary demon, perhaps," said Layareh, "but—"

"More than enough for an ordinary demon!" put in Istvan—though privately he had his own doubts about such home-cooked magic, the men's morale was low enough.

"—but—will it stop—that?" Layareh finished.

"We will hope so," said Arthfayel.

"Not by itself, no," said the Changeling. "But you have not yet seen the full fires of Rath Tintallain. When you have seen, you will understand its name: *the Fortress of Beautiful Fire,* it is called."

"Well, said Flann, cheerfully, "with all these marvelous spells and visions, not to mention fighting, the day is nearly gone, and no time to eat! I told you, Fergus, that we should have gone in before!"

"So that is why you are so strong," said Fergus mildly. "Nothing is so big that it takes your mind off your stomach."

"If you wait 'til yon gets here," said Carroll, "you might take a steak off it large enough even for *your* appetite."

"I don't think even the elves will have a sauce that would flavour that yonder to my liking," Flann rumbled. "You can have my share, Carroll."

"It won't be here before sunset, if then," said Istvan. "There should be time to eat. Some of us should stay here on watch. When you've eaten, Flann, come and tell me, and I'll go and eat then. Tahion, if you will stay, and—" he hesitated, trying to separate men who might cause trouble . . . "Ingulf? Karik? The four of us should be enough, I think. The rest of you—go eat."

Layarch frowned at him again, then turned with a sneer. The rest simply accepted the quiet authority of Istvan's voice without question.

"Tahion," Istvan said, when the others had gone inside, "I must speak with you." He rolled his eyes to indicate the two islanders, and Tahion went with him out of earshot.

"Tuarim tells me you are in command," Istvan said. Tahion's eyebrows rose.

"I wish he'd told *me*!" he laughed.

"When the attack began, Tuarim and I were on our way to speak with you. I had asked him about taking the command myself—no one seemed to be in charge, that I could see, and I do have experience—you know that I have commanded my own company now for five years."

"Indeed I do," said Tahion. "I've heard much of DiVega's Company—thought of hiring you myself, in fact, and may yet, if we get out of this alive."

"But Tuarim said that, as far as he was concerned, you were in charge of us mortals."

"Well, you have far more experience of command than I have," said Tahion. "I'll happily defer to you, if that's what you want."

"If we tried to tell Layareh and the rest of Conn Mac Bran's men that I was in command, I think we'd have fighting," Istvan said. "And we need more than one officer, anyway. We should be splitting up into watches. I think second-in-command should do. And as Tuarim told me, you do understand much that I do not, about the elves and their magic. If we advise each other and work together, we can accomplish much."

"Perhaps," said Tahion, with a frown. "There is one problem we both have, though—we are both outsiders. This is not our country—not even mine, though I was born here and spent part of my childhood here, and my student years in Elthar.''

"In one way, that's to our favour," said Istvan. "We have no stake in any of the feuds here."

"Perhaps," said Tahion. "Still, I think we need the advice of a local man. Fergus, perhaps. He's commanded the armies of Elantir."

"He and Layarah were close to blows this morning," said Istvan. "We'll have enough trouble getting Layareh to accept me. What about Carroll? They all seem to respect *him*."

"They do," said Tahion. "But I do not think he has much experience of command. All his deeds that I've heard have been done either alone or with a few companions. Starn MacMalkom, I'd say. His personal prowess is somewhat overshadowed by that bodyguard of his, but he has a good reputation for leading his Clan in war. And indeed, here he comes, with Flann—which means, I think, that you should go and eat. I'll stay out and talk with him, and you can send someone to relieve me."

"Right," said Istvan. "One thing before we go. We must divide into watches, so we can get some sleep, and we should use the watches to keep the troublemakers away from each other. Ingulf, Layareh, and Anarod, I think, are the most dangerous . . ."

Flann's voice boomed. "There you are! I'm finished now, and—"

"And I made him leave some food for you," said Starn, laughing. "But you'd best go in and eat it. Itself—" he nodded in the direction of *Tromdoel*, "hasn't flown away yet, I see."

"No," said Tahion. "I need to talk with you, Starn. Take Ingulf in with you, Istvan, and pick two others to relieve Karik and myself."

"Sir!" Istvan brought a hand up in the Seynyorean salute, smartly. It would be as well to establish Tahion's authority. But Starn only stared at him, and as he walked away he heard the Tumbalean muttering, "Well now, did you see that? Is it a disease he has, do you think? Or is it some new dance from the . . ."

Istvan's face still burned as he walked over to Ingulf and Karik, who stood at the wall, staring at the mountainous bulk of the *Tromdoel*.

"Come in and eat, Ingulf," said Istvan. "I'll send some-one out to relieve you, Karik."

"Eat?" Ingulf said, frowing. "What for? I'm a dead man. The elves have murdered me. There's no point to my eating. It doesn't matter."

Istvan blinked at him, and then looked back at Tahion for help, but he and Starn were deep in talk and not looking his way. Licking hs lips, he tried again.

"Come along now, Ingulf. It'll be an hour before you have another chance. If you do not keep your strength . . ."

"Why do you all try to trap me in this evil world?" snarled the islander, his face twisting. "I need no food, I tell you! It is all elvish illusion! All my dreams are broken! I have nothing to live for."

With a helpless glance at Tahion and Starn, Istvan shrugged his shoulders and spread his hands.

"Very well," he said. "Karik, you come along."

"I *am* hungry, sir, thank you," said the brown man. He had equipped himself with a sword taken from one of the dead of Sarlow, and he trotted along at Istvan's heels, leaving Ingulf staring off into the distance behind them.

"What can you do with—him?" Istvan exploded when they were safely out of earshot. "What is wrong with him? And what is he doing *here*? What good can a madman be?"

"I—I do not know," said Karik hesitantly. "I—I have heard stories. He was already a famous warrior in the islands, before he—he got that sword. Some say—some say that there was a curse that went with the sword; others say he fell in love with a woman he met in the City of the Sea-Elves. There are—many rumours. Perhaps you should ask Carroll Mac Lir. He knows him better than any of us."

They climbed the steps and went into noise and confusion. It took them a few moments to find food and dishes. The food seemed to be mostly nuts and fruit, and a strange kind of buttery stuff flavoured with fruit. But there was plenty of milk.

Istvan saw Carroll sitting with Fergus at one of the tables, and took his dishes there to eat.

"I tried to get your friend Ingulf to come in to eat," Istvan said after sitting down, "but he would not come. Said the elves had killed him, and he was dead already. What is—what *happened* to him? And why is he here? Why should the Hasturs summon a lunatic to defend this place?"

"I suspect it was the Sea-Elves, and not the Hasturs,"
Carroll said. "And it has to do with some promise that
Dorialith made him. But as to—his madness," he shook his
head, "he has told me the story, but it is not very clear. I
scarcely—it seems—that he was hunting in the northern
islands, and he speared a seal—only it was not a seal, but a
woman of the Sea-Elves. And then—well, *I* think she put a
curse on him—in any case, an enchantment, that made him
fall in love with her and follow her to the City of the
Sea-Elves. There, they placed more spells on him. He was
there a month, it seems, but he only thought he spent one
night. He tried to drown himself, or perhaps she ran away
into the ocean, and he tried to follow her. I *think*—" he
pursed his lips, and shook his head, "but I cannot be sure—I
think Dorialith punished her. In any case, she is now a seal in
the outer islands, and Dorialith has promised Ingulf that if he
does great deeds with the sword that they gave him, Dorialith
will make songs of them, and sing them to *her*. And Ingulf
seems to think that this will make her fall in love with him.
But—it is hard to say *what* Ingulf thinks . . ." He shook his
head sadly. "When I met him, he was—as bad as he is now.
He went into Sarlow to save the slaves. I followed. I still—I
should have let the fool go! But I helped him, and we did free
some slaves. And Dorialith—"

The room lurched violently. A strange moaning sound
seemed to come from the walls. Chairs fell and dishes broke.

"What? Let us go outside," said Carroll. "I will take some
food out for Ingulf, and try to get him to eat it."

"Tahion, also, has not yet eaten," said Istvan, gathering
up his own unfinished meal. "I should get some for him. . ."

"I'll take him some," said Fergus. "You have just hands
enough to carry your own!" And the black-bearded man rose,
catching his balance as the room rocked again; his chair fell
away behind him and clattered on the floor. Istvan let his bent
knees lift him from his chair without moving the chair at all,
and kept his balance with a swordsman's skill as the room
rocked around them. A deep, bass croaking sound vibrated
from the walls, and then a loud, crackling hiss.

The stairs swayed and creaked, the heroes clustered at the
door, but there was no pushing or crowding.

The twin suns were setting in a band of rainbow light. The
Tromdoel loomed nearer now, higher than the wall, higher

than the hill. The ground shook under foot. The fires burned steadily atop the wall.

As they watched, a great wave of need-fire washed over the surface of the black dome, and a deep, cracked rumble sounded, and they heard and felt it through the soles of their feet as it rang through stone.

Istvan blinked and rubbed his eyes. Was it illusion, or were the sunbeams that struck the fires on the wall making the flames grow brighter? And was it only the rippling of heat above the flames that made the sunbeams that passed above them twist down to join the leaping flames?

Another sound from the *Tromdoel* made the crag tremble. Yet, Istvan realised, none of the bundles of wood that fed the fires had fallen: they barely trembled as the stone throbbed underfoot and men's ears ached.

As the rumble of the *Tromdoel* died away, Istvan's pained ears caught another sound that it had hidden—a sound of singing voices, high and sweet in the distance.

Men moved toward the wall, and the monsterous shadow that loomed above it. Istvan joined them. Another flash of need-fire brought another droning peal of sound: the ground lurched underfoot.

Where were the elves? Surely, Istvan thought, they were not depending on this simple ring of fire alone to stop the grinding mountain that rolled down upon them.

Even with the thought, he heard the singing growing louder:

"*Beam and Bolt*" they sang,   " *'Round and 'Round*"
"*That the Spell*"   "*Be Tightly Wound!*"
"*Sun and Rain*"   "*Earth and Sky!*"
"*Power Rise!*"   "*Arrow Fly!*"

There was a loud ringing sound. Istvan, turning, saw that great doors had opened in the huge central building that they had thus far only walked around. He caught a hint of shadow and light through the open door, but before he could make out any shapes there, the ground lurched again, the stone humming under his feet.

Need-fire played all over the advancing mountain now. He saw the other heroes shrinking back from the wall. He ran to join them, not sure what he could do . . .

Behind him he heard the elves' voices again:

"Forth the Flame!"   *"Power Shine!"*
"Gather Power"   *"In a Line!"*
"Sunset! Lightning!"   *"Ring us 'Round!"*

The top of the wall flared with sudden light!

A ruby glow appeared above the wall like a solid ring, just above the flames.

At the same instant, blue-white lightning lashed above the wall, and jagged tongues darted down into the flames of every second fire.

"Bolt and Beam!"   *"Storm and Sun!"*
"Gather Together!"   *"Burn as One!"*

A crackle of thunder drowned the sound of singing—not the voice of the *Tromdoel*, but of the lightning that flared and faded above the wall.

Istvan flinched away, trying to blink coloured spots out of his eyes.

The twin suns had vanished behind distant hills. Lightning flared and faded, while the ring of ruby light hung steady above the wall.

"Bolt and Beam!"   *"Storm and Sun!"*
"Flame Together!"   *"Burn as One!"*

Out of the doors of the great round hall, Istvan saw lights come, and looking, saw a procession of elves in a long line, led by two who held torches together, left hand and right hand raised, so that their flames mingled in one flame.

Twilight gathered in the sky; a few stars appeared. But the light inside Rath Tintallain did not dim.

The trunks of the trees began to glow.

"Sun and Storm"   *"Ring us 'Round!"*
"Let the Ring"   *"Be Tightly Bound!"*

Now green leaf-light shimmered above the growing trunks: grass sparked underfoot. It was more like dawn than sunset, except for the early stars that began to twinkle overhead. Ghostly moons grew bright.

For a moment, it seemed to Istvan's bewildered eyes that a

moon came through the door of the hall. Blinking, he saw Tarithwen, and light like moonlight glowing all about her.

Behind her, Ethellin, Dorialith and Falmoran walked shoulder to shoulder, and the same white glow played over their white robes and their flowing hair and beards. Behind came Arduiad and Tuarim, and other elves Istvan did not know.

He felt the stone throb and shudder underfoot, and heard the deep croaking rumble of the *Tromdoel*'s voice.

"*Ring us 'Round*" sang the line of elves on the left.

"*Storm and Sun!*" sang the other line.

The heroes parted to let pass the elves whose torches were joined in flame, and they laid the flame into the wall.

"*Gather Together! Burn as One!*"

"*Light of Storm! Light of Sun!*"

"*Gather Together! Burn as One!*" both lines sang together.

Lightning flared again, crackling, and the red band widened. The snapping wood fires atop the wall surged up, hurling sparks high. Then it seemed that threads of light wove and mingled, and a wall of golden light rose, smooth as glass. . .

"Lay your swords into the fire, heroes!" cried the voice of Ethellin the Wise.

The Sea-Elves stepped up to the flame, drawing their own frost-bright blades. Gripping them with both hands, they thrust the points into the wall of light.

Ingulf was the first to follow, and then Carroll. Tuarim Mac Elathan stepped forward, and *Italindé* touched the light. The Sword of Kings flared more brightly than Istvan had ever seen it as Tahion laid it in the flames.

The wall flared brighter as each sword was added. Dair Mac Eykin motioned Karik to him, to share his new-forged blade; a hand of each held the long hilt as they set it in fire. Istvan's Hastur-blade slid into the light, and he sensed the need-fire flashing on his blade flowing to strengthen the wall before him.

Staring into the glare before him, he found that he could see through, now, into the night beyond.

The *Tromdoel* loomed like a black wave, and all around it, tiny flaming human figures flitted like fireflies.

It crushed the woods, grinding trees and earth together into the stone underneath its black shell. It surged forward, rolling toward them.

Out of the night sky stabbed a beam of silver, and the *Tromdoel*'s bellow of pain throbbed through the stone underfoot.

"*Strike!*" cried Ethellin! "Hurl the power of your bodies out through your swords! Aim at the spot where the swallows have struck!"

Now what does that mean? Istvan wondered in annoyance—

And suddenly he felt a power flowing through him, touching his mind, and as he stiffened, it was as though Tahion's hand were on his shoulder, and his quiet voice wordless reassurance . . .

And he *was* Tahion, hearing the trees scream as they were crushed, and feeling the deadly emanations of one of the Great Dyoles, remembering his power as Lord of the Forest, and linking together into one the minds of men and trees and beasts and all living creatures to strike as a unit against the monster, just as he would have done in the Living Forest that was his home . . .

And all in the same instant, his mind showed Istvan the skills he did not know he possessed—showed the energy channels of his body that he used without thinking when he fought, and Istvan thrust with blade and body, giving his whole being to the stroke.

And light lanced from his sword's point, stabbing at that silver spot on the black shell . . .

Flaming figures appeared and hovered in the air, and need-fire streamed from their hands to add power to the slender needle of light that drove into the black shell . . .

Suddenly, the blackness writhed, twisted. There was a sudden splattering of sparks as the shell altered, striving to keep out the light, rather than absorb it. Stone throbbed and lurched as it roared with pain.

Istvan felt wild elation surging among them all as the blackness sank down and shrank, dwindling down below the wall's level, until the lance of light slid harmless from its back . . .

No, a cold voice rang in his mind. *It is not harmed. But it seeks to dig down into the stone, to come at us from below* . . .

Flaming figures flew to the wall of light and into it, and hung there hovering above the heroes' swords. Their radiance streamed out, blending with the need-fire around them: the circle blazed more brightly, and the stones of wall and cliff began to glow . . .

One figure turned, swirled free of the flames and floated to the ground beside Ethellin. Need-fire faded, and Kandol Hastur stood there, swaying slightly, his face lined with pain and weariness.

Before he could speak, the cliff lurched and rocked beneath their feet. Men and elves reeled.

"Stand firm!" shouted Kandol.

Again Tahion linked the minds of the heroes together, and now Istvan felt other minds linked to theirs: the deep yet swift-moving minds of the elves; the passionless intellects of Liogar and Z'jar; the vast, mystic minds of the Hasturs . . .

Istvan braced himself, feeling the muscles of others as well as his own surging into the wide-spaced stance, while the solid stone rolled and rippled underfoot. Then an imponderable weight pressed against the tip of his sword.

His muscles strained against it. He could feel the steel bending, twisting the hilt in his palms. He saw the wall of need-fire bulging back toward him—the flaming figures who hovered within it, arms and legs outstretched, pushed back as by a mighty wind.

One of the glowing figures swirled suddenly 'round and seemed to vault to the ground at Kandol's side, and as the flames died, Istvan recognised Aldamir Hastur . . .

"Save your strength now!" he cried. "The *Tromdoel* can no more touch it than can we, and when it reaches the edge of the field—that will be the time to strike!"

"Let us guide your power!" the sweet voices of the swallows sang through the linked minds. "Feed it to us, and let us drive it through the shell!" The swallows whirled into sight, whirling around and around inside the wall of light . . .

Already Istvan felt his weight being forced back, his forward foot lifting from the ground. He let his weight shift and stepped back smoothly—and felt each of the other heroes stepping with him, all together.

For a second the pressure eased; then massive force drove against them, and Istvan felt rough rock slide underfoot like ice . . .

From somewhere in the linked minds came a sense of a line being crossed . . .

Pain shot up from the soles of his feet through his head. The linked minds shuddered: the fragile link shattered.

"Now!" shouted Aldamir, and Istvan, goaded by pain,

lifted his sword and lunged with his body, slashing the curtain of light with all his strength.

Fire leaped from the wall, and riding on it, the silver swallows. Suddenly, swallow-shapes swirled, became a lens, a cone—a pillar of fire that thinned to a needle's size as it drilled down into the undulating darkness below.

Other minds touched Istvan's, and he saw the needle of light piercing, tearing away the black shell. Something underneath writhed and knotted like a centipede in a fire, curling and uncurling.

Throbbing, roaring stone twisted sickeningly out from under his feet; then an inrushing wind slapped them all like a huge hand, down to the stone again with bruising force. Even the flaming figures of the Hasturs were tossed like leaves on that wind.

Istvan pushed himself up on one elbow in the sudden darkness. In the dim moonlight he glimpsed movement, and heard a crackling and crashing.

As he sat up, he saw the stone wall suddenly vanish, as the edge of the cliff crumbled and fell. He heard stones sliding and falling.

His sword glowed only dimly.

"Is it gone?" a faint voice asked.

"Yes." The voice of Kandol Hastur-Lord was weak with pain. "It has been hurled, wounded and weakened, back into the Dark World."

Demon voices wailed in the darkness.

CHAPTER TWELVE

Distant Dragons

Istvan's head throbbed; his bruised limbs seemed too heavy to lift. He laid his cheek against the stone and slept.

Whirling patterns of darkness and light . . .

Deep, rumbling voices broke through his stupor.

"Hah! He was right!" one said. "Is it not a stack of meat!"

"Some men are moving," answered another voice, just as deep. Istvan lifted his head, opening his eyes to a dimness where broad, squat shapes moved, like men wading in the ground.

"It will be the mortal men," the first voice answered. "It will not have been as hard on them."

Istvan braced against stone, and pushed himself up, blinking through dimness, shaking his head to clear it.

"Are we going to have to lug the whole lot up to the tower?" the other voice asked.

"Not until we've done what we came to do," said the first voice, and one of the broad shapes came walking past Istvan, and in a patch of brighter dimness he saw it was a dwarf, who walked to the ragged cliff edge where the wall had been, and leaned out over the void.

Istvan fought to draw a deep breath, but he felt as though a band were bound around his ribs. But it was the light that was uncertain, not just his vision: great fleets of cloud were sailing across the sky, and a looming bank of them had covered Domri and Lirdan, and only tiny, swift-moving moons were left.

He saw more dwarves coming up out of the ground.

"How bad is it?" one of them called.

"Bad enough," growled the dwarf at the cliff edge, shaking his head above the abyss. "The facing wall is shattered and piled up into a slope a child could climb, and just above it the ring tunnel's wall is open for fifty feet or more. There's no blocking that up! Easy enough to fix in peacetime, but if you listen, you'll hear their wolves."

And in the silence that followed, Istvan heard distant howling, and the low moan of a battle horn.

"Aye, and once they get in there, there are more than a dozen ways we shall have to hold against them," said another voice. Cruadorn's voice, Istvan thought.

"And more than a score of tunnels have been gouged open at the cliff's foot, where the Dyole tried to dig its way under," said the dwarf at the edge. "Those will be swarming with rat-folk soon."

"Can you not seal them off?" said another voice. Istvan recognised Prince Tyrin.

"We can seal the stairs to the next level, if we're lucky!" The dwarf pulled himself back from the cliff. "Aurothror was right. They already hold too much. The lowest levels will have to be abandoned. There are too many places they can force to come at us from two sides—more, in fact."

"There'll be men and wolves coming up that slide, soon," said Cruadorn. "And the goblins will find the chamber. We'd best get the heroes to the tower. I could never understand why Ardcrillon did not quarter them there in the first place. That's what they're here for, after all!"

"Ah, his Lordship doesn't want any sweaty old humans stinking up his nice airy aerie!" another dwarf said. "Nor any smelly dwarves either, I've noticed."

"It was he that had us dig the tunnel!" said Cruadorn. "If he'd left the old one . . ."

"Enough backbiting!" snapped the first dwarf gruffly as he strode back from the edge. "We have work to do! Where did that mortal go, anyway?"

"He was right behind us when we came up!" said Prince Tyrin.

"An odd one, he is," said another.

"He must be," said Tyrin, sweeping a hand around at bodies like piled leaves. "Look at the rest of them! Even the Hasturs—limp as lead!"

Istvan rolled over and tried to sit up, but found himself lying on his back, looking at the sky. Clouds wandered: cold wind-rivers wound between, filled with stars and tiny moons. A demon wailed somewhere in the night.

"The *Tromdoel*'s followers," snorted the first dwarf. "Not my favourite music! You healers get to work! But we'd best get the Hasturs to the tower, where their kin can reach them! Our healers have no skill for such! The elves, too."

"Who gets to carry her Ladyship?" asked Cruadorn.

"Not I," said several voices together.

"Ah, be still!" said the leader. "I'll take her myself, and put her into Ardcrillon's own arms! Let him complain if he dares!"

Istvan finally heaved himself up into a sitting position, though the sky reeled dizzyingly and the rock beneath him seemed to sway. He could see the stumpy figures lifting larger shapes from the ground.

"Here, Thubar! Take his feet, will you not?" said one. "This is the Hastur-Lord himself—it will not do to be dragging his feet all the way to the tower! But no matter how high I lift him, his feet still drag."

"You fool, that's not the way to carry him!" The gruff voice was scornful. "Have you never carried a baby?"

"Not one this size."

A chorus of deep, hooting laughter drowned the response. Istvan felt his eyes closing, felt the world sway out from under him. He fought desperately to hold onto consciousness, to listen to the deep voices . . .

Stars and worlds of profound blackness whirled before him: balancing worlds of flame . . .

"There you are, mortal! We were wondering where you had gone!"

Istvan rocked and drifted in darkness filled with bright visions, and fought to swim and claw his way back. After a while, he realised he was lying down again, and forcing his closed eyes open, saw starry streaks of sky between clouds.

Dwarf voices rumbled all around him: he struggled to hear what they said . . .

". . . him before! What! Svaran the Black risk himself on siege ladders? Not he! But now that the tunnels are open, he will be moving in with his men and his wolves."

"Well then, if nothing else, we can dent up those knee joints! Sharpen your axes!"

"There go the wolves!" another voice shouted, further away. "Back to their masters. Ah, they're turning away now, and going back into the forest."

"I thought as much," another deep voice said. "They are but scouting, and now they go to gather and attack in force."

"Here now, drink this." That was quieter—a man's voice that spoke from somewhere nearby. The voice that answered was surely the voice of Ingulf the Mad—though weak and shrill.

"What have the evil creatures done to us now?"

"All your strength was drained into your sword," the other man's voice answered, clear and resonant, "and the elves and Hasturs fed that power to the Birds of Morvinion; thus, when the *Tromdoel* twisted itself out of the World, and all space shook, you were touching it, magically, through the flame of your sword."

The voice was familiar: Istvan struggled to recognise it. Weariness clouded his mind. He drifted back into the dark behind his eyelids.

Against them he saw hanging galaxies—Universes—splendid weaving patterns of warring light and dark. He heard a distant crashing, as of thunder.

The thunder turned to the deep mutter of a dwarf-voice, very close.

". . . lug them all into the great hall. Sleep would be the best healing for them now." An arm went under Istvan's shoulders and lifted him as though he were a child. The deep voice throbbed through his bones, and a cup's rim pressed his lips apart. "Here, drink this now."

Berry-sweet fire on his tongue sent frenzied tingles to his brain. Eyelids lifted on a world grown sharp: sounds grew clearer, and he felt his blood throb with the sweetness, rushing in his veins to wake numb arms and legs.

He sat up. The band on his ribs loosened, and he drew a

deep, chill breath. Far away in the dark west, lacy lightning lit a cloudy cliff.

"*The dragons!*" a deep voice roared. "There! In the east! They . . ."

Thunder drowned the voice as Istvan scrambled up, turning to look. At first he saw only clouds and starlight, and wondered if this was some fool's joke.

Then, far down near the horizon, what he had thought a tiny red moon bobbed and dipped. Others near it caught his eye: a dozen dim lights like fireflies.

"Is Komanthodel with them?" a dwarf asked.

"Fool!" another snarled. "Who can tell at this distance? You can see as much as I."

"So the dragons are sent against us as well." Carroll Mac Lir's voice was calm.

"How fast do they fly?" Karik asked, from Istvan's side. "How soon will they be here?"

"A few days yet," one of the dwarves answered.

"Are they such slow flyers, then?" asked Fergus, his bull's voice muted and breathless.

"They are further away than you'd think," Cruadorn's deeper voice replied, "and they must stop often to eat and rest. Komanthodel himself flies swiftly, I am told, but the younger dragons cannot match his pace."

"Komanthodel would be here in a few hours," another dwarf said. "I remember when he came before. My mother let me stay up past sunset, and I saw the two flames coming out of the east, no larger than those yonder. They put me to bed then, but the alarms and the shouting woke me, and then the walls shook with the roar of the dragons. I still remember my mother's face as she snatched me from my bed. And I remember the smell as the dragon's breath began to poison the air in the tunnels. And I remember the rejoicing the day after."

"Dragons have attacked Rath Tintallain before?" exclaimed Fergus.

"Oh, indeed," said Cruadorn. "Four—nearly five centuries ago now, Komanthodel and Rianvari, his mate, both assailed us. Aurothror's father, Lorik, and Tuarim Mac Elathan, together slew Rianvari, and wounded Komanthodel so deeply that he flew back to their cave, and has lain there ever since, while his brood grew."

Istvan started, as his left hand slid over smooth cloth at his side, and hit the empty lip of his scabbard. His sword . . .!

Then, dimly glowing at his feet, he saw a dozen scattered swords, his own among them: swords torn from their owner's hands when the *Tromdoel* vanished from the World.

He reached for it. Its light was very dim. All the swords' were. Nearby he recognised Dair Mac Eykin's blade, and the swords of Carroll and Fergus. The Sword of the Kings of Aldinor lay nearby, and, looking around for Tahion, he saw him lying not far away, as still as a dead man.

His heart clenched, and he stepped quickly to his friend's side and dropped to his knees beside him. But the Forest Lord was still breathing, and his finger found a steady pulse in Tahion's wrist.

Looking around, he saw that although most of the men who were not on their feet moved feebly and seemed to be awake, there was a handful who lay as silent and as still as Tahion: Cormac, Alfth the Changeling, Layareh the Proud, and the wood-runner Finloq. Nearby, Anarod had lifted himself on one elbow and was feebly shaking the still form of Arthfayel, but the wizard's face flopped expressionless and limp from side to side.

Dwarves were still moving among the men, and one taller form, either man or elf: healers, lifting the weak but wakeful heroes, and pressing a drink to their lips . . .

Anarod collapsed across Arthfayel's body, and a moment later the taller form came up to them, and kneeling, lifted Anarod and pressed a cup against his lips.

"Here now," a man's voice said, "drink this. It will—"

"Calmar?" Anarod's weak voice squealed as he tried to shout. "Help Arthfayel! I don't matter! But Arthfayel's bad—"

"Never fear." Calmar's voice, stronger, drowned the other. "I will care for him, but first you drink this down and get out of my way." He pressed the cup in his hand firmly against Anarod's lips, holding him tightly against his shoulder. After a second of weak struggles, Istvan saw Anarod stiffen, and Calmar nod. "There, now." He took his arm away, and Anarod blinked around while Calmar, fumbling in the breast of his robe as though searching for something, leaned over Arthfayel. Then his hand, holding something Istvan could not see, stretched out above Arthfayel's forehead. A spark leaped in the dark. Light shaped a letter between eyebrows. The

wizard's eyelids fluttered: his body jerked. Calmar's arm slid
under his shoulder.

"Drink!" he commanded. Arthfayel kicked and twitched
as the cup forced his lips apart. "Easy, now," said Calmar,
soothingly.

"Calmar?" Arthfayel's eyes flicked open. "The—the
Tromdoel—is it—?"

"It is gone, indeed," said Calmar. "It twisted itself right
out of the World. It will be long years before it comes back!
But lie you still now; you've been badly shaken."

"Tahion?" Arthfayel asked, weakly. ". . . where . . .?"

"Over here," Istvan called, rising from Tahion's side.
"But he's numb as a log."

Calmar's dark head jerked up, his face a pale blur in the
night. He laid Arthfayel gently down upon the stone.

"Lie still now, and rest!" he said. "Do not try to get up
yet! And do not try to remember too much about the *Tromdoel*!
Healing means forgetfulness for you, and for Tahion." He
rose, and strode toward Istvan.

Istvan stepped back to make room as Calmar came up. The
black-haired man knelt beside Tahion, and, with a quick
glance at the stars, pulled from the breast of his robe something that glistened. Istvan saw the lustre of a yellow gem—
topaz, perhaps—set in silver. Calmar positioned it carefully
above the centre of Tahion's forehead, as though focusing a
lens. He jerked sharply as a shout rose from behind.

"Kilith!" a deep, dwarf voice roared. "Come help me,
quick. I think this one is dying!"

Istvan saw Calmar's head swivel, quickly turn back. Beyond,
one of the dwarf healers was bent above the body of a man in
islander's robes. Layareh, he thought; it was too light for
Fithil, and both Ingulf and Karik were already on their feet.
But the bearded face covered the man's as though in a kiss.

"Dying!" another dwarf exclaimed, rushing up on his
short legs. "What wrong is on him?"

The dwarf's face lifted.

"I know not!" It bent again to the other, rose a moment
later. "But his heart and his breathing have stopped!" The
voice was a gasp, and the face dropped again. The second
dwarf seized the islander's wrist, then laid a hand on his
chest.

"That's not just shock!" he exclaimed a moment later. "It is like poison!"

"Drink, now," Calmar muttered near Istvan's feet.

"Look for a wound!" gasped the first dwarf, lifting his head briefly from Layareh's face; then, breathing deeply, he bent to drive air down the islander's throat. The other dwarf began to strip away Layareh's robe.

"Who is hurt?" Tahion's weak voice asked.

"That islander—" Calmar replied. "Laira, or whatever his name is. They think he was hit by a poisoned arrow, or somesuch."

"Poisoned arrow?" said Tahion weakly. "Were there Irioch? I don't remember . . . help me up!"

"I will not," said Calmar. "Touching the *Tromdoel* as you have is a kind of poison itself, at least for an Adept! Lie you still now!"

His stronger voice overrode Tahion's weak protests, and the prince lay back. Istvan struggled to think: With Tuarim and the other elves unconscious, and Prince Tahion still too weak to rise, he was in command. Or Starn was. He wondered if Starn felt as weary as he. He could feel the effect of the potion draining slowly away, and weariness creeping back.

"Not a wound on him," the gruff dwarf healer's voice came. "Not a cut, not a scratch! 'Tis as though he's eaten strangleleaf, or heartsbane!"

The dwarf who cradled Layareh's now-nude body in his arms jerked his mouth from the islander's long enough to gasp—

"Have you pulsefire?" He jammed his face back over Layareh's.

"I have!" exclaimed the other dwarf. "Indeed, you've right, 'tis what he needs, poison or no!" He fumbled in the pouch at his side.

Just then Istvan heard the familiar voice of Fergus rumbling nearby. "Well, Flann! Did you have a nice nap?"

"A worse dream I've never had," Flann rumbled in answer. And Starn's lighter voice chimed in, "Aye, like a big black bubble it was, was it not? But a wee birdeen pecked it, and puff, it was gone."

Istvan turned toward the voices. As he moved, there was a curious sensation, as though he were swimming in deep water, and before his eyes hung strange patterns of swirling stars, both light and dark . . .

He blinked, startled, but the starry clouds, instead of fading, brightened, hiding away the world. He stared, and after a moment the vision began to fade, and through dusty clouds of stars he saw Starn turn laughing away from Fergus. Flann loomed behind, following like a faithful hound.

"Ah, outlander!" Starn laughed as Istvan came up. "I hope you've not been bored by your stay? You can see we're not without diversion entirely, even so far out in the country as this! Do your mountains dance as well as that? That one danced itself right out of the World!"

"One of us, Starn, must take command," Istvan said, ignoring the Y'goran's teasing. "Prince Tahion is too weak."

"And am I not?" asked Starn. "Why, man, do any of us have the strength to lift a sword? Do you? But what is on us? Is the enemy coming? Is it more goblins, or—what?"

"The dwarves who tended us saw enemy scouts," said Istvan, struggling to remember what he had half-heard in the dim waking. "Men of Sarlow, and their wolves. And dragons have been seen, but they are still far away." Lightning flared and faded, lit pallid faces.

"Let the dwarves fight, then," yawned Starn. "Let them stand watch! It's their city, after all, and I know not why they brought us! If I lifted even a straw now, much less a sword, I'd fall right down and—" Distant thunder throbbed and crackled.

"You go and sleep then," said Istvan. "I'll stand watch tonight."

"Good luck on finding any strong enough to stand with you!" said Starn. "But—where now shall we sleep?" He waved a hand at their quarters. Istvan stared through the darkness, and then a flash of lightning showed the ruined inner wall of the building leaning precariously over the gulf into which the outer had fallen.

"Now we know why they took away the wounded," Flann's deep voice rumbled. "Now if only we knew where they'd taken them . . ." Thunder muttered and boomed. Istvan gestured toward the gardens—that much, at least, he had seen.

"Into the big grey building," he said, "or follow the dwarf healers." He tried to remember, as he stared at the dark shape of the ruined wall, what had been in his saddlebags. Money was not important, or the extra clothes. There had been letters from Sylvia. Those could not be replaced. But he would see her soon, if he got through this alive. Others must have lost more important things. "I wonder if Cormac got his harp out?"

In the numbness, he felt sleep come drifting, tugging his eyelids gently down, and against their darkness he saw a splendour of Universes of light and dark . . .

He shook his head to clear it, forced his eyes open and stared through the vision at the factual night. Thick clouds swarmed across the sky, but great starry rivers of clear blue still cleft them into islands. Broad walls of starlight divided their shadows. In one beam of starlight, Istvan saw swirling and darting two tiny silver shapes: Z'jar and Liogar, playing like birds indeed.

". . . so I will follow them now," Starn was saying. "Are you well? Are you sure you can stand watch?"

"I—" Istvan hesitated for only a moment. "I am used to this. Sometimes, on the Dark Border, we must go without sleep for days."

"But—after a fight with a walking mountain?"

"Oh. . ." Istvan forced a grin while his memory called up the image of a day—was it only a year ago?—spent maneuvering his men out of the paths of three of the Great Dyoles, under the iron-grey magic-clouded sky of the Border. "Sometimes more than one of those." Starn's eyes widened. "You'd best collect the men who are going to sleep, and find them beds to do it in," he said. Starn nodded, subdued.

"Indeed," he said, "there go the dwarves! May you have a quiet watch!" He turned and strode away. Istvan, looking past him, saw beyond the two dwarf healers with a long naked body draped between them: Layareh the Proud. One gripped his shoulders, the other his feet; he breathed loudly and hoarsely.

Behind them, several Easterners staggered: the men who had followed Conn Mac Bran.

"Ah, Fergus, lad!" Flann's voice boomed nearby. "Will you be sitting up to help keep our Seynyorean friend from nodding off, or are you going to bed like a sensible man?"

"I know not," Fergus yawned. "I think he is right, and some of us should stay, but he will have to be more eloquent than I have ever heard him if his conversation is to keep me awake this night!''

"You go to bed, Fergus," the rich, melodious voice of Carroll Mac Lir chimed in. "There is strength in me still, and I can stay awake. But in the morning we will need your strength, for not only Grom Beardless and Vor Half-Troll will be on us, but Svaran the Black as well.''

"Grom Beardless and Vor Half-Troll are bad enough," said Fergus. "I do not fear them, but can any of us stand against Svaran?''

"I have fought him, and live to tell of it," said Carroll. "For all his speed and his size, he is an indifferent swordsman, and would have died long ago were it not for that armour. But if you look at his shoulder plates, and the metal that rims his eyeslit, you will see the marks of my sword. Strike for them. No matter how tough the steel, sooner or later it must break.''

Istvan felt himself drifting away from the voices. Swirling patterns of light once more filled his vision, Universes that glowed in Sylvia's eyes—or were they Tarithwen's eyes? He could not tell.

He shook his head savagely to clear it, fighting sleep; and the vision changed, and he saw crystal ships sailing on a sunlit sea . . .

He stamped his foot hard on the stone, and the pain drove the brightness from his eyes. He turned back into the night and strode savagely toward where he had left Calmar and Tahion, pounding his feet hard with each step.

He saw Fithil of the Curranach helping Tahion to rise. Arthfayel stood nearby, leaning heavily on Anarod. Calmar knelt beside Alfth the Changeling, and the jewel in his hand brimmed with light.

A spark leaped to the Changeling's brow: eyelids fluttered, lips moved, the limbs moved like a child disturbed in slumber—and, like a child, the Changeling settled back to sleep.

Frowning, Calmar muttered a low word and a second spark flared from the jewel, and burned as a rune above Alfth's eyes . . .

In a sudden blur, the Changeling was on his feet, glaring down at Calmar with blazing eyes.

"*What spell is this!*" he demanded, in a voice that throbbed with power even though he swayed on his feet like a drunken man. "*What would you do to me?*" The wizard shrank back, white-faced.

"I—I but tried to wake you . . ."

"Will not sleep heal?" asked the Changeling.

"Sleep can kill," Istvan barked, "when the enemy is awake! The outer wall is broken, the dwarf tunnels breached—" He broke off, as howling sounded out of the night. "Listen."

Wolf voices wove a curtain of wailing. But through the high, whining chorus burst another note, like and yet unlike, as though maniacal human laughter bubbled through a wolf's throat.

"Werewolves and true wolves bay," Alfth said, head cocked, listening. "I reckon we've fighting to do. I, too, have power. Cormac and Finloq still sleep: do you waken the harper, while I rouse the woodsman." Swift as a ground-skimming bird he was away, while Calmar crouched staring, white-faced, after him. The Changeling's sudden power had frightened him badly, Istvan thought. He watched dull red spread up Calmar's neck and across his face as the wizard slowly rose, teeth clenched, and stalked toward Cormac.

"Well now," said Carroll, from Istvan's side. "I never even guessed yon babe had teeth! Was it a bee that stung the lad? Or what happened?'"

"I know not," said Ingulf, low-voiced, "but I wish he had used his power to strike that lean sorcerer dead!"

"Ingulf! You loon!" cried Carroll. "Why would you say such a thing? The man is one of us, and an Adept of Elthar! And a healer! Why, was it not he who woke you?"

"And a cursed unclean waking it was!" Ingulf snarled. "I do not trust him. His skull leers under his skin. He is as bad as an elf!"

CHAPTER THIRTEEN

The Coming of Hastur

Tahion leaned on Fithil's arm by the gulf where the wall had been, listening to the gathering song of the Sarlow pack: long, sobbing wails broken by the mad, shrieking howls of werewolves.

Their speech differed from the speech of the wolves of Tahion's own forest, but he could understand enough. The werewolves, frantic to attack, bullied a reluctant pack. They would come, indeed—but slowly, driven only by the fear of their invulnerable masters, and it would take time for them to find their way through the tunnels.

Staring into the darkness of the treetops below brought bright fragments from Tarithwen's vision back into his eyes: white ships sailing on a strange dim sea, or, sometimes, swirling galaxies of cold, black suns. But that was only to be expected. When it got too bad he simply turned his face skyward to let starlight wash his eyes clear again.

"Listen to the wolves!" said Fithil, awe in his voice. "Is it not a sound to shake the forest? There must be thousands of them!" Tahion shook his head.

"No more than a hundred, if that. I doubt there are fifty in either pack," said Tahion. Fithil stared at him questioningly. Tahion sighed and tried to explain. "There are two packs, and a man in charge of each of them, and two werewolves that act as his officers. There is a fifth werewolf—I think he is a sorcerer—who is not part of either pack.'' Fithil still stared. Tahion met his eyes, and started over. ''Did you not know that in Aldinor, the land where my forefathers ruled, the king must be lord of beast, bird and tree, and not of man alone? At ten I was initiated into the Mysteries of Alden-Rah. In my own land, the wolves are my children, and so I know the meaning of each cry. These wolves here, though enslaved by evil, are only a little different.''

''I had heard of the Living Forest of Aldinor,'' admitted the islander, ''and I knew you had strange powers; yet, I—forgot. It is one thing to hear wonders in a song or a tale, and another to see them in a man you know.'' Lightning flashed.

The pack was still crying. Tahion glanced over his shoulder at the men behind him. Istvan DiVega stood talking with Ingulf and Carroll; Karik Mac Ulatoc stood nearby, looking at them as intensely as a small child watching an older child's game he dares not join. Close at hand, Alphth the Changeling knelt elf-fashion, one knee hugged close under his chin, his free hand stroking Finloq's temples as his soft voice crooned a spell. Tahion frowned: the boy still thought like an elf. That spell was for elves, not men. He would have to wake Finloq himself . . .

Further off, he saw Calmar's hand brimming with light as he focused starlight through topaz into the ghost eye in Cormac's mind. Thunder crashed.

Finloq sat up with flashing eyes and tossing hair.

''We've been circled 'round by foes, and close nearby,'' the Changeling said. ''Hear them yonder, howling? Led by blood-drunk beasts of sorcery?''

''The Hounds of Sarlow,'' snarled Finloq, groping for his fallen sword while Tahion stared. He found the dim-glowing sword and raised it. ''Ha! The demons must be gone, at least, or the fire would be brighter in my blade!'' Cormac stirred and groaned.

''They are not, alas,'' said Alphth. ''Prick up your ears! Can you not hear them through the wolf pack's voices? Demons wailing for their demon master?''

Tahion, too, listened, heard with effort the faintest whimper of a whistling keen that blended into the wolf pack's cry. Yet he saw Finloq nodding sharply.

"I hear them!" exclaimed Finloq, and was suddenly on his feet. Tahion blinked.

Was Finloq man or elf? Was he a Changeling, left in some human cradle?

Cormac groaned loudly: the light from Calmar's stone blazing runes in the centre of his forehead, as it poured through the ghost eye into his mind.

"My harp!" Cormac moaned. "Where is my harp? Bring. . ."

"Now, now," said Calmar, lifting him, pressing a cup to the harper's lips. "First drink this up . . ." Cormac swallowed obediently.

"Bring my harp," he said, after a moment, "or a pen. I must get it down. I must not forget it . . ."

"Forget what?" asked Calmer.

"The Fair Fires," Cormac answered, then began to sing in a weak voice—

> Lightning lances the rain-lashed sky:
> Fair Fires!
> Twin Suns in splendour sail on high!
> Fair Fires!
> Light was Life's Lover from of old:
> The Blades of the Bold, Fair Fires hold!

The harper struggled to sit up, fumbling with his clothing.

"My pen!" he said. "Where did I put—ah! the pen is with me! And ink is in my pouch!" Calmar rose, shaking his head, and walked to where Arthfayel leaned on Anarod's arm.

"Ah! What is wrong with my eyes?" Fithil exclaimed. "I see stars in the ground and stars in the clouds, stars where there are no stars! And some of them are black! It is like the vision that the Elf-Queen showed, again and again!"

"It is upon all of us," said Tahion, "but it will pass in time."

Nearby, Arthfayel laughed.

"Do not complain! You have learned at least part of the answer to a question that has been debated at Elthar and Carcosa for centuries!"

"You mean the question we all had to answer when we first went to study at Elthar?" Calmar sneered, and struck a comic pose. "*Why did the Elf-Lords come to the aid of Hastur?*" he said, in a voice shrill and cracked like the voice of an aged man.

"Master Failadon!" Tahion and Arthfayel exclaimed together, laughing. "Ah, yes," said Tahion. "I remember well the long nights we spend on that question."

"Yet it was never anything but a test," said Calmar.

"Indeed, the first question asked of every aspirant to the mysteries," said Arthfayel. "In Elthar, at any rate."

"In Carcosa, too," said Istvan, coming to join them. "I think," he chuckled, "I must have given the wrong answer."

"And what answer was that?" asked Calmar.

"Oh, let me think—it was long ago," said Istvan. "I was very young! Boredom was my answer. I said they were tired of eternal life in a land of eternal peace, and sought the excitement of war." He laughed. "Well, I was very young indeed, and lived at the foot of Hastur's Mountain, where no enemy could ever come. So they let me go off to the excitement I thought I wanted!"

"Pity was my answer," said Arthfayel. "Pity for those suffering on Worlds less fortunate than their own."

"Whereas mine," said Tahion, "was love: that love and responsibility that lies or should lie between all living things."

"That was much better than mine," said Arthfayel. "And what was yours, Calmar?"

"Mine?" The black-haired man shook his head and laughed. "Oh, I was young, too! Ah, I said that they were wise enough to see that the Darkness would be at their own door soon. That is not what I think now, of course."

"Of course?" said Finloq, coming up behind Calmar with a mystified Alphth. "Well, what do you believe now?"

"Why, now I believe that they wished to rule, and to spread their . . ." he smirked, "—goodness through another Universe, that they might make us over in their own image."

"I do not agree," Finloq said. "The answer I gave—and it was not so very long ago—was that they knew the oneness of all life."

"Some of those first elves still live in Elthar," said Istvan. "Has no one ever asked *them*?"

"Oh, often," laughed Arthfayel, "and gotten a dozen different answers! But those that live still in Elthar were not the leaders of the Elf-Host. Most of those died; others, like

Nuadan and Mananan, returned to the Living Land ages ago.
Those in Elthar may not know what was in their leaders'
hearts—and in truth, I doubt there was any single, simple
reason, such as these.''

"Perhaps we should ask the Birds of Morvinion" said
Tahion, with a yawn.

"Ask us what, Son of Raquinon?" a sweet voice trilled in
his mind.

Chill prickling thrilled spine and shoulders as he turned.
But instead of the bird-shapes he had expected, the beam of
starlight that squeezed through the narrowing gap between the
clouds had shaped itself to a slim pillar of silver light, and
near its base, looking into Tahion's eyes, was—a face!

Or a mask, perhaps, perfect as a statue's face: sculpted all
of light, calm, passionless . . .

"Forgive us," Tahion stuttered. "We—we were but
talking—asking why the—why the Elf-Lords came to the aid
of Hastur—we knew you were there. We thought perhaps you
knew . . ."

"We, too, have wondered," the sweet voice sang, the calm
lips motionless. *"For of all the wonders of two Universes,
courage is the most mysterious to us. We have none: we
cannot be destroyed; we take no risk.*

*"Ages we flew through that other Universe, observing
mortals of your kind and others, on a million million worlds.
And always we were deeply touched to see such frail, short-
lived creatures risk destruction to help others of their kind.
We thought it very beautiful, but we never interfered—indeed,
we knew not that we had the power to interfere.*

*"Until, a few short ages ago, the Dark Things broke into
our Universe. The greatest of the Eight Dark Lords ripped a
hole in the fabric of space, and burst through, and we, too,
were in danger, for we could see, beyond, this ruined Universe, where his Kin devoured the stars.*

*"Then, for the first time, we tested our powers, while all
the Cosmos reeled. Life was twisted and evil spawned on a
thousand worlds, mirroring the Dark One's thoughts. But
other powers came to our aid, others of our own kind, some
older and more powerful than we—Varvadoss, Kathugar,
Iod—and from them we learned our power and its use. And
together with them, and other, lesser powers, we wounded
the Lord of the Eight and hurled him back into this Universe.*

"*As best we could, we strove then, to close the hole the Dark Lord had torn between the Universes: even while we fought new evil, the shadows he had cast upon a million worlds. Yet we knew the Eight were still here: we feared they would come again, until Hastur reclaimed this world for the Light.*"

Wild chills raced up Tahion's spine, lifting his head.

"But—" he hesitated, heart pounding, "but—from whence did Hastur come?" He stared at the pillar of light.

"*Of all that lived here, only Hastur and Awan A' Towith escaped the ruin of this Universe.*" the silver pillar trilled. "*When the Dark Lord broke through the wall between the Universes, we saw two tiny shapes driven before it, lashing out with feeble flame as they were hurled into the dark between the stars. We paid little heed, for we were still trying to master our own power, learning to fight with the light of our star. But Varvadoss, older and wiser than we, wrapped his flame around the frozen bodies as they floated in space, life all but gone, and bore them to the Living Land, for he knew the skill of the elves.*

"*Varvadoss told us, long after, of those he had found. One was a giant of a race of giants: Awan A' Towith, last of an Immortal race, gifted by nature with great power over mass and gravity, and with the power to change his size and seeming.*

"*But the other that Varvadoss found was the body of a man like yourselves.*

"*But a greater spirit dwelt within it: the essence of some being or power that had grown with the galaxies, but was now fused into the body and spirit of some great mortal sage.*

"*Long, then, that body lay healing in the land of the elves, while the two spirits within blended and grew together into something new, greater than either had been.*" The slim shaft of light dissolved, and in a narrow beam of starlight, white swallow-shapes swirled.

"*Such was Hastur, and as he healed, he studied the elves' magic and added it to that which his two selves had known. Thus was he able to combine the skills and the knowledge of two Universes for the forging of the weapons from which the Dark Things fled.*"

"The Sword. The Ring. The Brooch." said Tahion.

"*And the Axe of Awan the Giant,*" the Swallows trilled.

"For Awan, too, desired to return. His power was great, though he had not changed and grown as Hastur had. But together they opened the Hyadean Gate, and hurled the Dark Lords back into the lightless Universes of the Abyss from which they had come. Thus they reclaimed this Universe, and Hastur repeopled it from our own."

The memories of long-dead ancestors stirred in Tahion's mind, and the living face of Hastur rose before him—a lined and ancient face at first, but with eyes that sparkled power—a face that had grown younger through the centuries, as power filled it, smoothing its wrinkles, turning the white hair red . . .

"Yes, son of Halladin," the Swallows sang, spiraling up and down the narrowing wedge of starlight, *"that was Hastur as we knew him when he opened the Gate into the Ruined Universe, and the Dark Lords fled his power. But time is short, your foes are near upon you, and the clouds are closing and soon will hide you from us. Arduiad knows how to open the clouds if we are needed."* Lightning flickered somewhere off in the night. *"The clouds close now! Fight warily, son of Halladin! Fight bravely and safely, all you mortal men!"* Suddenly, the silver shapes swirled up the beam—and vanished, as the clouds rolled together, sealing away the sky.

Distant thunder roared. Tahion blinked, suddenly aware of silence . . .

Silence! The wolves' howling had stopped. They were coming. He tried to reach out with his mind . . .

It was like reaching into fire. Touching the *Tromdoel* had seared his nerves raw, and now whatever lay under the stones of Rath Tintallain burned and throbbed at his rasped mind, and suddenly he knew why the elves wrapped themselves in illusion here, and what so tore the Hasturs' concentration that they could not use their powers. Somewhere beyond the pain, he heard Arthfayel's voice . . .

"Why, this is a secret that men have wondered and pondered for Age upon Age!"

"Much good may it do you!" said Calmar. "It would be of more use to know where Hastur went, and how to bring him back, would it not?"

Tahion swayed, fighting to keep his balance. Again the illusion of Tarithwen's vision was all about him, and now he seized it, hoping it would draw out some of the pain. He saw the vastness of the patterned Universes: fire and darkness balancing each other, throbbing in balanced harmony, until a flaw appeared in the pattern, and a Universe of light turned abruptly dark . . .

"*When doom from the Dark World devours the Land,*" a voice was singing softly, "*And Worlds laid waste by the*—no, no! That's not right!" It was Cormac's voice, and was followed by a rapid scrabbling of pen on parchment.

"Cormac!" exclaimed Arthfayel. "Do not tell me that you, of all people, did not hear the swallows? Were you so caught up in your own song that you could not hear another?"

Tahion could not see Arthfayel or Cormac; he was fighting the whirling patterns of light and dark that covered his eyes, and driving down the sickening pain. The pattern—pattern . . . there was a pattern here, too. Throbbing patterns of Light and Darkness that tore at him from under the earth. What was it? It burned his mind now, as it burned the elves and the Hasturs.

Patterns. There was a pattern to everything, he knew that. There was a pattern to this place, just as there was to his own Forest of Aldinor, but he did not understand it. Was it only to free an imprisoned Dark thing that the *Tromdoel* and the dragons and armoured might of Sarlow had come? Or was there some deeper reason?

"Oh, I heard them, indeed," said Cormac. "A great song it will make, when I have thought on it for a time. But the time for making that song is not yet. Now it is on me to make this song—

> "*Up rise the heroes, rarer than gold!*
> "*The blades of the bold fair fires hold!*"

"Hush now!" Alphth exclaimed in a whisper. "Can you not hear their paws on stone? The wolves are on the slide!"

Tahion pulled the Sword of Kings partway from its sheath, stared until its dim light filtered through the swirling patterns and drove Tarithwen's vision from his eyes. Then he sheathed it again, and rushed to join the others at the new cliff-edge where the wall had been.

A small stone rolled in the dark below, where dim shapes moved in the shadow. The faint musty smell of their fur rose, mixed with another scent, a foul scent. Further away there came a thudding of heavier footfalls, and a faint, lashing jingle.

"Goblins, too," said Finloq, beside him.

"And soldiers out of Sarlow," said Carroll.

"What shall we do?" Karik's voice was anxious. "There is no wall now! But can they climb the cliff?"

"They'll be coming through the tunnels," DiVega said.

Carroll added thoughtfully, "Should we not warn the dwarves?"

A wolf yelped in sudden pain: a yelp cut short. A horn rang: light flooded the slide, dyeing the broken stone, and leaping back in green and topaz from the eyes of the wolves and goblins.

"Perhaps we need not bother," said Carroll.

Deep shouts roared defiance from the stone. Wolves snarled and whined. On the red-lit rock the shadows of axes lashed, and the struggling shapes of wolf and dwarf and goblin were writhing blots, mottling the light through which the enemy rushed to the gap in the wall.

"Look!" cried Carroll, pointing. "Svaran!" He pointed at a figure in black plate-armour, toiling up the slope in the middle of a company of mail-clad men.

"And Grom Beardless!" Ingulf snarled.

Bloody corpses of goblins and wolves flew from the gap, to roll down the slide. Deep, triumphant war-shouts rang underfoot, humming through the ground mingling with screams and yelps of pain.

"It seems we may not be needed at all," said Carroll. "Indeed, we might as well be sleeping, for all the Seynyorean's —now where has he gone?"

"Ah, he made a mistake," said Ingulf. "He sat down to listen while the Birds talked. And there he sits now, snoring." He pointed. "And Fithil not far away." Istvan sat with his back to a tree, head drooping on his chest. The islander was sprawled on the ground nearby.

"And after all his talk about the need to stay awake!" Carroll chuckled. "Should we not wake him?"

" 'Sleep can mean death when the enemy is wakeful,' " Alphth quoted. "Those were his very words. We must wake him!"

"Let him sleep!" said Tahion. "Let them both sleep, unless the enemy comes." He paused, listening to the shouting and the snarling underground. "Stand guard over him, Alphth—you seem awake enough. Wake them both if any of the enemy comes up through the tunnels." He looked around, counting the men who remained. Alphth, Cormac, Finloq, Arthfayel, Calmar, Anarod, who else? Carroll and Ingulf, Karik: Dair Mac Eykin stood nearby, his reforged Hastur-blade drawn and glowing dimly in his hands. He seemed more alert than the others. Colin Mac Fiacron and Ailil Mac Ailil lounged nearby, but weariness weighted them: they were barely awake.

"Not many of us, are there?" said Carroll at Tahion's side, low-voiced. "Fourteen of us, if the dwarves cannot hold them. If they force a way through the tunnels, there may be fewer of us tomorrow. All very well to stand guard, but let us hope we do not have to fight! Or that the dwarves will come to help us! It is their fort, after all."

"Listen to the shouting and the snarling below there!" said Ingulf. "Dwarves fight well enough. If the goblins or the wolves do push past, is it not what we are here for?"

"I do not know why we are here," Carroll said somberly. "The dwarves fight, the elves fight, the Hasturs make magic. Why go to all this trouble to bring us? And where have those savages gone—the Ua Cadell?"

"They are all cowering at the foot of Ardcrillon's tower," said Calmar with a sneer. "When the *Tromdoel* appeared, they all ran like deer! It is a wonder they did not climb the wall and jump off the cliff at the far side!"

"Who could blame them if they did?" said Arthfayel. "They have no weapons for such a battle."

"But for such a battle as this they have, and they will be more rested than we," said Carroll thoughtfully.

"What weapons will they have against a werewolf?" said Arthfayel. "Indeed, if one of them is bitten, then we will have werewolves inside with us, and . . ."

"But they are safer from werewolves if they are warned and able to fight," said Tahion. "Finloq! Dair! You are both woodsmen, you have dealt with the forest tribes. Go rouse the warriors of the Ua Cadell and bring them back with you. Tell them to be ready to hunt wolves. And have them kindle fire and bring it."

"We shall," said Finloq, rising and darting off. Dair frowned, glanced at his friends, and stalked off more slowly, sheathing his sword and shaking his head. Cormac sang:

"When dreadful doors to the Dark World gape,
Fair Fires!
And barriers between Worlds break . . ."

The song broke off with a sigh and a muffled imprecation. Cormac's pen scratched loudly, and he muttered under his breath.

"And why is it the Ua Cadell are here?" Ingulf wondered aloud.

"They live in the forest below there," said Alphth, from where he stood beside Istvan and Fithil. "They have taken refuge here with us because their own land is now crawling with enemies."

"So I had guessed," said Carroll. He shook his head, and muttered, low-voiced, "But still I do not know what they need us for."

"*What?*" exclaimed Calmar. "Can it be that after all this time they have not yet told you what it is that you guard?"

"Well, we know, of course," said Arthfayel. "I had guessed some time ago, in truth. But since we arrived, there has been little time for talk, and—"

"*Hush!*" Alphth exclaimed. "Listen."

Wolf snarls and dwarf shouts were louder, echoing sharply from hollow stone.

"Up!" Alphth cried, seizing Fithil's arm. "Awake! The wolves come!" He sprang away as Fithil rolled up, sword in hand, reached to touch Istvan's shoulder, then sprang away, out of the sweep of the Seynyorean's sword. "Arise! They come! Look!" He pointed.

A double-bitted axe reared suddenly out of the ground, and fell again. Another rose where it had been.

Suddenly, Tahion was aware of a rhythm in the snarling and yelping from underground, a rhythm that was set by those lashing axes. He heaved up the Sword of Kings, and began to run.

There was a sudden change in the rhythm, marked by a deep shout of rage and a sudden thunder of growls.

A stumpy figure sprouted from the ground, frenzied axe heaving up and down. Behind him, Tahion heard the feet of the other heroes, and the light of swords unsheathing sparkled like stars on wet grass.

The dwarf sprang free of the ground, up out of the stair-

well. Great black shapes reared up to follow: skilled axe
strokes hammered them down.

But there were too many. The axe fell, and as it rose a dark
shape sprang under it. The dwarf leaped back: the great axe
smashed down, hurling the wolf-shape to the ground at the
dwarf's feet, skull and shoulder crushed. But already another
was leaping in.

And as he ran, Tahion saw the crushed wolf stir and roll
up, wounds healing, and knew it was a werewolf there.

Wolves surged out of the ground, flooding the stair. Even
as Tahion came up, the dwarf was hurled from his feet.
Tahion sprang in among the wolves, heaving the blade out in
great whirling sweeps, as he strove to drive them back from
the fallen dwarf. By the light of his sword he saw the
stairwell choked with glaring eyes, and his heart went cold.
Bone parted under his edge.

Then behind him he heard the voice of the Changeling,
chanting strange words . . .

"*Cuin qlaus rua! Cuimircor'm g'lua!*"

Werewolves bulked among the lesser wolves, red eyes
malign. "*Cuin shidarra Shinn!*" Alphth sang.

> "*Cuin foijarra Finn!*
> *White fair hounds!*
> *Bright-furred hounds!*
> *Red-eared hounds!*
> *Speed here, hounds!*"

A werewolf sprang, and the Sword of Kings whirred to
meet him, flaming with need-fire. The wolf tried to twist
away from the glowing blade, and the cut which would have
slashed it in half only sliced deep into the shoulder, and sent
it spinning away, screaming in a human voice. A torrent of
wolves rushed on Tahion: he hurled high his steel-and-silver
blade, expecting to be swept from his feet . . .

A new sound rose suddenly above the wolves' snarling—a
chorus of yelping like honey-toned bugles, and the wolf pack
was a sudden tangle of tumbling bodies as the lead wolves
veered, trying to stop.

Something white and lean flashed past Tahion's thigh, and
leaped to a wolf's throat. Tahion stared, his ears filled with
wild bugling cries. More sprang past.

Lithe white dogs with fox-red ears were darting, teeth snapping, into the ranks of the pack, dodging and twisting, elf swift.

"Where did—*they* come from?" Istvan exclaimed at Tahion's shoulder. Without waiting for an answer, he pushed past Tahion, and raised his shield to ward them both.

Where the slashed werewolf had fallen, a bleeding man rose. Clutching his wounded arm, he staggered to the steps, and plunged down them.

Wolves went down with torn throats; others fell back, grey fur stained with red where fangs had torn. Pack wolves fell back, but bearlike black shapes loomed.

Great jaws gaping, a werewolf lunged at a red-eared hound. The hound danced back while another leaped in, biting at the black-furred side.

As the hound's jaws closed, the werewolf whirled, and the hound yelped in startled pain as long fangs found flesh. With a shake of its head, the werewolf hurled the bleeding dog aside and leaped to meet another.

White hounds converged on the raging black beast in a biting, snarling mass. Istvan pointed.

"The dwarf!" he said, and began to sidle, shield lifted, toward the still form barely to be seen between paws. Tahion seized his shoulder. The fight surged toward them, elf-hounds clinging to the werewolf, their teeth dragging through invulnerable flesh.

"Dead!" Tahion's voice was flat certain, but he had to shout above the growls and snarls and yelps. "His face is half chewed away! Look how still he lies! Do you not see the caked blood in his beard?"

But Tahion's words were nearly drowned.

Fire-eared elf-hounds worried and bit. Teeth tore harmlessly through swift-healing black hide: bleeding white hounds whined in pain. The red-eared pack scattered as red-eyed black beasts leaped in. Blood-dappled white hounds dodged and twisted, darting to bite dark hide.

From the steps nearby came a crashing of feet.

"Back!" Carroll Mac Lir sprang to Istvan's side, and set his shield edge against the Seynyorean's to make a wall, as the biting, twisting battle swayed toward them. The three fell back. Each werewolf now dragged several elven hounds, dangling by their teeth from the night-haired hide, while other dogs darted and snapped.

But the werewolves' terrible jaws were crushing bones and slashing wounds, hurling hounds bleeding down onto the ground.

The men fell back, shields raised. Behind them, Tahion heard the voice of Alphth the Changeling crying strange words that sounded like the crowing of a cock.

"*Hig-a-foo-ca-doo!*" the Changeling crowed. "*Cu-roon-doo!*"

"Now what?" DiVega muttered. Behind them, Alphth began to chant.

> "*Dread Dog! Dire Dog!*
> *Dark Dog! Guard Dog!*
> *Cú-dú-roon! Cú-roon-dú!*
> *Hig-a-Fú-ca-doo!*"

The wolves that had fled to the stairs came pouring back out of the ground, and behind them came men with torches, wet blood dripping from their swords. Lightning flared off mail-rings.

Wounded white hounds crawled, bleeding. Their wounds healed, but not so swiftly as the werewolves'.

Alphth's chant went on:

> "*Fierce-Eyed, Fire-Eyed,*
> *Haunt-Hound: Help-Hound!*
> *Quimirkar'm g'loo!*
> *Cú Ru'n Du!*"

Tahion felt it then—some power rising, flowing upon them, rushing upon them like a cold wind. Chill swept the back of his neck. Thunder drowned the chant, then it swelled again . . .

> "*Cara Shi agum!*
> *Cara Rún agum!*
> *Cara Gar'g agum!*
> *Cara Gar'v agum!*
> *Bale-Hound: Black Hound!*
> *Fierce Hound! Friend Hound!*

> *Fierce Friend: Faerie Friend!*
> *Come Friend! Come!*
> *Hig! Afúca! Hig!*
> *Come, Friend! COME!"*

As the Changeling's voice rose to a wild crowing: *"Hig a-foo-cu doo!,"* something black, huge as a calf, bounded from the bushes.

Istvan and Carroll raised their shields against it and shrank back against Tahion, glowing swords ready, thinking it another, larger werewolf. Great eyes like goblets of golden fire turned to regard them, and they saw the drooping dog jowls, and Tahion sensed in its eyes intelligence and a power untamed and alone . . .

Then it had turned and was leaping over the white dogs, the teeth in the great jaws glowing with need-fire.

A werewolf reared to meet it, white hounds still clinging to its sides. White dogs scattered as the black beasts met. Growls like thunder hummed through stone and bone.

With a snarl, the jowls closed, the great head jerked up, and the howling werewolf's paws kicked and struggled above the ground.

"Fight, A' Fucca! Fight!" cried Alphth, and he sprang past Tahion and the others, a long, slim blade flaming in his hand.

"Follow Alphth!" Tahion exclaimed. "Quickly!" Bright swords waved behind him as he ran.

The men of Sarlow had shrunk back into the stairway as the great black hound had sprung; but now they rushed out, some waving torches, while the rallying wolves raced beside their knees.

Four werewolves fought to come to their comrade's aid, dragging the thin, pale dogs who clung, snarling, on rear, loin and shoulder.

A wounded hound barked. Suddenly dozens of the pale shapes dropped away from the black shoulders and wheeled to the stairs, voices raised in a chorus of shrill, clear yelps. Wolves shrank against their masters' knees: soldiers waved torches and shouted.

The werewolf in the great jaws screamed in a human voice, and Tahion blinked to see the outline of the body there shifting and flowing. The other werewolves came charging in, white hounds still clinging to their sides.

Now a man hung screaming from the black dog's jaws, and then a contemptuous shake of the head hurled the changed shape spinning. With a bark that sounded like a command, the black hound whirled to fight, while the thrown man sprawled among milling white hounds, his scream cut short.

Two werewolves went down under the black dog's leap; a huge paw pinned one on the ground. Fiery fangs found the other's throat. Two other werewolves checked, snarling, wild red eyes searching warily.

Beyond battling black shapes, swords and torches lashed at twisting white hounds. The belling chorus swelled. Men shouted: wolves snarled.

The mailed ranks split. A robed man came from the stairs, a slick black stick in his hands. Behind him, torchlight glimmered blue on a following dark shape—like a man carved all of black steel . . .

"Svaran!" Carroll snarled.

Two free werewolves sprang at the black hound's haunches. Tahion blinked, doubting his vision even as he felt the surge of magic: the black bulk shifted shape and a black horse stood there, teeth in the throat of a struggling werewolf while another snapped at the foreleg that held it down.

Lashing hooves met the werewolves in the air. Human voices wailed in pain as they flew.

Alphth sprang to the horse's side, sheathing his glowing blade in the heart of the werewolf that writhed snapping under the hoof. The horse reared. A dark shape hung from its mouth, screaming in a human voice. A flash of distant lightning showed a man-shape dangling there. The horse leaped and came down in a gallop, running straight into the fight.

Fallen werewolves ran cowering, tails pressed tight between legs.

White hounds fought men and wolves: their merry caroling barks swelling. The robed sorcerer's black staff lashed out: a hound fell back howling in pain, a great black patch seared on the white hide.

"Hastur's flames!" Carroll exclaimed. "It's alive, that dog is! But those sticks kill!" A second hound yelped and fell back, burnt, as snarling werewolves tore a lane through the line of hounds. Fangs tore at them. They bled, shrieking, and

Tahion saw that they were changing as they ran. Mailed men leaped to their aid, driving the hounds back: lifting the bleeding were-men—still shaggy, but stumbling now on two feet—and helped them back into the ranks. The black horse tossed a human shape at the sorcerer's feet.

A sword slashed at the horse; he reared, eyes blazing golden fire and the soldier reared back with dented helm. A wolf fell, skull crushed. The black rod lashed out.

Need-fire flared where the black beast stood. The sorcerer reeled back. When the flame died, the black dog glared with eyes of golden fire: the white hounds bayed in triumph.

The soldiers locked shields into a wall: the black-steel shape like a statue in the centre. The wolves cowered behind, with the staggered sorcerer.

Recovering, the robed man raised the deadly staff high, and screamed strange words in an unknown tongue.

> "*Kumto Kunturn K'thuggdarn!*
> *Yiier Yugkonth Yarlothp!*"

His voice shifted pitch eerily, breaking in a shrieking howl

> "*Yizjoth ek Yogzthoth Yugibstmoc!*
> *Fressec'hu i'ker'thro Fol'kmoc!*"

A sudden sharp bark stilled the chorus of the hounds.

Out of the dark came a whistling keen, pulsing nearer, clearer . . .

"What is it?" asked Karik's voice. The hounds whimpered.

"Demons!" said Fithil. "Coming up the cliff."

Tahion turned, and others with him. Filmy veils, blacker than the night around them, writhed up over the cliff's edge.

"A' Fuca?" Alphth's voice whispered.

A strange voice answered, high and clear as a harp string, humming in all their minds.

"*No power have I over such creatures,*" the voice said. "*Only the swords of the heroes can help us now—or the Birds of Morvinion, if the clouds will part to let them pass.*"

Wearily, Tahion raised the Sword of Kings. Lightning flashed, off in the distance, and by its light they saw the fleshless black wisps gliding hesitantly toward them.

Would dawn ever come? Tahion wondered, feeling the endless fight weight his limbs, his bones heavy as though laced with lead. Flaming swords made a glowing fence against the demons. Karik Mac Ulatoc looked about helplessly, the plain steel blade he had snatched up drooping from his hand.

"Kill them!" a muffled voice shouted from the Sarlow line, and there came a rush of feet from behind.

"Istvan, Carroll, turn!" Tahion shouted. "Karik! Fithil! Anarod! Cahir! Fall back and help them! The rest, hold your ground!"

Then, in surprise, he heard Alphth's voice chanting.

> *"Arduiad, Archer!*
> *Archer come quickly!*
> *Quickly rise, reaching,*
> *Raise the bow, bend it.*
> *Bind string on strong bow:*
> *Strung now, come quickly,*
> *Quickly Bold Bowman:*
> *Bring Birds, Cleave Clouds!"*

The chanting was drowned in the hammering of steel. Istvan's shield gonged at Tahion's back, but he held the Sword of Kings steady, watching the blots of drifting black mist that moved toward them, keening. He heard hounds barking and he heard men shout.

Then, from behind, came a glow like moonrise, and the demons drifted back, eddying . . .

A deep humming, and then soaring above the shouting of the battle and the demons' shrill whine came another, sweeter sound, the high shrilling music of elvish piping.

Tahion glanced over his shoulder, saw DiVega's Hastur-blade wheeling like a hawk, and beyond, above the trees, the crystal tower that had sat still and dark through the night, glowing now as though moonbeams filled the walls.

And atop the tower a figure swayed on its feet, but it raised a great bow above its head. Near it another figure stood, pipes rising above its shoulder.

"Arduiad!" Alphth cried.

Flaming arrows shot skyward, one after another, and they heard the elf's voice crying in the distance.

Wet drops struck Tahion's forehead as rain began to fall. A cold wind swayed the treetops. A great moonlit river appeared between the clouds, and a wide strip of moonlight like a glowing glass wall.

And out of the starlight the swallows came swooping, silver shapes wheeling in the moonlit air.

One swallow-shape flared, and a glare like full sunlight shone on a demon. Black film dissolved.

And at that sight Tahion turned his back to the demons, shouting for the others to do the same, and, trusting in the powers of Liogar and Z'jar, sprang to the aid of those who fought the men of Sarlow.

The shield-wall reeled before them, outnumbered though they were; had they all had shields themselves, it would have broken. Razor-edged, glowing blades slashed away. Lean white hounds darted under shields to tear at legs. Tahion saw a few of the hounds bleeding from sword strokes, but only a few: they were too quick.

"Beware!" Carroll cried. "Svaran comes!" Tahion looked, saw the black-steel shape, gleaming in the light of their swords, stride toward them.

Anarod leaped into its path.

"Anarod!" Carroll shouted. "No!"

Anarod's flaming blade glanced from a black-steel skull: the sword's light showed a filmy shimmer of speed-blurred steel.

Anarod's shield split with a loud *crack*, and he flew from his feet. Steel death came swooping back.

Ailil Mac Ailil leaped into its path, shield and sword together crashing with the impact.

Wild war cries wailed; weary, cursing men paused, swords in the air. A thrown javelin took a soldier in the throat; breathing blood, he crashed to the ground.

Dair Mac Eykin sprang from the leaves. The thin, steel wire of the "woodsman's needle" in his hand slipped through mail rings. Behind him, dozens of savage, naked warriors burst from the brush.

Panic seized the mail-clad men; the shield-wall broke as they rushed for the stairs, the wolves cringing among them, white hounds snapping at their heels.

Only three stood beside the black-armoured figure; they wavered as heroes converged on them, swords poised like a wave crest. Anarod rolled to his feet. Ailil's point grated on black steel above one eyeslit: a steel-clad arm and shoulder whipped around in a blur, and blood and brains gushed above Ailil's left ear. Svaran wrenched his sword free from the crushed skull.

Anarod's shriek blended with the shouts of Finloq and Dair, and all three hurled themselves toward the tall steel shape. But Istvan and Carroll were there before them, and their blades made bright scratches on invulnerable armour as their hammer blows battered him back toward the stairs.

Two mailed men fell back, shouting Svaran's name as they cowered behind their shields. The third sprang to his aid. Tahion leaped into his path, crashing the Sword of Kings down across a whistling cut, and found himself staring into the cold blue eyes of Grom Beardless.

Steel clanged as Tahion hurled back another cut, and then the sudden wall of Grom's shield blotted his vision and he was swept aside.

Reeling back, he saw Istvan's shield driven against his helm by Svaran's savage strength, while Istvan's own blade scraped harmlessly across black steel. Carroll fell back as Grom joined Svaran: the two stood back-to-back.

Grom was shouting. The white hounds snarled around them, darting in to snap at their legs. A white hound went down, slashed in half by Grom's sword; another sprang back yelping, blood welling from a deep cut where Svaran's sword had struck.

Suddenly, the air around Svaran's helmet was filled with splintered arrows.

With a last shout, Grom sprang for the stairs, covering himself with his shield: in a moment, its great wheel bristled with arrows.

More slowly, Svaran fell back, moving with measured arrogance. Hounds and heroes followed, but stayed out of the range of that deadly sword. Arrows still shattered on Svaran's helm; he kept his head turned to keep them from his eyeslits.

The great, black dog moved among the white pack, growling, but it too, hung back. Svaran gave a short laugh and backed down the stairway, Grom Beardless at his side.

Music sounded. Elves came rushing up, Tuarim Mac Elathan at their head. Tahion leaned wearily on his long sword. Svaran and Grom vanished down the stairway.

Dawn stained the clouds.

CHAPTER FOURTEEN

Patterns of Power

> *"I am patterned Power:*
> *I am patterned Atoms:*
> *I am patterned Metal:*
> *I am patterned Silver . . ."*

Tahion woke, listening. A hammer beat: a tiny hammer on a little anvil, somewhere outside. A high voice pulsed as it chanted with the hammer . . .

> *"Patterned silver shimmers:*
> *Shimmering wire, weaving*
> *a woven web of waves . . ."*

Tahion opened his eyes and sat up, blinking. The faint chant faded, and other sounds drowned it: the voices of men. Tahion rubbed his eyes. Daylight was gloomy in the great stone room.

He had been too tired to see much when he had staggered in at dawn. Only Garahis of Ordan had seemed to be awake. He had gone out willingly enough to stand watch with Dair and Karik, who still seemed to have some strength—perhaps because they had shared a single blade between them when they had held off the *Tromdoel*. Reluctantly, Tahion had wakened Starn before wrapping himself in his blankets.

The gloomy light filtered through arrow slits high in the walls, and showed a vast, round, indoor space like a cavern: dim in grey distances he saw chairs and chests and cabinets, but near at hand the heroes were sleeping on pallets on the floor. Beside him, Tahion saw Istvan sleeping with his hand on his sword, his face peaceful. Nearby, Carroll's arms were flung across his face, and beyond, Tahion was startled to see Cormac's harp, with the harper's body curled protectively around it.

Turning his head, Tahion saw Calmar sodden, the blanket over his face, and Arthfayel snoring loudly. Anarod's blankets, beyond, were piled and empty.

Soft-footed as a beast from his own forest, Tahion rolled to his feet. Fergus' voice boomed laughter somewhere outside: Flann's voice joined and blended, and then Starn's higher tenor laughter chimed in in musical counterpoint.

Catlike, Tahion slipped between the sleeping heroes to where Layareh lay, still and pale. Shifting his sight, Tahion saw the islander's aura, steady but muddied: poison, right enough, he thought, and frowned. He looked for a wound, but could see none. Still, poisoned weapons from Sarlow should be no surprise . . .

As boisterous voices faded outside, he could hear again the hammer banging on the little anvil, and the elf-voice chanting . . .

> *"Metal ocean shimmers,*
> *Shining rage ripples,*
> *Rippling silver sea . . ."*

Beyond Layareh, Tahion recognised the wounded young Easterner in whose mind he had nearly drowned. As he stepped to look at the wound, the chanting swelled, and now he recognised the voice of Falmoran the Sea-Elf . . .

> *"See lightning leaping:*
> *Lapping spirals spreading:*
> *Spreading pulse of power . . ."*

The boy lay curled, knees drawn up like a child in the womb. Tahion dropped to his knees beside him. There was something wrong. He looked at the wound: the fresh dressing bound it well, the blood had stopped, yet . . .

The boy's face was still, peaceful. Too peaceful. Tahion set his hand on the cool forehead and slowed his breathing, shifting it to match the too-regular breath of the other. Slowly, he breathed himself into trance . . .

Into the boy's mind . . .

Into peace . . .

Into emptiness . . .

Into sweet warm milk . . .

There was no future here, no past, only peaceful warmth, comfort, homelike, womblike . . .

Tahion felt himself drift away again in the warm sea of milk, nameless, drowning . . .

He caught himself, kicked out, struggled to remember. He was—he was . . .

He was the Lord of the Forest . . .

He was Halladin, Lord of the Forest . . .

Halladin, born under a single sun, fleeing and fighting with his ancestral sword against the evil that threatened to whelm his world . . .

Riding into a circle of flames that drove the pursuing shadows back: carrying him into a strange new world where two suns shone, and a great voice roared into his mind and the minds of all men "I AM HASTUR!" . . .

But another voice, under that, wordless, wonderful, calling, calling . . .

Halladin, wandering, wondering, answering . . .

The Forest, the young Forest, root and branch, leaf and bud: growing, sprouting . . .

He was Halladin, King of the Forest when all the world was new. King of root and branch, of leaf and bud, of bird and beast: Halladin, the king, calling, as the stag calls in spring . . .

Young Ong-quenna, answering that call, slipping timidly between trees, night-black hair over dawn-red breasts . . .

He was Halladin King of the Forest, and Ong-quenna his queen, and Onakar their son: Onakar King of the Forest . . .

He was Onetaquo, King of the Forest . . .

He was all of the Kings of the Forest . . .

He was the Forest . . .

He was the Baranor, King of the Forest, slain by a mob, his crown torn away . . .

He was Raquinon, Lord of the Forest, exiled King of the Forest, crossing the broad sea, dwelling at last in the Elfwoods, a world away from his soul in the Heart of the Forest . . .

Raquinon, meeting at last a woman of the half-elven Clan Gileran: getting a son . . .

Tahion, son of Raquinon and of Eolavra of Clan Gileran, standing at the Heart of the Forest, while a harp woke ancient memories . . .

He was the Lord of the Forest, Tahion, Lord of the Forest. . .

Far away he felt the Forest wake, beyond the sea. The Tree That Walks Like a Man stirred in the darkness, shaking his mighty limbs with a rustle of leaves: King Stag rose from his thicket, sniffing the air; deep in the roots, under the soil, Aldenrah pulsed, the Heart of the Forest, waking trees and men and beasts . . .

Faint and far away, the Forest: the Lord of the Forest knelt half a world away. Yet its power anchored him as he reached into the sea of milk, through milk into the womb where the nameless spirit floated, babe-helpless . . .

Somewhere under the milk, its memories slept, and the ancient Lord of the Forest reached for them, seeking the name . . . through seething milk the name . . .

The name HRIVOWN!

The milk-sea seethed: the nameless child waved little fists and kicked feet drawn up, elf-fashion, knees near chin. Tahion's mind called again the name: *HRIVOWN!*

The shape uncoiled as the name throbbed through Tarithwen's milk. Phantom hands clasped Tahion's. Together they rose through the sea of milk: drained and drank the milk . . . Tahion rose out of the boy's mind, gripping tightly the phantom hands . . .

Eyelids flickered. The still face stirred. The boy's eyes opened.

"I am Hrivown," he said. "You called me?"

Outside, a tiny hammer clamoured on a tiny anvil.

> *"Wavecrest to Wavecrest,*
> *Power is pulsing.*
> *Pulsing in patterns.*
> *Patterns of Atoms . . ."*

"I called," Tahion answered. "You have slept two nights and a day since you were wounded. Do you remember the fighting?"

"I—" the boy's brow crooked, frowning, "I remember— did we win? Did we drive them back?"

"We drove them back," said Tahion. "You must not worry now. Now you must sleep. You are very tired. Sleep is what you need." He put his hand on Hrivown's forehead and his will on his mind. "Sleep will make you strong, now . . ."

> *"Channeled the Power.*
> *Pouring through metal:*
> *modeled these atoms,*
> *Atoms of Silver!"*

The chanting and the hammering stilled. The boy's eyes closed. Tahion watched until he was sure Hrivown only slept, and would not slip back into the elf-spell. Then he rose, and left the boy slumbering. Sunlight through the door glittered on tiny chips of ruby and emerald.

This great gloomy room had been rich long ago: it was cluttered with gold and with jewelry still. Even through dust, Tahion could see the lines of fine workmanship.

A leather pouch burst as he stumbled over it, and his foot sent chips of sapphire and emerald skittering through the dust. Old leather crumbled to powder. He frowned, perplexed. A half-carved face stared at him from a rough block of marble.

By the look of things, no one had been here in a long time. He walked toward the door, noticing the stands beneath the arrow slits, the heavy crossbows and racks of quarrels that hung beside them. The heavy door was forged of steel. Why had so strong a fort, still filled with treasure, been abandoned?

His foot shied suddenly from the stones of the floor before him: senses scorched and numbed, he swayed and almost fell.

He looked down. Through the thin layer of dust, his eyes could make out only the faintest difference in the stonework of the floor. But the newly wakened senses of the Lord of the Forest had plunged through those stones into an aching void, where freezing cold fought fire at the edges of a blankness his mind could not pierce.

Dropping to one knee, he lashed one hand across the dust, sweeping clean a long strip of stone. Here the edges of the stones had been carefully carved to fit the curving lip of a circle in the floor: other stones had been carved to fit inside them. But the mortar inside was different.

There had been an opening here, a well, or, more likely, one of the sudden spiral staircases that the dwarves seemed to like. But it had been blocked, sealed with great, if hurried, labour.

The pain was lessening now, as his mind drew back into his body. No wonder the elves hid themselves in illusion, and the Hasturs avoided the use of their powers! The pain would be far worse for them . . .

Rising to his feet, Tahion skirted the circle, his mind guarded in his body.

And so he had no warning or defence when the change came.

It began as green veins growing in the walls, writhing through rock. Twisting vines branched and twined, green leaves widened, lifted . . .

Trees fountained from the floor. He smelled pine needles under his feet, and green leaves that glowed bright with sunlight shining through. A forest-scented wind was in his face.

Sailing on that wind came a rainbow-feathered bird, and its voice was an elf's voice . . .

"Brithlain!" it cried. *"The baby is hungry, and Anarod comes!"*

He stared after the bird, dazed, and began to stumble after it through the sudden forest glade. The bird vanished among the great trees.

A sharp pain lanced up through his foot, jarring him. He looked around.

This was all wrong. There should be no leaves nor pine needles under foot—only bare stone and chipped gems. There should be no trees—only the vast stone hall.

He tried to see through the illusion, but searing pain surged from the floor and his scorched mind drew back. He staggered, every nerve burning. But he had a glimpse of the door. He reeled toward it, though it was now the arch formed by the crossing branches of two great oaks . . .

He passed under them and the forest vanished. He blinked in grey daylight: the sunlight that had illumined the emerald leaves was a lie: the sky was sombre white.

Savages in ragged plaids swarmed around the door, their faces tense with fear. Women clutched their children fiercely, protectively.

Beyond, Tahion saw dwarves leaning on wet red axes or dripping swords: their rent mail oozing red. Steel gates barred the gap in the thorn hedge, and there he saw Flann towering behind Starn, who stood talking to Tuarim Mac Elathan, while other heroes clustered around.

Tahion drew a deep breath to help shake off the illusion that had trapped him, and stepped down from the door. Scowling savages drew aside to let him pass. Their women stared, love and fear in their eyes. Was battle then so near?

He heard a little hammer begin to beat: Falmoran's voice chanted, off to the left . . .

> *"I am patterned Power!*
> *I am patterned Atoms!*
> *I am patterned Metal!*
> *I am half of salt . . ."*

He turned toward the voice to look, but all he could see was a swirling fountain of bright-winged butterflies, crimson and golden wings whirling in a funnel, while the chanting swelled . . .

> *"Sealed in a silver sea:*
> *Silver Sea seething.*
> *Seething ocean sunders—*
> *Split salt Islands wander*
> *A woven web of waves."*

Just for a moment, the butterflies thinned. Tahion glimpsed the elf kneeling beside his anvil, beating fine wire. He had stripped to a sea-green kilt: his long beard was thrown back over his shoulder; something like a large, green cheese lay on the ground beside him. The little hammer rose and fell as he sang:

> *"Waves of whiteness washing*
> *Whirl around the Islands:*
> *Islands linked and locked . . ."*

"Tahion?" Fergus' bull voice drew Tahion's eyes away

from the whirling curtain of butterflies. "Have you seen Anarod? Is it well with him?"

"His blankets are empty," said Tahion, startled, "or were when I came out. Why? What do you fear for him?"

"He tried to throw himself off the wall," said Fergus, "and cursed me for keeping him from his beloved! Flann and I held him back, and later we saw him go inside. We thought he was still there."

Tahion remembered the words that the rainbow-feathered bird had cried.

"I think the elves know where he is—or perhaps I should say, I *fear* they do." He frowned. "I will have to look for him. But there are other duties first. What has happened while I slept? I see there has been fighting." He gestured at the dwarves ahead.

"In the mines," said Fergus. "The goblins drill like rats in the walls, and the Sarlowaq and their wolves roam where they will. They have driven the dwarves out of the lower levels of their own city: King Aurothror and his warriors have just come from battle in the tunnels under our feet."

"Do you mean the city itself has been taken?" Tahion asked.

"Only the deeper tunnels," said Fergus. "The core of the city is still theirs. But Sarlowaq gather in the wood below, with Vor Half-Troll at their head, and Aurothror believes they mean to attack from both above and below the . . ." A deeper voice drowned his.

"Is it not the man who guides elves through the woods? Do you think you can find your way out again?" Looking down, Tahion saw Ogar Hammerhand, resting his chin on the crosspiece of his tall, two-handed sword. Tahion and Fergus were now in the midst of the dwarves.

"Why, finding my way out is easy enough," Tahion answered, "but I am choosy about what company I keep on the road."

"Indeed," Ogar rumbled. "Even inside, the discourse has been less pleasant than I might have wished. Why, below stairs there, we've been discussing the same subject for days!"

"There have been some sharp points raised, though," said another dwarf, who leaned on an axe beside him.

"I admit it," said Ogar," and I have taken more than one of those points." He gestured at a wound under a rent in his mail. "A point of my own I have driven home a time or two," he added, shifting his great sword so that the point squeaked on the stone. "Yet I think I have spent evenings in more pleasant company."

"More polite company, no doubt!" laughed Tahion. "Well, perhaps together we can improve the quality of the company here about! But I fear I must consult King Aurothror and Tuarim before we make such plans, so I had best be at it!" And with a smile he walked on, Fergus at his heels.

". . . of no use now," he heard Tuarim saying as he came up. "The dragons, at least, would follow, and you would have no hope and no defence upon the road. But I think you are right, Prince Tyrin, and once we have beaten off this attack, I will tell Kandol myself it would be wise to accept your offer. But for now, all we can do is defend this fort, and hope."

"You say *we*," said Aurothror, "but it is my people I see dying in the mines."

"We offered our aid when we first came!" Starn exclaimed, hotly. "Carroll Mac Lir offered our swords to you, and you laughed at us! There has been fighting up here, too, and if you will trouble yourself to count, you will find nigh half of us are gone!"

"It was not of you mortals that I spoke," snarled Aurothror, but Prince Tyrin's voice broke in—

"I have seen Tuarim fighting in the mines, and not so long ago! You know well, Aurothror, why the elf-folk avoid the main part of your city! You gain nothing by blaming them! And well might they ask: where were we, while they fought against the *Tromdoel?* They have done their part, while we have done ours."

"Well, when Vor Half-Troll leads his men up the cliff, then we must all do our part," said Aurothror.

"Aye, and when Svaran comes up out of the mines," said Starn, grimly. "With men and wolves at his back and Grom Beardless beside him, then indeed we shall need every sword."

"Swords are of little use against Svaran," Prince Tyrin growled. "It will take an axe tempered like a Hastur-blade to cut such steel."

"Grom Beardless I have fought," said Tuarim. "But Svaran I know not. Who is this Svaran, and why is he spoken of in such tones?"

"He is the most deadly of Sarlow's fighting men," said Starn. "Not so fast, perhaps, as Grom Beardless, and certainly less skillful, and not so strong as Vor Half-Troll; but he wears a suit of magic plate-armour that no sword can cut. It is said that no man can face him and live."

"Well, I am no man," Tuarim said. "I must meet this Svaran, and put his armour to the test. We will see how it fares against *Itelindé*, which was forged before Hastur drove the Dark Things from this Universe, by the greatest smith of the Living Land."

"His armour was tempered to resist a Hastur-blade," said Aurothror. "The dwarves have their own grudge against Svaran the Black. Only one other such suit of armour has ever been made—for the Emperor of Airaria: an army could have been equipped with half the treasure he paid. The five greatest smiths of my people worked together on it; such steel has never before been wrought or even imagined. This second suit was made by order of the King of Devonia, across the sea, for his son. He must have beggered half his kingdom to raise the price they named. Yet the price was paid: the prince was measured; the suit was forged. A Nydorean ship sailed with it; but a raider from Sarlow chose that ship as quarry, and captured it."

"Some say Svaran was captain of that ship," said Prince Tyrin.

"Not likely," said Aurothror. "A sailor, perhaps. But most likely, the armour was taken back to Sarlow before they could find any that could fit it. For remember, such an armour fits closely to the body of the wearer, and this had been forged to fit the limbs and body of Prince Ascelin. By sheer chance, Svaran could wear it."

"And it is only since he has gotten the armour that men have heard of him," said Starn. "Five years ago, no one had ever heard of Svaran the Black."

"Aye," said Aurothror, "and during those five years my kinsmen have haggled with the King of Devonia over whether to give back the treasure, or to make another armour. There seems little hope of reclaiming this one."

"We shall see," said Tuarim. He turned. "Well, Prince Tahion! You have been quiet and patient while we talked."

"Ears hear more than mouths," quoted Tahion, "and there is much I need to know, both about our enemies and

ourselves, and our plans for this battle. But first: one of my men is missing—Anarod.''

''Anarod?'' said the elf. ''Fear not for him. Brithlain, the virgin daughter of Artholon, nurses his child, and now has taken Anarod also in her care.'' Tahion made no reply, but his heart went cold: this was what he had feared. In the silence, he heard Falmoran's chanting voice and hammer:

> *''Half-salt holes.*
> *Hollows holding Power;*
> *Power pours pulsing;*
> *A pulse of lashing lightning . . .''*

Much has happened while you slept,'' said Prince Tyrin. ''The Sarlowaq and their wolves, whom you drove back into the city, scattered in their panic. Many of the wolves, indeed, fled the tunnels and escaped down the slide; some men, also.

''But Svaran and Grom kept a part of their force together and came down on our rear as we battled goblins in the deeper mines.

''That was grim fighting. Many died there, and those that survived were forced to flee into narrow corridors where the men could not come, while wolves and goblins swarmed after them. I owe my life to Ogar Hammerhand, who lives, and to Tamun, to Favi Helmcrusher and to Rokhad Keenheart, who do not; for these took the rear guard when we were driven into the tunnels, each of them standing alone.''

Prince Tyrin fell silent. The Sea-Elf's hammer beat.

> *''Power burning brighter*
> *Brightens into lightning . . .''*

Still Aurothror leaned on his axe. Now he spoke, his voice bitter.

''Death took many. Sons I lost, as well as comrades, and more will die. Our lowest halls swarm with goblins; in the walls we can hear them, boring through the stone. And soon now Vor Half-Troll will scale the cliff.''

''Why then do we not defend the cliff?'' Tahion asked, looking out through the gate. ''Why are our forces drawn back behind this hedge, leaving undefended ground we have fought over for so long?''

"I ordered it thus," said Tuarim Mac Elathan, "and Starn, your comrade, has already protested. But look you—there is no wall there to defend; the stairways run down into tunnels already opened to the enemy. If you stand at the cliff's edge to defend it, then you may well be cut off by foes coming up the stairs. It would waste lives, and you would be forced at last to fall back to this redoubt.

"But the cliff-edge is not undefended. Arduiad Mac Artholon stands on the tower, and beside him four famed archers, Sithglas, Rithcugal, Suleric, and Sithewn, all skilled and deadly: not easily nor unscathed will the foe reach this wall of thorns!"

"But then what?" said Aurothror. "Then they will have to chop down your hedge—unless we chop it down ourselves— before we can chop them! And then it will be the same as if we stood on the hedge's other side. Except that the hedge will be gone."

Tahion reached to the trees: the whitehorn's bright throbbing filled his mind, their life flowing through him . . .

"It will not be easy to cut these trees." The air in the leaves throbbed with Tuarim's voice. "Elves have planted these trees and nourished them: our magic flows through them; our magic grows in them. They know when they are threatened. Their branches can move, their spines are sharp; they can strike out an eye or break a bone."

Tahion was one with the trees, part of the trees, feeling sap flow and leaves tremble; feeling the light that glowed through the sap; feeling the roots reaching for the light under the ground; the brightness at the heart of Rath Tintallain . . .

He felt the roots recoil. Pain gnawed like a cancer at the heart of the light; a poison that blighted and killed; a rot that reached for their roots . . .

His flowing mind charted the root-web, finding bright, healthy roots growing in the glow, nourished by sweet, live underground light; found, too, black and withered roots, blighted and dead, in dead soil where no insect crawled—dead soil that ran like a corridor cut straight through the root-maze. Corridors that alternated in frightening symmetry with the channels of bright life where healthy roots grew thick and strong . . .

He pulled himself back into his body, swaying, aching with the pain of the roots withered by dark rays.

"If the trees will fight," Starn asked, "what do you need *us* for?"

"Indeed," said Tuarim. "We could all go home, if the trees could stand by themselves. But they cannot: they will only fight to keep from being cut down. My people will aid them, fighting from within the hedge and in the branches of the trees, but sooner or later the enemy will break through, and there will be need for swords and axes!"

A hand touched Tahion's arm.

"Ah, Tahion! There you are!" The voice was Arthfayel's; it was his hand on Tahion's shoulder. "Know you where Anarod is?" Tahion reeled, his mind still mapping the root-web, charting the pattern of life and death . . .

"Are you well?" Arthfayel asked. Tahion blinked at him. "You look—pale, and tired."

"I do not know—wait!" Tahion shook his head savagely, trying to clear it. For a moment the dark stars of Tarithwen's vision swirled before his eyes. "I do not know where Anarod is, but I fear I can guess. Come!" Still reeling with shock, he staggered away from the voices of Tuarim and Aurothror, with Fergus and the mystified Arthfayel following, around the wall of the great grey building, and into the swirling butterfly cloud that rang with hammering and Falmoran's voice:

> "Night flees Need-Fire:
> Fire fed by ferment.
> Metal atoms dashing.
> Lashing half-salt islands:"

Butterflies flew up out of a little open fire. Falmoran sat beside it, beating braided strands of wire with his hammer, his face was haggard with strain. Beyond the fire they glimpsed another elf, who stood with hands raised in the heart of illusion, eyes remote: the two wizards could dimly sense the strands from which he wove the spell. They hurried on.

"Why butterflies?" asked Fergus.

"I think," Tahion said, "to protect Falmoran's mind while he does magic."

"Against—whatever it is—*that which we guard*, as the Elf-Lord called it?" said Fergus.

"Whatever it is that is under the ground," said Tahion. He

turned to Arthfayel. "I have not known Anarod for very long. But if you will picture him clearly in your mind—"

"What? Tahion! Do you think I cannot do so simple a magic for myself?" Arthfayel snapped. "But what is it? What fear is on you?"

"Tell him, Fergus," said Tahion. When Fergus finished, he added, "I fear the elves are trying to help. Tuarim said the daughter of Artholon had taken him into her care."

Arthfayel nodded, biting his lip; then, closing his eyes, began to breathe slowly and deeply. After a time his hand came up, pointing. Tahion's mind, joining Arthfayel's, sensed Anarod walking between crystal walls.

Throbbing under the earth made the contact vague. After a moment pain forced Tahion back to his body.

They circled the great round building, and the glittering towers rose beyond the trees. The little wood was quiet and peaceful about them as they strode purposefully between beech trees and hazel trees along the gravel path. There were no birds now: all had fled the coming of the *Tromdoel*. The smell of apples and apple blossoms grew around them: a rose-scented breeze blew in their faces from Ardcrillon's gardens.

In the maze of paths between the rose bushes, they met Anarod himself, humming a cheery tune, striding the gravel with a broad smile, like a hero who has achieved his heart's desire.

"Anarod, man!" Arthfayel stared at him. "Why—man, it's good to see you smile again! But where have you been?"

"Oh, I went to see Eilith and the baby," said Anarod, carelessly, "and we were talking of us, and what we would do after going home. And we played with the baby, and talked of the next baby and what we would name—"

"Anarod!" Great tears ran down Arthfayel's face as he stared at his friend. "Have you gone mad, too? What are you talking about? You know well that she is dead!"

"Dead?" For a moment something horrible and bleak stared at them through Anarod's eyes. "No! It is you that is mad! I was with her just now! It is you that is mad! Come see for yourself!"

Arthfayel's mouth opened, but Tahion's fist clenched on his arm, commanding silence.

"Indeed, I would like well to see her again," he said

calmly. "Very much, for my mother, Eolavra, was the daughter of Ericru, whose sister, Luriana the daughter of Dorial, was the mother of Crioran, Eilith's grandfather. Her father and I were boys together, but I have not seen her since she was ten."

"Why—" Anarod started, and stared at Tahion. "I had forgotten! But indeed, she has spoken of you! You are the most famous man of her kin since the death of Cugarvad! Why, she will be pleased to see you indeed! Come with me!"

He touched Tahion on the shoulder, and led the way through the maze of roses. Arthfayel and Fergus followed, unnoticed.

The door beyond the thrones was still shut. Anarod turned to the left, and they went sunwise around the tower. Toward the tower's back, a low white wall jutted from its side, and the walk ran under a rounded arch into a small, enclosed garden.

"Eilith!" Anarod darted through the arch ahead of Tahion. "Eilith! See who I have brought! It is your famous cousin, Tahion Mac Raquinon, that you were telling of!"

A golden-haired girl looked up with laughing blue eyes from the bench where she sat holding a red-haired babe to her breast; and Arthfayel's face went dead white.

"*Eilith!*" he groaned.

Then Tahion caught his arm, and hurled his thought through flesh and blood and sinew: *Not another word! His mind will break!*

"Fortune be upon you, Tahion," the girl said, smiling. She was rosy-skinned and sturdy; big-boned, wide-hipped, deep-breasted, wrapped in a faded green plaid. But there was an eerie sweet beauty in her voice. "It is happy I am to see you here. Give me your hand, and let me be your true friend, for the sake of your mother and our kin, as well as for the sake of your kingdom of the wood."

She stretched out her free hand: the baby's mouth lost its grip on the rosy nipple, and it made a little mewing noise, not quite a cry. She hugged it to her, and slipped the nipple back into the little mouth, singing—

> "Hush, health of my heart!
> Suck up sleep from me!
> Drink and dream, my dear!"

As she sang, the human quality left her voice, and it took

on an uncanny, wild beauty like the crying of birds across far marshlands. Tahion dared to open his mind, for here the pain underground was fainter and further; and he saw the pink-skinned, strong-limbed woman grow ghostly to his added sight, and faintly a slighter, paler shape showed through . . .

"It is I that would be a true friend to you, kind girl," he answered her, "for the sake of that man and his child. It is on you that his health and his mind depend. Do you understand me?"

The blue eyes leaped to meet his, but under the blue there was a sudden glint of silver-grey.

"I understand," she said, low-voiced. "There is no mischief on him!" Again her hand stretched out, and now Tahion took it. "We will speak more after," she said, then began to croon to the child . . .

> *"Health and wealth of heart to thee;*
> *Strength of stream and stone to thee;*
> *Might of Mind and Heart to thee—*
> *Blessed babe, take from my breast!"*

"Anarod, my love!" she cried, "were you not telling me it was on you to go to the battle?"

"Alas, my heart," he answered, "it is true, that is on me."

"Leave, leave my love. I will not be happy until you return. But a spell of power I place upon thee!" Her eyes met Anarod's, held them, as she sang . . .

> *"Strength of Steel be thine.*
> *Strength of Stone be thine.*
> *Strength of Storm be thine.*
> *In all thy striving—*

> *"Force of Fury with thee.*
> *Force of Fire with thee.*
> *Force of Fortune with thee.*
> *In all thy fighting!"*

"Now go, my beloved, my lines and my binding go with thee! Come back to me, my heart!"

Anarod turned away, but did not seem to see either Tahion or Arthfayel. Yet when he passed Fergus near the gate, he slapped him on the back and laughed.

"Fergus! Are you coming? Is evil at the gates yet?"

Fergus stared a moment, then the two strode out together, leaving Arthfayel and Tahion alone with the girl and the baby.

Carefully, aware of the dangerous, slumbering power he could rouse, Tahion gently parted the illusion around her. The merry blue eyes widened, while frost turned them silver: shadows darkened the gold hair. Flesh faded: hips and breast shrank, and the rounded limbs thinned until they seemed like the bony limbs of a coltish thirteen-year-old. And yet she grew more beautiful instead of less.

The healthy skin paled to pearl-white: the hair turned black and grew longer. The tartan faded off the cloth around her, and turned a simple green.

"You see deeply, Forest Lord," she said. "I am Brithlain, the daughter of Artholon. No harm will come to him."

Tahion was stern.

"And how long, do you think, must this masquerade go on? And what will happen to *him* when you tire of the play?"

She huddled down, head drooping, shoulders curving around the baby in her arms. The nipple slid out of his mouth again, but he only opened a bright blue eye, sighed faintly, and closed it again in sleep.

"Men do not live that long," she said. "Even my little one here, my beautiful one, will probably not last even a full century!" Her flaming silver eyes filled with tears. "The man would be dead now but for this! It was Grandmother's idea, anyway! She took this shape first! Go blame *her*, if you dare!"

"You would not be the first," he said, "to wonder at what I might dare. I might dare things that would surprise you! But what has been done is done, and I have no heart to blame you further. You meant well, and have done the best you could do. And it is true, the depths of despair in a mortal's heart are beyond any pain an elf can bear. Weep no more! We shall know in time what the fruit of your pity will be."

She smiled shyly up at him. A drop of milk hung at the tip of one nipple: it dripped to the baby's face. He squirmed, but did not wake. Carefully, she set the baby down, and blinking the tears from her long lashes, reached down to lift from beside the bench a covered silver bowl.

Already another white drop was forming. Lifting the cover

from the silver vessel, she squeezed a stream of milk into it with her other hand.

"I think Grandmother made this spell stronger than was needed," she said, calmly and with no shyness, milking herself into the sweetly ringing bowl. "Even by myself, there is too much for my poor little motherless one to drink!"

Arthfayel spoke.

"It is your milk, then, that we have been drinking?"

"Mine and my Grandmother's," she said. "Between us there is enough for all the fort! When our kin first found Anarod wandering in the forest, with poor little Liam starving in his arms, Grandmother went there at once, and made the spell to bring milk to her breasts, and nursed him. Then she said it was time for me to learn to be a mother, that I was a child no longer, and must learn a woman's magic."

Arthfayel knelt beside the baby, looking at him.

"He has his father's hair."

"But his mother's eyes," she answered. "He is such a good and happy baby! The last mortal child we had here—indeed, it was Alphth, when he was a baby—cried always until we took him away. He could not bear the pain of that which is under the ground."

CHAPTER FIFTEEN

The Hidden Chamber

Istvan woke out of a dream-filled sleep, hearing a sound like running water. In his mind, memory fought crystal fragments of dream.

A thousand fantastic images mingled behind his eyes: swaying nightmare swords; armour even his Hastur-blade would not cut; blood and brains oozing from a shattered skull; dragons like distant fireflies; werewolves fighting white, red-eared hounds; a particoloured unicorn; the *Tromdoel* crawling toward the fort, grinding the forest underfoot; Universes black and white, linked like Anthir's legendary Stone; a fire-eyed black dog that changed to a horse; Tarithwen glowing with moonlight; kentawrs singing on the moon of Lirdan; a bird feathered like the rainbow; dwarf healers talking of poison; Layareh's ashen skin; elf-ships sailing on a far, strange sea. . .

He opened his eyes on green sunlight filtered through screening leaves. Shadows moved on leaf and branch as cool winds swung the tree above his bed to and fro.

He was not in his bed in the chambers built into the wall, so maybe that part was true, and the building fallen with the outer wall with Cormac's harp and the letters from Sylvia, when the *Tromdoel* came, and all now buried in the pile of rock.

But where was he then? Was this the wood by the rose garden? He had thought he remembered—but it must have been a dream—going into the great round building to sleep. But he did not remember hearing running water in the wood. Perhaps he was on a part of the hill where he had never been. . .

He stiffened. What he heard was not the sound of water. It was the voices of men . . .

He rolled up on an elbow, listening. But it did not sound like men fighting. He lay back again. He could take his time, and do the sword exercise that he had been forced to neglect— what, two days now? Or was it three?

He had thought himself alone, but suddenly a voice rang out nearby—the voice of Ingulf the Mad.

"Ah! The evil creatures are doing it to us again!" the islander cried. "And I still trapped in this evil world!"

Istvan whirled toward the sound, saw Ingulf sitting up in some bushes nearby, rubbing his forehead with a clenched fist.

"They are murdering me!" he moaned. "Why do they hate me so? Why will the evil creatures never leave me alone?" Istvan felt an aching in his chest. The poor lunatic!

"Leave me be, evil elves!" Ingulf screamed, shaking his fist at the sky, as Istvan started to roll to his feet.

Istvan's right hand and left foot touched soft, fragrant green grass, but his right foot came down on dusty stone. Grass, trees and leaf-strained sunlight alike had vanished, leaving only the shadows of a vast dim hall, ill-lit by arrow-slits.

His startled hand flashed his sword free. All around, men cried out, as the greenery vanished. But among the voices Istvan heard a low laugh, and, whirling to face it, saw Calmar kneeling on the stone floor, a drawn dagger gripped in his fist.

"Up to their old tricks again!" Calmar said, sheathing the dagger and rising as Istvan came up. His laughter echoed noisily from the walls. "Another elvish illusion—to make us comfortable, no doubt, to protect against that which they guard. But—" he dropped his voice so only Istvan could hear, "it did not make our crazy friend more comfortable. He has no wits to lose, after all!"

Istvan frowned and looked away. He sensed annoyance under the sardonic humour; but to mock Ingulf seemed cruel.

Then, at Calmar's feet, he saw deep scratches in the mortar

between two stones, and the fine powder spread into the dust where Calmar had been kneeling, across the curiously laid circle of stones. Calmar's eyes caught his as he looked up, startled.

"Indeed," the red-faced wizard said, "they had me fooled so bad I started to dig for—worms, yes! Worms so I could go fishing in that stream we all heard!" He laughed. Istvan looked down, a furious blush burning in his skin. *A lie,* he thought—but why would the wizard lie?

"What was I drinking last night?" a voice exclaimed behind him. Turning slightly, he recognised Layareh the Proud lurching toward them, fastening his sword belt over his robe with one hand, and the other pressed against his temple. "It's destroyed I am, with the grandmother of all hangovers, and I not even remembering a drink!" Carroll's booming laughter echoed, and the islander winced.

"Indeed, it is upon us all, Layareh!" laughed Carroll. "It is the heady drink of victory over the *Tromdoel,* and even the Hasturs found it too strong!" The echoing laughter grew as others joined, but Istvan remembered; sharp and clear, the dwarf healer's voice in the night. *That's not just shock! It is like poison!*

Yet the dwarves had found no wound, so it could not have been poison. Not unless someone had slipped it into the islander's food . . .

Such a fantastic suspicion was best kept to himself, he thought. It would not take much to rouse the ancient feuds that divided Clan from Clan all across the continent, and there was already too much distrust between the Easterners and the rest . . .

But no—Tahion, at least, must be told. Too much was at stake here. A quick glance showed him that Tahion was nowhere in the hall. Outside, then. With a nod to Calmar, he turned and strode for the distant door.

Behind him, jesting and laughter faded: beyond the door were other voices. As he approached the arch of daylight, he heard a voice that cut easily through the voices of men: a dwarf's voice, ocean-deep, lion-deep, thunder-deep . . .

". . . silver to nickel, aye, and nickel to iron, that's clear enough. Iron to cobalt. But . . . ?"

Now another voice broke in, a high, rich voice, trumpet-clear, that sang with power; an elf's voice.

"The wires must be woven most carefully," the new voice sang, "with each new metal in proper order, linked and melted into the next. For if two metals that do not meld touch, even by the breadth of a bee's wing, the blade is flawed."

"You have right indeed!" the dwarf voice thundered, as Istvan reached the door. "That is why most elf-blades break, I'm thinking! Linking steel with tungsten is nothing new, nor nickel nor cobalt, but all these metals, platinum and all . . ."
Looking out the door, Istvan saw the ragged women of the Ua Cadell staring toward the hedge where their men were gathering. By the locked gate, Istvan recognised Starn and Tuarim Mac Elathan: Tahion would be there as well, no doubt.

"But it is the pattern that matters," the elf said, off to the right, and turning, Istvan saw the brown-bearded Sea-Elf that he had seen before with Ethellin and Dorialith, but whose name he had forgotten, if he had ever heard it, kneeling by an anvil, before an open fire, near the wall. Only his long beard covered his chest.

"It is that I do not understand," said the dwarf, whom Istvan now recognised as Cruadorn. "It is there that magic is in it. You say that it is the order of the weaving metals that shapes the power out of sunlight, and moves the power . . ."

"It moves, and more," the elf said. "It stores the spells in the patterns of atoms, just as your body does, to sense and react to signs of dark—but here now, listen while I enchant the core. All the runes are cut, and the grooves. After, we'll fit the inlays, and wind the first layer of wires, nickel and silver, and fuse them all. Hand me the lodestone there, if you please?"

The Sea-Elf put a cloth in his hand, and used it to lift a slim thread of metal like a yard-long needle. Cruadorn handed him a small lump of rock, and the Sea-Elf began to stroke the bright strip of metal, his seal-brown beard swaying with the motion as he chanted:

> *"I am Patterned Power:*
> *I am Patterned Atoms:*
> *I am Patterned Metal:*
> *I am Patterned Iron!*
> *Crystals of Wisdom:*
> *Spine of the Spell!*

Spread Spirit's will
South to North:
North to South!
Power in the Pattern
Dances in and out!
Crystal to Crystal,
Hear the holding hand!
Listen, Crystal Wisdom,
One with the hand,
One with the Will!
Net of spirit nerves
Knit the spirit's will:
Spine of the Spell:
Crystals of Wisdom,
One with the Will!
Listen, Metal crystals,
Spine of the Spell!
Listen, Crystal Wisdom:
Listen for the Cold!
Listen for the looming
Cold cruel Craving!
Feel Evil nearing,
Feel with the field—
East and West,
North and South:
Power in the Pattern
Dances in and out!
East and West,
North and South:
Dance between Crystals,
Summon Sunfire!
From South to North
Need-Fire flies,
From Crystal to Crystal
South to North!
Crystals quiver:
Tremble in tumult:
Swaying Waves:
Rippling Radiance:
Lines of Lightning:
A growing glow
Rippling in Runes,

Glistening in graven
Paths of Power!
Spirit of the Steel!
Crystals of Wisdom!
Spine of the Spell!
You are Patterned Iron!
You are Patterned Metal!
You are Patterned Atoms!
You are Patterned Power!
You are Patterned Spirit:
Spirit of the Steel!"

As the chant ended, Istvan realized that he was only a few slow steps from the door: the spell had held him. Shaking himself, he quickened his pace and tried to fix his mind on business, searching for Tahion with his eyes, trying to ignore the elf's voice behind him.

"Quick, now, the nickel. Let us link the layers . . ."

But as he walked past the clustered women of the Ua Cadell, cold crawled on his back to see how closely they clutched their children, how tightly they gripped spears and knives while they stared at their men. He knew that look. His hand closed around his sword hilt as he hurried to the hedge.

Dwarf-mail glinted dully under the grey sky. Savage men in ragged plaids knelt, long spears ready, trying to peer between thickly-woven thorny branches. By the steel webwork of the gate, the heroes crowded around Tuarim Mac Elathan: Istvan rushed to join them.

Garahis and Fergus turned at the faint grind of gravel under Istvan's hurrying feet; and another man turned with them, a face that Istvan at first did not know. Then his heart lurched as he saw that it was Anarod—but Anarod changed.

Gone the twisted face and tragic, haunted eyes: a smile transformed lips and the lines of brow and cheek; the eyes glowed with humour.

"Here's the wild hero!" the strange Anarod said. "Is it not the swift foot, and the strong hand on the sword? Do you fear you will miss the fighting?"

"What is happening?" Istvan asked.

"Only a few wolves, so far," said Fergus. "No sign yet, to tell whether they are with Svaran's force, or Vor's."

"So I am taking wagers," said Anarod, "as to whether it

will be Svaran or Vor Half-Troll whose face first pops up out of the ground. What do you say, Seynyorean? I'll stake a golden Skioth on Vor!''

"Um—not just now," muttered Istvan. "Is Tahion here?"

"He is not," said Fergus, but Istvan saw a strangeness flit across his face. "But come, I'll show you where he is." With a sidelong glance at the changed Anarod, Fergus stepped to Istvan's side. Anarod moved as though to follow, and Istvan saw a baffled look of despair in the big Elantirian's eyes.

But just then a voice spoke out from the trees of the hedge, and looking up they saw an elf leaning out of the thorn-thick branches.

"Tuarim! It is my belief that the wolves there are naught but scouts. They are going back into the ground now, and I do not think we will be seeing their masters for a while." Anarod turned back into the crowd, and Fergus grasped Istvan's arm and hastened him back along the path.

"I left Tahion, along with Arthfayel, in a garden around toward the back of Ardcrillon's, talking with—" he threw a quick glance over his shoulder, and his voice sank, "—Anarod's wife!"

"What?" Istvan stared. "I thought she was—"

"Hush!" Fergus hissed. "And so she is, but do not say so in front of—himself! But there she was, nursing the baby, seeming solid enough. Some phantom of the elves, of course! And now, himself, that I had to stop from jumping over the cliff this morning, is as cheerful as a robin with a worm, as you can see! But to forget—that—he must forget what has happened since; much of what has happened in the past several days. And whenever anyone speaks of anything that has happened these past few days—then you can see madness like a ghost in his eyes, and then he is dangerous. I fear death will come of it, for he will kill rather than admit that she is dead—and almost any innocent remark may remind him." He let go of Istvan's arm and waved a hand at the crystal towers rising out of the trees. "So I will not go with you to Tahion, but will watch Anarod and try to keep him from harm."

"Good!" Istvan nodded grimly. "Thank you! But try to get Starn aside and warn him of this. Also . . ." he hesitated, uncertain. Fergus was a man to trust, he thought, but should he trust anyone with this? He looked back at the men gathered at the gate, saw Starn's arms and hands move as he argued.

He wanted to find Tahion, but Starn also should know. But he could not tell him now. And indeed he felt he knew Fergus better than Starn . . .

"Also—if you can, without any other hearing, warn him that—that we may have—a traitor or—at least, a murderer among us. Someone tried to poison Layareh."

"No!" Fergus gasped. *"What*—why? That's madness! Not that I can blame anyone for wanting the man dead, mind! Yon is an easy man to hate. But a fort under siege is a bad place for foolish feuds! But what makes you think—?"

"The dwarf healers said he was poisoned," Istvan answered, "but there was not a scratch on him anywhere. They may have been wrong—I hope they were wrong, and that I am wrong—but if it was poison, it would have had to be in something he ate or drank."

"Indeed, I must be careful that none overhears this!" Fergus shook his head. "There is enough ill-will among us as it is! But this could set us all to killing each other. But what of Layareh? Will he not be telling everyone, or at least his friends?"

"Layareh does not know," said Istvan. "He was dying when the dwarf healers found him. He did not wake then, and remembers nothing this morning."

"It is good that he does not." Fergus bared his teeth. "But what of Tuarim? Should I not tell *him,* as well as Starn?"

"Let Tahion decide how much to tell Tuarim," Istvan said. "He understands elves. I do not."

"You're right there!" Fergus laughed. "Nor do I! Go and tell Tahion! I myself will watch over Anarod!"

He turned back toward the hedge: Istvan walked on toward the door. Cruadorn and the elf were braiding strips of wire beside the wall. Suddenly, the dwarf sprang to his feet.

"Fool!" he exclaimed. "For that I need the other forge—Deepheart forge, outside the zone! Am I to gather an army to retake that one corridor? It is only the forges in the main part of the city remain to us, and none of them can build up that kind of heat!"

The elf's reply was softer-voiced, and Istvan had other things on his mind. He would go quickly through the hall and out the door on the far side—unless, by chance, Tahion had returned while he was out—and go to Ardcrillon's triple tower.

In the doorway he came close to colliding with Ingulf. Istvan stepped courteously aside with an easy swordsman's sidestep and waited for the islander to pass, but Ingulf turned on him angrily.

"Is it a ghost I am," Ingulf raged, "that no one speaks to me, or sees me?"

"I—I am sorry," Istvan stammered, "I did not mean—"

"It's destroyed I am, surely!" Ingulf's voice was shrill with passion. "The evil people have murdered me again! Mortals do not matter to them! They do not care!"

"Calm yourself!" Istvan's voice was sharp, trying to break through the other's madness, as he might have tried to reach a soldier hysterical on the battlefield. "The illusion is gone, and—"

"All the world is an illusion!" Ingulf shrieked. "It is all an evil cheat and a deception, and will remain so until the daughter of Falmoran has mercy upon me!"

Falmoran? Istvan felt a sudden prickle of unease. Where had he heard that name?

But as his mind groped for the memory, everything changed.

Through the door he saw a lace of ghostly green light.

Green veins glowing in stone turned to green vines, growing, inset into ornate carving, writhing like emerald flame, eerily alive, veiling the wall with leaves. Startled men shouted as trees rose up from the stone floor.

Between the sudden trees flashed a rainbow-winged bird, and its voice was a sweet fluting that sang human words . . .

"*Carroll Mac Lir!*" it cried. "*Istvan Di Vega! Ingulf Mac Fingold! Fithil Mac Moran! Hurry, mortal heroes! Come to the crystal tower! Ardcrillon now calls you! The time of need has come!*"

The bird whirled and swooped by the door and flew back the way it came, false sunlight flashing on the colours of its wings.

"You see?" whispered Ingulf. "They are doing it again!" But even as he spoke he was turning, and *Frostfire* flashed glittering from its scabbard. Istvan's hand had flown to hilt, too, and both of them were running then, following the rainbow-feathered singer.

"*Layareh Mac Lohar!*" that bright bird sang, spiraling and

swooping between trees. *"Larthon Mac Keharn! Cormac Mac Angdir! Dair Mac Eykin! Need is on us now: heroes, heed our call!"*

Heroes rushed from the phantom forest to join Istvan and Ingulf, racing after the bird. They followed it out of illusion and into the wood outside before they were aware, into a pattern of spells that swept them like a river toward the gleaming towers.

They burst from the wood, and ran between singing roses, while tiny, winged flower-spirits watched and whispered.

"Why are they so evil?" Ingulf groaned. "Oh, let me be! My grief! Why? Why will they drive us thus?" The islander's breath was ripping in and out of his lungs like a saw. *Panic breathing,* Istvan thought, carefully controlling his own lungs, drawing air in long, power-filled breaths that held his mind calm as a windless lake, despite the faster pattern of his running feet, then letting it out as slowly.

He forced words into the long, slow, controlled exhalations.

"Breathe slowly!" he gasped out, and filled his lungs again. "Ingulf!" Pent breath boomed in his voice. "Swordsman of the Isles!" He breathed in, legs pounding. "Would you shame your master?" Ingulf turned hurt, startled eyes on him.

"Where is your training?" The towers loomed near. "Master your breath!" Istvan saw Tahion and Arthfayel running by the wall. "Master your mind!" Tahion and Arthfayel turned, and sprinted up the steps just ahead. "Breathe peace!" Istvan's running feet sprang up over five steps. "Not panic!"

Ahead, the door to the shimmering magical tower gaped wide, opening on supernal light, where Ardcrillon stood at the tower's heart, robed in majesty, glowing with wisdom. . .

"Goblins tunnel into the secret chamber," the wild, sweet voice sang. A finger pointed. "Down this stair, heroes! You are our only hope! Hurry!"

They ran. Where his finger pointed, a heavy steel door hung open on darkness that led downward.

Istvan almost ran into Tahion and Arthfayel as both stopped short at the door. Then magic faded around him: the force that had driven him was gone, as though a cold wind from that door had stripped away all illusion.

Slipping past Tahion, Istvan saw by his sword's light steps that led down through the crystal floor. He took the lead, running at an easier pace, feeling a weary ache in his legs, and his heart pounding from the wild race . . .

But no—it was not the strain from the speed the elves had forced that made his heart pound so. His veins and his nerves beat in time with some hidden throbbing ahead, as every step took him closer to the aching mystery that pulsed in the secret heart of Rath Tintallain.

At first he thought it was his eyes. The crystal walls seemed to flicker in the light of his sword, fading and flaring with his pulse.

The steps ended in a long tunnel that sloped down.

As he dashed down the tunnel, the throbbing increased. It was not his eyes. The need-fire on his Hastur-blade pulsed: its glow flared and dimmed, keeping time with that rhythm that throbbed along his nerves.

Behind him he could hear the sound of heroes' feet following. Now faint echoes rang ahead, of shouting and of screams. Strange light began to flare and fade, faint as yet, far ahead down the crystal corridor. Istvan increased his pace.

Dull streaks broke the crystal sheen of the walls. Further on, bands of crystal dwindled into slender veins like roots, anchoring the tower firm as a tree.

They could see, brighter now, the glaring light that flared and dimmed ahead. They hurried down the corridor, hearing more sounds of war: deep dwarf-voices shouting ancient war-cries; goblin squeals; metal weapons hammering, deafening, echoing!

Glancing over his shoulder, Istvan wondered to see need-fire on the Sword of Kings changing hue, gold to blue-white, then fading suddenly to a dim red.

Light flickered at the tunnel's end, glaring off brownish stone: the tunnel ended in a wall, lit from below. Louder now the sounds of war from the floor swelled. Before them, they saw a stairway leading down into the light.

Metal echoed clamouring, mingled with battle-cries, and goblin squealing answering the shouting of dwarves.

From the gap beyond the stair, glaring light leaped and flared. Deafening, the echoing battered their ears. Gazing from the stairway's lip hurt their eyes.

Battle-wise, Istvan slid his Hastur-blade back into its sheath, then went leaping down the stair, into the glaring light, both hands free for balancing on the steep steps.

At the bottom of the stair, shadows pulsed through the glare—a band of throbbing, greasy black crossing the room.

Through the darkness and the light raged the fight. Istvan's eyes, dazzled by mad shadows, saw only dim forms.

Down from the ceiling ran the stair. Istvan saw, suddenly, to his left a towering pillar of flame: blazing white like curdled light, almost a solid thing, stretching up, pulsing from floor to roof.

He neared the bottom of the stair. Through the glare, shapes appeared: twisted goblins scurrying, rust-red blades in their hands, circling round a smaller force armoured in heavy mail, where several dwarf warriors fought in a ring.

From its heart, towering, the fiery, glowing pillar rose, a blaze of flaming diamond, stabbing the roof. Dwarvish axes rose and fell, dripping blood.

Goblins yelled. Iron weapons hammering echoed like deafening bells from off the solid bedrock of the walls.

At the bottom of the stair, goblins were gathering. Istvan's hand was on his hilt, ready to draw. He was thankful that his boots were strengthened with metal strips. But he knew that all the Y'gorans' legs were bare.

Goblin eyes were staring up out of the shadows at Istvan and the other men running behind. Hordes of them were scuttling rapidly in and out as Istvan saw the shadow's edge shift.

Suddenly he realised that the flaring of the light alternated with the pulsing of dark, making up the maddening rhythm that gnawed at his agonised nerves and made his head ache. Darkness throbbed, a flare of light following; flare of black—flare of white, endlessly on. And the beam of darkness ran through the dwarves' armoured ring.

Goblins clustered eagerly at the foot of the steps, rusty blades waving, awaiting the rosy blood, as Istvan neared the bottom-most course.

Suddenly he hurled himself from the steps, leaping high, down into the middle of the lashing thicket of swords. Flaring, his Hastur-blade flew from its sheath as he landed, crouching low, to face foes tiny as evil little children armed with poisonous knives.

Whirling in a deadly slash, scything necks, his sword cleared space enough for him to stand. Goblin squealing shrilled. Rusty blades hacked at his boots. He cursed the elves and their spells, wishing they had left him time to get his shield.

Tahion leaped down the stair, the Sword of Kings changing hue with every alternating flare of dark beams and light. After him came Ingulf, *Frostfire* glittering. Istvan, whirling swiftly, sprang to their side, terribly aware of the vulnerability of their bare legs.

Fighting together then, the three, battling furiously, drove their rat-like enemies back from the stair. Fithil of the Curranach, Karik Mac Ulatoc and Arthfayel came hurrying down to their aid.

Istvan by now had fallen into the familiar rhythms of the goblin killing training dance of the Three Swords School; stooping low, point near the ground, whirling around his legs, guarding in a fiery blur.

He risked glancing over enemy heads toward the embattled dwarves and the light's uncanny source at the centre of their ring. Above the dwarves, a glaring-bright beam of white flared from wall to wall.

A goblin blade lashed at his knee. He jerked it back, thrusting down, and was for a moment too busy for a second look.

Other heroes rushing down the stair were changing the odds. Istvan began to cut his way toward the dwarves. Now the glaring line of light was right across his sight. From it, the flaring pillar rose at right angles.

Suddenly, he realised that the black beams crossed the white.

This was no time to dwell on mystery: goblins swarmed around.

Steel rang. Foes died. Fithil staggered suddenly, blood running from his thigh.

Deep shouts roared out. A new force of dwarves swarmed into the fight. Like trapped rats, foes ran. Some men leaped to follow. But Istvan let his sword's point drift to the ground, and stood staring.

The black beam crossed the white beams atop a pedestal near the middle of the room. The dwarves had fought with their backs to it, defending: many now lay bleeding around it, some groaning, others still and dead.

Istvan walked toward the pedestal. Something solid lay

where the beams met, something like a tiny scrap of metal he could have held in his hand . . .

Light flared from three faces of a cube. Two other faces projected beams of greasy black that throbbed and cast a shadow about them, as the other beams lit the room.

His sword flared violently, throbbing with the rhythmic pulse, the alternate flare of light and dark.

"Now what have we here?" It was Anarod's voice.

"The Stone of Anthir, perhaps?" said Tahion.

"What else could it be?" Arthfayel said, wearily.

CHAPTER SIXTEEN

The Secret Trust

Istvan wondered why it should surprise him so to find yet another legend true.

Shrieking goblins still ran around the room, hotly pursued by men and dwarves, but Istvan stood staring at the queer throbbing light of the stone. Tahion was trying to staunch the blood that stained the plaid skirt of Fithil's robe: Arthfayèl knelt beside a groaning dwarf.

Sheathing his sword, Istvan reached into his memory, trying to recall the story that every wizard he had ever known—and he had known many—had scoffed at as a moral fable.

Some goblins climbed the walls like flies. Others ran to one of the corners, jumping into the hole out of which they had come.

Istvan could find in memory only bare bones of the story of Anthir Hastur—the only one of the Hastur-kin ever to try to use the Dark Ones' own magic against them—and of the talisman he made, that held the essence of both black and white magic.

But he recalled that there were many different endings to the story. Most versions had Anthir corrupted by his Stone, and turned to the service of the Dark Lords—as so many mortal wizards had been, in truth. Some versions wove Anthir's story into the grand fabric of the Fall of Nardis, telling of Anthir stories more often told of Nargil, or Thale the False-Hastur. In these stories, Anthir's kin were forced to hunt him down and destroy him. But there were other stories that the Stone itself had destroyed its maker.

"Do they not say," asked Anarod, sheathing his Hastur-blade, "that if a man held this thing, that he could command both the Dark Lords and the Hasturs themselves?"

" 'Tis what they say," said Arthfayel, looking up from the wounded dwarf. "But whether they say truly—that is another question."

"Little, is is not?" Anarod took a step forward, and reached out his hand toward the Stone.

"*Stop!*" Tahion and Arthfayel shouted together. "Do not touch it!"

But already Anarod's fingers had closed around the shining little thing.

Suddenly, the light in which they had stood was swept away, as a beam of throbbing black rolled across them, with shadow forming around it. A sickening cold knotted Istvan's stomach. The wounded dwarf groaned. The room itself seemed to spin.

On the walls above, goblins who had huddled in the comfort of the dark shrieked as light glared on them. Many dropped from the walls, others scrambled higher.

Anarod's laughter echoed above the screams and shouting.

"All this fuss over such a little thing!" his voice boomed. He tossed it lightly in his palm.

The flaming pillar toppled from the ceiling, and burned like desire through their flesh. A dark roof formed above their heads as shadow sprang in a spreading cone from Anarod's hand, hiding his face. From the back of his hand, white light flared upon the floor. Again he tossed it, laughing, and white flame and black spun above his palm.

Istvan lunged.

His speed-blurred swordsman's hand closed above Anarod's; he felt his fingers press cool metal against his palm . . .

Sudden heat and cold numbed his arm, burning through a ghostly hand, shaped of translucent cloud, pulsing with white and black light . . .

"*Anarod!*" The breath sucked into his lungs as he lunged became his best parade-ground roar. "That is enough now!"

The stone burned through his hand's translucent flesh, seeming to hang in the air. Three beams of light pulsed from his hand, one a slanted pillar that hit the wall just below the ceiling: goblins scrambled away. Istvan stood chest-deep in darkness, near-blinded by the light. A white beam burned along his right forearm, but his left shoulder was chilled by the shadow around a throbbing black beam.

Out of that bar of darkness, a second ghostly hand closed over his own.

"And who do you be thinking you are, man?" Anarod's voice was coolly dangerous; there was no laughter in it now.

A thin ribbon of flame appeared in the darkness: Anarod's Hastur-blade was sliding from its sheath.

"I am a DiVega of Carcosa—"

A sudden hoarse roar of pain drowned Istvan's voice, and the other ghostly hand that gripped his own burned on his skin as though made of flame.

It fell away, and at the same moment the glowing ribbon of steel shortened and vanished. Anarod staggered out of the shadow, cradling his sword-hand against his chest.

"Burned me!" he gasped, his voice thick with pain.

"—and the Hasturs of Carcosa are my kin," Istvan went on, coldly. "They have set us to guard this thing, not to play with it!"

The room still reeled about him: he hoped it was only an illusion that the floor underfoot was throbbing with the pulse of light from the Stone—and his aching head.

Slowly turning, he stretched his arm out to return the Stone to the pedestal where it had rested, on a smooth-topped stone column that jutted out of the rock of the floor, hewn jointlessly of the same stone when the chamber was quarried.

Behind him, from the corner where fleeing goblins had run like an ebbing tide back to the hole they had come from, a sudden chorus of frenzied squealing swelled. Then the echoes thundered with deep dwarf-voices, mingled with the shriller shouts of men.

Istvan's ghostly hand passed over the lip of the pedestal, and the floor reappeared under his feet as the stone column drank the black beam.

Stabbing through the back of his hand, the pillar of fire wavered across the roof as his translucent, near-invisible numbed fist dragged the cross of light and dark toward the pillar's centre.

His still-shadowed fingers touched smooth, cool rock. Slowly, he worked them carefully out from under the little block, settling it back to rest. The constant flare and fade of light and dark still hurt his eyes and dizzied him, but at least the areas of light and shadow were stable again.

Flesh reappeared as he drew his hand back. He half expected to find his palm seared black, but as far as he could tell in the weird light, the skin was unhurt.

Anarod seemed less lucky; moaning, he cradled his sword-hand against his chest, his face fallen back into its old tragic lines.

Half-rising from the dwarf he was tending, Arthfayel, anguish in his eyes, stared anxiously at his foster-brother. Then the dwarf gasped, and Arthfayel sank down beside his more gravely injured charge, mouth set firmly.

Calmar walked out of a black beam's shadow, and strode to Anarod's side.

"Give me your hand, Idiot Boy!" he snapped. "We'll soon have you healthy and happy as a blackbird full of blackberries!"

But now the shouting and screaming behind had reached such a pitch that Istvan turned—to see men and dwarves scattered and driven back as an irresistable tide of goblins flooded back out of the hole at the edge of the room.

Goblins ran frantically hither and thither. Some swarmed up the walls. Others raced to the heavy stone doors through which the dwarves had come. Many scuttled up the stair toward the tunnel that led to Ardcrillon's tower. Their foes were driven to fighting back-to-back in tiny clumps.

"But why?" Anarod was saying. "What would make Narthron—what could make my sword burn me like that?"

"Oh, it's common enough," said Calmar's voice. "It happens all the time to—" he paused a moment, as though choosing his words carefully, "—to those wizards foolish enough to—to experiment with the powers of the Dark Things. If your hand is on a talisman of evil, and then you touch so strong a talisman of light as a Hastur-blade, its need-fire will react against the dark force in your body. You were standing in—"

But Istvan had no time to hear more, for the first wave of

goblins had reached them. His Hastur-blade flew from its sheath and lashed across a row of throats, turned in the air and flew back as more goblins trampled over the bodies of those he had killed.

A long lunge took him in front of Arthfayel and the dwarf he tended. He saw a goblin leap onto Tahion's back as he struggled to draw the Sword of Kings, saw Fithil roll up on one arm, the other lashing out with his bright blade, but swarming goblins blotted both from sight.

Then Layareh came leaping through the press, whirled, and slid to one knee, his sword looping and skimming like a bird.

"Fithil!" he shouted above the squealing echoes. "Is it alive you are, under there?" A pile of dead goblins stirred, and a figure drenched in goblin blood sat up, spat, and spoke in Fithil's voice.

"Phui! Life is in me yet, if I do not drown! Where is Tahion?"

"Here!" The Sword of Kings shimmered and shifted colour above the swarming goblins. "Watch your backswing, Layareh; you nearly bobbed my nose for me!"

Layareh's blade had swirled and flickered around him all the time he had spoken. Now Fithil pushed himself to an awkward sitting position, and the two blades of the master swordsmen wove over and around each other in a complex, deadly dance, and made a wall of goblin corpses before them.

Karik Mac Ulatoc sprang to Istvan's side. He had snatched up the double-bitted axe of one of the fallen dwarves; its edge, black with goblin blood, hummed in the air.

Behind Istvan, Arthfayel crouched above the dwarf, short blade drawn and glowing in his hand. Beyond the reach of Istvan's sword, goblins streamed past. Thrice Istvan had to whirl his blade behind him, while Arthfayel worked to staunch the flow of blood.

A mound of bodies three yards wide was piled at his feet: a mound that rose with each slash of his sword. Already the goblins climbing on it stood nearly his own height, so he was no longer slashing at waist level.

A similar wall of the dead had grown before Layareh and Fithil, forcing Layareh to rise to his feet to fight over it, while Fithil watched with a wry grin. He attempted to rise and fell back.

"It's sorry I am to leave all this work for you now," said

Fithil, "but it is on me to watch and bear witness to your deeds, it seems."

"Do they not teach you how to guard your thigh in your school?" asked Layareh, with a faint hint of malice in his tone.

"They do indeed, but—ha!" A goblin darting around the end of the mound of dead met Fithil's sword-edge across its throat. "But not how to have one sword in three places at once. But I will be guarding *your* thighs now, so do you pay attention to the top, there, and just leave the bottom to me."

Ingulf came wading through the goblin ranks, *Frostfire* a milky shimmer of moonstone light around his hips, the sleeves and hem of his tartan robe stained by goblin blood. Dirty-furred hordes seethed round him, rushing in behind, rusty blades reaching for bare legs; but he moved in a whirling dance, turning and turning between falling bodies.

Anarod stood with the beam of light blazing through his heart, his Hastur-blade sparking and flaring in his hand with each bright pulse, beside the piled corpses over which Layareh fought. Ingulf, turning and twisting, cut his way to them and stepped into place between Anarod and the end of the swing of Karik's axe.

Goblins howled against a line of whirring blades.

Istvan felt his arm tire. Now that the dead were piled high enough that they could not get at his legs, it was more butchery than fighting: rarely did he need to do more than slash out at the right height to take the heads off a whole row. They seemed, indeed, to be fleeing something behind, attacking only what stood in their way. They were so frightened, Istvan realised, that they were not even stopping to eat their dead and wounded.

And still they poured out of the hole in the floor. Yet fewer sprang onto the piled bodies to die by Istvan's sword: they began to turn aside from the wall of the dead into the shadow of the black beams on either side.

The flood of goblins thinned. Goblins with blood-matted fur turned and hacked with crude blades at something in the hole beneath them.

A massively muscled arm thrust up out of the well, holding a short, spike-backed hammer that met a spindly goblin arm in mid-swing.

The goblin dropped its sword and reeled back, arm bending at a new joint. Other goblins scattered and fled.

Prince Tyrin's face lifted over the lip of the shaft; then a surge of long, powerful arms swung the dwarf up onto the floor. His axe was slung at his back; he lost no time in pulling it free and sliding the hammer back into his belt.

Doomed goblins fled wailing toward the dark. Many surged up the stairway to the tunnel that led into Ardcrillon's tower. More swarmed up the walls. But only a few threw themselves against the swords of Istvan and his companions.

More dwarves clambered out of the hole behind Prince Tyrin. Istvan recognised Thubar, Ogar, and Cruadorn. At a word from Prince Tyrin, they formed up into a deadly line and attacked, axes and swords scything goblins down. Scattered groups rallied: the grim line extended from wall to wall, with the floor behind covered with bleeding goblin bodies.

Starn MacMalkom came crashing through a packed mass of goblins, with Flann and Fergus on either side. Carroll Mac Lir and Larthon Trollslayer fought their way to the great staircase and took places at its foot, cutting off that line of retreat. Dwarves rushed from Prince Tyrin's line, with shields to guard the long, bare legs of the men.

Suddenly, Ingulf shouted, pointing. Istvan could not make out the words. His eyes followed arm and finger, but the bright light flashing above his shoulder made him half-blind. Ingulf and Anarod both vaulted the rampart of bodies and ran toward the stair, goblins scattering from their path in terror.

"What is it?" Istvan called, but they were already beyond his voice. Karik pointed up toward the stairway rearing out of the room's heart.

"Someone fighting. Up there." Again Istvan looked, but the glare still blinded him. "Alphth, I think, or perhaps Finloq." Istvan squinted past the glare, made out at last a flurry of dark bodies, a flash of light from some bright sword.

At the stair's foot, Ingulf and Anarod were shouting and pointing. Carroll and Larthon turned and bounded up the stair: the dwarves' shield-wall opened to let Ingulf and Anarod follow, then closed again.

Istvan had to turn: a handful of goblins came fleeing the grim line of dwarf-axes. Spinning, he whipped his blade across the throats of half a dozen who sprang onto the pile of bodies. One threw itself under the glittering arc, and slashed at Istvan's arm. He leaned back, his stroke missing the last in the line, and the crude iron blade rang against his own. Istvan's wrist twitched, flipping his point into the throat he had missed. Another blade hacked from the side. He dodged away from its edge, his fingers spinning his sword to slash the skinny arm. A lightning lunge ended the goblin's pain in a spray of blood. Karik's axe was busy: the mound of dead grew.

Perhaps a dozen more goblins leaped up to meet Istvan's sword or Karik's axe, and Tahion and Layareh killed as many. Several sprang through the gap where Ingulf and Anarod had stood, and dodged past the pillar where the Anthir Stone throbbed, into the shelter of the black beams, making no attempt either to seize the Stone or to molest the wounded.

Then the dwarf-line reached them, swords and axes dripping. Istvan's arm was aching as he leaned upon his sword, and all his memories of comrades savaged by goblin teeth could not keep him from pity for the vermin. He could hear their shrill squeals diminish as they ran in the spreading shadow, no doubt making for the walls.

From the stairs came still fierce squealing and battle shouts. Ingulf, Carroll, Anarod and Larthon toiled like reapers in a field, their blades clearing the steps above them. Goblin bodies rained down.

Dwarves came climbing over the rampart of corpses, to form ranks again on his side.

"Karik!" a familiar voice boomed, waterfall deep. "Still living and sound? Good! By dawn we'll have done forging your sword, and a fine sword it will be! Already Falmoran has finished braiding the core of the blade, and now that we have taken back the lower levels—"

"*Falmoran!*" Istvan broke in with a start, his voice cutting shrill through the dwarf's deep roar. "Cruadorn, who *is* Falmoran? What does he here?"

Clear in his mind, he could hear Ingulf's voice: *It is all an evil cheat and a deception, and will remain so until the daughter of Falmoran has mercy upon me!*

"Why?" Cruadorn stared up at him, scowling. "Falmoran is the Sea-Elf who labours with me to forge the sword—or so he was named to me. They say he is a great sea captain, from the Living Land, and he told me himself that he is a friend to Govanon, and has worked in his forge—where do you go?"

"To speak to Tahion," Istvan said, over his shoulder. "Your pardon! Tahion must hear this, as quickly as may be!" He strode rapidly to where Tahion stood by Layareh's mound, leaning wearily on the Sword of Kings.

The line of dwarves had formed again, and was marching past the stone. Already the ends of the line were hidden by the spreading cones of shadow that grew around the black beams.

Eerie wails came out of the dark. Istvan started as hammerings metal clanged. He whirled, sword ready, but could only make out dim shapes swaying.

Goblins had gathered in ambush where the black beam ran under the stair. Now they sprang in force against the dwarves, trying to break through.

For an instant Istvan stood poised, drawn sword flaring in his hand, watching short figures sway in the dark. He glimpsed lashing dim blades, and great eyes that glowed like moons.

The dwarf ranks reeled. Istvan thought they would break. Starn and Flann rushed down the surging row of mail-clad backs. Bright blades flashed, setting dwarf-mail aglitter and showing dirty brown and grey fur beyond.

Fergus and Garahis ran to join them, and the dwarves became a rampart over which they fought, with their swords swooping down like the wings of attacking birds.

The dwarf ranks held. Istvan sheathed his sword.

"Tahion!" he called, and strode toward where the Forest Lord stood with Layareh, swords raised, above Fithil. "I must speak with you. Alone." He saw Layareh frown. "This is important. It must be kept secret."

"No doubt." Tahion shook his head, and sighed. He looked sick, Istvan thought. "I will come. As soon as I find someone to take my place guarding Fithil . . ."

"I am here!" Layareh interrupted. "I need no help. Fithil will be safe enough!"

"Indeed," said Fithil. "It was not my sword-arm that was wounded! I need run no footraces today."

"Let us go, then," Tahion said wearily. "But talk softly." He sheathed his sword, swearing under his breath. Istvan studied him as they strode around the mounds of the dead.

The smell of the dead goblins was enough to make anyone sick, Istvan thought. Now that there was no fighting to distract him, his flesh crawled.

But more than that was wrong with Tahion. From the first steep rush down the steps, the Forest Lord's fighting had lost its fire. Indeed, all the Eltharian Adepts—at least Cormac, Dair, Arthfayel and Tahion himself; he had seen neither Finloq nor Calmar fight—had gripped their swords awkwardly, fighting on a level of bare competence.

It must be the Stone. It made *his* head ache: it must be far worse for a trained and sensitive mind.

"I was looking for you," Istvan said when he was sure they were out of earshot, "when the elves—summoned us. There was only one thing I needed to tell you then, but that was bad enough: someone poisoned Layareh."

"I'd have thought him poisonous enough already," laughed Tahion, then sobered and stared. "But—you are serious? He looks well enough now!"

"We can thank the dwarf healers for that," said Istvan, and quickly repeated what he could remember the healers saying.

"Then Layareh himself does not know," mused Tahion. "Who does, beside us?"

"The healers, of course. And I told Fergus, and asked him to tell Starn. I do not know if he had time. No one else—except, of course, the one with the poison."

"This is madness." Tahion shook his head. "But then, this is Y'gora, and where the old Clan feuds are concerned, Y'gorans are all mad."

"Yes," said Istvan, quickly, "but that brings up the other matter I had to tell you about. Ingulf. The girl that drove him crazy . . ." He paused. "You know more of elves than I. Am I correct in believing that the elves have no common names, as we know them—that each name is unique?"

"Nearly so," said Tahion. "Immortals expect to have their name a long time."

"The girl who drove Ingulf mad," said Istvan, "was the daughter of Falmoran; and Falmoran is the name of the elf—the Sea-Elf—who helps Cruadorn to forge Karik's sword."

"So! Is *that* what he is doing here, then?" Tahion straightened, his eyes thoughtful. "Indeed, that answers questions in my mind about some curious things I have heard. But now I must talk to Ingulf and get the true story from him. I must talk with those healers, too! I do not suppose you have their names?'' Istvan struggled to remember, but at last had to shake his head.

There came shouting, and the sound of feet. Goblins had crept like flies across the ceiling, down the walls far enough that they could drop to the floor behind the line of dwarves. A few threw themselves on the backs of their enemies. Most scattered across the floor, scuttling for their hole.

''If I do not get out of here soon,'' said Tahion, an odd, strained shrillness in his voice, ''I will be as crazy as Ingulf!'' He looked up at the stairs, at the battle there. Istvan looked, too. It was hard to see, with the blazing pillar so close to the stair, but, by squinting, Istvan was able to make out the tartan of Ingulf's robe and *Frostfire's* moonlight shimmer. He could not tell Anarod from Carroll at this distance, but beside them fought another, slighter figure.

A tide of goblins fled up the stairs: other goblins rushed across the ceiling toward the opening that led to the long tunnel under Ardcrillon's tower.

Cruadorn waited for them beside the rampart of piled goblin dead.

''Ah, Prince Tahion,'' said the dwarf, a faint, malicious grin shaping his beard, ''the name of the healer ye'll be wanting to talk to is Kilith.'' The grin changed to loud laughter as their faces changed.

''You mortal men!'' the dwarf chuckled, after a long and thunderous laugh. ''Just because you are half-deaf yourselves, you assume other folk have no better ears than your own! No matter. But it was Kilith who led our healers that night, and if he did not tend—him you spoke of—himself, he will be knowing who did. But as for Falmoran, I know no more than—ah! Master swordsman!'' He turned, and bowed as Layareh came up walking quietly between the bodies. ''What is it that you wish?''

Layareh stared down at him, haughtily.

''Tell me, smith,'' said the islander, pointing into the glare, ''is this thing, as they say, truly the Stone of Anthir?''

''Indeed, it is,'' said the dwarf.

''Then at last I know what my king died for,'' Layareh said bitterly. ''But why here? Why is it not guarded at Elthar, or Carcosa, or some other great fortress, where the full power of the Hasturs and the resources of a kingdom could be brought to its defence?''

"It was made here," Cruadorn said. "The Hasturs have no power to move it—nor would it be safer in the Hasturs' citadels. Have you not seen how it weakens them?"

"But *why* was it forged here?" Layareh persisted.

"Why, indeed, was it made at all?" Tahion added.

"Anthir Hastur hoped," said Cruadorn, "that his Stone would enable his kin to bridge that gap between Universes in which the Dark Things placed the lost city of Astormin, where the Ring of Hastur is hid. Ours was the nearest dwarf city, and from here he thought he could walk to the pit, the poor fool!" He shook his head.

"What happened to him?" asked Istvan.

"My great-grandfather found him lying unconscious by the forge, and this thing beside him, after a night and a day in which the solid bedrock had shuddered and groaned. When he came to himself again, all his powers were gone, and he was no more than a mortal man, and in time he died as a mortal man does, of old age.

"He had not reckoned on the intensity of the conflict between the powers he had united. No Hastur could touch the Stone, nor could it be unmade without releasing forces that would shatter the Universe, and spread the four walls of this room across the furthest stars.

"And so the Hasturs perforce placed it in our care, and we have guarded it here, as you see. Although, indeed, at first there was no one to guard it against. Three thousand years ago, the savage tribes of the Sarlow and their allies were still wandering the Norian Wastes: the Gates to the Dark World were well guarded; the Hasturs kept secret the Stone's existence, and, although rumour got out somehow, the tales never mentioned us.

"Centuries passed, and we grew careless. We built this chamber as our treasury, and the fortress above. In the centre of our treasure we set the Stone, so that the flame rising from it lit not only this treasure-room, but rose through the stair-well to light the fort—its dome we polished to reflect the flame. So bright was its light, that the fort became the favourite place of working for artists, especially for sculpture and the cutting of gems.

"Then Ardcrillon Crystalweaver came to us out of the forest, drawn by the fame of one of the great smiths of that day, Ontar Gem-Maker, who made rubies and emeralds in his furnaces.

"He studied Ontar's gem-making long and long, and at last he laughed, and said he would never be able to make such fine stone. 'And yet,' he said, 'I am not without skills of my own.'

"And to show us, he dissolved various metals and pebbles of the hillside with acids, and then poured them out as long crystal spars, and laid the first foundations of his tower.

"Then the dragons came: Komanthodel and his mate.

"Ardcrillon's kinsmen came to our aid—Artholon his brother, and Arduiad, son of Artholon, and Tuarim the Son of Elathan. And Ardcrillon and Artholon wove spells to cloud the dragons' minds, enabling Tuarim, and Lorik, who was our king then, to slay Komanthodel's mate, and to wound Komanthodel himself so sorely that he flew back to his hoard.

"But now the Hasturs were afraid, for the dragons are a people with strange powers of their own, and they feared what Komanthodel might have done with the power of the Stone. And Kandol Hastur-Lord got Lorik to agree that the elves should aid us in our defence, and that Ardcrillon, son of Ioldan, should be co-ruler with Lorik, as the Mortal and Immortal Kings rule jointly in Galenor.

"Then, slowly, over many years, the Sons of Ioldan wove the crystal wall of their towers, shaping the crystals with music and spells. At each corner they set a rod of adamant that Ontar wrought and through all the walls they wove rods of ruby.

"And Ardcrillon bade us wall up the stairwell that rose into the fortress, and dig instead a tunnel that ran from his tower's foundations. And indeed, as the years passed, we became loath to dwell in the fortress above the ground, for whenever the elves walked there, they sheathed themselves in illusion to shield them from the pain the Stone causes them—and it is unnerving when the jewels you are working on turn to butterflies and fly away, or when a statue you are carving rolls its eyes to look at you, and begs you not to strike.

"Yet neither Ardcrillon nor any of his kin can enter the chamber of the Stone—not even Tuarim, despite his mortal blood.

"The Norian savages founded the kingdom of Sarlow and their sorcerers sensed the power hidden here. Spies came, then goblins and demons, led by a sorcerer. But demons can no more approach the Stone than can the Hasturs, and when this was realised, Ontar Gem-Smith, who had been studying the magic that is practised among your kind, took the Stone, and went to face the sorcerer, and spoke to the demons through the Stone. At his bidding they turned on their master and devoured him. But Ontar went mad, and died raving.

"But from that day," Cruadorn went on, "the forces of evil have gathered about us. Always there are more goblins in the woods, and Sarlow's southern border marches toward us. Thrice we have beaten off attacks by their soldiers within the last fifty years. The Hasturs . . ."

The dwarf broke off, as Tahion swayed and almost fell. Istvan threw an arm around his friend, staggering as the heavier man lurched against him.

"Sorry . . ." the Forest Lord mumbled, fingertips squeezing the bridge of his nose. "So sorry. The pain . . . worse all the time. I thought I could—but it keeps getting worse . . ."

"It is the Stone," said Istvan. "If Arthfayel and Calmar suffer as badly, we'd best get them out of here." He looked up the long flight of stairs that led to the ceiling, and groaned inwardly at the thought of lugging Tahion's weight up all those steps.

"There is another way," said the dwarf, almost as though he could read Istvan's thoughts. "The door yonder, where the guards came in. Not shorter, perhaps, but more easy."

"Layareh," Istvan turned to the islander, "if you will, see to the others. I fear that Arthfayel and Calmar may need help, too, and Fithil, of course. Get Karik to help you. There is no more need for us here."

"Indeed!" said Layareh. "It is time that we left!" He dashed off, while Istvan wondered to find the islander agreeing with him for once.

Layareh returned a short time later, carrying Fithil in his arms like a child, and behind, Arthfayel came leaning on Calmar and Karik, moving slowly and stiffly, like an old, blind man.

"Follow me," said Cruadorn, and gestured toward the door through which the reinforcements had come.

"Cormac?" Istvan asked. "Finloq? Dair? They all studied at Elthar, I'm told."

"I saw Dair fighting beside Sir Garahis in the line," said

Karik, "and Cormac too, earlier. But I've not seen Finloq at all."

"Let us go then," said Istvan, turning to the dwarf.

"But wait!" Calmar exclaimed. "What of the Stone? Should we not mount a guard over it? Or even take it with us? There are more goblins in the deep places of the earth, and that tunnel they made will lead them right up to it . . ."

"That tunnel is being blocked now," said Cruadorn. "If you go to the shaft and listen, you will hear the masons at work. In time, the well will be blocked from bottom to top. And my people have mounted guard over this thing for three thousand years, so I think we can manage for tonight!"

Cruadorn touched the rune-adorned door, and it swung back. Beyond, the pulsing flare of the Anthir-Stone glared on smoothly polished marble.

Staggering under Tahion's weight, Istvan followed the dwarf through the door. Arms and shoulders ached from fighting, and Tahion, lurching against him, seemed heavy as a horse.

The noise of battle echoed. Distorted scraps of sound rang shrill and distant. But there was something strange about the din, as though the echoes spoke of a larger space than this narrow corridor. He looked at the flicker-lit marble, then let his eyes grope higher.

Where he had expected a roof there was a sudden blur, and after a moment he realised that he was seeing, above the top of a slab of marble, the distant, half-lit ceiling of some vast room.

Cruadorn was waving them all past. The dwarf stepped back, and the closing door set echoes crashing. The pulsing light vanished. Cruadorn passed again, gesturing for the men to follow.

The dwarf turned left, and Istvan saw that the slab ended. The steady light of the room beyond seemed strange and dull to eyes that had grown used to the frenzied shifting light in the room they had left.

Dwarf warriors' mail-shirts rippled in the hall's still light. Piled white blocks at his left eye's edge shaped themselves, when he turned his head, into the steps of a dais, and the topmost block blinked to a low throne of mottled marble: jewels blossomed on its pink and purple veins.

On the smooth white stone behind the throne, gold-filled grooves were tangled into symbols he had no time to unravel, though he did see a gold anvil and a gold-handled hammer with a silver-outlined head. But Cruadorn was trotting on across the room, and short, bearded warriors in glittering mail were courteously drawing aside. He had to hurry on, with Tahion's weight lunging against him with every step . . .

"Am I not strong enough?" Shrill echoes thinned Layareh's voice. "I will carry him! Leave me be!" A glance behind showed the islander, frowning and glistening with sweat, holding Fithil in his arms, fronting a row of dwarves who bore a long stretcher between them.

"You have strength enough, surely," a dwarf-voice rumbled like an avalanche, echoes whispering like sliding snow. "But we can bear him together with less trouble. It is a favour to us if you let us help."

"And to me, if you will let me lie down," said Fithil.

"Well, no harm in that," said Layareh, gently laying his rival into the stretcher as carefully as a father putting a child to bed. Yet Istvan could see relief in Layareh's eyes as he straightened.

He wished they had brought a stretcher for Tahion.

The marble stair rose before them, with a low railing of gold too low for a man to reach, and Istvan dreaded the ascent. But at least it was shorter than the long stairway out of the secret chamber would have been . . .

"The vision!" Tahion mumbled. "Tarithwen's vision!" The Forest Lord's voice was thick and slurred.

"What?" Istvan's foot came down painfully on a higher step than he'd expected, jarring him as Tahion came down against his shoulder. "What are you . . . ?"

"The vision Tarithwen showed us, of the Universes of Light and Dark!" Tahion exclaimed. "It was like the Stone! The balancing forces, light and dark, precisly matched . . ." His weight seemed to lessen, as though the excitement of his thoughts strengthened him. "That was how Anthir was able to join the powers! And that was how he hoped to reach the Hidden City!"

Istvan could remember the vision, but that did not allow him to make sense of the wizard's ravings. But at least Tahion's full weight was no longer upon him. Indeed, both Tahion and Arthfayel seemed to gain strength as they climbed.

". . . a fool I am!" Arthfayel's words came up to the stairs to Istvan's ears. "So sure I was, that the Stone of Anthir was a silly tale, and so sure that I already knew what was here! So wise, I thought I was!''

"The Children of Hastur worked many a year," put in Calmar's voice, ''to make you believe it all a lie! They fear that a mortal might gain the power over them that the Stone would give!''

'And they are right to fear it!'' Tahion said over his shoulder, voice strong now. They were almost at the top of the stairs, and Tahion took his hand off Istvan's shoulder and took the last step by himself, turning at the little balcony at the stair's top. ''A mortal who used the Stone would be all too likely to summon the power for purposes at best selfish, and at worst harmful. And who will guard the World while they dance to some fool's calling?''

"It is more than *that* that they must fear!'' Cruadorn's voice was a genuine roar. ''In unskilled hands, so the wise say, the Stone's balance could tip, the powers escape control. Then Anthir's Stone, balanced no more, would burst—'' he paused. ''And—no one knows for sure—but the Hasturs say— that should its balance fail, a whole new Universe of stars—a *Universe!*—would burst from the stone, and the walls of our town would as atoms be borne by wandering suns beyond its ends . . .''

CHAPTER SEVENTEEN

An Arrow in the Dark

There was silence after that. They had walked down long corridors of polished stone and were mounting the stairways to the outside before any of them spoke again.

"Cruadorn," Istvan said at last, "it is good that you have made Karik's sword—but will that sword cut through the armour of Svaran the Black?" The dwarf looked up at him, startled, and shook his hairless head.

"At least one of our enemies," Istvan went on, "wears the finest armour your people can make. Yet, among us, your allies and friends, only Garahis and myself and a few of the Easterners are armoured at all! The rest go bare-legged against goblins, and clad only in cloth against invulnerable Svaran and his mail-clad soldiers, many without even a shield! We need shields more than swords, and armour more than either!"

The dwarf's eyes sparked under the stubble on his singed brows, but before he could speak, Layareh's voice burst in.

"What nonsense is this, Seynyorean? Do you think that I will weigh myself down with an iron shirt, and fight hiding behind a door, just because there was someone willing to give me one? Think you I have such concern for my tender flesh?"

"I would not know what to do with a shield," said Karik.

"You see!" sharled Cruadorn angrily. "if we gave these men armour they would not wear it! Islanders are too proud even to use shields!"

Silently, Istvan berated himself for forgetting: his cousin, Raquel, who had long ago studied under one of the sword-masters of the Isles, had told him that, deadly as their long-weapon and single-sword techniques were, islanders scorned the shield.

"We like our own weapons better," said Fithil. "And we who fight so much in boats would rather swim than sink. Yet look you, Layarch! Because I did not fear for my skin, I am now but a burden upon the rest of you! Not dead, but no help in the fighting to come!"

"I will be happy to wear mail," said Tahion, "but I fear most of the Y'gorans will not. Men who fight in thick forest, where stealth is an important weapon, have little use for armour that squeaks and jingles to tell the enemy where you are, and betray you in an ambush. So, although most of the mainlanders would be willing to carry shields, I fear you will have no luck getting them into armour—unless it were elf-mail, maybe."

"Elf-mail?" Istvan asked.

"Long ago," said Cruadorn, "the great elf smiths made mail out of tiny rings, so small a straw would barely pass through. Such rings would of course have to be of the strongest steel in order to stop any blow at all, but they would stop a thrust, certainly, and were no doubt good against knives and arrows. The stories *say* that they stopped swords and spears, too, but—I have my doubts. In any case, the mail was very flexible, and then the elves would weave threads through the links, and more threads through those, until you had what looked to be a shirt of ordinary cloth—until you tried to use a knife on it. And because of the cloth, they made no noise in the woods. They were priceless—indeed, legend said that they were never bought or sold, but only given as gifts."

They came out into sunlight and greenery while the dwarf spoke, and found the men of the Ua Cadell all around them. A babble of voices rang out, and then Tuarim Mac Elathan came through the wild men.

"Ah, Tahion!" the sweet voice chimed. "It is yourself I would rather see just now than my dinner, even though a great hunger is on me, indeed!" His words reminded Istvan of his own blazing hunger. "I take it all is well below stairs, there?"

"The dwarves are shooting goblins off the walls," Tahion said wearily, "and their tunnel is being blocked up, if that is what you mean."

"Indeed, it is!" The elf nodded. "We have not been idle here. A large company of soldiers came up out of the ground and met Arduiad's arrow-storm. Many fled, but some formed a shield-wall and charged the hedge. But they could not chop through with their shields locked, and we killed nearly half of them. The rest fell back to the stair, and there's been no sign of them since. But when they come back—and they will be back—they will be better prepared. And I have been thinking that I will want your advice then."

"Istvan's advice may be better than mine," Tahion said. "He has more experience in this kind of war than I." His voice was growing fainter again; Istvan looked at him sharply.

"I thought you were better," he said.

"I am," Tahion said with a smile, "but *better* is not the same as *well*, as they say. My head is still ringing like an anvil."

Istvan frowned. He stepped away from Tahion, and the wild men got out of his way as he strode to the hedge and looked out. The trees were sorely hacked. Beyond them lay corpses in spear-gashed mail.

Many had faces torn by thorns; eyes had been clawed from the sockets of one, and lay like pearls on the dead cheeks. With a little shudder, Istvan turned away and studied the ragged savages who stood leaning on bloodied spears.

"Are these not also your allies, Cruadorn?" Istvan's voice was sharp. "They are in worse case than we!" He whirled on Tuarim. "Convince Cruadorn—or Aurothror—to give these men decent arms, shields at least, and armour if they will wear it— and *then* we can talk about making a stand here!"

He did not wait for an answer, but turned and strode back to Tahion's side. Tahion met him with an approving nod and a weak smile. Much to Istvan's surprise, Layareh also nodded at him grinning, then murmured at him, low-voiced, "*Good!* Make them beg! You have the right!"

Both Cruadorn and Tuarim stared.

"*Wait!*" a hoarse voice broke in, and one of the wild men stepped toward them. The man's dark hair was streaked with grey, though the body was lean and hard. There was the unmistakable dignity of a leader in the dark eyes as they met Istvan's own.

"Starn MacMalkom I have spoken to," the man said, "but you I do not know. Nor you," he added, turning to Tahion.

"I am Tahion, the King of Aldinor, beyond the sea. And this man—" Tahion rested his hand on Istvan's shoulder, "is a war-chief of the Clan DiVega, who live upon the slopes of Hastur's Mountain. All his life he has fought in Hastur's service, the world over, and no man alive knows more of war than he."

The savage's eyes widened for a moment, then narrowed in a frown. "I am Yolaru, high-chief of the Ua Cadell," he said. "I, too, have fought many battles. I have fought men in iron shirts. I lived: they died. Iron could not hide them from hurt. Why should I wear iron now?" His eyes locked with Istvan's.

"In the forest," Istvan said, choosing his words carefully, "you know how to fight, and as long as this hedge holds, you can kill men on the other side with your spears. But once there is a hole in the hedge, it will be a different kind of battle. They will make a wall of their shields, a wall that moves. A light stroke cuts flesh: only the strongest will cut armour. Your foes need not strike as hard to kill you as you must to kill them."

"He speaks the truth," said Cruadorn. Yolaru's eyes still rested on Istvan's, and his face did not change.

"Listen to him!" Tuarim Mac Elathan said. "I have known war far longer than he, yet I find his advice good."

"Words are wind," said Yolaru. "Deeds are steel. Though bards sing, death is real, and the wounds of dead men never heal." His eyes were still fixed on Istvan's, unblinking, challenging. "This would be a new way of fighting for my people. If we give up the way that we know, how can we learn the new way in time? Who will teach us?"

"I will stand with you," said Istvan, "and show you all I can. But you cannot learn all at once. Yes, men will die." He met the war-chief's gaze calmly. "Even so, with armour you will hold them longer than without." Yolaru's eyes dropped at last.

"So. Men die. That is war." He nodded. "Old men know life is short. Will you give us the armour, dwarf?"

"Armour and shields both," Cruadorn said, "if my words can move Aurothror. And swords of good steel.

"But this will be a costly war for us," he added, low-voiced, to Istvan. "Kings would pay highly to equip their armies so."

"When are we going to eat?" said Layareh. "And *what* are we going to eat?"

"Ah!" said the dwarf. "That, too, I had best see about! I will have some food sent up to the fort—good, plain food—none of these elvish sweets! I will send it up as soon as I can!"

"Good!" said Karik. "Let us go inside, then."

Tahion and Arthfayel, leaning on each other, were walking slowly toward the door of the fort. Fithil and his stretcher had already been borne inside. Cruadorn ran a few steps after them.

"Tahion!" he called. "I will be sending the healer Kilith to you." Tahion looked back, and nodded to show that he understood.

Istvan looked at the sky. The twin suns were already westering, and he had eaten nothing since before the *Tromdoel* came! Who had poisoned Layareh, he wondered, and would they try again? Would the food be safe now?

And yet he had not been hungry until Tuarim had spoken. The elves again, he supposed. Their summons, surely, had put his mind on other things.

"Well, there will be milk, at least!" Arthfayel said, as Istvan walked through the door and into the shadows inside the fort.

"There is a bowl of nuts here, too," said Fithil.

"Is this what the elves expect us to live on?" exclaimed Layareh.

"We should be glad they are giving us real food at all," said Tahion, "and not just hiding our hunger from us, or giving us illusions to eat." He dropped to his blankets, cracking a nut. He shook his head. "It feels as though there was a boy with a drum in my head!"

"And mine also!" Arthfayel said. "And I am tired!"

As Istvan walked toward them, he felt a sudden familiar, pulsing twitch at his nerves, and looking down, saw that he was standing on the odd round pattern of stonework at which Calmar had been scratching with his dagger.

Suddenly, he guessed that he was standing right above the stairway: this must be the sealed entrance to the Chamber of the Stone, and the pillar of fire blazed against the ceiling somewhere under his feet.

"Did you see?" Carroll stormed angrily through the far door. "The boy was lying on the ground, and the blood pouring from him onto the grass!" Behind him Anarod, Larthon and Ingulf came, their faces grim with rage.

"Who?" Tahion asked.

"Hrivown!" Larthon snarled.

"That boy who was lying over there," said Carroll. "The wounded boy that seemed as though he'd never move again! He was lying on the path, halfway to Ardcrillon's tower! The elf-call must have reached him, but he was too weak to go far!"

"Just far enough to tear his wound open!" said Larthon bitterly.

"Ah, no!" said Tahion. "Will he live? Where is he now?"

"The dwarf healers are taking care of him," said Larthon, "and will be bringing him soon. Youth is healthy: boasting follows battle. The wound has closed, the bleeding stopped; I have no fear for him."

"Here are the healers now," said Anarod.

Dwarves entered bearing a stretcher, then more dwarves with a second stretcher, Alphth the Changeling hovering behind. Istvan saw in surprise that Finloq lay on the second stretcher, his leg swathed in red-stained bandages.

Tahion went to the other stretcher and placed a hand on the boy's forehead. His face went blank.

"Was that—who was it that was on the stairs?" Istvan asked.

"Did you not see?" said Anarod. "Alphth fought there alone, straddling his friend."

Tahion drew a deep breath, and took his hand away.

"Finloq fainted on the steps," said Alphth. "I stayed with him and tried to rouse him, but he would not stir. Then the goblins came. I drew my blade and fought. See how his leg is bitten! I thought us both dead."

"Death was close," Larthon agreed, "had those killers been left alone. They bit Finloq to the bone!"

Tahion sat back.

"Well, Hrivown will live," he said. "But this is the

second time elf-magic has nearly killed him!'' Finloq groaned on his pallet: Alphth rushed to his side. Tahion rose more slowly, like an old man.

Finloq's wide eyes opened, and he caught his lip in his teeth. Tahion touched the bandaged leg with his fingertips, and flinched. Layareh poured a cup of milk and held it to the injured man's lips.

''I stood over him,'' said Alphth, ''to protect him, but they swarmed over us. And one that I wounded, and thought I had killed, started chewing on his leg. And still he did not wake!''

Again Tahion touched the blood-soaked bandage, and his frown deepened. He looked into the wide grey eyes.

''Finloq, are you a man, or an elf?'' he asked. Finloq's face was troubled.

''I—I do not know!'' His voice was shrill. ''My mother was mortal, but . . .''

''You are a Changeling, then?'' Arthfayel interrupted.

''Indeed I am not!'' snapped Finloq. ''Not I! My mother bore me, of that I am sure! But she was a woman of Clan Gileran, with as much elf-blood as mortal blood in her veins. And my father—'' He paused.

''My mother called him *Alangal*, but that is only a made-up name from the Old Language, meaning *Beautiful Stranger*. For she called him out of the forest one night, when her loneliness was more than she could bear. For she was not considered beautiful among the women of Clan Gileran, and her elf-blood had made her a powerful witch—many feared her.

''And on a night she put all her longing and her need into a song of power. And my father came from out of the trees, and she loved him in the moonlight. But when she woke he was gone, and she never saw him again, or ever knew his true name. None among the elves will admit—'' He paused, and sighed. ''I cannot find him, nor know if he is elf or man; alive or dead.

''If he was an elf, then I have more elf-blood than mortal. But the only way I shall ever know is to wait and see if I age and die. If I die, I will know that I am mortal!'' His voice was bitter.

''Others of Clan Gileran have doubted their mortality,'' said Tahion, ''and changeling elves, raised among men, must—''

"I did not ask you for sympathy!" Finloq snarled. "You asked whether I were elf or mortal, and because I thought you a healer trying to help, I told you as much as I know! If you cannot heal my leg, leave me be!"

Tahion stiffened as though stung, then shook his head and sighed.

"I am sorry," he said. "And you have a right to your anger. But if you are a mortal man—" he paused, "then I fear your leg will not heal. At least, *I* cannot heal it. Were you at Elthar or Carcosa, then perhaps the Hasturs, or some of the great mortal healers they have trained, could grow back the damaged flesh, and knit the nerves and sinews chewed away. Perhaps the dwarf healers have more skill than I. But as far as any skill of mine goes, you will walk with a limp for the rest of your days, if you are a mortal man . . ." He paused then, and looked down at the floor.

"If you are an elf," he said, slowly, "then the same force that keeps you from aging will make you heal more quickly. And it might even be that a mortal man with as much elf-blood as you have will heal as an ordinary mortal would not . . ."

But what else Tahion said, and what Finloq answered, Istvan did not hear, for just at that moment the rich smell of hot food filled the room. Istvan turned, his mouth watering: he smelled potatoes and butter, hot bread, mushrooms and sausages and roasted birds.

Dwarves were coming through the door, platters piled high in their hands.

Two great trestle-tables were borne into the hall. The heroes hung back while the tables were set up, then formed themselves into a line with all the eagerness of hungry fighting men.

Knives and spoons clattered on plates: the din was deafening. In the midst of the confusion, Starn, Flann, and Fergus appeared at the door, stared a moment, then hurried to join their comrades at the tables. Cormac came limping in close behind, leaning upon the shoulder of Garahis of Ordan, and then Dair Mac Eykin and the three surviving Easterners.

"How is Hrivown?" one of the newcomers asked, a slender, hawk-faced man in mail, pale-skinned and dark-haired.

"He will live, Peridir," said Layareh, "or at least," he jerked his chin toward Tahion, "that one says he will."

"There are only us six left, out of all who followed Conn and Laemon on this journey," said the stocky, red-faced Easterner. "Curse the elf who brought the message!" Layareh took a bite of the sausage he was eating, and chewed thoughtfully.

"And what will you be doing now, Gurthir?" he asked. "After all this is over, I mean?" The red-faced man tugged his black beard.

"I suppose I will be going back to Ualfime," he said frowning, "unless Peridir wishes to take me into his service."

"If we both live through this," said Peridir, "I will be both pleased and honoured for you—or any of you—to join me."

"I may well need to," said Layareh. "I am an outlaw now in the Empire."

Istvan sat eating quietly, and counting the men left alive. There were barely twenty, besides himself, able to fight.

At least the other Easterners, beside Layreh, all wore armour and carried shields. He remembered what he had said to Yolaru. That made six armoured men he could use to show Yolaru's tribesmen how to fight in formation.

He went to find Tahion. The Forest Lord looked tired and worn, and Istvan saw pain in his face.

"You need sleep," Istvan said. Tahion nodded.

"I am weary indeed, and would gladly lie down, if there were not things which I must learn, and folk I must talk to. Ingulf first, I think." He rose to his feet, and swayed, clutching his head, then stepped over to Ingulf, who sat a little apart, brooding. "Ah, Ingulf!"

"What now," said the madman testily. "What do you want of me? Why will you never leave me alone?"

Tahion dropped to the floor beside him, studying him intently.

"Men do not go to the City of the Sea-Elves, not even the men of Clan Gileran, who have close kin among the elves. Yet I hear that you have been there?"

"I have." One corner of Ingulf's mouth twitched.

"Whatever were you doing there?" asked Tahion. Ingulf blushed.

"I was searching for Airellen, the daughter of Falmoran."

"And who is she, Ingulf?" Tahion asked. Ingulf was silent, brooding. "Why did you search for her?"

"She is a seal!" Ingulf snarled, and sat silent, staring into blankness. Tahion looked at Istvan, shaking his head slightly, and suddenly Ingulf's voice burst out again, hoarse with passion. "She is the most beautiful of women, with long dark hair, and eyes like . . ." His voice died, and he wrapped his arms around his knees elf-fashion, and rested his chin upon them. After a long, baffled silence, Tahion prompted him again.

"Where did you meet her, Ingulf?"

"In the Scurlmard Islands. I was—" Suddenly he threw his hands in front of his face, and his voice rose to a shriek. "— it was all my own fault! The folk of the Scurlmards warned me about the seals, but I thought it all a lying story. And when I saw her swimming in the sea, I—I remembered their warnings! But I did not believe them!" His frame shook with sudden sobs, and he pulled his hands away and turned toward them a haunted face wet with tears.

"Is *that* the sin for which I am being punished?" he asked, his voice shrill and wild. "I do not know why I must suffer so! They will not tell me!

"I saw the seal! I raised my harpoon, and I threw! But on the shore, the seal turned to a woman—a woman there, and my spear in her, and she wailing and bleeding . . ." He hid his face again, and rocked back and forth, back and forth . . .

"I love her! Day and night her eyes are looking at me, and I have no peace! How could I have hurt her so, she who is all the world, and all the joy in life? Why must a man hurt her he loves most?

"Her wound healed and she left me," he went on after a silence, his voice quieter, "and my life was empty. What was there for me to do but to seek her?

"And so I searched through the islands, and then sailed to Elthar, and there I hunted through old lore, until I knew where to search for the Sea-Elves' city . . ."

He was silent again. Istvan looked around, saw other men gathered, listening: many blushed and looked away when they saw Istvan's eyes were on them.

"Tell me of that city, Ingulf," said Tahion softly, placing a gently hand on Ingulf's shoulder. But Istvan saw his eyes go blank, and knew that Tahion watched the wakening memories through Ingulf's own eyes.

"All white stone it is, white and cruel as bone. The roaring of the sea is there, and the chiming of harp strings, and the sea wind blows ever between the towers . . .'' He shivered in memory, hunching further into himself; and Tahion beside him hunched and shivered.

"And did you find her, Ingulf?" It was Anarod's voice. Istvan started.

Ingulf gasped like a strangling man.

"There she is at last in her blue gown! Airellen!'' His voice rose to a scream, and he heaved suddenly to his feet, his eyes wild and staring. Tahion, too, heaved up, but now his hand clenched on Ingulf's shoulder.

"Ingulf! Come up to this time now! It is only memory! It is over! It is past!"

Ingulf looked wildly around him, and sank suddenly to his haunches, his shoulders heaving as he sobbed, his face hidden by his hands.

"I spoke to her!" he cried. "I spoke to her! I touched her hand, and I screamed her name! And she would not turn, she would not look at me! She would not speak, and would not turn and she would not see me . . .'' And as he spoke his voice grew higher and shriller, until it was like a wind whistling through an arrow slit.

"And I followed like a ghost . . ." Ingulf whispered. "A lost ghost, and a lonely ghost. Oh Airellen, will you never turn the beauty of your eyes on me again?" His voice broke once more into sobs. Loud above them came a snort of anger.

"Have we grown so bored now we have nothing better to do than sit and stare at the poor loon?" It was Layareh's voice, and was followed by the noisy scraping of a bench. Ingulf did not seem to notice: his voice went on, a thin fluting. . .

"And now I am lost and destroyed! I am the ghost of a drowned man, for when I saw there was no hope, I went and drowned myself in the sea . . .''

"Ah, the poor loon! Drowned, is he!" Layareh stalked to the door. After a moment, the other Easterners rose and followed. The door slammed loudly.

"And *is* there no hope, Ingulf?" asked Tahion, softly.

"Only one hope!" Ingulf said. "The sword. *Frostfire*. Dorialith . . . Dorialith gave it me. At the end of the night. And she spoke to me then. She asked if I was a hero. But then she said—she said . . .'' His voice broke again, and again he huddled down into himself. "She said it was only a spell she had put on me! Yet she said she loved me, and then—and then she ran away into the sea, and swam away as a seal. I followed her, but the other seals dragged me back to the shore. And Dorialith promised me—but it means *nothing!*" His face twisted, his voice rose angrily. "I went into Sarlow, and fought to free the slaves, and killed werewolves and fought against the sorcerers, but I am still only a lonely ghost! My life is meaningless . . ."

"*Arm yourselves!*" Gurthir shouted from the door. "While you sit and listen to this fool's story, Vor Half-Troll has come out of the tunnels and is chopping at the hedge! It looks like they will break through!"

Ingulf leaped to his feet.

"*Good!*" he cried. "I can kill! Killing always helps. And Dorialith will sing of it to *her*—" He ran for the door, *Frostfire* sliding from its sheath. Tahion stumbled up after him, then reeled, clutching at his brow, and almost fell.

"No, Tahion!" Istvan seized the Forest Lord's shoulder as he tried to rise. "Go to bed now! You're in no condition to fight! Neither are you, Arthfayel! Starn! You were up all day while the rest of us slept! You and Flann get some rest now! Some of us *must* sleep! Fergus—?" But Fergus was already gone through the door. So were the rest, except for Cormac and the wounded.

Istvan snatched up his shield and ran. Outside, he could hear shouts and screaming, and the rhythmic *thud* of steel on wood.

Sunbeams slanted just above the ground, laying long black shadows over grass. He saw trees shaking, and he heard wood crack.

Ragged tribesmen were kneeling by the hedge, long spears thrusting between trembling leaves.

Even as his foot passed over the doorsill, he saw a tree leaning. A rain of elves leaped from its branches as it toppled with a rustling roar.

Men's voice shouted in triumph beyond the hedge, and mingled with them was another, shriller sound, like pigs squealing.

Thorn branches thrashed wildly as the thudding began again. As Istvan sprang down the steps, he saw both Layareh and Tuarim Mac Elathan run toward the fallen tree.

Mail-rings glimmered through swaying leafy boughs. A cloud of arrows hummed between branches. A bass voice screamed. But the leaves continued to sway as the tree moved outward, and great, arrow-furred wooden shields filled the gap.

Another tree lurched drunkenly beside the first. Half-naked clansmen scrambled back as it fell. Fading sunbeams sparkled on shifting rings of mail.

Sunset painted the sky with rainbow colour as the twin suns slipped past the world-rim. Arrows flew. Mailed men shouted and milled.

New shouts rose as the shadows grew. Armoured men poured through the gap, circling the fallen trees. Tiny, shaggy brown figures raced among them, sheltered by their shields.

Layareh's blade flew from its scabbard, hid its point behind a shield, then flew above it, dripping red.

Great wooden disks loomed over him. One lifted a little, and wheeling steel blurred from under it. Layareh leaped high in the air, over the blade flying to slice him asunder at the waist, his own sword stabbing skyward—

It snapped back down as his feet touched, down past the curve of the shield-edge. Blood splashed.

Rainbow flames were fading from the sky: twilight gloomed in the east. Dim moons loomed there: Domri a ghostly dome above the line of jagged peaks; Lirdan, a haggard fruit, hanging higher. Firefly stars blinked.

Istvan's feet beat stone: he saw Tuarim Mac Elathan spring at the shield-wall, his blade lightning.

A half-naked savage staggered back, clutching the dripping red stump of his arm. Women were screaming above men's shouts and the high pitched goblin squeals.

Ahead of Istvan, other men were running: Karik with raised axe; Garahis, armour dull in twilight; Carroll, Anarod, and Fergus shoulder-to-shoulder behind their shields; Ingulf springing ahead of Gurthir, moonlight sword in hand.

Larthon sprang to Layareh's side, his sword crashing on wood while his heavy shield boomed. Layareh dodged another whipping sword-stroke, his point lancing the wrist sticking past the shield-edge. Tuarim danced and darted like a bird, death flying as a flicker of light from his hand.

The ragged clansmen were falling back, the thorns of their spears prodding at the wall of wood that pressed them back.

For a spear to catch in a shield was death from lopped limbs' bleeding.

Now Peridir and his companion, whom Istvan had heard addressed by some name that sounded like Shluwethlin, reached the enemy line, shining swords swirling in eddies of light that hurled splintered shield-chips high.

A sword and a dripping hand went flying. A man's voice screamed. Still the shield-wall pressed ahead: the foe closed ranks over the fallen. Heroes and clansmen fell back.

Frostfire, glittering in a long, deceptive arc, scored a deep, straight cut across one shield, then slid from its edge to slash above the next in line, across a face below the helmet. Ingulf leaped out of the swing of a falling sword.

The ends of the shield-wall lengthened, as more soldiers poured through the gap. Arrows flew like flocking birds, pecking round shields till they bristled like fur.

Turaim Mac Elathan raced in a blur from end to end of the line, his ancient blade flickering death. His eyes glittered cold and gay.

Istvan ran off the stone walk. Soft grass soothed his running feet. He raced to catch up with Garahis.

Istvan ran. Both left and right, arrows fell like hail. He saw shaggy goblin figures rushing the clansmen, cutting at naked legs. Layareh leaped in among them like a cat among mice, his deadly blade lashing in a murderous slice that laid six, headless, on the ground.

And now Istvan ran beside Garahis.

"Link shields now, and hit the wall!"

Already Anarod, Carroll and Fergus were rushing to the left: Istvan turned right, Garahis running with him, the edges of their shields pressed tight.

Where are the dwarves, Istvan thought, *and where is the armour Cruadorn promised?*

Shield met shield with a crash like doom. The men from Sarlow reeled. Istvan's hand flew on the wing of his sword. He felt metal part under its edge. Swords crashed loud on shields as strong men raged against the dying light. Steel split wood and rang on mail with deadly hammer-blows: death shouts brayed as red blood gushed. Battle-clamour rose: shrill echoes pealed.

The advancing shield-wall slowed. But men still poured through the gap in the hedge.

Istvan and Garahis fell back together, shield-to-shield: new foes replaced the men they had slain. A goblin ran in to cut Istvan's legs: he lowered his backstroke enough to take off its head. But quick glances over each shoulder showed dozens of tiny shapes scuttling, shadows in the deepening twilight, and tribesmen down, hamstrung, with goblins swarming over them. He tried to suck the whole sky into his lungs.

"Fall back and rally!" he roared. "Men with shields! To me! Form a line! Yolaru! Gather your warriors behind us!"

He paused, trying to think, to plan. Where were the dwarves? His brain swam. He had meant to send Fergus, Anarod, Karik, Garahis and some of the others inside, but they were too few now! With too many enemies. All their bravery and skill would barely slow down the army against them: without their help, the tribesmen would have been slaughtered already.

Of the elves, only Tuarim Mac Elathan seemed willing to stand with the men, although elvish arrows swarmed in clouds. But they could not pierce the huge, table-like shields.

While he thought, his feet were moving, and he and Garahis were backing toward the center, shields edge-to-edge, swords poised to strike. Other men were moving to meet them.

He saw *Frostfire* catch in a shield, and a sword sweeping toward Ingulf's head.

It glanced from Layareh's steel as he made a long, dangerous leap and lunge. Karik's axe split the shield from top to bottom, and *Frostfire*, freed, darted to the mailed throat, lifting the curtain of rings like a veil, and darting under.

The three islanders sprang back, their weapons whirling as goblins tried to close in, slashing at their knees.

High, eerie howling sounded beyond the hedge.

The shield-wall advanced another ponderous step, all together. Layareh leaped toward them, point rising, spiking the starlit sky. Shields lifted, and the islander threw himself down, lashing out ankle high.

Men screamed and fell, their feet slashed away. For a moment there was a great gap in the wall, then others came rushing to fill it from behind.

Beyond them, Istvan saw a bearded head and mailed shoulders rearing above tall men. Vor Half-Troll had come.

Black, red-eyed wolves rushed out from under the shield-wall. One leaped at Karik's throat—his red axe met it in the air and hurled it down with a shattered skull.

It rolled up, snarling, red eyes askew, and Istvan could see bone and flesh knitting, reforming, as it pulled itself up to spring at Karik again . . .

Frostfire glimmered in its path: point driving deep into the black-furred chest.

"My thanks!" Karik was close enough now that Istvan could hear his voice above the sounds of battle. "If they would only finish my sword! Then I could show you what I am worth."

"Indeed, you've already shown us, Karik," Carroll's voice answered. "You showed us that when you faced Grom Beardless with only a pair of broken sticks in your hands. And with a magic sword it will be harder, not easier, to find any deed as brave as that one."

Tuarim Mac Elathan flitted out of the dark, and laid his shield edge against Istvan's.

"What is it you would do?" he said. "You must fall back farther! Can you not see that the dwarves will be cut down one by one?" Istvan blinked at him. The elf pointed. Istvan strained his sight in the dimness, until at last he saw the dark pit in the ground where Tuarim was pointing, and realised it was one of the stairwells to the tunnels.

The long line of shields advanced.

"Steady!" Istvan barked. "Together now, fall back two steps—one—*two!*"

Shoulder-to-shoulder and shield-to-shield, feet stepping all at once, the heroes fell back. Only ten had shields. Behind them, savages milled confused, spears raised to thrust.

Suddenly, behind them, women's screaming mingled with goblin squeals.

Yolaru and his men turned at the sound and went running back, and the shield-wall wavered as even Istvan looked over his shoulder, to see the women of the Ua Cadell wielding long knives against moon-eyed shadows that dodged and danced in the twilight.

A voice cried out in the Sarlow line, and with a shouted roar the steel-crested wave of shields rolled down upon the little band.

The war shouts drowned the startled cries of two men at the end of the line as they toppled into the mouth of the stairwell.

Istvan and his men braced for the shock: the three islanders shrank behind the shield-wall, blades poised to cut above or between their comrades' heads.

Dim, stumpy figures sprang up behind the Sarlow line.

"Now!" cried Tuarim. *"In* now! Hit them hard!"

Tensed knees lunged with the word. Shield-wall crashed on shield-wall with a *crack!* like mountains falling: stunned men staggered, while the soaring swords swooped down like hawks, hunting the blood of men.

Then from the end of the enemy line came curses and screams and the clamour of metal. Grim dwarves rushed from the foes' rear flank, lashing axes felling men like trees, with lopped legs spurting blood on the ground.

Istvan's sword-arm whirled in a circle, his swords' light flickering before his eyes as its flat stroked the top of his enemy's shield. Twice he felt it skitter off a helmet.

He let it hang in the air a moment, then cut again as the shield came down—feeling mail-rings grinding as his edge slashed under the helmet's iron rim, driving tiny bits of wire through the thin temple bone.

He saw trees sway in the hedge, heard a musical *thrum* of strings, and something shook the rear of the Sarlow line like a great wind.

"A trap!" a deep voice roared. *"Fall back! Back to the tunnels!"*

At Istvan's right, invisibly fast, Tuarim's blade ripped through shields and armour: three men fell, blood flying from torn ring-mail.

On his left, Garahis and Fergus battered their foes back. Beyond, he glimpsed Carroll's sword pulling free from a bloody, cloven helmet, and other flaming blades whirling.

Dwarf-axes came dripping out of the night, splitting shields, hewing legs and helmets, and before them the wall dissolved and scattered.

Istvan caught sight of Vor Half-Troll standing by the gap in the hedge, trying to keep some order as men collided there, too many now for the narrow way.

A werewolf sprang into the storm of dwarf-axes; fell gashed, only to leap up again, bloody wounds healing as he moved. Istvan turned, but Tuarim Mac Elathan was there before him, and *Italindé*'s flaming steel-and-silver blade slashed the wolf in half while Istvan blinked.

Where the shield-wall had stood, a tangled snarl of fighting swirled and eddied, as little knots of men surged and reeled and battered at each other, rousing thunderous echoes with the booming of steel.

"Garahis!" Istvan shouted. "Fergus!" The two dropped back to his side. "Get you back to the dwarf fort, and take the women and the wounded of the Ua Cadell—and any of the warriors you can get out of the battle and the children—inside. When you've got them settled, I want you two to go to bed. Someone will have to be awake tomorrow! Take Anarod and Karik with you, if you can find them."

Then he was striding on through the shouting and the clamour. A werewolf sprang at him: its weight sent him staggering, his shield holding back the fangs, while red eyes glared into his own. He slashed across the top of the shield, between the grinning jaws, and jumped back from the fountain of blood.

At the edge of vision, a red-and-silver streak arced at his arm. He twisted his wrist to bring his own blade in the way, and the impact chimed through his bones as the falling sword glanced.

The battle spun around him as his head turned, and his blade dropped to catch the second stroke that lashed at his ribs, while his eyes locked with the pale blue eyes of the soldier who had cut at him. Then he was pivoting on his right foot while his shield whirled 'round his body, the brown leather of its back rising, blotting out the enemy eyes as it belled and shuddered on his arm.

The same motion pulled his sword behind him again and lashed it across the eyes he had seen—but too late; even as his shield fell, he felt his edge catch in the wood, and ripped it savagely free and back.

But the enemy's sword was not aimed at his momentarily exposed wrist; it was falling toward his legs.

He jumped back and felt the point of the other blade snick painfully but harmlessly across the metal that covered his shin. The huge shield was high, the other's shoulder well back—there was nowhere to cut.

He waited. The other moved in, sword-arm swinging over head and shield, hurling the dim blade at Istvan's eyes.

Istvan's own sword flew under the other as his shield rose and quaked on his arm. He felt metal and bone break under his edge a second before he felt the shield bend his blade.

As he wrenched his sword free, he saw *Frostfire's* cold glimmer nearby and rushed toward it, vaulting the slashed halves of the naked human body that lay where the werewolf had fallen.

Ingulf fought to guard Carroll's back, and Istvan blinked in awe at his mastery of the sword.

Carroll traded cuts with two of Sarlow's soldiers, his shield crashing and his bright blade flying about him. At his back, Ingulf stood just beyond the reach of his backswing, holding *Frostfire* two-handed, drawn well back to keep the enemy from trapping it with the huge shield.

As Istvan watched, *Frostfire* snapped down across the islander's body, clanging as it met the other blade in front of Ingulf's shoulder.

With a long lunge to the left, Ingulf tried to stab around the edge of the shield, following the returning arm, but the enemy pivoted, the shield brushing *Frostfire's* point aside as the other blade swept in a circle above the iron helm, whirling low toward the ribs on Ingulf's exposed side.

Istvan expected to see the islander cut in half, but with a supple twist of his body, Ingulf brought *Frostfire* tumbling back over his shoulder, point down, and the glittering blade quivered and chimed as it bent under the stroke, driven right against Ingulf's flesh.

All this, while Istvan filled his lungs. He shouted and ran, as the armoured man whirled his blade around to the other side. *Frostfire* spun down, and met the other sword as it came out from behind the shield, knocking its point to the ground.

The armoured man backed away, seeing Istvan coming, and turned and ran, rushing to join the crush at the gap in the hedge. Ingulf wasted no time on thanks, but ran in a wide circle to Carroll's left, and rushed at the sword-side of the nearest, *Frostfire* brandished high above his head.

The soldier whirled, and got his shield around, barely in time. *Frostfire* sank deep into wood.

With a savage wrench, Ingulf pulled it free, and threw himself to one knee to escape the sweep of the enemy's steel: the wind of the cut ruffled his hair.

Carroll, freed from the double menace, sprang at his remaining foe, his flaming sword flashing under the foeman's chin, and before the flying head could fall to earth, he had turned to Ingulf's aid.

Istvan, too, was running. The soldier, seeing two more coming at him, backed away toward his comrades.

Ingulf came back to his feet, and wiped the sweat from his eyes.

The enemy was in full retreat, ebbing back to the stairs. Flights of arrows harried them, but could not pierce their mail.

Carroll hugged Ingulf with his shield-arm.

"Well done!" he gasped, out of breath. "I'd not have held out much longer! My thanks!"

"And what was the use of it all?" Ingulf asked, his voice bitter. "With Dorialith nowhere in sight!"

"Well, you saved my life!" Carroll exclaimed. "Do you call *that* useless, you loon?"

"I might!" jeered Ingulf. "I saw you live through a worse fight!"

Istvan opened his mouth to speak—closed it again.

"Then I'll not thank you, loon!" Carroll shook his head, with a half smile. "I'll not look for Dorialith to tell him about it, either! And I'll waste no more time chattering with a loon in the middle of a battle!" He turned away, and in an instant Ingulf had reached and caught his arm. His face showed panic, and pain.

"Ah, Carroll, Carroll, you know that—you know I did not—indeed, I only meant you did not need my help—you—you—you would not turn from me? You would not desert me? *You* are still my friend, are you not? Forgive me!"

Carroll turned back to him, and for a moment Istvan saw the pain and sorrow in his face before he put on a cheerful grin, and beamed at Ingulf.

"Ah, my poor friend! Let us forgive one another." His voice was somber. Ingulf was trembling.

"It is alone I am. *She* will not forgive—I do not even know what—" his voice sank to stuttering murmur, his eyes were pools of pain. Carroll looked at Istvan then, and his eyes narrowed.

"And what is it you are staring at, outlander? Have you no business of your own?"

"Did you wish me to interrupt?" Istvan met his eyes calmly, though his ears felt hot. "Now that the shield-wall is broken, and Sarlow's hosts have fled, and the dwarves seem to be ready to share the work ahead," he hesitated, then went on, defiantly, "I need to find warriors with brains enough to see that they can fight better against men in mail if they are willing to armour themselves. I'm told the men of Y'gora are too proud to wear mail. Layareh is, I know—it does not make me think more highly of him! I've seen your skill, both of you. I know what you can do. Will you wear mail, or are you afraid of what Cormac might say of you?"

To his relief, Carroll laughed.

"I have fought in mail before. I wore it as a disguise in Sarlow, when I followed Ingulf there. I wore it when I fought Svaran and Grom Beardless!" He bared his teeth in a grim grin, and waved a hand at the mailed corpse near their feet. "So, you want us to loot the dead!"

"That might be quicker than waiting for Cruadorn to bring the armour he promised me," said Istvan.

"Good enough!" Carroll said. "What about you, Ingulf?"

"It makes no difference to me," said the islander mournfully. "I am lost upon the land: *she* swims in the sea! And if I drown, it will not matter." His voice grew muted, the shrillness fading into toneless despair. "I will do whatever you say."

While they had spoken, the clamour of battle had lessened and faded. Goblins still squealed in the dark; wolves or werewolves snarled, but the men of Sarlow had fled.

"Ingulf," Istvan asked, gently, "where did you last see Karik?"

The islander jabbed a thumb back over his shoulder, toward towers and fort and fighting.

"Back there somewhere," he said. "Killing goblins, he was, he and Layareh."

"Good," Istvan said. "We should all kill goblins. Anyone know where Anarod went?"

"No knowing," Carroll said, leaning down, kneeling by the body of the soldier he had killed, tugging on its mail-shirt, lifting up the mail-skirts to drag it off the corpse. "We were shield by shield when we hit the shield-wall, but once they broke I saw him no more. Ingulf, come lift his feet!"

Istvan was elated. This would change their notions; no one would sneer at Carroll with derision! This would be a force to reckon with: mailed men unmatched in skill—and he would be their leader!

A werewolf snarled nearby. He heard goblins squealing

and he heard men shout—the rat-folk still dashed and scuttled through the shadows, but they kept well away from the flaming swords.

Soldiers were squeezing through the hedge. More every moment came running from where the dwarf-axes hewed. Vor Half-Troll loomed beside the fallen trees, a giant's axe gripped in his fist, a grim guard over his fleeing men.

Toward them, the four mail-clad Easterners rushed, with Larthon the Troll-Slayer leading.

As Istvan watched, Gurthir, Shluwethlin and Peridir hurled themselves at the mob of men that wove past the fallen trees, but Larthon darted away and sprang straight toward Vor's vast form, his burning sword a comet's tail behind him, his heavy metal shield poised and braced.

Istvan heard the crash as the great axe fell, belling on Larthon's lifted shield with the power of a toppling tree. Most men would have been crushed to the ground by such a blow.

Now Istvan saw the reason for Larthon's fame, and why men named him "Troll-Slayer." Knees bending, he sank under the weight of the stroke, spread feet braced, while his bright sword reached for the massive arm behind the axe . . .

The great wood shield drummed. Splinters flew from its edge. Then rapidly hammering axe and sword were thundering angrily. Gurthir, Shluwethlin, and Peridir battered back men who tried to rush to Vor's aid. Steel crashed echoing on shields. Istvan ran to help.

Looming over his foe, Vor heaved his great axe high— then, as Larthon's shield lifted, lunged with shield and shoulder to send the Troll-Slayer staggering. The heavy axe lashed down, ringing Larthon's shield like a gong.

Already reeling, Larthon was driven to his knees. He crouched there, fighting for balance, heavy metal shield ready, sharp sword poised, but Vor was already backing away.

Larthon scrambled to his feet, but Vor had turned and was rushing to his men's aid.

The huge axe split Shluwethlin's helm; a blow from the shield sent Gurthir reeling. The remaining soldiers, hiding behind Vor's vast shield, squeezed through the hedge.

Running up, Larthon sprang to follow, but Peridir caught his arm as Istvan came up.

"Are you daft, man?" Peridir cried. "It is on top of you

they will be before you can come out from under the trees!
You cannot fight an army!''

"I'll kill him!" snarled Larthon, his voice wild as he
looked down at Shluwethlin's corpse. A werewolf snarled
somewhere nearby.

"Not if he has fifty other swords to help him!" Istvan
snapped. "He may be as big as a troll, but he fights like a
man, and a skilled man, too! If you are to match him at all, it
will only be on even terms. You cannot fight him and an
army at the same time."

Larthon glared at him. "I could if you would follow me!"
he burst out, turning back to his friends.

"What?" exclaimed Gurthir. "The three of us! Four, with
the foreigner? I am your friend, but it would be better to walk
over that cliff with you. We would—"

"Here Shluwethlin lies!" Larthon exclaimed, angrily. "Our
friend who followed Conn to the end, loyally—" He gestured
with his sword. "His helmet rent, his brains oozing from his
head, Shluwethlin lies here dead, yet you"—his eyes flashed—
"bid me stop, for dread I might join those who are gone?
Shluwethlin dead—dead is Conn—what matter if I live on?"

Dwarves shouted. Goblins squealed. Steel pealed steel.
Noise filled the night.

"You talk as though we had finished the fight," said
Istvan. "Have you no ears? This battle is not over! We have
driven back only a small part of the enemy army: there are
still werewolves and goblins loose here, and our allies of the
Ua Cadell have no magic swords to fight them with—not
even ordinary armour! Always we grieve for friends after
battle, but we must not forget our duties to the living. Come!"

Turning, he found himself facing the lifted axe edge of the
leader of a rank of dwarves. He flinched back, shield and
flaming sword coming up: the dwarf-axe lowered.

"Forgive me," the dwarf rumbled. "I expected to find
only men of Sarlow here, and saw your mail-shirt . . ."

"If you seek for men of Sarlow," said Istvan, "you must
search the other side of the hedge. Is Cruadorn among you?"

"I am here!" the deep voice called from further back. The
ranks parted, and a sturdy form strode through.

"We'll need healers now," Istvan snapped impatiently,
terribly aware of the sounds of fighting behind, "to replace
the mail-shirts you forgot to bring." He turned to walk away.

"I did not forget!" Cruadorn exclaimed. "The Sarlowaq came before we could get them! King Aurothror said to give you shirts of the finest steel, and—"

"Where are they then?" said Istvan, wheeling back. "And when *will* we get them?"

"They are under the ground, of course, down in the city. Some have been sent to get them from the Chamber of Bitter Axes, and before long . . ."

"Did it never enter your mind to take mail-shirts off the dead?" Istvan raged, and hurried to join the Easterners. He heard Cruadorn's voice rolling behind him, but he had no time to listen.

Goblins darted away as the bright swords approached. The bodies of the dead of both sides were marked by their teeth. Again and again, clusters of crescent-shaped eyes would shine out in the light of the swords, and then dozens of dark figures would scatter, and there the poor gnawed body lay.

Istvan shuddered, hoping they had all been dead before the goblins arrived, and ran to catch up with the others.

Great hills of cloud floated in the dome of night; below them, Istvan saw a moving light, like wings of flame, cast a ruddy glow on the bottoms of clouds.

He had no time to stare. Ahead of him, dim shapes scurried in the dark. Flaming blades flashed. Elves and goblins scrambled fighting through the brush, and the men of the Ua Cadell huddled together, their spears fending off swarming goblins. Carroll and Ingulf had joined them.

Among the goblins, Layareh danced.

The flaming film of his steel looped and wheeled, trailing blood and fire as goblin heads flew. A leaping werewolf died, sheared in half. Larthon shouted, and Istvan, leaping forward, linked shields with the others and rushed with them, crashing through the milling mass. Goblins scattered, squealing; were-wolves lunged and died.

Istvan wheeled sharply away from the others. Shield-wall tactics were worthless here: the goblins simply scattered out of the way and closed behind again.

He leaped among them, slashing. A few feet away, Layareh twisted, his blade whipping around to slice an arrow from the air. Istvan heard him cursing.

"That is the third arrow tonight!" Layareh snarled to

himself. "Why will those elves not watch their aim?" Goblins rushed him: his sword became busy.

Something tugged violently at Istvan's mail from behind. He wheeled, but there was no enemy there. A goblin leaped in, slashed at his leg, and died.

The goblins milled screaming about them: flaming blades flew humming.

Then Istvan saw Layareh, fighting boldly in the middle of a knot of goblins, stagger suddenly, sway, and fall. Goblins swarmed over him, hiding him from sight.

Istvan sprang shouting, slashing his path through the foe. Peredir, Larthon and Gurthir came hurrying. Tuarim Mac Elathan flitted out of the night, *Italindé* burning in his hand.

Istvan's Hastur-blade lashed through the biting, squealing, pack that quarreled over the fallen islander. He kicked dirty-furred corpses aside and straddled Layareh, blade sweeping the air, until the others arrived. Whirling, then, he knelt by Layareh's feet, slashing above his booming shield while goblins howled and cut at him with rusty iron swords.

Layarch the Proud lay gasping on the ground. A slim feathered shaft jutted from the back of his red-dyed robe. His death rattle sounded in his throat even as Peridir dropped to his knees beside him.

"And I thought you elves were such fine archers!" Peridir snarled, pulling the arrow angrily free.

"Let me see that!" Tuarim snatched the arrow from Peridir's hand, and lifted the feathers to his nose. A ruby drop of blood gathered on the finely chipped blue crystal of its point as he sniffed.

" 'Tis an elvish arrow, right enough," he said at last, "but it was a man that shot it. This one too, I think." He reached toward Istvan's back, and touched something.

Craning his neck, Istvan saw a second arrow, dangling, its crystal point caught in his mail.

"I fear," said Tuarim, grimly, "that you have a traitor among you."

CHAPTER EIGHTEEN

Against Friend and Foe

Tahion woke around the middle of the night, hearing a silent voice, throbbing with power, that called. *Ingulf! Come here!*

He rose from his bed, and saw in the dimness that Arthfayel, also, had risen.

"It is Falmoran's voice, is it not?" Arthfayel said.

"It is," said Tahion. He sighed. "And it is upon us to follow it, and to be there when Ingulf comes."

"It is upon us." Arthfayel agreed. He looked around. "Where is Calmar?"

"I do not see him," Tahion said. Again the voice throbbed, and in it was the crashing of waves on the shore, and the crying of sea birds, and the wild voice of the cold salt winds.

The two wizards stalked into the night.

"Keep your shoulder back when you make that cut!" Istvan heard Carroll saying, somewhere behind him. "If I see it, I can cut it!"

"Aye," said Ingulf, "but I *am* heavier." It was mail that weighed Ingulf down, as he and Carroll circled with shields and scabbarded swords, striking and guarding in slow motion, as Carroll tried to teach Ingulf the basic principles of shield-work.

Istvan had been helping for a while, showing some of the simpler tricks and exercises from the Three Swords School, but now he stood staring into the night, watching the dragons that glowed steadily brighter and larger in the sky.

Great cloudy mountains floated, snow-topped under the stars; once he thought he caught a faint flicker of distant lightning.

The silver swallows spiraled playfully, chasing each other like real birds.

Under the mountainous piles of cloud, dragons soared above the forest like bats of flame, dying the clouds red above them. One, larger than the others, circled around the rest, flying ahead, then wheeling back: *old Komanthodel himself,* Istvan thought.

Dragons! He shook his head. He had known there were dragons here, and in Noria: there was even a legend that one still lived in the Mountains of the Shadow. But he had never expected to see one. Let alone twenty or more . . .

"What are you doing, Ingulf?" he heard Carroll's voice, sharp with annoyance.

He had never expected he would have to fight dragons. Tuarim had fought dragons before—had fought Komanthodel himself, indeed. But Tuarim was not a leader of men. Whatever experience he had . . .

"Ingulf! Where are you going? What is it? Can you not hear me?"

. . . there was no leadership there. And Aurothror had made no attempt to link the heroes with his own forces: Istvan suspected that the dwarves resented the intrusion of men and elves into a trust which had once been theirs alone . . .

"Ingulf, am I a ghost? Answer me!" Carroll shouted. Then, "Istvan! Come quickly! Something is wrong with Ingulf!" Istvan turned, saw the islander walking away, sword sheathed, shield on arm.

"What is it?" he asked.

"I do not know!" Carroll exclaimed. "We—I was striking and—and then he was away! I called, but he walked on—I believe he is in a hurry—I—I think it is some spell upon him."

"Yes," said Istvan, "I expect so."

They rushed after the gaunt figure circling the round dwarf hall. The door opened, and Garahis stepped out, yawning, and stretching his arms.

"All quiet, is it not?" he called to them cheerily.

"It is not," called Istvan. "Keep watch out here!" He dashed on, hurrying to catch up with Carroll. Ingulf had already vanished in the shadows of the trees.

They hurried after him, hearing the jingle of mail, and the crashing as he blundered into the bushes in the dark.

"There is no woodcraft in him at all," muttered Carroll. "I think he would have starved to death in the woods had I not met him. He should never have left his island!"

They hurried on, into the bright moonlight of Ardcrillon's garden. Ahead, the tower glittered like ice, and they saw Ingulf striding toward the doors.

They caught up with him at the steps of the tower. Carroll caught hold of his shoulder above the shield, and Istvan was just in time to grasp his sword-hand as it closed on *Frostfire's* hilt.

"Ingulf!" Carroll cried. "Do you not know us? We are your friends!"

"If you are my friends, why are you murdering me?" Ingulf's voice was wild and shrill. "Let me go! Can you not hear them calling me above the waves and the gulls? The Sea People are here—they are calling me! I must go! *She* will be with them . . ."

"Airellen is not here," said Istvan, "but Falmoran, her father, is." He paused, and caught the wild eyes with his own. "Let us go with you, Ingulf. You may need friends with you, Ingulf."

Staring at Istvan in amazement, Carroll let go of Ingulf's arm, and now Istvan lifted his fingers away from the islander's wrist. Ingulf climbed the stairs, and they followed.

"I do not understand," whispered Carroll. "What did you mean about—about Airellen's father?"

"He is here," Istvan said. "That brown-bearded elf who was helping Cruadorn forge Karik's sword? That is he."

The great door opened soundlessly, and white light flooded to meet them.

Ingulf walked straight to a crystal stair and began to climb. Istvan and Carroll followed, more cautiously.

The door behind them swung shut.

The floor above was softly carpeted, and confusing—a maze of tapestries and corridors and growing things. But Ingulf went without hesitation through the maze, with Istvan and Carroll hurrying to keep up with him. Three staircases led upward, but Ingulf went directly to the one at the left, and began to climb.

There were three towers, Istvan recalled. This must be one. They passed two doorways. Ingulf kept on, then turned to the third.

The door opened.

Ingulf went through. Istvan and Carroll went to follow. At the door, light blinded them. Istvan felt his body pressed back, as though by a great wind.

"And who bade you hither?" the wind cried.

"The Hasturs," he answered, stubbornly pushing against it.

"Hasturs!" The wind laughed. *"Beggars! I sail the Sea of Infinity, to bear from World to World the gifts sent by the Lords of the Living Land! What care I for the Hasturs?"*

And the wind rose wildly, pushing him back. Istvan crouched, bracing himself against the wind, and his hand groped for and found the frame of the door. The blinding light turned to darkness now, and he could hear the whispering crash of the ocean. Wetness poured over his face: he tasted salt.

Suddenly, he could see again: but all he saw was waves. His heart lurched within him, but he tightened his grip on the invisible door frame.

This was illusion then, he thought, wind and water both. Another wave broke over him, salt stinging his eyes . . .

He felt his clothes still dry, and heaved himself forward. His arm felt as though it were tearing from its socket, but he held onto the frame and thrust himself through the door of the room.

His sight cleared: the waves vanished. The brown-bearded Sea-Elf turned startled eyes on him, and raised a hand. Istvan tried to step forward, but his feet would not move.

Ingulf stood facing the Sea-Elf, longing and wonder in his eyes, his mouth open in a wide smile. There was no sign of Carroll.

Falmoran held out a goblet: light pulsed through its crystal to fill the room.

"Take it!" Falmoran said, his voice music. "Your sorrows now are ended. Here is the end of your quest. Take it! Drink!"

Ingulf's hand stretched out.

"Do not drink it, Ingulf!" Istvan shouted.

Ingulf hesitated, and the Sea-Elf glared at Istvan. Blinding light flared, blotting the room from Istvan's eyes. When he could see again, the room was empty, and he could move neither hand nor foot.

Tahion and Arthfayel had seen Ingulf and the others on the steps of the tower, but when they reached the door, it was closed.

Tahion struck the portal with his hand.

"Open!" he cried, but there was no response. He looked at Arthfayel. "Shall we beg them to let us in?"

"No," said Arthfayel, "it is time they were taught a little respect."

"But can you use your power?"

"This far from the Stone I can—I used it in the Chamber of the Singing Fountain, did I not?"

Stepping to the door, he raised his staff. A moment he stood still as stone. Then he moved the tip of the staff gently over the door, until it reached the spot he wanted. Then he was still again.

Tahion set his hand on the wizard's arm, and linked minds with him to lend him aid. This was a magic few mortals mastered.

Arthfayel had sunk deep into himself, and there the power built and built: wheeling, whirling, throbbing, growing. Arthfayel's mind focused steadily on the sequence of symbols he had been taught.

Tahion focused on the symbols in Arthfayel's mind also, and let the two minds fade into one, into a single crystal clarity in which vagrant thoughts were wisps to be blown away. The four elements whirled, earth changing to air, air to fire, fire to water, water to earth again. The breast of earth swelled with air, lightning flashed, and rain poured down. Plants drank the rain and ate the soil, and breathed out . . . .

Around and around, now a stone, a wind, a flame, a wave, a tree . . .

And suddenly the focus changed and the stored power flowed. An avalanche, a cyclone, a lightning stroke, a river hurled through nerves—through wood. Bars bent. The door sagged back.

Tahion felt a stir in the tower above them.

"Come!" He strode in, Arthfayel following, a flame of wrath burning plainly within him.

No elves appeared, but on the second floor they found Carroll staggering, blundering into walls. Tahion caught the man's arm, and the still air of the tower was shaken by the power of a great wind that almost hurled him from his feet . . .

He drew the wind out of Carroll's mind, into his own lungs, and held it there until it stilled. Carroll blinked and stared at him.

"Ingulf," he said, "Ingulf is under spells—he went in—"

"Where?" said Tahion. "Where did you last see him?"

"Up there—" Carroll waved at the three flights that led up to the towers. "The left-hand stair. The third level—" He was breathing rapidly and shallowly, panic working his lungs. Tahion smoothly slid into the muscles of Carroll's chest, relaxed them, and slowed the pace of his breathing.

Arthfayel was already striding toward the stair. Tahion hurried to catch up with him. Carroll followed. As they climbed, Tahion heard a shout from above.

"Do not drink it, Ingulf!"

They hurried up the stair. The third door hung open. Istvan stood just inside, eyes staring blindly past Falmoran and Ingulf.

"What, more mortals?" The Sea-Elf gestured at Ingulf, and he stiffened into trance. A phantom ocean rose: great waves rolled at them. Tahion only smiled. Arthfayel raised his staff and rolled the waves back upon Falmoran.

"Is it a contest of power, then?" laughed Falmoran. "So be it!"

In the phantom waters, phantom heads appeared: an army of ghostly seals. They gathered around Falmoran, and Falmoran changed.

Bone and flesh shifted: Tahion sensed clearly that *this* was no illusion. He linked his sight with Arthfayel's, to be sure the wizard saw also.

Falmaran reared up as a bull seal, in the midst of a host of seals, and launched himself at Arthfayel's throat.

Arthfayel had raised more power than he had needed to break the door. Now that unused power surged up; plucked the real seal from the host of phantoms and hurled him against the far wall.

The seal struggled: Arthfayel held him pinned. But Tahion could sense the wizard's strength draining away.

The seal-shape melted, shifted. Something like lightning leaped, and pain surged through both wizards: their hair crackled and stood on end. Arthfayel staggered, but still held Falmoran pressed against the wall.

The Sea-Elf, in his own shape again, ceased his struggles. He crooned a low and wordless tune, and Ingulf and Istvan whirled together, facing their rescuers, hands on sword-hilts. The flaming blades slid from their scabbards.

Tahion knew that it was not Arthfayel and himself that the two warriors saw, but some enemy.

Arthfayel's strength was ebbing rapidly. Tahion's mind leaped out to Istvan's Hastur-blade, and used its power as he surged into the Seynyorean's mind, striking the illusion away, then flew to *Frostfire*, and flowed up the nerves of Ingulf's sword-arm to clear his sight as well.

Ingulf and Istvan straightened, surprise on their faces, then turned to see Falmoran against the wall—but the Sea-Elf's eyes sought theirs, and they stiffened again into trance.

The air around Falmoran rippled with power, and Arthfayel reeled, near the end of his strength. Falmoran stepped away from the wall. Power gathered around him . . .

"Falmoran! Stop!"

It was the voice of Ethellin the Wise.

He entered like a king, or like the master of a school of wizards come to quiet erring children. And Tahion sensed that he entered in power, with all the potency of ancient magic about him.

Behind him came Dorialith and Ardcrillon, but they were silent while Ethellin spoke. "What means this?" he asked. "What do mortals in Ardcrillon's tower, breaking his bolts and unsealing his door, and contending with his guests in magic?"

"One of my men—Ingulf, whose story you know," said

Tahion, "was summoned here by a glamour laid upon him by Falmoran the Sea-Elf. You may know better than I what lies between Ingulf and—Airellen, the daughter of Falmoran." He met Ethellin's eyes then: saw the Sea-Elf flinch. "Ingulf's companions came with him, to try and protect him, and were themselves attacked by Falmoran. Arthfayel and myself heard Falmoran calling Ingulf. We came, and the door was barred against us.

"By what right would you elves bewitch one of my men for private vengeance?" he stared straight into Ethellin's eyes, and folded his arms, waiting for an answer.

"Justice is in your words, Prince Tahion," Ethellin said with a slow nod, but his eyes were troubled. "But . . ."

"But it was *my* door that was broken," said Ardcrillon, suddenly. "And I am the Lord of Rath Tintallain! You bear yourselves proudly, you Sea-Elves, you who come from the Living Land. Falmoran, by what right do you act upon a private grudge within my halls, against *my* mortal allies?"

"The right of a father!" Falmoran said. "*You* have no daughter exiled upon the cold ocean, eating what she can catch in seal-shape, with no music but the cry of the gull! Why should my daughter's life be ruined—and why, indeed, should this man's life be ruined—because none of you can brew a potion of forgetfulness?"

"*Forgetfulness!*" Ethellin cried, angrily. "What? You would dare tamper with this mortal's mind and memory?"

"You said you would consult with me," said Dorialith, "before you laid any judgment upon Ingulf. Or upon Airellen."

"Beware, Dorialith! Do not try to twist my words so!" Falmoran straightened. "You know well that was not what I said! I thought then that I would want your council, and said so! What you had told me had made the question seem far harder than it is."

"And you think it simple now?" asked Dorialith.

"If I undo the harm done by my daughter's spell, and free him from his madness, will that not end the matter?" Falmoran exclaimed. "Then my daughter can return to the Secret City, without fear that this mortal lout will come to haunt her: he will be as he was before he met her. I will have my daughter again: he will have his mind. What harm, then?"

"Will you force her to drink, as well?" asked Dorialith.

"Did you not hear when I told you that she loves him; that she could have undone the spell herself were it not for that?"

"And how will you brew a potion for a mortal man, Falmoran?" snorted Ethellin. "You never saw one before you came here! You will have him forgetting his own name, and how to speak and dress himself!"

"Do you think me a fool?" exclaimed Falmoran. "Have I not been at watching and listening? I understand them, and their weakness! I made sure of that before I began. I am tired of fools! Wise, you call yourself, Ethellin, but you are only a child. I am far older than you—and it is I who am wiser!"

"I will not allow you to tamper with this man's mind," said Ethellin.

"Not *allow*, is it? And who are you to forbid?" snapped Falmoran. "Am I not a noble of the Living Land? Am not I, too, of the ancient blood? Who has given you authority over me?"

"Manannan gave it, and Nuadan," answered Ethellin. "And most particularly was I bidden to guard the race of men, that the tragedy of Ranahan might not occur again! I speak with their voice to all that come here from the Living Land—even to you, Falmoran! And both in the name of Nuadan, and in the name of Manannan, I forbid you to rob his memory, or bind him in any way against his will."

"Against his will?" said Falmoran. "And have you asked what his will is? Have you asked if he wished to suffer from my daughter's spell, or if he would rather go back to what he was before? You have not asked *his* will, at all! Let us let him choose!"

And before Ethellin could answer, a wave of Falmoran's hand had brought Ingulf out of trance, and the gaunt, red-haired man was suddenly glaring around, sword lifted.

"Ingulf," said Falmoran, "I am Airellen's father." Ingulf stared.

"You love my daughter, because of spells that she put upon you without meaning to. This love has brought you suffering and sorrow: there is no hope of happiness. I am here to make amends." He held out the cup. It glowed no longer.

"This has the power to cure your grief. Drink this, and forget my daughter. It will be as if you had never met."

"But beware, Ingulf," Dorialith's deeper voice cut in, "it

may make you forget more than that. It is brewed by a wild elf who knows little of men. It may make you forget the speech of men and the very face of your mother. It might leave you an infant again, lost, with no memory, in a strange world where you understood nothing . . .''

''That would be no change!'' Ingulf snapped angrily. ''Indeed, and I already lost in this evil world! I have understood nothing since first I saw Airellen.''

''Drink, then, and forget!'' said Falmoran.

''Forget?'' The larynx bobbed in Ingulf's long throat: strain pinched his face to the bones. His hand stretched toward the cup, but pulled back. ''Never to have met—Airellen?''

''You would be happy now,'' said Falmoran, ''had you not met her. You can still be. Drink!''

''No hope?'' Ingulf asked, staring at the cup. ''To forget her—never to dream of her again . . .'' His hand moved. Fingers closed on the goblet, wrenched it from the Sea-Elf's hand, and in a frantic spasm hurled it to the floor: the priceless potion staining stone. ''Give up all I live for? My one dream, my last and only hope?'' shrieked Ingulf wildly. *''No!* She is my life, my soul, my dream! She is my heart, and the desire of my heart!''

''Well, he has chosen,'' said Ethellin.

''Aye, he has chosen!'' Falmoran snarled, glaring with eyes like the eyes of a spitting cat. ''Now I go to find my daughter, and when I have found her, we shall sail together to the Land of the Ever-Living, where this loon cannot haunt her, and such troubles can touch her never again!'' He strode from the room. Ingulf covered his face with his hands.

''They will not let me live!'' he cried, his voice shrill and high as a child's. ''Why will they torment me so? Again I have chosen wrong, and they will punish me, and take her away and destroy my only hope! They trap me, they always trap me!'' The voice shrilled to a whistling squeak that grated the nerves.

Carroll pushed past Tahion and, wrapping his arms around Ingulf, pulled him against his shoulder as though he were a child, indeed. Dorialith, too, stepped foward, and laid a comforting hand on Ingulf's arm.

''It is a sad thing that has happened,'' said Ardcrillon, ''and I beg you to forgive that I could not stop it. But now this tower's door is broken, and the dragons coming. Can you mend what you have broken?''

"Alas," said Arthfayel, "I cannot."

"Then I must go in haste to the dwarves," said Ardcrillon, "that they may straighten the bolt and strengthen the door before the dragons come." With a sudden flitting blur, he was gone.

"Are the dragons so near, then?" Arthfayel asked, blinking.

"No," Istvan answered, "they fly slowly, and should not be here for at least—"

His voice stopped as a single, high, pure note of music came out of the night.

They all listened: even Ingulf's sniveling stopped.

"What was that?" asked Dorialith.

"Sir Garahis!" exclaimed Istvan. "That was his horn! An attack!"

Red light flared in the crystal wall.

They stared, startled, at this new spell. Dorialith hummed some strange, short word, and the room was dark, save for that ruby glare.

Now in the dark they could see more clearly: in a square in the wall, like a window, trees were blazing up, leaves flying like sparks . . .

"The hedge!" Arthfayel exclaimed. "The dragons have set the hedge aflame!" Again the bugle rang out in the night.

"Not so!" Dorialith said. "Do you not see the torches beyond? It is the men of Sarlow. They have come up out of the dwarf-tunnels and fired the trees."

Istvan sprang to the stair and went leaping down, shield on shoulder, blade bright in his hand.

Anarod stood at the stair's foot, with his wife's ghost pressed in his arms: Istvan almost collided with them. As he fought to balance on the step where he stopped, he glimpsed for a moment Tarithwen's face beyond the lovers.

Their embrace broke. Anarod looked up, a trace of irritation on his face.

"The enemy has fired the hedge!" Istvan exclaimed. "If you cannot come, at least let me pass!"

"I will come!" snarled Anarod. "I will be with you!" Catching the ghost-woman to his breast, he kissed her hungrily. Istvan's skin crept.

Dimly, he heard other men's feet on the stair above.

"I will be coming back!" Anarod said. The ghost-woman crooned some soft spell. Anarod gazed into her face a moment, then turned to Istvan. "Let us go, then!"

They ran down the stair to the floor below, through the door, past Ardcrillon and a dwarf—out into a night lit by the orange flare of burning trees.

"All this foolish fuss over that silly chunk of slag!" Anarod grumbled. "My cousin is right; they should throw it away! or the two of us take it, since we do not cringe as—"

A great, dark shape bounded out of the tree-shadows. Red eyes blazing, it hurled itself at Anarod's throat. Long teeth closed on the edge of his shield: wood and leather splintered and tore in the massive jaws as his Hastur-blade lashed across its eyes.

A huge piece tore from the shield edge, gripped in the great jaws as the beast fell, blood pouring.

The horn-call of Sir Garahis rose again. Suddenly it stopped. Red light outlined the squat dwarf-fort: rolling smoke glowed.

More werewolves were running under the trees. Istvan's heart sank. Did this mean the men and dwarves who had watched by the hedge were all dead?

Flaming eyes rushed under tree-shadows: leaves crackled under heavy pads. As the eyes flew up at his own, Istvan's shield rose before them, and he stabbed under it and felt his point drive deep. A shrill yelp changed to a human scream: he slashed his blade out and free, and turned to help Anarod.

Anarod needed no help. He dropped to one knee as the werewolf sprang, and his flaming blade flew in a looping arc above his head, slicing the beast in half. He stabbed back sharply as another tensed to spring: its leap spiked its throat on his point.

A third whimpered, backed away from the two glowing blades, then ran, paws rattling dead leaves.

Istvan and Anarod ran on, around the curved wall of the closed fort. Ahead, trees were pillars of orange flame, sparks swirling from them, dark smoke rolling slowly to the ground.

Through the smoke, men in mail came running.

Other men poured from the door of the fort: heroes mingling with warriors of the Ua Cadell. Istvan cursed as he saw savage women, too, rush from the door, long knives bare.

The bugle of Sir Garahis rose above the fray.

Water burst from the ground by the hedge. All up and down the row of burning trees, sudden fountains spouted from the ground. Startled cries rose. Steam thickened the smoke.

Through the stinging, grey clouds came a black metal shape, whirling a sword two-handed among near-naked men who scattered and fell back before him: Svaran in his invulnerable armour. Behind him, ranks of huge, round shields marched.

A sword glowed through the smoke. A figure sprang into Svaran's path: a wood-runner, with only the light of his sword to distinguish him from the half-naked clansmen around him.

Smoke stung Istvan's eyes as he ran at the ill-matched fighters, already foreseeing the end.

The fiery sword fell on the black helm: a frail, leather-covered wood targe met the wide blade's lashing hammer-blow.

Smoke swirled. Through it, Istvan saw it was Colin Mac Fiacron who stood against Svaran, his flaming blade flailing, harmlessly glancing from the black helm, while his light shield splintered under Svaran's heavy sword.

Rolling smoke hid them both from Istvan's eyes as he raced toward them: it parted to show Svaran's sword sunk like a cleaver in Colin's shoulder, a welter of blood and splintered bone.

Over the body, the black steel shape strode on, unhurt. Now before him Larthon reared out of the smoke, bright blade poised. Svaran's two-handed cut gonged on the Troll-Slayer's shield: practiced knees eased the shock as Larthon's shining sword sang down.

The black helm rang. The blade sprang back: the helm held, but even Svaran reeled under such a stroke, and staggered back to crash into the shields behind.

A huge wooden disk swung out like a door to let the steel shape through. A wave of shields surged toward Larthon.

Garahis, Gurthir and Peridir raced out of the smoke, hurrying to Larthon's side.

Istvan and Anarod ran to join them: Ingulf and Carroll ran up from behind. Others came rushing from the smoke: Dair Mac Eykin threw himself down by Colin's corpse, and knelt there, grieving. Starn and Flann MacMalkom raced up, shields linked. Cormac and Fergus were close behind.

Dair leaped up from beside his friend's body, and with a wild cry, raced at the wall of shields, heaving high his new Hastur-blade.

There was more coughing than shouting as the smoke thickened: the lines met with a thunder of steel on shields. The firelight dimmed as fountaining water soaked the burning trees: pillars of dense smoke shrouded smouldering orange trunks. Istvan could barely see the man at whom he sprang: but when by instinct he hurled his shield high, it boomed as a sword hit.

His blade sank into wood and stuck there; his forearm prickled with fear. He launched his shield out to cover: it rang on his arm like a gong.

The sword hilt jerked and twisted, almost pulled from his hand. He lunged forward, striking blindly with his shield-edge, and felt the buffet as a sword's flat skittered off his scalp.

His shield-edge struck wood: he hurled his weight back to pull the sword free. A keen edge whistled past his ear. His point pulled free, and he cut at the sound.

Mail jingled but held as his sword knocked an arm aside: a voice cursed. Smoke glowed around his sword: his eyes and throat stung.

His forearm whirled over his head in a flat cut: he felt a shield-rim lift his blade; but then his edge chopped into bone, and he felt the steel bend and straighten as the rising shield fell.

He wrenched his sword from the skull. Already through the smoke another huge disk loomed. Istvan drew his sword back and coiled behind his shield . . .

A sudden blast of wind nearly tore him from his feet: his shield pulled at his arm like a sail. He staggered, and saw the enemy swept helpless by his larger shield. The smoke was rolling away from around him: he saw stars and clouds in the sky. Trees blazed up.

The wild blast softened to a normal wind that rolled the smoke back through the hedge. The trees' blaze died in the fountains' spray. In the now-clear night, he could see the rough line of huge, table-sized shields that faced him, and the handful beside him; saw, a little way off, a second line facing a square of raised dwarf-axes.

In between, goblins scuttled in hordes. White, red-eared hounds chased them.

And then a bearded face looked over the helmets of the enemy before them, like a grown man looking over the heads of children; and at that sight Larthon shouted, and hurled himself at the line with such sudden violence, his sword slashing like lightning before him, that the shield-wall crumpled as he leaped toppling bodies to rush the vast form of Vor Half-Troll.

"Follow him!" Istvan shouted, springing forward, sword whirling. Gurthir, Garahis and Peridir were already moving, their swords hammering and battering the great wooden shields.

Istvan heard the booming of Larthon's shield, as Vor's giant axe crashed down. Even as Larthon's blade lashed back, he sensed the air lightening. Dawn was breaking, slowly.

Vor's shield drummed in the dim half light, every stroke louder. Maddening, the domed hollow metal of the Troll-Slayer's shield answered, booming above the din.

The shield wall shattered as heroes drove into the gap Larthon had made: the battle splintered into little scrambling fights. Stars faded: shields drummed in the dawn.

Istvan caught a brief glimpse of Vor and Larthon battering each other's shields: sun-bright sword and giant axe. But a sword-edge sang at his temple, and his own crashing shield hid the two away as he stepped and turned and slashed.

Then, as he ripped the bloody sword free, he saw Cormac on the ground, trying to rise, while a bloody sword lifted above him . . .

Istvan ran to help, but Carroll Mac Lir was nearer: his shield caught the falling sword that lashed at Cormac's neck.

Carroll sprang like a tiger: the two shields met with a clash like thunder that hurled the soldier staggering back. Carroll leaped after him as Istvan came up.

But a great, black, red-eyed shape lunged at the bard as he groveled bleeding on the ground. Istvan was there to meet it: the silver-flaming blade slashed, and the beast screamed in a man's voice.

Cormac struggled to his knees and got his shield up. Carroll's sword flew out from behind his enemy's table-sized shield, spattering blood. But other mailed shapes gathered, rushing him all together. He fell back before them. Istvan, after a quick glance at Cormac, rushed to Carroll's aid. Cormac could protect himself now; there was no more to be done until he could be gotten off the battlefield.

From somewhere nearby, Ingulf came running, *Frostfire* whirling above his head like an eddy of moonlit water. The three of them met the foe shoulder-to-shoulder.

Istvan's shield boomed; his sword flew high and ripped through the mail-rings covering the enemy's arm. A hoarse voice cursed: the sword fell to the ground. The wounded man ran. Another sword whirled down at Istvan's right; spinning, he glimpsed men fighting, and, high above all, a giant axe crash. His blade soared and swooped—he felt the edge catch. . .

As the man before him fell, Istvan saw, through the crowd, Larthon reeling in a cloud of blood, Vor's axe sunk in his shoulder.

The giant stooped, stepping on the corpse to rip his axe free, and Istvan found his tongue.

"Fall back!" he roared, shaping tones of command in his throat. *"Rally and reform!"*

Quickly, he backed to where Cormac knelt in his own blood; after a startled glance, Carroll and Ingulf joined him, and the three shouted to gather the others.

But Gurthir and Peridir rushed Vor Half-Troll: Garahis hesitated, looking back at Istvan, then followed the Easterners.

The giant's axe lashed down like a toppling tree: it split Peridir's shield. Peridir staggered back with a cry, broken arm and shield dangling, useless. Gurthir cut at Vor's huge arm: the flat of the axe hit the side of his helm and hurled him flying.

Garahis leaped in front of Peridir as the great axe whirled to fall on the helpless man. The axe blade hooked over his lifted shield rim, pulling the shield down with such force that the young knight was wrenched to his knees, while the axe rose up for a second stroke . . .

There was a sudden, blurred flicker of motion, a flash of light—and the head of the axe flew like a thrown stone across the lawns, to crash loudly against the dwarf fort's wall.

Sudden as a dancing shadow, Tuarim was there; and now the blurred flame of *Italindé* sheared off the top of the giant's shield.

Cold prickling swept Istvan's neck; his heart soared as he remembered lines from the *Song of Fendol*—

> . . . *More swift than any mortal man*
> *Tuarim, Son of Elathan*
> *Bounded in among the foe*
> *And over Fendol's head did throw*
> *His ringing shield* . . .

Vor staggered back; another huge wooden shield moved between him and the elf. *Italindé* vanished in another lightning stroke, and the top third of the shield fell away, to reveal the black-plate armour of Svaran.

The steel arm shot out, elbow first and hand and blade blurred in a whip stroke nearly as fast as the elf's. Tuarim's shield clanged and shuddered from the power of that blow; *Italindé*'s lightning glanced from the rounded helm as the elf was hurled from his feet.

He was up again and moving before Istvan could blink or open his mouth, running almost too fast to see. Again the invisible blade sprang back from Svaran's helm.

And again Svaran's whiplash return boomed on the elf's shield. Tuarim was lifted and thrown through the air.

"Dair! Stay with Cormac!" Istvan snapped. "The rest of you, follow me! Keep together!" He raced toward the fight, the others at his heels: mailed men scattered before them.

Werewolves and goblins went hurrying past, running through the twilight toward the hedge. Some of the werewolves were changing as they ran, staggering up on two uncertain legs, human features already visible through fur.

Istvan saw the dwarf-square advancing, and more dwarves came marching up out of the ground. The mail-clad soldiers were falling back, regrouping among the smouldering trees, with water from the fountains spouting all around them.

Svaran slowly backed toward the hedge, sword raised, shield ready.

Tuarim had risen to his feet, but he made no move to follow.

"Well met, heroes!" Prince Tyrin's voice called as the dwarf ranks neared. "And well fought!"

"We thank you, but there is more fighting ahead," Istvan called back.

Tuarim turned to help Peridir take the broken halves of his shield from his dangling, hurting arm. Garahis had driven his sword's point into the ground, and was using his sword-hand to support the shield. After a moment, he leaned forward, laying the shield flat on the ground, and used his sword-hand to carefully work the other free of the straps: Istvan saw him wince with pain.

Gurthir lay still, not far away. Fergus Mac Trenar went quickly to his side and knelt down.

"He lives," said Fergus, looking up. "He is breathing, at least, and I think that—"

"Murdering dog!"

Fergus threw his arms in front of his face. Gurthir's shield came up from the ground: its flat caught Fergus on the heavy muscles of his raised forearms and knocked him sprawling. Gurthir rolled toward the sword that lay a little way off.

But Istvan's foot reached it before Gurthir's hand. He stepped on the blade, then set his own point above the Easterner's throat.

"Have you gone mad?" he demanded. "Lie still! Answer me!"

"I saw him sneaking away from the battle! It was he that killed Layareh!"

"Are you saying I would put an arrow in a man's back?" Fergus snarled, reddening.

"That's no Fergus' way," said Starn. "If he'd had a reason to kill Layareh, he'd have fought with swords—"

"And then it would have been Fergus Mac Trenar lying dead!" Gurthir shrieked. "And well did Fergus know it! So he went inside and found the bow, and then—"

"Let him up!" Fergus roared, *Aibracan* flashing from its sheath. "I am not so great a coward as to kill a man so! Nor am I a liar!"

"That's enough!" Istvan roared as Flann MacMalkom's huge hand closed around Fergus' wrist.

"Be still and listen!" Flann's gruff voice rumbled. "Can you not hear the Sarlowaq laughing? Look over there, fools!"

He pointed, and as the screaming voices stilled, they heard indeed the sound of laughter. Turning his head, Istvan saw the soldiers of Sarlow laughing and joking among themselves as they formed into a line, preparing for another charge. He looked down then, and spoke.

"Listen to me, Gurthir! If I must take men out of this battle to lock you up somewhere, I will do it! I do not know who killed Layareh. Neither do you.

"Fergus did not sneak from the battle. I ordered him to go. That much of your suspicions, therefore, can be answered. For the rest—after this battle there will be time to try and find out who *did* kill Layareh—and whoever did it will pay. I will see to that! But this is not the time.

"If I let you have your sword, will you give me your word to fight only the enemy? Be quick! Their line is forming!"

Gurthir sank his face to grass, eyes screwed tightly shut. His fist clenched above the sword hilt beside Istvan's boot, then opened.

"You have the right of it!" he said. "I am sorry. I did not—I will swear—I do swear—to be at peace with Fergus, and all here, until Grom Beardless and all with him are driven from the fort, or dead. But then, I will—"

"*Then,*" a dwarf's deep voice boomed, "you will bring your charges before King Aurothror for justice. This is his city, after all!"

The speaker was Prince Tyrin: he had stood leaning on his blood-stained axe, listening quietly, but not intruding into the affairs of the men—until now. Istvan bowed, but did not yet take his foot off the sword.

"You heard," he said. "Do you agree?" Gurthir's lips were tight against his teeth, but he nodded.

"You have my word."

Istvan stepped back, and pointed his sword away from Gurthir—but did not sheathe it: already the enemy was advancing from the trees.

"You will be on the left end of the line," he said, "Hurry now, get to your place!"

"My people will take the brunt of this part of the battle, Lord DiVega," said Prince Tyrin. "We have a special grudge against Svaran the Black. That is *our* armour he is wearing. Hold your men in reserve." Istvan bowed again.

Dwarves were already spreading out in a double line between Istvan's little band and the enemy, who were moving at a slow walk out from the hedge. The light of the rising suns flashed from helms and sparkled on mail: their broad shields were lapped in a moving wall; their swords rested on their shoulders, points skyward, some flashing, some dull with drying blood.

Garahis and Peridir were led away by healers. Prince Tyrin stumped off to his battle line. Most of the dwarves in his front line bore small, round shields and short, heavy swords suited to their height; here and there among them, one leaned on a two-handed sword, or rested its blade on his shoulder. The second line was shieldless, but here were spears and axes and two-handed swords aplenty sitting on their owners' shoulders, waiting.

Istvan looked over the dwarves' heads at the slowly advancing foe. In the center of the line, Svaran stalked, black-plate armour gleaming behind the cut-down shield he still carried. On his right, Vor Half-Troll loomed behind a new shield. And the man on Svaran's left had no beard . . .

CHAPTER NINETEEN

Dragon-Fire

"Ah, look, Carroll!" Ingulf laughed and pointed. "Svaran has not forgotten you! Did you see his new sword-hilt?" Carroll chuckled. Istvan shaded his eyes, peering under his palm, and after a moment noticed that curved bars of steel or iron ran from guard to pommel, covering the back of Svaran's hand.

"What is the joke?" he asked.

"Ah, I broke Svaran's hand when last we met," said Carroll. "That is why I am here alive today. He exposes his hands recklessly, counting on his armour. He is not really a very good swordsman—fast and strong, but if it were not for that armour, he would be dead long since. When he bothers to fight with a shield, he exposes his shoulder and his arm—he cuts too far. I could not cut through his armour—through you will see scratches on his shoulder and by his eye slit where I tried—but the best steel in the world will not keep the little bones of the hand from breaking if a sword comes straight down. But those bars will." He shook his head.

Dair came running up—healers had taken Cormac inside.

Suddenly from behind came a wild, laughing screech. Turning, Istvan saw Karik Mac Ulatoc capering wildly outside the door of the fort.

A mail-shirt hung unbelted from his shoulders: a helmet held down black, wild hair. And high over his head he waved a sword, pulsing and flaring with rhythmic bursts of silver fire.

Leaping in the air, kicking bare heels together, shaking his new blade and laughing like a madman, he rushed toward them. Behind him, through the door, came Tahion and Arthfayel, glittering in hauberks, with steel shields gleaming on their arms, followed by Yolaru, swaggering in unaccustomed armour, and a long line of the men of the Ua Cadell.

"It's done!" Karik cried, between wild braying laughter. *"Now* you'll see! Isn't she a beauty?"

"She is indeed," said Istvan, watching the mirror-bright steel flare and fade as the fire in the blade pulsed with the same rhythm as the Stone of Anthir. "But I wish you'd grabbed a shield as well."

"I—" Karik's black eyes fell. "I—there was one, but I—I still do not know how to use one . . ." Istvan felt his taut nerves tense to shout at the man, and drew a deep breath and held it, then forced himself to say, gently, "Go and get it then, and with luck I—or someone—will have the time to show you. I have to teach the Ua Cadell. If not, watch me—you have seen me fight in the last few days!" Istvan turned to Yolaru.

"I fear there is little time for teaching! Line up your warriors, let them watch what I do and try to do the same."

The dwarves shouted, and with that shout the air hummed with arrows from the tower.

The great wooden shields rose, arrows drove into them: two soldiers staggered back, dying, arrows jutting from their faces.

Dwarves with two-handed swords leaped from the front rank, slashing under shields.

Legless men fell screaming: their comrades roared and charged.

Dwarf-axes shattered wooden shields. Dwarves with shields scuttled suddenly to close quarters, stabbing low. Elf-arrows swarmed above shields.

But swords could kill, too.

Dwarves died all up and down the line; and where Svaran stood in his ringing adamant armour, with Grom and Vor at right and left, piles of the short dead grew.

Dwarves swarmed there, filling the gap: not yet was the line broken. Yet, Istvan knew it would not be long. Then he must fill it—but had he, or any of the men, a better chance against Svaran then these dwarves?

Swords and axes hammered shields: death shouts rang echoing; men and dwarves roared as they killed and died.

Slowly, the dwarves' battle line bent back before Svaran and Vor and Grom Beardless: dead dwarves piled around them. Elsewhere, dwarves and men were more evenly matched, and the battle swayed back and forth.

Tahion, Starn and Fergus helped Istvan get the tribesmen into a line, and showed them how to stand behind their shields. With Fergus, he went through a short mock battle in slow motion, showing them the most basic cuts and guards. Then, facing them, he went through a simple exercise that took his sword through every plane of attack that could be done without exposing the shoulder, then turned away from them and went through it once more, hearing dimly above the metal clamour of battle the whisper of many sword edges slicing wind behind him, wondering how many would die . . .

And then there was no more time. Through thinning ranks of dwarves, the black figure strode. His shield had been hewed to his arm in places, but he paid no heed. Arrows splintered on his armour: dwarf-axes sprang back. With each stride, his heavy sword blurred and crashed into a dwarf's helm, or the head just below the helm. Its edge was chipped and broken, but it still killed.

On his left, Grom Beardless was a whirling, dancing cyclone; on his right, Vor Half-Troll swept dwarves aside with lashing strokes of a sword as long as a young tree, with a blade as broad as a board.

The steel figure's stride quickened, blade flickering like a wingbeat. Suddenly, the thin rank was gone, and Svaran, turning, struck the back of a dwarf's neck, and another step swept steel death against the helm of a second; the blade twisted in his hand and did not bite, but the struck dwarf staggered, and Grom's grim blade wheeled down.

Istvan shouted as he raced toward the black shape. Behind him, feet pounded: Starn was close at his side.

But with a bound like a panther's, Tuarim Mac Elathan was there before them. Lightning flickered from his hand.

Again, *Italindé* rang on the black helm, flickering in a whirl of cuts at the eye-slits.

Svaran's heavy blade blurred. The elf's swift-moving shield caught it; the force of the stroke threw him back. Cat-like, he landed and sprang back, the blurred flame of his blade rasping the helm's black steel.

Again Svaran's blade sent Tuarim flying: he twisted in the air to avoid a dwarf-axes's backstroke.

Ponderous armour strode rapidly after him. Another heavy blow battered him back again before *Italindé* could strike.

Istvan rushed to Tuarim's aid, then hurled up his shield as Grom Beardless sprang into his path, sword slashing.

Istvan's shield pealed on his arm as his own blade wheeled above his head toward the mailed shoulder. His edge touched mail-rings before the wooden shield pushed it away.

The other sword swooped in the blue sky, to dive at his right ear. An explosive dance step took his right heel left, pivoting his body, carrying the shield up to meet the falling edge, sword-arm swinging round, edge winging at Grom's cold blue eyes.

As his shield belled on his arm, he saw, past its quivering rim, Flann MacMalkom spring in front of the reeling elf, his sword slamming into Svaran's helmet.

Grom's shield rim brushed the Hastur-blade, sending it skimming high; his sword lashed down toward Istvan's head. Istvan's shield lifted.

Brown wood blocked Istvan's sight as Grom's shield rammed into Istvan's with all Grom's armoured weight behind, hurling Istvan staggering back.

Istvan was sure he was dead. Almost by instinct, he flailed his shield down. It rang like a bell as Grom's blade appeared and hit it, inches from his side.

Past the wooden shield's rim, Istvan glimpsed Vor Half-Troll looming, giant, bloody sword looping high.

Staggering back from the press of Grom's shield, Istvan cut over his head for the shoulder, knowing that the Sarlow men, perhaps because their shields were so large, often rolled their shoulders further forward than any civilised sword-master would allow. His sword stroked mail-rings.

They jerked away, and Grom's edge whispered near his right ear, then boomed on the gong of his rising shield.

Suddenly, the wood shield grew as Grom launched his full weight at Istvan.

Bracing himself to meet the shock, deepening the bend in his knees, Istvan laid his blade atop his braced shield-rim and crouched low.

Grom's shield was a hammerblow on the spike of Istvan's point. He felt wood give, then mail-rings spread, the softness of flesh and the shock of bone . . .

A strangled voice roared behind the shield.

There was a tug at Istvan's point, and he pulled it free. Blood oozed through the slit wood. For a hand's breadth down from the point, red smeared his steel.

Istvan cut as the shield fell away from Grom's pain glazed eyes.

The dazed eyes focused: Grom stepped back, swinging his blade to sweep Istvan's sword aside. The useless shield dangled from his arm—oozing blood coated the rings that covered his shoulder, where Istvan's point had driven through muscle into the joint itself. Grom's face twitched with pain as he let the shield fall off his arm.

Soldiers of Sarlow swarmed around him. Bleeding, Grom vanished behind the great round doors of their shields.

Off to the right, Istvan saw Flann's targe splinter under Svaran's heavy blows. Starn leaped in, a red thread running down his face.

To his left, Istvan saw Arthfayel go down before Vor's long blade. Anarod sprang to stand straddling him, and Tahion and Karik leaped to his aid.

Two warriors rushed Istvan, blades singing. His shield rocked. His Hastur-blade's point sliced through bone into the eye of a blond-bearded man.

The other was black-bearded: his face and fighting style familiar. With a chill, Istvan remembered that this man had nearly killed him once before: *Vildern,* Carroll had shouted . . .

But Istvan had been shieldless then . . .

Shields thundered under swords: each stroke matched and met. Then rings flew from Vildern's linked mail as Istvan's edge brushed his shoulder. The nearness of death drained Vildern's face: he fell far back behind his shield, blade raised, wary. A cautious and a crafty fighter, Istvan saw.

Steel crashed all around them. Starn staggered back as strokes of Svaran's blade battered his buckler to pieces on his arm: Flann, shield already shattered, sheltered behind his chief's, striking past Starn's shoulder at the steel-clad foe.

Not far away, Fergus fought three men, *Aibracan* flaming in his hand.

Karik Mac Ulatoc cried out and staggered back from Vor Half-Troll, his shield dangling, his arm broken.

Vildern's edge hissed at Istvan's face. Istvan's steel shield rang, and he shot his point explosively skyward, knowing the cautious fighter he faced would already be coiling back behind his shield . . .

Before the note of the stroke had died, he was springing to the right, his blade falling and whirling in an underhanded wheel.

He felt hanging mail-rings clog his edge, and his heart sank—then the shock of impact, metal parting, a softness of flesh. Then, above his falling shield-rim, he saw Vildern stagger, saw red stain the rent rings on his thigh, and his heart sang. Not a deep cut, not deadly or even dangerous, but enough to slow the black-bearded man and keep him from following while Istvan ran to his friends' aid.

Even as he turned, he saw Starn stumble and almost fall. Flann caught him, guarding with his sword the cut that would have split the young chief's skull, but without a shield, all he could do was fall back, guarding helplessly.

Istvan ran toward them, but Fergus Mac Trenar was closer: two of his foes were dead, and the third falling back swordless, clawing pitiously with his shield at his mangled, dripping sword-arm.

Whirling, Fergus sprang in, *Aibracan* crashing on the black helm. The force of the blow sent Svaran reeling back.

Fierce whirling blows battered Svaran, but the slick black armour held, though it pealed like a bell in pain.

Now Svaran's shield, already cut down to the size of a buckler, leaped to catch the deafening sword, and his own heavy blade leaped again, and now the shields of both men roared as the thrashing swords swayed faster and faster between them.

Even as Istvan rushed to help Fergus, Arthfayel's voice cried out behind.

"*Anarod!*"

And whirling, Istvan saw Anarod collapse across Arthfayel, his shoulder crushed and red. Tahion sprang in front of them, the dwarf-made shield on his arm tolling as he swept aside cut after cut of the giant sword, while the Sword of Kings, glowing dully, chopped away the edge of the great round shield.

Beyond, he saw a milling mass of mail-shirts, where dwarves and newly-armoured Ua Cadell warriors fought the tide of soldiers that had swept away the formation of the dwarves.

Carrol, Ingulf and Gurthir fought shield to shield among them: Dair Mac Eykin, still unarmoured, darted rapidly through the press and was lost to sight.

He did not see Calmar. Karik Mac Ulatoc, broken arm dangling, fought over the heads of three dwarves with shields who had formed a line, and were trying to rally their comrades.

All this in a quick glance, and for a second Istvan hesitated, unsure whether to help the fight against Vor Half-Troll, who seemed more dangerous . . .

Then Svaran's feet steadied. More swiftly now his blade snapped out. Fergus still caught each whiplash blow on his loud crashing shield, while his own blade whirled in a constant sequence of cuts: some drumming on the wooden shield, some clanging deafeningly on black steel.

For a moment they stood, toe-to-toe: blades flying between them. Then Svaran took a long stride forward, sword lashing as his leg moved, and Fergus reeled back.

Istvan sprang toward them, plan already in mind. He would jump between them, catching Svaran's cut on his shield, to let Fergus rest. Then the two of them could batter the invulnerable armour.

Svaran's blade whipped above Fergus' shield, and black hair and beard were soaked with blood and brains.

Svaran ripped the sword from the shattered skull.

Istvan sprang in, his point driving for the eye-slits in the rounded black helm.

The helm jerked aside. Istvan's point slid harmlessly over smooth steel, and the blurred blade whipped at Istvan's left ear. His shield thundered on his arm: the power of the blow rocked him back. Even as he moved to cut, a second whiplash stroke came.

His shield boomed and crashed. His left arm throbbed from the impact through the steel of his shield. His own blade, almost of itself, whirled down on the exposed shoulder, and bent nearly double on the invulnerable armour as he pulled the stroke through.

Then he saw that the shoulder plate on that side was already warped and dented and lined with faint scratches where swords had fallen before.

He stabbed again for the eye slits. As always, cold prickles swept over his wrist for the moment it was exposed, but Svaran made no attempt to reach the arm. The dented plate moved: the steel-clad elbow stabbed, the sword came flying out—not for the wrist as expected, but for the ribs exposed as the shield lifted.

Bent knees brought Istvan's shield down, even as Svaran's struck his point away. But the loud stroke on his shield threw him backward.

Now he saw that the black helm, too, was covered with fine silver scratches.

A sudden stillness filled his mind. Even while he guarded with his booming shield, part of him sat rapt in contemplation, like an eagle hanging motionless in the sky, studying those bright lines, while around him the ghostly battle clamoured.

One was far deeper and wider than the other: a groove at the centre of several scratches that pointed to Svaran's right eye slit.

Like an eagle wheeling, his blade swooped above his head, and his edge stroked the length of the groove with a rasping sound.

His shield-arm was leaping to catch Svaran's sword: the battering blows still bore him back. But with each stroke, Svaran pressed his face into the continuing whirling movement of Istvan's sword, and the edge slid again and again through the groove.

Then Svaran felt the danger: the wooden shield rose, and Istvan's edge suddenly twisted and skittered as wood splinters cushioned it, pushing it up.

He glimpsed Starn and Flann running by. Svaran's blade ceaselessly battered and hammered his shielded left arm. Bell-like, the rounded helm knelled as Istvan's Hastur-blade glanced across the steel skull.

Back and forth the swords flew, flickering in sunlight despite the dark-brown, dried blood stains.

Beyond Svaran's helm, Istvan caught glimpses of Vor

Half-Troll's huge sword rising and falling. He tried cutting low to draw the shield down, but Svaran ignored him. Invulnerable leg armour clanged; the splintered wood of the shield was still in place when Istvan's edge swept at the eye slit.

Would the man's shield-arm never tire? Istvan could feel his own muscles slowing, wearying. Svaran's quick cuts kept his shield leaping, booming.

A sudden shadow flitted beside him: a blade blurred to a lightning flash lashed above his own as Svaran's booming shield fell, and *Italindé* rasped through the groove.

"Fall back now," said the voice of Tuarim Mac Elathan. "Fall back, and I will finish him."

"No," Istvan answered. "It will take us both." His blade lashed just above the rising shield and rasped on metal. As his arm wheeled back, *Italindé* was a flicker of fire, a translucent spiral.

Svaran's shield lifted higher, hiding his eyes, while his whiplash steel hammered Istvan's shield-arm. Istvan began to feel pity for the man who was trapped inside that black, nightmare suit of armour.

As the sword drew back, Istvan followed with his shield, and pressed against the arm.

"*No!*" a shrill voice screamed, hollow in the helmet. "*You're* supposed to die! *Not me!*"

The shield fell away. Istvan's sword stroked along the groove, and suddenly reversed in a thrust as it left the steel, through the eye into the brain.

The armour twitched: the dead weight collapsed against him. He stepped smoothly back, and his point slid free.

"Ah, very good!" said Tuarim, but Istvan was not listening. His gaze had flown across the field, where Vor Half-Troll's tree-long blade lashed like a branch in a storm.

Tahion was reeling, weary though unwounded. Gurthir and Dair Mac Eykin came running. Behind them, the injured Arthfayel still cradled broken, bleeding Anarod like a child in his arms.

Vor was bleeding from a dozen rents in his mailed sleeve. At his heels were stacked dwarf corpses: a handful of his men guarded his flanks.

Dair, bare hide red-streaked, staggered back, dazed—arm and buckler broken by a stroke of the tree-long sword.

Tahion's long swing only sheared another chip from the

chopped shield-edge. Vor Half-Troll's voice roared with laughter as the massive steel flew.

Starn and Flann MacMalkom were hurrying toward the fight. Istvan followed, Svaran's blood still dripping from his point. Tuarim sprinted past on feet as fleet as skimming birds; and dancing on past Starn and Flann, raced to where the swords were hammering.

Istvan slowed, breathing hard. Deep within, his body cried: *Let the Immortal Hero, then, rush on to deal with Vor Half-Troll! Was not killing Svaran deed enough?*

His eyes swept through milling mailed ranks, to see who was still alive. A faint shimmer of moonlit frost hinted at Ingulf, but he saw neither Carroll nor Calmar. He saw Dair and Karik fall back together, their broken arms dangling.

Garahis and Peridir and Cormac had all gone wounded into the fort . . . Everyone else he could remember was dead. He forced himself into a run. Above reeling foes, Vor loomed like a bear.

Tuarim sprang into the air. His sure feet lit on Vor's shield rim, *Italindé* whirling in a wheel, but before it touched the grim killer's face, Vor's arm violently shook the shield, making Tuarim reel as Vor's long, sharp sword cut. Tuarim leaped above the steel, to land, balancing valiantly, on the shield edge again.

Tuarim stood, but the giant shook the thin wood more, and turned his arm to make it spin, making the elf miss with *Italindé*'s edge. Tuarim sprang down from the shield, and at once Gurthir lunged in past the shield edge, slashing at the throat, and Tahion cut high with the Sword of Kings. Vor leaned back, his huge sword lifting, as Gurthir's point snickered through his beard and jingled mail-rings on his shoulder.

The Sword of Kings sank quivering deep into the giant shield of wood. Then the giant's sword snapped down, and Gurthir's helmet broke beneath it.

Cruel laughter rumbling loudly, Vor ripped his blood stained weapon free from Gurthir's corpse, while Tahion tugged at his trapped sword's hilt.

Istvan ran. Starn and Flann, nearer, got there first. But Tuarim Mac Elathan had landed on his feet, and now *Italindé*, like a lightning-flash, slashed through the wood that trapped the Sword of Kings.

The wood crescent fell against Vor's chest. Tahion reeled

back, his sword, suddenly freed, pulling him back with its swing as Vor's heavy blade drove into the ground where he had stood. Tuarim sprang for the cut shield-rim; Starn MacMalkom hewed at the giant's shoulder.

Vor twisted free; the flat of his shield sweeping up caught the elf in mid-air and hurled him flying, stunned. Starn's edge sliced mail-links and skin from Vor's shoulder as it twisted from under the stroke, whirling the great blade up.

Vor's sword fell, driving deep into Starn's body. Flann shrieked and leaped: his elf-sword slashed through Vor's blade, cutting through the steel and leaving the hilt useless in Vor's hand.

Flann leaped like a panther at Vor's throat. Vor dropped his shield and used his left hand to grab Flann's sword-wrist. For a second, the two glared into each other's eyes: Flann's face twisted with pain and grief, Vor's with a sneering smile.

He surged erect, pulling Flann's feet free of the ground, and squeezed and shook the smaller man's sword-wrist. Flann opened his hand and let his sword fly: but his other fist clenched on Vor's wrist.

Istvan, running up, set his point against Vor's side.

"No!" Flann rumbled, "He is mine!"

Vor stared, then gave a grunt of pain. Bones ground in his wrist, and the hilt fell from his hand.

Flann suddenly twisted around, swinging his legs out. Vor tottered. Flann's feet touched ground, and he hurled Vor over his hip. The giant sprawled, stunned: Flann knelt on his chest, and his left hand flew from wrist to throat.

Then, more slowly, his right hand dragged Vor's arm down.

"Back!" a harsh voice shouted. "Back to the tunnels! Retreat! The dragons are coming!"

Flann's right hand joined his left on Vor's throat. Vor's eyes bulged: his free hand struck at Flann's face.

"Fall back!" the harsh voice shouted; and now another voice, lighter, joined it, shouting through the hammering of steel.

"Run, you fools! The dragons are coming now!" This time Istvan looked up. Vildern Blackbeard leaned on the uninjured shoulder of Grom Beardless, just beyond the blackened row of soaked and smoking stumps. "The dragons are here!" Grom shouted.

Mail-clad figures began to back out of the battle, backing toward the hedge behind the hacked remnants of their shields.

"Hurry, you fools!" Vildern's harsh voice croaked. "Run, or you'll be cooked!" And with that, they both turned, and Vildern hobbled off, leaning on Grom. The mailed mass swayed, and the soldiers of Sarlow surged out of the press, hacking at dwarves and men who followed.

Vor's face darkened and his eyes bulged. He thrashed frantically and, with a wild surge, twisted under Flann, hurling him off his chest. His rolling shoulder knocked Flann's hands away from his throat: he heaved up on his hands and knees . . .

Flann planted a knee between Vor's shoulders, and wrapped his hands around his throat again. Vor struggled; Flann wrenched up and back. With a crack like a snapping stick, Vor's neck broke.

The soldiers of Sarlow backed into the fountains and between the black stumps. The Ua Cadell raced after them, whooping wildly. Deep, dwarf-voices shouted.

A red light glowed atop the eastern cliff.

Grom Beardless lifted Vildern from his feet and ran, carrying the armoured man like a child on his hip. Other soldiers, turning, shouted at the sight of that light, and ran. Some threw down their shields.

The rank that was still falling back in order turned and ran, too. The wild men of Ua Cadell leaped in pursuit.

"Let them go!" Prince Tyrin's voice shouted, and Tuarim's chiming voice echoed the dwarf's, weirdly.

"Let them go! Save yourselves! Get underground, or inside!"

But many of the Ua Cadell still ran, slicing at the backs of the fleeing men.

Grom reached the stairway and ran down, still carrying Vildern on his hip. Other mail-clad men raced after him.

A fountain of fire rose above the cliff.

On each side, something lifted into view, and vanished again. Istvan was startled by what at first seemed a homely sound. Like strong winds among blankets hung out to dry. Like the flapping of sails in a ship's rigging . . .

Again the fiery fountain was framed by heaving, vast shapes that rose above the cliff on either side.

Tahion was trying to lift Arthfayel. But Anarod, incredibly, was not quite dead. He coughed blood wildly, pitifully, and then coughed words with the blood—

"Promis—Arthf—" Blood spattered from the mouth.

"I swear it!" Arthfayel's voice was broken with weeping. "He shall be as my own son!" A weak smile came over Anarod's bloodied lips: the face stiffened; the eyes rolled up . . .

The fountain of fire split in two.

Something like a great, glowing log appeared at the cliff's edge. Two huge knobs, each larger than a man's head, glowed with brighter flame. Behind them twitched two gigantic, triangular stalks as long as swords, and between them, beyond the glowing saddle between the knobs, what seemed a sword blade rose.

Two smaller knobs came into view, each spouting fire. Between these knobs and the others was a bridge large enough for two men to walk abreast, but floored with a bed of coals.

Gigantic wings rose and fell, with a crash like sails.

The great flat face lifted, ears twitching. Istvan opened his mouth to shout, and found he had no air in his lungs, and his mouth was dry. But other voices were shouting . . .

The glowing head lifted above the wall: fire hid the gaping jaws. The great wings crashed: dark wings like bat wings that reached from end to end of the cliff . . .

Then the fire-golden serpentine body, tiny between those vast wings, wafted over the edge of the cliff, little legs dangling.

Voices were screaming and shouting. The men of Sarlow were running toward the stairs leading down. Dwarves were dragging the body of Svaran away. Arthfayel wept over Anarod: Tahion pulled him to his feet. Blood ran down the wizard's leg.

"*Back!*" Carroll's voice was shouting. "Back to the fort!"

With that, Istvan came awake: shame filled him. He had never seen a dragon before, but that was no reason to stand gawking like some lout from the provinces on his first service . . .

Ua Cadell warriors still pursued the fleeing soldiers, hurling javelins and striking at their unprotected backs with well-sharpened dwarf-blades.

Ingulf gasped at Istvan's side.

"Look there!" He pointed, high up. Istvan looked. Another dragon circled, high above the towers. How high it was, he could not be sure. How big it was, he could not be sure.

But with a cold chill he was certain that next to it the winged serpent that had flown over the cliff would seem tiny, indeed. . .

"Komanthodel!" he said.

"Indeed it is!" said Tuarim Mac Elathan. "Follow me, now!" And he was rushing, like a cloud scudding across the sky, swifter than a bird . . .

Suddenly, a handful of the soldiers of Sarlow whirled on their tormentors, hurling up a wall of their great shields against the Ua Cadell. Men shouted: steel clattered and glittered between them.

The dragon at the cliff's edge saw. With a rapid, supple twist of its body, a lash of its tail and a flourish of hundred-foot wings, it swerved, and swooped on swords and men. Men screamed and scattered.

Flame flared from its jaws. Men screamed as white-hot-mail-links burned their flesh. The great wooden shields were charred black. But behind them, men lived. Those who threw down their shields to run, died.

The others backed behind their shields to the seeming safety of the stair.

The tiny, dangling legs stirred, lifted paws like hands, and landed on the palms. The swaying neck lashed out and back in a serpent's strike. One scream stopped short, and a full-grown man hung like a mouse from the great jaws.

It threw its muzzle skyward: flame flickered eerily while great teeth crunched metal.

And there was still red light rising at the east wall.

"Back to the fort quickly," Tahion exclaimed. "Yolaru! Get your warriors inside! Come along! Flann! Arthfayel,—Flann—"

Flann rose from his knees, holding Starn's broken body to his breast as tenderly as a mother with her child. His head was bowed, and tears fell from eyes filled with a hurt beast's despair.

Jets of fire appeared at the cliff's edge.

"Flann," said Tahion, his voice filled with pity, "leave him now. There are not enough of us to carry all our dead, and you know well that the elves will—"

"We know nothing of what the elves will do!" Flann snarled. "But I never expected to hear you lying to me so, Tahion Mac Raquinon! Look there, and tell me that the dragons will leave one bone unpicked when they come over the wall!''

The dragon had lowered its head and was muzzling the burnt, armoured skeletons that lay all round it. A leathery tongue licked as Istvan watched, and a blackened mail-shirt and steel dwarf-shield and sword all vanished with the bones. Istvan blinked. Did the beasts truly eat the metal?

Suddenly, with an incredibly swift motion, it had put its long snout down into the hole where the men had fled. While it had eaten, its huge wings had folded and folded again along the veined fingers, until they seemed bundles of rods wrapped in black and laid along the body.

The head went all the way into the hole, and suddenly, quick as a ferret after rats, the red-gold rope of the long body slid glowing into the hole, and was gone.

There was a wilderness of grief in Flann's dark eyes.

"And even without that," he said, "what rest will he be having here, so far from his fathers and his land? I must take him home, to rest in the tombs of his fathers!" Istvan and Tahion looked at each other, helplessly. The big man was mad with grief . . .

"Flann," said Tahion, gently, "it will be a long way to your home, and—"

"Fool!" snapped Flann. "Do you not see Kandol Hastur-Lord, standing atop yon tower?"

Carrying the corpse in his arms, he turned and trotted away, even as two more winged serpents rose above the cliff edge, scales glowing like red-hot iron, hunger flaming in their eyes.

"To the fort!" Istvan shouted.

"Run!" Tahion added, lifting Arthfayel from the ground again with a last, sorrowful look at Anarod.

With a loud *clang!*, steel doors snapped shut over the stairs that led down into the dwarf-town. Water burst from sudden fountains at their feet. They staggered as the cold spray hit their eyes.

On the far side of the fort, trees burst into flame. Tahion reeled. Fiery beasts darted through the air, trailing fire, hundred-foot wings fanning the flames . . .

From above came a hissing, croaking roar, and a blast of fearful heat. Rhythmic bursts of wind buffeted the tops of their heads, and Istvan, blinking cold water from his eyes, looked up to see the burning gold belly of a dragon overhead, forepaws dangling like tiny hands, great wings blotting out the sky on either side, rising and falling as the monster climbed.

As one of the great wings lifted, he saw another dragon circling beyond.

Ingulf turned to face the dragon, *Frostfire* glinting in his hand.

"Aye, fly away, evil animal!" his voice raged. "Evil, murdering animal! I'll not run from you more! You'll not destroy me without a fight. *Frostfire* and love will destroy you surely!" He waved the white blade high. Carroll caught his arm, and after a moment the madman turned and trudged sadly through the fountains toward the fort.

Ahead, the surviving Ua Cadell were swarming through the door, but Flann had turned aside and was trotting around the wall of the building, toward the flaming trees beyond. Istvan watched him run through the cold spray, and shivered. Hurrying, he caught up with Carroll and Ingulf.

"When you're inside, go to the other door," Istvan said, "and be ready to open when I—when we come. I'm going after Flann. I'll try to persuade him to come back inside."

"I'll come with you!" said Ingulf, but Istvan shook his head. One madman at a time was enough.

"No, you stay and help Tahion," he said, and hurried off before the islander could answer.

Ahead, Flann had vanished around the curve of the wall. Istvan raced after him, wondering if perhaps he was crazier than Flann—or Ingulf.

Here were more fountains. Water soaked him. Ahead, he saw a forest roofed with flame. Fountains were soaking the trunks of the trees, but the leaves still burned, and the higher branches. But the Tumbalian trotted on, his chief's body in his arms, ignoring the fire as he ignored the water.

Smoke rolled down from the burning roof: the constant spray of water made a mist all about him. Istvan hesitated, then raced after the big man.

"Flann!" he called. "Turn back now. Bring him into the fort. The dragons will never let you cross the garden alive. . ."

"And what of that?" rumbled Flann, looking down at him.

"Do you think there is any wish to live in me? Turn back yourself!" He trotted on, Starn's head bobbing. Istvan hesitated, looking back at the safety he had left behind.

Great wings beat above the flaming leaves. Through a gap, he saw a red-gold dragon settle on the domed roof of the fort.

Smoke blotted it out, but he heard it roar. Another roar answered, blending with it. Smoke and flame blew away for a moment, and he saw the dragon on the roof, and then the head of another lifted over the dome . . .

Smoke hid them again. It rolled all about him. He slid his sword free, not sure what use even a Hastur-blade was against a fifty-foot winged worm, and then plunged into the smoke and mist after Flann.

Through the smoke he saw him, but it was hard to see. The flaring roof glared the eyes when mist and smoke did not hide it.

Then he saw another figure, a pale, slender shape that sped between the trees.

"*Anarod!*" a woman's voice cried—a voice that sang— and through the rolling clouds of smoke, the slim shape sped up to Flann.

He stopped in surprise, and Istvan saw in the lurid light of the fire above them a rosy, blue-eyed face, crowned with yellow hair, but drawn with suffering.

"*Anarod?*" the voice cried, and she looked down into Starn's dead face, and touched it with slender hands.

"No, it is not he!" she said, and her face came up again— but now it was a pale and slender face, with wide elf's eyes, and when she whirled, a cloud of dark hair spun around her.

"*Anarod!*" she sang. "*I am coming! Where are you?*"

"Anarod is dead!" Istvan called, as the graceful figure glided past him, through smoke and flame . . .

The ghostly shape did not stop, but a cry tore Istvan's heart, both too beautiful to bear, and too filled with sorrow.

She dashed on and vanished in mist and smoke, but her lonely voice came floating back, singing above the roaring crackle of burning leaves.

"*Anarod!*" she sang. "*Are you dead now, truly? Anarod! Is she with you? And now, has your sorrow left you?*

"*Anarod! Has your sorrow left me?*"

Istvan realised that Flann was far ahead of him now, and he turned from staring after the voice to catch up. But as he ran, he still heard her song behind, slowly growing fainter. Leaves roared overhead.

> *"And now, there is only Brithlain:*
> *Brithlain, whom you never met, never saw:*
> *Brithlain, whose name you never heard.*
> *Ah, what will become of me now?"*

The roaring fire drowned the words, but still he could hear the song, her high voice keening like some wild bird. Burning branches fell hissing into the spray around him: a burning leaf singed his wet hair. Smoke and mist blinded him as he ran. The unbearable loneliness of her voice faded slowly into the roar of flame.

Through the dense fog, he caught glimpses of Flann, and blundered after him through the smoke.

The smoke thinned—the flame-roofed wood was coming to an end. He blundered on, and wind blew smoke aside. He saw sunlight ahead, sparkling on a field of leaping water: Ardcrillon's garden was filled with spray.

He looked back over the burning wood. Beyond it he saw the dome of the fort; dragons coiled there, others circled.

There were fountains every few paces, all across the top of the hill, it seemed, and the dragons did not like the water . . .

Flann strode though rising showers, his dead chief's body cradled in his arms. Istvan followed.

Suddenly, between the branching towers, his worst fears rose up alive, as brazen, glowing forms looped and twisted like giant, red-hot worms, and lashed the air with ponderous, beating wings.

Istvan ran to Flann's side, wondering what harm his puny sword could do against such things.

One winged snake lifted into the air, beating pinions echoing.

Istvan and Flann ran for the tower's shut door. They dashed through spray up wet steps.

A flare of heat dried the clothes on their backs and the steps ahead of them. Istvan whirled, and brought up his shield.

This dragon was smaller than the other: its head like some huge chest. Its great wings beat, holding it hovering above the water.

Flame flared. Istvan hurled up his shield to meet it. Steam rose all around: Istvan felt heat that made him cringe. Cold water washed away the worst: hot mail would have cooked him like meat, had he not been cooled by the fountain's spray.

Wing-wind rocked him as the beast swooped to seize its prey. Staggering in water, he struck wildly, blindly with his blade.

A bell-clear voice chimed as his steel struck stone-hard armour: the trumpet-trill of Tuarim Mac Elathan.

"Inside!" the elf sang. *"Swift, now, Flann!"*

Istvan staggered back, steam and water blinding him. Blinking, he saw the blazing worm coil warily, wings cupped and spread . . .

Lightning lashed across one leathery wing. Tuarim twisted away and sprang over the crippled wing onto the dragon's back as a flare of fire dried his footprints.

Istvan ran in, slashing at the bent neck as the dragon twisted its head around, blowing flame across its own back. Tuarim leaped high, above the flame and above the looping neck. Istvan staggered back as fiery blood like molten metal gushed from his cut: the dragon's bellow hurt his ears. Tuarim landed on his feet by the dragon's wing shoulder, and lunged with *Italindé*, stabbing deep.

Great wings throbbed in the sky.

"Quick!" Tuarim shouted, springing away as white-hot heart's blood spouted. "Run for the door now! Get inside!"

Istvan turned and ran through jetting water. Tuarim sprinted past him in a blur. The door opened: Tuarim stood waiting. Then, as Istvan reached the door, the elf blurred away, and Istvan heard his shrill war-cry ringing behind. Whirling, he saw a second dragon come down on the steps themselves. Tuarim leaped over the fire that hissed from its mouth, and plunged *Italindé* into its eye.

Roaring flame, the dragon reared: Tuarim leaped in under its clawing foreleg, stabbing deep.

He sprang up the steps to Istvan's side, and was pushing Istvan through the door even as white-hot blood seared the stone where he had stood.

The door closed, and two dwarves lifted a heavy iron bar and laid it across.

"My thanks," muttered Istvan to Tuarim. He looked around

for Flann. Elves surrounded him, staring with huge, beautiful eyes. Walls glowed with white light: great transparent squares showed dragon-fire, and the flaming woods outside.

Flann was already halfway up the stair, still bearing Starn's body in his arms. With a muttered apology, Istvan slid through the silent crowd.

As he dashed up the steps, he became aware of another behind him: a quick glance showed Tuarim Mac Elathan, following like a shadow.

At the top of the stair the walls vanished, and it was as though the ceiling floated above them, with only the slender stairways to hold it up. Between roof and floor he saw only sky, and dragons flying, the distant dome where dragons crawled, and the burning tops of the trees. Here bright-eyed elves sat silent and subdued on soft pillows and chairs, watching lava-red dragons in the blue, while flowers bloomed around the room.

Flann hesitated only a bare moment, then took the right-hand stair.

Istvan followed, wondering at Flann's stamina as the stair wound up and up, until his own breath dragged into aching lungs, while Flann, burdened though he was, bounded ahead.

As Istvan climbed, he became slowly aware of pain on the back of his sword-hand, and looking down, saw the skin red and the hair singed away, and realized that the dragon's heat had seared him when he had cut at it.

Pain does not hurt, he told himself, *fear of pain hurts,* and he put his mind on the business of climbing this stair.

The steps seemed endless: they climbed and climbed. Istvan had known the tower was tall, but it was only now, with aching feet winding around this rising spiral, that height meant anything . . .

At last they came out in the sky: forest and fortress spread out below, and the backs and the shadows of dragons. The red roof lifted on a pierced crystal stalk: a walkway around it crowded with elves. The roof glowed with red light: it seemed a single piece of red crystal stone.

Kandol Hastur-Lord brooded over the parapet, chin resting in his hand as he watched the dragons circle far below.

Nearby, Ardcrillon stood and stared down intently, and beside him Arduiad the Archer, and another elf Istvan did not know, his face as like Arduiad's as one bluebell is like another, but as much like Ardcrillon's as two flowers on one stalk. All three held bows as they stared intently into the smoke and flames below.

Flann strode to the Hastur-Lord and laid his chief's corpse at his feet. Kandol looked down, compassion in his face. But Istvan saw no trace of the pain he had seen earlier.

"We obeyed your summons, lord," said Flann, "we have done your bidding. Here lies my master, all hewn down, young and good, put to sleep by the sword."

Aldamir Hastur appeared out of the air, his round face troubled.

"We have done your bidding, lord," said Flann, "but I do not understand. Why did you call us here?" His face twisted. "What good have we done here? Why did you summon my master to his death?"

"In truth," said Kandol, somberly, "we did not summon your master at all. We asked him to let you come. It was his own pride that called him here." He sighed, and shook his head. "We could not forbid his coming. But what would you have us do now? We do not trouble the dead. There is nothing we can do to help Starn MacMalkom now."

"There is something for you to do!" Flann snarled. "You can bear him and me across the miles to our home, that I may lay him to rest among his fathers, in the tombs of Clan-na-Malkom. You owe us that much, surely. And my work here is done."

"Done!" cried Aldamir. "How can you say your work is done with the Stone still in danger! On path after path of the future, I still see the Stone in the hands of the Council of Sarlow, or, worse still, of Komanthodcl!" The young Hastur shivered. "Now, with the dragons upon us, we need your strength! This is no time to abandon us! We count on you!"

"Count on Tuarim Mac Elathan," said Flann. "I am no dragon-slayer!"

"Yet you slew S'thagura."

Flann frowned, pondering.

A sudden shout from the strange elf who stood beside Arduiad drew all eyes.

"There she is!"

"I see her, Father," said Arduiad, raising his great bow.

"Courage, Brother!" said Ardcrillon.

Istvan stepped to the parapet and looked down. The elf had pointed . . .

Then, among the fires and the fountains below, he saw someone running.

He could see little more of the runner than a dark cloak spread on the wind, the little figure moved so swiftly through the smoke and the fountain's spray.

But a circling dragon saw it. It stretched a dark wing and dipped sideways, and fell into a swooping glide downward.

Arduiad's bow came up.

His bowstring strummed swift as harp strings, loosing shaft after shaft in the air.

Other elves' bowstrings were humming too: their faces tight-set. The swift shafts flew.

The brightly burning dragon dived toward the runner below. It suddenly swerved in its steep path. A hole had been torn in its wing. It fell from the air like a wounded bird, struggling and fluttering its one sound wing.

The little figure ran on. Swift as it was, Istvan sensed it staggering, as though it carried a heavy burden. Peering down through the smoke and spray, he saw that it carried another in its arms.

Through guarding spray in the garden it ran, to the steps where the dead dragons sprawled. And always Arduiad's bow was ready, and he leaned far out over the parapet to watch the door.

"Artholon," said Ardcrillon, "put away your fear. Brithlain is safe now."

"Soon she'll be here," Arduiad added.

"S'thagura was no dragon, for all the bard's lies," Flann rumbled, his voice avalanche-deep and harsh after the sweet chiming voices of the elves. "It was but a bird bespelled, grown by some sorcerer's magic to monstrous size, and trained to hunt men. Were my chief alive, I would fight for his sake, but now the heart is gone out of me. Have I not fought enough? I fought in your war! Did I not kill goblins and men? Did I not lay my sword in the fire when the *Tromdoel* was coming? What more need is there for me here?"

"Now our greatest need is on us!" Aldamir cried. "Now on path after path I see the Stone taken by the dragon—by Komanthodel—and of the futures I have seen, that I dread the most."

"Why?" Flann scoffed. "What good would the Stone be to such a beast?"

"Komanthodel is no beast." Aldamir shook his head somberly. "Do not be fooled by his shape. His mind is as keen as my own. Or did you think there was no room for brains in a skull the size of a house? If only they were but beasts! Then we could control them! But they are proof against our magic. Do you not see now how greatly we need your help?"

"I do not!" Flann said. "Now even more, indeed, do I feel myself useless and lost. Neither strength nor skill is in me to fight such creatures! You have power: the greatest heroes of the elves are with you—what need have you for me?"

"We cannot even—" Aldamir began, but Kandol's voice cut him short.

"Leave be, Aldamir!" The Hastur-Lord stepped to face Flann, and met his eyes calmly, as one man to another. "You have right: burial with his fathers is the least that we owe to Starn MacMalkom." As he spoke, there was a sudden flurry by the door of the stair. Turning, Istvan saw a slender, black-haired girl spring through the door. She looked as frail as a flower, but she carried Anarod's poor, hacked body in her arms.

Kandol paid no heed, but went on speaking.

"And a safe journey home we surely owe you. Lift Starn up, now. You must carry him." Grief twisted Flann's face, and the dried tracks of tears around his eyes were flooded anew as he lifted the corpse of his chief from the floor, and cradled it tenderly against his chest.

The elf-woman staggered under Anarod's weight: her face, too, was wet with tears. Artholon pressed toward her, Tarithwen and Arduiad close behind. She knelt before them, laying the broken body down. Her voice was wild with grief, yet even so, sweet as music—

"Father! Oh, Grandmother! I loved him! I loved him!"

Kandol placed one hand on Flann's shoulder, and the other on Starn's body.

Aldamir had turned to stare, brooding, over the wide forest. Suddenly he started as though stung, stepped behind Flann, and laid one hand on top of Kandol's on Flann's shoulder, and reached to take the other . . .

. . . And the air was empty where they had stood.

Istvan blinked, then looked around. He *was* used to it, after all, he reminded himself. No need to stand gawking like a provincial.

But no one had been looking at him. The elf-woman still wept over Anarod's body, while Tarithwen, her face torn by pity, all glamour gone, knelt across from her and reached a hand to her shoulders.

"Oh, Daughter," she groaned. "It is hard with me that I put this weeping upon you! Better for me to have given him myself for his healing . . ."

"What is this?" asked Artholon. "Why do you say—Mother! Is it that—?"

"Leave her be!" the girl flared, sitting up, eyes flashing through the tears: her beauty chilling, wild. "Are you not her son? And are you not the one who was saying that we must make our magic to help these mortals and not for our own pleasure? You should be proud of me—or do you think there is pleasure for me, knowing this man Anarod never knew I existed, never knew I was not his dead wife! Yet, I could have made him forget her! I could have made him as mad for me as Ingulf is for Falmoran's daughter!"

And at this, Falmoran himself appeared, looking down at her.

"Do all tongues have this story now, in this World, then?" he asked. "Well, we will both be out of it soon." He sighed, and looked down on her. "But do not think me cold. I grieve for your sorrow, so close to what my own daughter has escaped. Indeed, you are much like her. But mortals die, daughter of Artholon. It may be no comfort to you now, but sooner or later this would have happened, and at least you have no more to sorrow for than these few days of your life. The longer he had lived, the harder it would have been to lose him."

"Yet, if I must live upon memories, is it not a pity there are so few?" The girl's voice was bitter. "Only a few days, when I could have had years to look back on! It is cold comfort you offer, whether *you* are cold or not." She shook her head, scattering tears from her face. "Yet, at least for a time, I have his child to nurse . . ."

Falmoran looked at her strangely. Istvan, embarrassed at finding himself in the midst of a family quarrel, was edging around the tower, but their voices followed.

"But surely," said Falmoran, softly, "it would be worse for you if you had been together longer. You will forget—"

"It is too late for that!" sobbed the girl. "But it is not of myself that you are thinking, but of your own daughter, Airellen!"

Falmoran stared.

"It is foolish you are, girl!" he snapped, drawing himself up and turning away. "You do not even know my daughter!"

To Istvan's great relief, Kandol returned. Istvan went to join him at the parapet.

"Is it foolish I am, old elf?" she laughed. "Listen to him, Grandmother! It is a wise elf who would bear his daughter away to the Living Land, with the heart gone from her empty breast? Oh, he is filled with wisdom, filled with mercy!"

Kandol looked down at the domed dwarf-fort below. More dragons had settled on the dome: they writhed over the roof, drooling fire down the walls.

Others had settled in the clear space below, where the three towers split. They writhed around the bases of the towers like glowing worms. Others still circled.

"It is a young girl full of opinions you are," said Falmoran. "My daughter is dearer to me than anything in this world—or any world!"

Only the wounded dragon, whose wing Arduiad's arrows had ripped, still flopped wearily on the ground among the acres of fountains that sparkled in the sun.

"They do not like water," said Istvan.

"No," said Kandol. "It would kill them, eventually, cooling the molten stone of which their flesh is made. But that takes a long, long time. Indeed, the dwarves have the right idea, but they must have help."

He turned away from the wall, and blue robes flickered into being there. Before they vanished, Istvan recognized Herstes Hastur and Earagon Hastur, but they were gone before he could make out more. Kandol turned, and looked down again upon the dome.

"The elves called up a storm, almost by accident," he explained, noting the question in Istvan's mind, "when they raised their magic against the *Tromdoel*. The storm is still there, but it has been allowed to drift away. We will bring it back, and feed it clouds and moisture from the sea. We can make it rain for days, or months, if need be. That will drive them away—in time.''

Istvan watched the dragons crawl like bats on the fort's roof. The fire of their breath rolled down the walls.

''That will not help my friends trapped in the fort there,'' he said. ''It must be getting hot inside.''

''Oh yes,'' said Kandol. ''The dragon-fire will poison all the air, too. They will have to retreat down the shaft that leads to the Chamber of the Stone, and down into the dwarf-city.'' Istvan stared at him.

''But lord,'' he said, ''that passage was sealed! Ardcrillon ordered it blocked with stone! Did you not know?''

Now Kandol stared.

''*Ardcrillon!*'' he shouted, whirling. ''*Come here!*''

The Elf-Lord obeyed, meek as a dog.

''This mans tell me—and I see in his mind it is true—that you have bricked up the passage between the dwarf-fort and the Chamber of the Stone. What means this?''

''Why—'' Ardcrillon was plainly taken aback. ''I believed that if we closed the hole, the Stone would be more safe—''

''Fool!'' Kandol exclaimed. ''Now the heroes we brought to guard the Stone are trapped! Send at once for Aurothror. The hole must be opened and the men let free!''

''I will go now!'' said Ardcrillon, and in a blur of running, dashed down the stairs and was gone.

Istvan looked out over Rath Tintallain, and saw more dragons circling beyond the wall. He began to count them. Behind him, he heard Tarithwen's voice suddenly raised; never, he thought, had any woman scolded in so sweet a voice.

''Listen to him, the great elf, filled with knowledge; but little of grief—or women's hearts!''

Istvan had gotten up to twenty-six dragons by this time, and now another flew into his sight—but far higher, far larger than others—old Komanthodel himself . . .

There was a sudden blur, and Tuarim Mac Elathan sprang up onto the rampart and stood balancing there easily, *Italindé* flaming above the drop.

''Komanthodel!'' the elf shouted. ''Do you remember this sword?''

The answer was a sheet of flame.

Istvan shrank back, scorched: Kandol Hastur-Lord was

suddenly on the wall beside Tuarim, his arms around the elf
as fire washed over them.

Washed over them, but did not consume them. For an
instant they stood in the heart of the flame, the Hastur's face
rapt in concentration while he absorbed the dragon's flame
into his own need-fire, then both vanished. Hands seized
Istvan and pulled him away.

Arduiad Mac Artholon was dragging him to the tower's
door. Kandol and Tuarim had reappeared there. Artholon and
Falmoran were shepherding the women through. Tarithwen
and the girl were dragging Anarod's corpse. Istvan sprang to
help them.

"Inside!" shouted Kandol. "All of you—yes, you too,
Tuarim! Quick now! Inside!" shouted Kandol. "He comes!"

Then they were all on the stairs. A bellowing roar made the
stone around them tremble.

Kandol stopped and spread his arms wide, just above shoulder level.

"Down the stairs!" Kandol shouted. "This stair will be
dangerous—the tower will be rocked and shaken when he
strikes, but it will not break while my power holds! Get down
the stairs!"

The Hastur rose in the air. Istvan, staring, for a moment
half sensed lines of force running from the Hastur's hands to
the walls—beams of power, bracing the stone around them . . .

"Let me remain!" Tuarim cried. "I defied the dragon in
order to draw him within reach of my sword. I will—"

"He will not come near your sword!" Kandol snapped.
"He will try to bury you in the rubble of this tower! Go! I
must remain: my body at least must stay above the field. It is
bad enough to reach down through the walls—hold fast! He
comes!"

The tower rocked. The steps flew from under Istvan's feet.

He pulled his knees to his chest and made his body a ball,
and then, somehow, struck out with his feet and found himself standing on them again, swaying. Anarod's corpse rolled
down the stairs: the girl sprang after him, her long dark hair
flying like a cloak behind her.

"Brithlain!" Artholon shouted, following.

"Down the stairs!" Kandol shouted. *"Quick now!* I have
summoned my kinsmen to brace the other towers. Hurry!
Ardcrillon has built well, but had I not been here, Koman-

thodel would have snapped off the top of this tower like a twig! Make haste! He is turning to come again!''

Istvan bounded down the steps. A door opened before him; Artholon was helping his daughter lay Anarod's body out in the room beyond.

"Come, Brithlain," he said as Istvan ran past. "Come away now."

"No!" she sobbed. "No, Father. I want to stay with him!"

"Do not stay, Daughter. Come with me now, Brithlain. Hurry! He will be safe enough here!"

The stairs rocked. Istvan caught hold of the door, and held on.

And now the crystal throbbed with the voice of the dragon—a roaring, deafening bellow, that hummed in stone and bone.

Then, mingled into that thundering rumble, soundless words roared in all their minds.

"DIE!" the mind-stunning silence shouted. *"Fall Stone! Shatter and Break!"*

"These stones shall stand!" answered another silent voice in the calm tones of Kandol Hastur-Lord.

The tower swayed like a tree in the wind, and even the elves fought for balance as the steps writhed under them. When the dragon's bellows ceased for a moment, they heard a distant rattle of thunder, but then the dragon drowned all out again.

They staggered down the stairs while the tower trembled with the fury of the dragon's attack. Istvan used all his training to keep his feet, and twice bruised his shoulder against the wall.

At last the steps ended. Istvan sprang from the reeling staircase and managed to land, swaying, on his feet. Dozens of pairs of wide elfen eyes dropped, stared at him a moment, then rose again to the ceiling. Istvan looked up.

The glowing, red-hot scales of a dragon's belly met his gaze.

They were flat against a roof Istvan could not see: the long, tapering fingers on the clawed hands were spread out, palms flat.

He saw in wonder that the roof had faded, and walking out from under the belly of the dragon, he saw past it the tall towers swaying, and the wildly beating wings and lashing tail of Komanthodel.

The lesser dragon that coiled around the tower flattened itself against the roof as its furious parent battered the tower above with wings and tail.

Istvan stared in awe. The towers were reeling back and forth like masts on a ship as the dragon's monstrous weight hammered them, and he knew that they would have broken, had it not been for the powers of the Hasturs.

Komanthodel turned in the air: the great wings flapped and the dragon soared into the cloudy sky. In the sudden silence, Istvan heard Brithlain weeping. A quick glance showed her kneeling on the floor close by, looking back up the stairs, while Artholon stood beside her, looking helpless, and Tarithwen conferred with the three Sea-Elves.

Lightning flashed. The distant shape of Komanthodel wheeled in a sky rapidly filling with clouds, and came diving back at the towers.

The great head drove between two of the towers: his shoulder struck and the roof reappeared as the whole building rocked. Istvan was hurled to the floor. The dragon's angry roar throbbed in the stone.

Again the roof faded. The towers still stood, though they swayed back and forth like reeds in a high wind.

The great wings rose and fell, battering the towers while angry roaring swelled. The dragon flapped back from the towers and circled. Then it arrowed away, with a final, ear-splitting bellow.

In the sudden silence, Istvan heard a familiar voice from the floor below.

''. . . from these evil animals!'' the shrill, wild voice of Ingulf the Mad raged. Turning, Istvan saw the red-headed scarecrow figure striding up the stairs from the floor below, with Carroll and Tahion behind. He had stripped off his mail, and wore his shabby tartan robe again.

Suddenly Ingulf froze, staring, his foot on the top step, his face filled with hope and terror . . .

"Airellen!" he gasped. "Airellen! Why do you weep?"

He was staring at Brithlain, who sat with her back to him and her long, dark hair draped about her.

Just then the dragon on the roof stirred and stretched its wing.

The movement drew Ingulf's eyes upward. With a wild shriek he ran toward the girl. *Frostfire* flew gleaming from its sheath.

"*Airellen!*" he shrieked. "I come!"

Elvish laughter rippled through the room, and even Istvan felt his lip twitch, even though he felt sick with pity.

Dorialith called to Ingulf, but the madman paid no heed. Instead, he sprang to the stairs and began running up.

"Stop him!" cried Dorialith. The roof became suddenly solid again, but Ingulf did not stop. Carroll and Tahion ran after him.

At the top of the stairs, Ingulf turned, and clawed at a door there.

It opened. Ingulf dashed through. Istvan leaped after Tahion and Carroll and sprang back onto the staircase he had escaped with such effort. At the door of the room, he collided with Tahion. Before them, across a richly furnished room, they saw an open door, and beyond it the islander, running straight at the red glow of the dragon's side.

"Evil beast!" Ingulf shrieked. "You'll not harm her! It's destroyed, you'll be!"

The dragon whirled. Istvan and Tahion cringed back as a sheet of flame met them at the door. But Ingulf had leaped to the side as the fifty feet of molten stone had turned, and now ran in under a neck as thick as an old oak log, both hands locked on the sword hilt above his head.

Frostfire's moonlight gleam flashed beyond the red glare, and suddenly the dragon's head twisted as the elf-sword chopped through the spine and more than half the neck.

A flare of liquid fire spattered over Ingulf's sword-arm: his robe and hair caught fire. Ingulf screamed.

The cut neck swayed toward him, fiery blood flooding out. They ran, knowing full well that, before they could reach him, the dragon's molten-metal blood would have poured over him . . .

A figure blurred past them and sprang to Ingulf's side. One of the Sea-Elves, Istvan saw: Dorialith, he thought, come to protect the islander.

The flames faded from Ingulf's arm and hair, and the Sea-Elf caught the madman up in his arms and darted back through the door. They turned back, saw the bearded elf lay the islander down on a comfortable bed. A rich voice crooned some swift spell, and the islander's screams and struggles stopped, and the elf looked up.

It was only then that they saw that Ingulf's saviour was not Dorialith, but Falmoran.

CHAPTER TWENTY

The Peril Within

For days, Calmar and Tahion laboured over Ingulf's burns, while rain hammered down steadily outside. Istvan shuddered as they struggled with the pain.

On the second day of the storm, the tower rumbled with dragon-voices. The elves made part of the wall and ceiling transparent. Dragons came flocking, settling like vultures around their dead kin on roof and step, tearing at the bodies until they had stripped the stony flesh from great metallic bones, and gnawed those, as well as molded piles of hardened metal blood.

"Well, you dwarves should get some good out of that," said Falmoran to Cruadron. "It is said that the greatest of the Swords of Power are forged from dragon's bone. Dragon's blood, too, they say, can be forged into strong steel!"

"And what spells would be needed," asked Cruadorn quickly, "for the forging of such a sword?" And for hours they discussed smithcraft then, while outside the dragons gnawed the bones, and finally flapped back to their perches on the roof—except for the dragon Arduiad had wounded, who crawled through the rain and the fountains' spray, flapping his one good wing, dragging the other. Idly, Istvan counted twenty-eight dragons.

But these were only the lesser dragons, the children of Komanthodel. The great dragon himself was nowhere to be seen.

"The Hasturs say he is near," Dorialith said later when he came down to look again at Ingulf's burns. "He is in the forest, waiting for us to grow careless, perhaps." Only the three Sea-Elves and Tuarim ever came down; the bottom floor now was left to men and dwarves. Dwarf healers came to add their skill to that of Tahion and Calmar, while craftsmen tinkered with the lock Arthfayel had broken. The folk of the Ua Cadell were being housed in the dwarf-city: they were too frightened of the elves to enter their tower.

Fithil was able to hobble around now, leaning on a stick. Arthfayel's wound was more serious, but he would have been up had Tahion allowed it. Cormac kept to his pallet, playing the harp until Istvan thought he would scream.

> *"Ranahan rode out one fine summer's day,*
> *Down by the windy sea-strand:*
> *And there he met the hosting of elves*
> *As they came wading up to the land.*
>
> *Where do you come from, Elvish King?*
> *How long in this world will you stay?*
> *From the Land of Life with no sorrow or strife*
> *We come to drive the Dark Things away."*

Tuarim taught the song to the harper, and though Istvan liked the song the first time he heard it, he grew to dislike it long before Cormac had the entire thing by heart. Still, there were compensations: hot baths, good food, and time to sleep.

Hrivown was slowly mending, but still slept most of the time. Garahis still had his arm in a sling, for though his shoulder was back in its socket, the muscles and ligaments had all been torn. Yet he seemed likely to recover before any of the others. But Ingulf's burns were horrifying, although Istvan knew they could have been far worse—would have been, had not Falmoran rushed in. A small patch of skin on the forearm had been charred and would scar badly: the rest of the arm, a sizable section of ribs and neck, and a thin strip in front of his ear were raw and blistered.

Dwarves told them goblins still prowled the lower levels of

the dwarf-city, but only in small bands that attacked lone dwarves, but fled from any organised resistance.

Carroll, growing restless in the confined space of the tower, joined the dwarves who went to hunt the goblins down and rid the city of them. He was gone for two days, then came back with a tiny scratch on his sword-arm.

"Killed three," he muttered, rolling himself in his blankets.

For five days, the injured dragon flopped through the rain and the fountains, dragging his wounded wing.

On the sixth day, all were wakened before dawn by a chorus of hoots and hisses that made the tower shake.

Again, elf-magic made a window in the crystal of the tower, and looking out, they saw a dozen dragons flame in darkness as they fluttered to the ground and gathered around the injured one.

For hours, then, hooting and honking and groaning rang through the tower's walls, while the huge dragon heads swayed back and forth on their long necks, as though they spoke in council. Watching their long necks bobbing made Istvan think of a flock of geese. At last, after hours of debate, they fell upon their wounded brother and devoured him, while he struggled and hooted piteously.

The next night, a sudden, crashing shock hurled them from their beds. The roof above them writhed as the whole hall shook. From the floor above came screams and shouts. Istvan rolled to his feet, his useless sword flaming in his hand, and ran to the stair's foot to shout—but then all sounds were drowned in a roar, and a silent voice chanted in his mind.

Crack Rock! Walls Fall! Down, Stones! Kill All!

Another silent voice answered.

Stone Stands, Kandol Hastur-Lord's calm mind replied, *Walls Whole! Power Holds Tower's Mold! Strong Crystals, Woven Well, Spoil your Spell, Komanthodel!*

Give me the Stone! Komanthodel's mind roared. The towers swayed and rocked. *Give me Anthir's Stone and I need serve your enemies no longer! With the Stone I can be free! Give it to me! Give it to me!*

For a moment the dragon's bellowing stilled: the building ceased to sway . . .

Go home to your cave, Komanthodel. Kandol's thought was sad. *There is no help for you here.*

A bellow of rage rumbled through the walls. Istvan, from

the foot of the stair, saw through the clear roof, far above, the great glowing wings lash, and was prepared for the crash when it came. Walls and roof rocked as he walked back to his blankets, sheathed his sword and lay down. The walls shook with the dragon's rage.

"So that is why he wants the Stone!" said Karik. Calmar gave a low laugh.

"Well, that—and so that he may rule all the rest of us, and eat us when he pleases! Oh yes, the dragons resent the power the Dark Ones have over them, never doubt that! But do not think them any kinder than the Dark Lords, for all that!" The dragon's roaring went on as he battered at the towers above their heads.

"Istvan?" Tahion's voice said. "You cannot really be asleep, with that dragon shaking the walls and trying to knock the whole place down?

"No reason not to try," said Istvan without opening his eyes. "If Kandol Hastur-Lord cannot hold the tower together, nothing can, and certainly not my staying awake worrying! I lost enough sleep last week! And we may still have to go without before we go home again. So I may as well sleep if I can." Tahion chuckled. Istvan lay in the dark behind his eyelids, forcing himself to breathe slowly and ignore the fear that clawed with each new shock.

Toward dawn the shaking stopped, and the dragon's roaring drew slowly away. Then Istvan slept, indeed.

"All this fuss over that silly chunk of metal!" Calmar said the next day. "Why do they not take it further from Sarlow? Perhaps we could help them."

"Indeed," said Cruadorn, who was working on the lock, "that is what Prince Tyrin has been saying, is it not?"

"It is," said Thubar, who had also come to try to rebuild the broken lock. "And now King Aurothror has come to agree with him. They have spoken to the Hastur-Lord, and so, most like, we will take the Stone south to Dunsloc when we return. After this is all over, and the roads are clear again."

"Indeed?" said Calmar, an odd note in his voice. "Well, it will be further from Sarlow there, right enough! But it will still be in the Forest of Demons. Would it not be safer in the Three Kingdoms?"

"It would not," a new voice said from the stairs, and looking up they saw Dorialith descending, coming to see

Ingulf. "That would be foolish! It would not make the Stone safe, but would put the Three Kingdoms in danger! The Stone would break the net of mind by which the Three Kingdoms are protected: it would be like a flaw in a sword, or a weak link in a shirt of mail."

"A dangerous thing to guard," said Calmar.

"Why do you go to the trouble?" Istvan asked. "Why not throw it in the sea, or bury it—not merely in earth but in stone, so deep that no one would ever dig it up? It's no use to anyone! None of you can use it!"

"None of *us* can use it, no," said Dorialith. "But some day—some day, some day, the one will come who can use it. . ."

"Use it for what?" Carroll asked.

"For the purpose for which Anthir made it," said Dorialith. "To pass through the Dark World to reach Hasturmina—Astrimna, I believe men call it now, Hastur's Lost City—and to recover Hastur's lost Ring."

Carroll frowned; so, too, did many of the others.

"I remember the legend," said Carroll, "but it never made much sense to me."

"When Hastur's Brooch," said Dorialith, "was stolen from the Tower of Carcosa by a mortal—"

"Rethondo DiSantos," said Istvan.

"Ah yes, I had forgotten the name," said Dorialith. "He stole the Brooch and pried out the gems to sell them: that broke the spell that held the Dark Things from the World.

"The Eight Dark Lords attacked the Hastur-Cities, and the sons and grandsons of Hastur fought them. They drove them from Carcosa and Idelbonn and other cities, but Astrimna was surrounded and—taken away. One of the grandsons of Hastur escaped to bear the tale. But the city was cast out of the universe, or partly so."

Dorialith paused, stroking his long, fine beard.

"Or partly so," he said again. "Deep in the heart of the Forest of Demons, beyond the Dragon Wastes, the place where the Lost City stood is sometimes only a great dome of darkness, a hole into the Dark World. And yet, sometimes, it is said, the towers of Astrimna can still be seen; and it is believed that in some strange dimension beyond that hole, the ancient city sleeps untouched, still protected by the Ring. Yet no Hastur who has attempted to pass that barrier has ever returned.

"There are times," Dorialith went on, "when we elves see brief glimpses of things to come—so indeed do men and dwarves alike. But we have foreseen—both Ethellin and myself—that if the Ring of Hastur is ever recovered, it will be by the use of this thing. Who will use it, and when, and how we will know when the right person comes—these are mysteries to us still."

"And when the destined person comes, you will no doubt guard the Stone against him as well!" exclaimed Calmar. "Perhaps *I* am the one destined to use the Stone! Will you give it to me?"

"Not without great thought and care," said the Sea-Elf. "Be sure that the Hasturs and elves would be long in council over that, and the dwarves too!" Calmar made no reply, and then then Ingulf woke, moaning with pain, and Dorialith went to help Tahion calm the islander, and soothe his pain and put healing balm upon him.

But Istvan noticed Calmar's brooding face, and when he looked over at him a moment later, he saw that he had risen and was at the door of the tunnel that led to the Chamber of the Stone.

Istvan rose and followed him into the maddening, throbbing pulse of the Anthir-Stone.

Dwarves passed them in the corridor: healers bringing salves and bandages, and others with food—for Aurothror had ordered his people to make sure there was other food for them—Ingulf in particular—besides the apples and nuts and milk that the elves provided. And when they reached the stair that led down to the Chamber of the Stone, Istvan saw that there was a strong guard of dwarves about it. The pillar of fire no longer flared against the roof, but rose into the smoke-filled fort above. Calmar smiled at him, but Istvan sensed something else behind the smile.

"Not much for so many men to have died for, is it?" Calmar said, waving his hand at the throbbing pattern of light and dark down below. "You had the right of it—it is not good for much."

"It gives me a headache," Istvan said. There was surprise on Calmar's face.

"Does it now?" he said with a smile. "Is it true, then, as they say, that there is Hastur-blood in the Seynyoreans?"

"Hastur-blood and elf-blood, too, in my line," Istvan

coughed, as the scent of dragons came from above. "But it's not as though I had powers, or anything of that sort. There have been seers and wizards in my family, but I always thought myself the most ordinary of men." Calmar grunted and turned back up the corridor.

Later that day, Istvan went up to the second floor. The elves there were in merry mood, dancing wildly to Oranfior's piping. Istvan, looking through the clear patch of wall, could find only fourteen of the dragons.

Still later in the day, dwarves brought word that several dragons had crawled into the opened tunnels in the cliff broken by the *Tromdoel*. Tuarim Mac Elathan, already fretting in his captivity in the tower, was wild to seek them out—but the only way into the dwarf city led through the Chamber of the Stone.

The next day, dwarves bringing food found Tuarim Mac Elathan unconscious on the stairs leading down into the Chamber of the Stone. When he came to himself he was very weak, and complained that his head throbbed with pain like waves of the sea. But he denied that he had tried to get past the Stone, saying that he had only meant to go partway, but had been overcome before he realised how close he was.

Meanwhile, the music and laughter on the floor above grew louder and wilder. Tahion shook his head.

"I am thinking that perhaps we should all move down into the dwarf city," he said. "It is in such moods as these that wild elves are most dangerous, and most careless of mortals."

"Is it an old woman you are, Tahion?" Carroll snorted. "Can we not hear music without your dithering about the danger that is in it? Move down with the dwarves yourself, if you have such fear on you!"

"*I* am in no danger!" said Tahion, sharply. "I have lived among wild elves for many years, and my own powers are enough to counter their magics. It is *you,* Carroll, who should beware!"

From the floor above came the sound of bagpipes, wild and beautiful, that wove disparate melodies into a blended splendour of sound, then, suddenly, sped into a rapid dance tune. Carroll shook his head.

"A mother hen you are!" he snapped. "Do you think I've never been among elves?"

"I do not think you have been among them enough to have

learned respect for their powers!'' Tahion answered. "Look at Ingulf! You call him 'Loon,' and pity him, and treat him like a child. What will keep you from becoming as he is?''

"Why—'' the big man blinked at him, and shook his head, "a man with his wits about him, and a strong enough mind, can always see through illusion! Ingulf—''

"Ingulf's mind was as good as your own, before this came on him!'' Fithil pushed himself from his blankets. "Better, I would say, indeed, listening to you! But I knew him well. His father is a master swordsman of my own school, the Wheeling Gull School, and so I learned to know the boy when he was young. There was no weakness in his mind then.''

"But he knew little of elves, by his own admission,'' Carroll said. "And I know at least enough to beware of the elf-women!''

"Do you now, Carroll?'' They all started guiltily, for it was Ingulf's own voice that broke in upon them. The islander lay still, and did not try to move, his eyes were feverishly bright, but his voice was steady. "And how would you do that, if one of the women up above decided to make you fall in love with her?''

"I know my own mind!'' Carroll answered angrily. "I would know! Then, I would come to Tahion, or seek out the Hasturs. Or I could even go to the tunnel yonder, and let the power of the Stone drive the illusion from me!''

"Let us hope you are right,'' said Tahion. He turned away from Carroll and went to Ingulf.

Later that day, there were a dozen dragons left on the roof of the dwarf-fort, and by the next day there were only five. The music and gaiety in the tower grew wilder still. Tahion went down to the dwarf city and spoke with Aurothror.

The next day the last dragon flew from the dwarf-fort's roof, and Tahion called them all together.

"The time has come, I think, for us to return to the fort,'' he said. "Leaving aside other reasons, I think Ardcrillon, our host, will be happier—''

"And why would you say that?'' sneered Carroll.

"Because Ardcrillon,'' said a deep, booming voice, "for all he will be hospitable, and polite, does not truly care for the company of mortals—whether men or dwarves.'' Turning, they saw King Aurothror standing at the tunnel's door.

Behind him were a dozen others of his folk, including Cruadorn and Prince Tyrin. "We are, after all, *cruder* than he. I have known him since I was a child, remember! Not all elves are like that, but Ardcrillon is terribly . . . fastidious, and none of us can ever be—clean enough for him."

There was an angry murmur at this. Tahion raised a hand for silence.

"So," he said, "any of you that wish may remain, but Aurothror tells me that the fumes of the dragons have cleared away now, and these dwarves will carry men back at least as gently as you were carried here—more gently, most likely, since there will be less haste upon them."

"Well, it is the best exercise I am like to get for a while," said Hrivown, who was awake, though still too weak to move. "At least there'll be a different roof to look at!" There was laughter at this, but Finloq rolled to a sitting position, and then, slowly, with Alphth's help, struggled to his feet.

"I do not think that I will go," he said. "I think, Prince Tahion, that you can see why. You know much of wounds, Istvan DiVega. Have you ever seen one heal as quickly as mine?"

Istvan considered carefully before he spoke.

"Vampires and werewolves heal faster. So do the Hasturs. But ordinary mortal men—no—except for once, when the Hasturs were doing the healing, and put forth all their power."

"So, it would seem then, that I am not truly one of you. And in truth, I dread being carried through the Chamber of the Stone. So, since it seems that the elves are to be my people, I had best become used to them."

"And I will stay with him, I think," said Alphth. "These are still my people, the only friends and kin I have ever known. And though I must go out into the mortal world, it will be hard for me, and I will be glad of this time with my kin."

The music from the floor above grew wilder and more gay. Cormac looked up with longing.

"It would be the height of folly for *me* to stay, I suppose. Still—" he sighed, "—still, I cannot play my harp here, and if my fingers—ah well . . ." He shook his head sadly.

Istvan put on his mail-shirt while they talked.

"It will not matter whether I go or stay," said Ingulf, his voice spiritless. Tears were in his eyes. "Airellen will not see me, will not come to me, even though I saved her from the dragon . . .''

"*Loon!*" cried Carroll. "*I* have told you, and Tahion has told you, and Falmoran himself, that it was not Airellen that you saw . . .''

"You are all trapped in this evil world," said Ingulf, sadly.

Istvan lifted his shield from where he had leaned it against the wall, loosened the buckle on its long strap and slid shoulder and head through, to sling the shield on his back. Buckling it tight across his chest, he walked toward the tunnel where the dwarves stood. They made way for him.

"Well, now!" laughed Carroll. "What's your hurry?"

"No hurry," said Istvan, turning around in the door. "But everything I own is over there, so I thought I might as well put this with it. I'll see you when you get there, I suppose, or when I get lonely and wander back; whichever." He turned away, and walked on down the hall's throbbing light.

The air in the fort was indeed still bitter and smoky with the dragon scent, like the scent of a forge, but mixed with some strange smell—a vaguely tarry stench, unlike anything he had smelled before, that made him cough. Rain drummed on the roof.

The hall that had been so dim and gloomy was bright now, lit by the pillar of fire from the Stone. The great domed ceiling mirrored the light throughout the vast room, and Istvan understood why gem cutters and sculptors had once loved to work here. There were still beautiful statues in odd places around the hall.

It was considerably sooner than he expected that he heard voices below, and going to the irregular hole in the floor where the dwarves had torn out part of the stonework that had blocked the old round entrance, stepped down into the throbbing light and waited on the stair, seeing by the pulsing flare at his back the long files of stretcher-bearing dwarves in the crystal corridor. Carroll walked by Tahion, but a frown was on his face.

Istvan went back up the stair. Very soon afterward, bustling dwarves came carefully carrying their charges up through the jagged hole.

An hour or so later, Tahion and the dwarves were still busy

getting the wounded men settled and comfortable, when Istvan heard a sudden, new noise from outside. He stiffened.

Carroll heard it, too, and they both moved toward the arrow slits beside the great door that looked back toward Ardcrillon's tower.

Long before they reached the window slits, they were sure that it was a wild screaming of voices they were hearing, but they were not sure whether the voices screamed in terror or in joy.

Suddenly, a strange light crept over the wall, veiling the harsh flicker of the flame that came through the floor, and sudden vines and flowers twined over the stone.

''Ach! They've started again!'' a gruff dwarf voice grumbled behind them.

Then a wild burst of elf-music, rapid, fluttering, filled the air—a wild mingling of instruments. And out of the flowers that bloomed in the stone came whirling tiny winged figures that darted everywhere, gamboling and spinning in the air, and their singing blended with the music.

Come out! they sang.

> *Come out and see!*
> *Come out and see our Victory!*

Drolly comic figures somersaulted across the floor.

> *Far, far away the dragons fly!*
> *Come out and count them in the sky!*
> *Rain and the fountains' spray*
> *Have made them fly away,*
> *So now we dance and play . . .*

Trumpets bugled triumph. Istvan pressed his face against the arrow slit, and saw through the trees the doors to Ardcrillon's tower wide open and brimming with light, and everywhere rushing white bodies danced and laughed and pointed at the sky.

Drawing back, he caught Carroll's eye, and the two of them stared at each other, silently.

The flowers that had covered the walls were changing hue, shifting, crawling, spinning. They began to glow, to cast off the vines that had held them floating free, and suddenly the room was filled with stars.

"Well," said Carroll. "Let us go and see!"

They threw aside the monstrous heavy bar, and drew back the complicated bolt, and opened the door onto night. A clean wind smelling of fresh rain blew in to sweep the dragon scent away. Cold water met them driving in their faces.

But the elves seemed to mind neither the rain nor the fountains that still spurted all about as they danced and sang, moving almost too quickly to see.

Tuarim Mac Elathan came dancing up, and Arduiad with him, and they laughed wildly, and pointed up into the clouds. Istvan had to blink cold water from his eyes before he saw what they pointed at.

Strung in a long line across the night sky, the dragons glowed against clouds that reflected their fire as they flew, and softened their ruddy glare with a misty blur.

In that long string, Istvan counted twenty-seven dragons.

Trumpets sang golden triumph in the icy rain. But, Istvan wondered, was it victory? He looked again, blinking cold rain from his eyes. Twenty-seven dragons, but none was spectacularly larger than the others.

"Come!" cried Ardcrillon, leaping past them. "Let us feast now! You too, mortals! Come, share our joy!"

The cold rain did not seem so bad now. He must be getting used to it.

White bodies leaped and spun in the rain and the spray, light-footed, beautiful: leaping wildly, almost too fast to see. Music swelled triumphant around them.

The warm, pleasant rain began to glow with a golden glory, as though the water had caught fire, or as though sunlight shone through it. The elves were rushing all about him, and he and Carroll were caught up in their rush, moving with them. Other men too: he saw Garahis for a second, his face bright with wonder, and then Brithlain Ni Artholon moved between them, and a dozen other elves he did not know, whirling in a wild dance. He smelled flowers all around them, the smell of Ardcrillon's rose garden that he had seen withered by dragon's breath and too much water, and with the large patches where the dragons had trampled it into mud while they had torn the bodies of their dead apart . . .

He had seen all this, and yet now there were flowers everywhere—flowers with faces, and great blue-and-golden eyes that watched him kindly, laughing . . .

The golden glory brightened, and Istvan knew suddenly the danger they were in. He seized Carroll's arm.

"Carroll, *wait!*" he cried. "The wild elves—they already have hold of our minds. If we go with them, feast with them— already we are in their power, inside their dreams. . ."

Carroll twitched his big-muscled arm out of Istvan's hand with a snort of contempt.

"You've been listening to all those womanish tales! Is it a mouse you are?" He laughed. "Run along to your hole, little mouse!"

His scornful laughter brought a surge of anger to Istvan's mind. That helped. He looked back, trying to see the dwarf fort . . .

All he could see now were sparkling fountains of golden glory, and flowers, flowers everywhere. Even the clouds had erupted into gold . . .

Where was the fort? They had been on one of the stone walkways that ran from it through the little wood—all blackened and leafless now. He stamped his foot, but felt only soft grass. He looked around, trying to see. But the fountain's spray had thickened to gold-glowing mist.

Elves crowded around him, child-eyed, laughing. Carroll strode gleefully ahead in their midst, but Istvan forced himself to stand stock-still, while the stream of laughing elves parted and flowed past. He could feel the music plucking at his muscles, beckoning, caressing . . .

Its beauty tore at his heart, but he stood firm, holding himself against the sweet compulsion, until all the elves had passed; then he bent down and felt the grass with his hands. Could not even touch be trusted?

He looked around wildly, but nothing met his eyes except grass, and flowers that sang and watched with tiny eyes. He sat down. Little winged people came out of the flowers and fluttered around him, singing, their voices a tiny, chiming chorus.

He pulled off one boot, then another. Perhaps his feet could find the stone of the path, and find his way back . . .

Singing roses changed colour all around him. The golden mist began to change, with creeping washes of other tints . . .

He crept, spread arms and legs over the ground, like a spider, feeling with fingers and toes.

He drew his Hastur-blade and stared at its need-fire, hoping the flame would wash the illusion from his mind. When that did not work, he set its point to the ball of his thumb until he saw blood welling. But there was only the slightest throb of pain. He sheathed the sword again, and went back to groping across the grass. The golden mist was all around. He could not see Ardcrillon's tower any more than the dwarf-fort. He should be able to see the throbbing light that came up from the Stone of Anthir . . .

As he thought of that, some of the glory faded. He fastened on that, and forced himself to remember the Stone, remember its hateful throbbing, and the sickening bands of dark that radiated from it . . .

His groping foot found hard, cold smoothness where his eyes saw only grass. He crawled to it, dragging his boots with him.

He crawled onto wet stone and stood, tentatively. A little cloud of singing lights swirled around him, beckoning, red and blue and green. He stamped his bare foot hard on the walk. The singing of the roses faded: the pain jarred their harmony. Stubbornly, he stepped backward, away from their beckoning.

After a few steps, the flickering colours of the mist began to fade. He turned around, then, and saw dimly through transparent, enchanted beauty the black bulk of the building he sought.

He staggered toward it. Roses called him back. Transparent green fog pulsed with dawn-red sparks, dancing, calling, summoning. Stubbornly, he forced his feet on.

The phantom building was right before him now. He threw himself at it: sharp pain shot through his shoulder, and then the door flew open and he was falling through, into the throbbing, painful light of the Anthir-Stone. Tahion and Calmar and the dwarves looked up at him. A voice moaned something slow and strange, like a long song sung on one note, and then many voices joined . . .

"Tahion!" he cried, his voice sounding strange and wild in his own ears. "The elves—the wild elves! They have Carroll—they put an illusion about us—" He paused. Tahion was moving toward him—but so slowly and so strangely. And the faces of the others—they writhed, slowly moving from one expression to another, but so slowly. Tahion's legs bent deeply as he walked on his toes, and he rose in the air and drifted down . . .

"What are you doing?" he cried. "Are you mocking me? This is no time for foolishness!" Tahion had reached him, and now his arms stretched out, so slowly, and his palms moved toward Istvan's face, as though to slap both cheeks in slow motion. Istvan jerked his head out from between them. Tahion spoke, and his voice was strange and deep, each word slowly chanted—

"*Iisst-vann! Lisss—senn too mee!*" His hand groped slowly for Istvan's face. "*Youu arre un-derr spelllss!*"

"I know that!" Istvan snapped.

"*Eye cann not Uunderr Sstaannd youu!*" the strange voice said. Tahion's head turned slowly to the left, then back slowly to the right. "*Toooofasst! Youuumusst'ssslow downn! Breeeathaaaaahsssssloow leee ahsss youuu cahnn!*"

Breathe slowly. That, at least, made sense! His breath must be rattling in panic—

But no! As he became aware of his breathing, he realized that it was slow and laboured. He was fighting for air! He realized that there was an ache in his chest, as though it was squeezed by a giant hand . . .

His heart, too, was beating so slowly . . . a beat at a time . . .

He closed his eyes and concentrated on his breathing, drawing air slowly into his lungs. It was as though the air was thick . . .

He let Tahion's hands settle against his cheeks, holding his head firmly. They were so still, those hands! So immobile!

He concentrated on breathing. He drew breath in and in and in, until it seemed that his lungs should be filled to bursting—but they were not. He kept sucking air painfully into his aching chest. It did not seem to want to expand fully. At last he felt he had enough, and began to breathe out—

And out and out. He could not seem to get his chest empty . . .

Deep, slow, wordless thoughts boomed in the deeps of his mind. Yet it was a familiar touch. Now he felt Tahion's heart tolling, far, far more slowly than his own.

He breathed, slowly, fighting each breath . . .

His mind seemed to split, and now with one mind he felt his heart and breathing slow—but with the other he felt his breath rasping rapidly in and out of his lungs, and his heart battering . . .

He had a sudden vision of himself as Tahion had seen him, hurtling through the door, and then hopping about twittering like a bird, his every small movement blurred, jerky . . .

He had been aware of deep, slow voices chanting in the background: now, through the new part of his mind, he heard them as ordinary voices speaking clear words . . .

". . . only outside for a moment!"

"It is one of the worst spells the elves can put on a man!" That was Arthfayel's voice. "It must have seemed like hours to him, out there. And there are tales of men who have aged and died in a few days."

Istvan concentrated now on slowing that rapid-breathing part of his mind. Gradually, the tightness in his chest eased. He felt his heartbeat slow toward normal. He opened his eyes, looked into Tahion's, nodded. Istvan realized, suddenly, that he was drenched, sodden.

"I—think I'm all right now," said Istvan, hearing his words with Tahion's ears as well as his own. Tahion sighed and dropped his hands away from Istvan's face. Istvan felt weak and sick. "They have Carroll," he said. "He went with them, to their feast."

"I'm afraid they have Garahis, Dair, Karik and Peridir as well," said Tahion. "Just after you and Carroll went out, they all wandered over to see. I was busy, but I looked up and they were gone. Then you came crashing back in. Did you see them at all?"

"I saw Garahis. He looked—excited."

"I'll have to go after them," Tahion said, and started for the door. Aurothror's deep voice stopped him.

"Not that way!" the Dwarf-King said. "Take the tunnel! That way at least you will get as far as the tower without their spell trapping you!"

"And do not go alone!" Arthfayel called after him. But Tahion was already striding into the white flame pulsing from the jagged hole in the floor. Istvan, soaked through, shivered. His teeth chattered, his hair and beard dripped.

He headed for his blankets and his pack.

"Calmar!" Arthfayel called fretfully. "You should not let him go alone! Go with him!! Help him!"

"And let this man freeze to death, I suppose?" Calmar's voice answered, and then, closer to Istvan: "Here, let me help you."

"I will help," came a deep dwarf-voice, and Aurothror himself was at Istvan's side. Istvan's mail hung heavily as he bent to let it fall over his head. Friendly hands lifted its skirts, and its weight jerked on his shoulders as it fell down his arms to the floor.

He dumped the dry clothes out of his pack, too exhausted to sort through them. He stripped clammy cloth from his body: other hands helped him, he scarcely noted whose . . .

"Someone help me up!" He heard Arthfáyel's voice raging. "Where is my staff?"

But then another voice rose: a dwarf's voice roaring from under the floor, shouting for the king.

Istvan turned. Out of the flame that leaped through the cleft, a dwarf sprang. Aurothror strode to meet him.

"Goblins gather in the lower caves!" the dwarf cried, dropping to one knee. "There is a werewolf there, too, I think. They hammer at the doors of the West Branch, and we can hear them drilling in the stone near the Tilted Seam."

"What a time for the elves to be playing tricks!" the Dwarf-King snarled. He turned back to the men. "I must go, and gather my warriors." He rushed down the stairs and all the dwarves followed. They could hear his voice ringing in the chamber below.

Calmar suddenly left Istvan's side and dashed to the cleft in the floor, and crouched over it, his flesh glowing with the flame glaring up through him, head down as though listening.

"What now?" Arthfáyel grumbled, but Calmar was already coming back, and helping Istvan into his best doublet.

It was warm and dry, but Istvan was still shivering. There was a fireplace somewhere, he remembered, and if he had to hunt for wood, the effort would warm him up. He must keep moving . . .

Then, out of the cold fire rising from below, other figures appeared, and Carroll Mac Lir staggered out of brightness, his head lolling like a drunkard's, his eyes open, unseeing. He staggered a step and stopped, rapt eyes fixed on emptiness before him.

Karik reeled from the flame behind him, and stood staring at nothing. He had pulled his broken arm out of its sling: it dangled as his side as though unhurt. Behind them Tahion glowed, light pulsing through his flesh, as he stepped wearily out of the fire of the Stone.

Ingulf came up out of his blankets, despite the pain of his burns, and rushed to Carroll's side.

"Carroll!" he exclaimed. "What is it? What is on you?"

Carroll did not answer, but only stared.

"He is deep-wound in their webs," said Tahion, wearily. "They both are. I could not reach either of them. Nor did the Stone's fire have any effect. I think time is moving faster for them, now, as it slowed for Istvan. And there are still three more I must find!" He shook his head wearily.

Ingulf cursed, angrily and at great length. He slapped Carroll's face hard enough that the head rocked; but Carroll's idiot grin was unmoved.

"He feels no pain," snarled Ingulf, his scared face twisted with passion. "The evil creatures! Ah, Carroll, Carroll, such foolish pride was on you! And now you are trapped." He wilted, his hand straying involuntarily to the seared skin of his neck, and Istvan caught him as he swayed.

"There are still three that I must get, somehow, away from the elves!" Tahion shook his head wearily. "I could not find Ethellin, or any of the Sea-Elves. I do not know if the Hasturs are still atop the tower. I thought of going up to see—"

"You should have!" snapped Arthfayel. Tahion shook his head.

"If it were not for Anthir's accursed Stone, I would gladly have run to the Hasturs, and let them find the men! Do you not see, Arthfayel? This close to the Stone, their Powers are less than my own! The Stone blinds them. I do not know what to do."

"Let me see what I can do with Car—with these two, and do you go and find the others," said Calmar. "Perhaps I can use the Stone's power."

"I tried that already," Tahion said. "It did no good. A lesser illusion will be stripped away, but they are both deep-sunk in strong enchantments. But see what you can do." He turned away, dispirited.

"Wait, Tahion!" cried Arthfayel. "Let me come with you!" But Tahion had already stepped back into the light of the Stone, his bones showing dark in his glowing flesh. "Calmar, you know well you should be with him! DiVega, help me up!"

Istvan had led Ingulf, unresisting, back to his blankets. The madman's teeth gripped his lower lip, but a whine escaped them at times. Istvan helped him down.

"DiVega!" Arthfayel demanded. "Calmar! One of you help me! Someone must go to the Hasturs! What is wrong with you, Calmar? I do not understand you at all!"

A strange, sad expression crossed Calmar's face as he stood, hand pressed against Carroll's forehead. "You never did understand me very well, Arthfayel," he said, with a sorrowful frown. "And it never was any good arguing with you. You were always far too certain that your own opinion was the only one."

Istvan saw pain in Arthfayel's eyes at that. He helped the wizard up. The cast on the wizard's leg thumped on the floor.

"Give me my staff," he said, weakly. When the wood was in his hand, he straightened painfully. "Calmar," he said, "forgive me—"

"Ah, be off with you!" The anger in Calmar's voice was startling. "Forgiveness is it? Forgiveness between old friends! Be off with you, womanish loon! I'll not forgive you! No, not I! You fool! Forgive you! Aye, I'll forgive you, and do you then forgive me—when—and—be off with you! Do what you feel you must do! Leave me to—to what I must do." He turned back to Carroll, and taking him by the hand, led him into the flame and down the stair, while Arthfayel stared after him.

The wizard hobbled toward the stair, staff and cast thumping alternately on the stonework. Istvan caught up with him and took his arm.

Karik still stood staring into space where he had been left. Ingulf sat on his blanket, rocking back and forth, weeping from the pain of his slowly healing burns.

The light of the Stone flared around them blindingly as they went down the stair. Istvan felt it pulsing through him, maddening, painful. Dimly, through the blinding light, they could see Calmar leading Carroll down the stair ahead. Calmar did not seem troubled by Stone, Istvan thought, feeling Arthfayel cringe next to him.

Anarod, too, had seemed unaffected by the Stone . . .

They turned off the stair, into the corridor: far in the distance, Tahion was dwindling ahead. Arthfayel's staff and his cast rang on rock loudly as he hobbled after Tahion down the crystal corridor. The pulsing light cast shadows, flickering ahead of them, darkening and fading with the pulse of the Stone.

Now music sounded far ahead, faint at first, then gradually swelling. Its rhythm fought with the Stone's rhythms, plucking at their minds and their muscles, caressing insistently.

Arthfayel's breath rasped. Istvan's bruised shoulder ached, and the pinprick in his thumb throbbed. His feet hurt, and the joints of his knees.

Yet the music pulled at his nerves, made him want to dance.

Now there was another light ahead of them, and Istvan was not sure whether to be relieved or frightened. The new light was far more pleasant and friendly than the flare of the Stone, yet he knew the danger in that pleasure.

He heard the rhythmic beating of Arthfayel's staff and cast changing. He had noticed before that they had been keeping time with the throb of the Stone, but now he heard them shifting, changing to the beat of the dancing music ahead . . .

"Careful!" he said, squeezing the wizard's arm. "Don't let them get you!" The wizard drew a deep breath, held it.

"Ah! A Scynyorean you are, indeed!" he said. "And a good thing, too! I will need your strength."

"My strength was not enough before!" said Istvan, grimly.

They came up into a bewildering swirling of lights and music and beauty. Istvan tried to fix his mind on the hateful throbbing behind them—tried to find real things in the room he had spend days in . . .

He knew the walls were plain crystal rock, and not overgrown with vines and strange flowers. He knew that the stars that swirled and danced around him were illusion, and the sudden, wild changes in colour and form . . .

He knew this, and yet he smelled the flowers, and the sudden wind that sprang up smelling of pines and blowing through open skies upon a hilltop near the sea: and the blood in his veins began to leap and dance with the music, even as he fought to keep his legs still . . .

Arthfayel struck his staff on the floor: light flashed like lightning around them, and sharp pain snapped through Istvan's flesh. The music faltered for a second, then went on. But Istvan could see now the glittering white crystal of the walls.

Dancers reeled wildly all about them. Arthfayel began to force his way through them, Istvan holding onto his arm, moving with him, no longer supporting him. Elves swerved and darted around them without missing a beat of the dance, whirling like leaves eddying in the wind.

There was no sign of Tahion, or any of the missing men. Arthfayel clumped across the dance floor toward the stairs.

It was hard to fight the rhythms of the music: they changed and shifted maddeningly while Arthfayel made his slow way across the floor. Now bagpipes and oboes played together, in slow and stately chorus; now drums burst suddenly into a frantic rapid patter, while the fingers of the pipers wove a wild dance; now all these stilled, and the tune, without pause, flew to the fleet fingers of a harper, blurring upon the strings. Now and again a lightning-fast hand would flash to the pegs: a tuning key would swirl as the harper retuned even while he played, and the music shifted again . . .

Now pipes joined the harp, and the voices soared as all the elves sang . . .

They reached the stairs, and climbed, Istvan holding tight to Arthfayel's arm as the wizard heaved himself up clumsily, cast thumping on the stairs.

On the next floor they found Tahion, dancing with Garahis.

The Cairanorean had let the sling slip from his injured arm, and was tossing it about carelessly, all pain lost to him in the wild joy of dancing.

Arthfayel stomped angrily toward them, but the dancers whirled away. Arthfayel stood, baffled.

"Can you catch them when they come round again?" he asked.

"I—I think so," said Istvan, wondering if, when he let go the wizard's arm, he also would be caught up in the dance, swept helpless before the music.

The music shifted, and he felt his body's rhythms shift in answer. This was harder than any battle with a sword. Yet many of the rhythms were simple enough—many of them reminded him of children's games and the songs sung with them, this one for instance . . .

The rhythm shifted, but he clung to the thought: fought to keep the simple rhyme in mind, use its rhythm to down the new rhythm that plucked at him . . .

> *"Hoppity-Skippity over the sea!*
> *What have you brought back to me?"*

Tahion and Garahis came whirling around in the dance, and Istvan sprang, bawling out the words to hold the rhythm, clapping his hands as he lunged . . .

> *"Hoppity-Skippity onto the quay!*
> *Gold and jewels so bright to see!"*

At the last second they veered from his hands, but with a perfect swordsman's balance he twisted, and with a perfect swordsman's judgement of distance sprang directly into their new path. Both crashed into him, and he threw his arms around them both, shouting against the music's rhythm—

> *"Hoppity-Skippity home from the war!*
> *What have you brought to my door?"*

Arthfayel's staff crashed on the floor.

Lightning flashed around them, hair crackled and every muscle twitched with sharp pain.

The music stopped. Garahis cried out, clutching his shoulder. The elves drew back, staring

"Up the stairs!" Arthfayel shouted, limping toward them, pushing them ahead of him. "We must ask aid of the Hasturs!"

"We do not even know that the Hasturs are still there!" groaned Tahion, groggily.

"We did not see Komanthodel leave!" said Istvan. "If he has not left, the Hasturs are still here!"

Behind them, music began again. Istvan led the way as they scrambled up the right-hand stair. After a moment he had to stop and wait for his companions. Arthfayel's pounding staff and cast faltered. Tahion dropped back to help; Garahis staggered with the pain of his arm.

Swift, darting music followed them like angry bees with honey dripping from their stings. It plucked softly at their minds, insistently at nerves, twitched muscles as it tried to make their bodies dance.

Garahis ceased to claw his shoulder and swung about on the step. Istvan sprang, and catching his arm, dragged him quickly up the stairs. Garahis did not resist. He seemed to have no will, like Karik and Carroll.

The irregular thumping of Arthfayel's staff upon the steps helped fight the rapid, fluttering rhythm that followed them.

The wizard's face was tight with pain. Still he staggered on up the endless stair, leaning heavily on Tahion.

The music slowed.

Its calling changed, though still its sweetness summoned them. Istvan climbed on, feeling the sweet notes calling him back.

Up and up, and yet the calling music never seemed to fade, but stayed in their ears. Their breath grew short. Exhaustion closed their ribs on their lungs. The stair went on, up and up, around and around . . .

A blue robe flashed into being on the step above, as Kandol Hastur-Lord appeared from the air.

The hunting music haunting them sank and faded into the depths of the tower beneath their feet.

"You are safe now." Kandol laid his hand upon the face of Garahis. "Wake now, good knight, be free from dream!" Garahis started, and stared at him as though seeing him for the first time. He clutched at his shoulder: Kandol set his hand upon it, and then helped him to put it into its sling. "There. The healing is upon it; that is true healing and no illusion, and the pain should stop soon."

"Well done, Tahion! Well done, Arthfayel! I fear I can do nothing for your companions until they are brought here to me, for if I descend more than ten steps from this place my powers will desert me, and I will myself most likely be caught in Artholon's spells. But I have called to Ethellin the Wise, and though he cannot restrain Artholon, he will at least be able to find your friends and bring them here. I feel—"

His voice fell suddenly silent, and he stood still as stone. Then, after a moment, he went on. "I feel him coming now, with Dorialith; but that is a very strange thing, for they are both so deep in the aura of the Stone that it should blind me to them. Something very strange has happened. We must wait."

And they waited, the Hastur-Lord standing on the steps above them, cloaked in a silence they did not dare to break, looking down into the invisible aura that blocked his senses, until the two Sea-Elves came leaping up the stairs, long, fine beards flowing with a wild beauty of their own that still had something in it of the mane of a wild horse running . . .

"The Stone!" cried Ethellin. "It's been stolen! It is moving! Can you not feel it?"

"It is going away," said Kandol, "down into the earth. What has happened?"

"By Nuadan, I know not!" cried Ethellin. "Mortals! Can you tell us what is happening?"

"Goblins have attacked the lower levels of the dwarf city," said Istvan. "They must have broken through."

"Listen!" Ethellin exclaimed. "I think one is coming now who can tell us. Listen!"

Istvan listened, but all he could hear was the faint music.

Then, under it, he heard something else, a shrill voice that shrieked and screamed and raged.

"Let go of me, you evil creatures! Mad things! Evil animals! Let me go! Let me pass! Take your fingers from my mind! Let me go! Stop trapping me in your evil worlds! Leave me alone! Let go of me! Evil monsters, evil . . ."

"Ingulf!" Istvan exclaimed.

"But his burns!" gasped Garahis.

"Why are you doing this to me?" Ingulf shrieked. *"This cannot be happening! This makes no sense! Leave me be, you evil murdering creatures! Let me go!"*

"The pain of his burns disturbs the joy of the feast," Dorialith smiled. "I do believe Ardcrillon is angry!"

"And Artholon, too!" said Ethellin. "And the spell he sets on Ingulf now is no mere innocent mischief!"

Kandol Hastur had his eyes closed.

"I see him now," he said. "Yes, Artholon weaves nightmares . . ." And suddenly his eyes flashed open. Even Istvan felt the sudden use of power.

"Perhaps Artholon will learn, now." Kandol's voice was very soft. Dorialith's laughter was a wild screech.

"I would think he would!"

Then, running up the stairs, weaving, staggering, catching himself with his hands on the steps while the dressings tore off his burns, came the bony, scarecrow figure of Ingulf. He looked up, saw them, and screamed.

"There you are! Why have you done this to us? Why did you leave us alone with that evil one? Carroll walks like a doll under his will, killing the guards—and he has taken the Stone!"

"Who—what are you telling us?" exclaimed Tahion. "Who has taken the Stone?"

"That black-headed, evil-hearted sorcerer friend of yours!

He has Carroll under a spell, and made him kill the guards while he stole it!'"

"You—you cannot mean—*Calmar?*" Arthfayel's voice was almost as shrill as Ingulf's own, but muted with disbelief.

"Aye, that was the name, Calmar it was!"

"Who—?" The Hastur-Lord's voice was startled. "Calmar Mac Tahal, of the Ua Eamon?"

"Indeed," said Arthfayel. "He was one of the wizards you summoned here, was he not?"

The Hastur-Lord shook his head. "We never summoned him," he said grimly. "Calmar Mac Tahal is traitor, *morijtar*, outlaw, these many years! He studied the forbidden magics, and was driven mad by them. He fled into Sarlow, and it is believed he now has a high place on the Council of Sorcerers."

"It cannot be true!" Arthfayel swayed. "He studied at Elthar with me!"

"And with me," said Tahion.

"Tell us what happened," said Istvan.

"He took Carroll down into the place of Lights and Shadows," said Ingulf. "The rest of you all left. I did not trust him—I never trusted him—and when I could, I followed.

"From the stair I saw them, standing in the Stone's shadow. At first I thought Carroll was better, for the evil animal spoke to him, and Carroll answered. The two seemed to be talking normally, and then, when I crept closer, I heard the evil murderer saying: 'Do you not see those goblins there?' And Carroll said he did. 'Out with your sword then!' And Carroll—" The madman stopped, shaking his head.

"There were only two dwarves left on guard, the others had all gone away. Carroll sprang at them shouting, and they barely had time to turn before both their heads were off! I shouted at him: 'Carroll, you loon!' I shouted, 'What do you think you're doing?' And Carroll started to turn, and the evil one laughed, and said: 'Look, Carroll, another goblin!' And Carroll turned and looked at me, and I knew well enough it was not me he saw! And me without my sword, naked except for bandages! So I ran, but before I ran I saw him take the Stone—"

"It is lost, then!" said Ethellin, a sob in his voice.

"We are all lost," Kandol said. "He will take the Stone back to Sarlow, and use it to make himself undisputed master of the Council. Then—" he looked at the elves somberly, "then he will use it on us."

"I cannot believe it!" said Arthfayel.

"So I ran to find you down the tunnel," Ingulf said, "and the elves attacked me, and they tried to draw me into their dances and trap me again; then, when I fought them and struck them, they came after me as hounds and horses, they chased me as stags and cats—"

Istvan turned to Kandol Hastur.

"You can feel this thing as it moves." His voice was firm. "Let us follow it then, and catch him before he reaches Sarlow—before he reaches the soldiers, who must be waiting for him somewhere near the fort."

"Follow—?" Kandol looked at him. "I can feel the edge of the field moving, but as for finding him in the heart of it—I could not guide you close enough . . . and if I could, there would be another danger. For if the holder of the Anthir-Stone ordered me to destroy you, Istvan DiVega, there is no doubt that I would obey."

"I can feel it moving," said Tahion. "And I can feel it well enough to follow."

"Then let us go!" Istvan said.

"*Does no one listen when I speak?*" cried Ingulf. "*Is it a ghost I am?*"

CHAPTER TWENTY-ONE

He Who Dares

For hours they followed dwarf-tunnels deeper and deeper into
lonely, deserted corridors, lit only by their swords. They had
long ago left the section of the city which the dwarves had
troubled to defend.

Deeper and deeper into the rock of the hill the way took
them, down long, echoing stairways. Tahion could sense in
the walls the ghostly radiance left by the passing of the Stone.
Several times they came to branching corridors where both
passages had been so marked, showing plainly that Calmar
was as lost in this great maze as they were. Twice they had to
try to guess which way Calmar had gone, and which was the
false start he had abandoned: once they had guessed wrong,
and spent nearly an hour backtracking to pick up the trail
again.

But the rest of the time they did not have to guess, for
Tahion could feel the Stone throbbing plainly ahead of him.

It was only this that allowed them to gain on the thief at all,
for both Istvan and Tahion were tired from their struggle with
the elves, while Calmar was still rested. At first they had
hurried, trying to catch up, but soon settled into a steady,
even pace, which they knew they could keep up for days if

need be: trained warriors both, they knew that this race would
not be won by speed.

More and more often they came across traces of the goblins: broken goblin weapons, and the scattered bones of dwarves
or men, marked by fangs.

The only dwarves they had seen had been the two dead
guards in the Chamber of the Stone. They had paused there
just long enough for Istvan to run into the old fort and snatch
up his shield. Karik had still stood there, staring blankly into
the darkness, but there had been no sign of Carroll. Most
likely he was still with Calmar.

More stairs led downward. Tahion suspected that they were
now deeper than the base of the hill itself.

Soon he was sure of it. At the foot of the steps, the light of
their swords rippled on water: the passage was flooded, almost ankle-deep. A sudden breeze hit their faces: air from
outside.

They splashed along the passage, and the water rose. At
intervals, they heard the mutter and whistle of wind through
the labyrinth, and now and again ominous splashes echoed in
the distance.

Beyond the light of their swords was utter blackness. Tahion
could feel the throbbing of the Stone of Anthir; now he
sensed, faintly, something else.

As they waded past the mouth of an intersecting passage,
the sense became suddenly very strong, and he whirled,
pointing his sword up the corridor, staring into its darkness.
Istvan whirled also, but he asked no question.

For a moment, Tahion wondered if his nerves were suffering under the long strain, but then they heard faint splashing
sounds, and suddenly fiery eyes blazed in blackness.

For a moment the eyes stared at them, another pair appeared beside the first—then, suddenly, in a wild chorus of
shrieks and squeals, the eyes vanished. Loud splashing receded into the distance.

"Goblins!" Istvan said.

"There are bands of them roaming these tunnels," said
Tahion, wondering if Calmar had met them; and, if he had,
what had happened to Carroll.

They went on, and after a time the faint trace of Anthir's
Stone turned up another corridor, that rose off to the right,
and the wind still blew fresh in their faces.

The water receded as they climbed, although the floor was still wet. The passage ran straight as an arrow, and dim in the distance before them was a faint glimmer of light. Tahion felt the aching pulse of the Stone grow stronger.

The wind was wet. Ahead of them, the roof of the tunnel vanished and they saw a narrow strip of naked sky, with torn and broken clouds, and faint, misty beams of moonlight.

After a few moments they were standing under that sky, with the wet wind tugging their hair, looking up at gaps in the tattered clouds, where moons and stars flashed. The rain had stopped.

Soon after, they were able to turn and look back at the shattered cliff looming over them: they were at the bottom of the great trench gouged out by the *Tromdoel*.

They went on down the roofless corridor. Even had they been able to climb the sheer sides, Tahion could feel the ghost of the Stone in the walls, and the Stone itself ahead.

Soon, in the distance they saw a tiny, pulsing star. Now they increased their pace, not yet running, but jogging steadily. Now was the time to gain. The light grew, but they could still see nothing else.

Still it grew, and now they increased their pace a little more.

The light winked out. For a moment more they ran on slick wet rock, then slowed, and began a steady plod, breathing in great gulps of the cold air.

Overhead, clouds parted, and a great river of clear sky opened between them. Two wandering moons poured light down, and near them, Aldebaran and the Hyades.

And on the wings of that light, the silver swallows came riding, shaped from starlight, whirling around the heads of the mortals as they walked.

"*Well run, heroes!*" the silent, sweet voices trilled. "*The Hasturs have sent us to guide you, but you have already seen that your quarry is straight before you.*"

"What?" Istvan exclaimed. "When the light vanished, I thought they had turned off into some side passage."

"*No,*" the swallows sang, "*the Stone only turned, so that its shadow is toward you, and hides the shimmer where its beam hits cliff.*"

"Then, let us run," Istvan said, sheathing his sword. Tahion sheathed the Sword of Kings, and the two, somewhat rested now, increased their pace again, gradually. Now, with their guides, there was no fear of their losing the trail, or running into a trap.

"Tell us," asked Istvan, "do not *you* have the power to take the Stone from Calmar?"

"We know little of this Stone," the swallows answered, whirling around the heads of the running men. *"We have not seen it before. It was always underground, where the starlight cannot pass. Tonight, when the clouds parted, we saw the two men with the light in the cleft, and we went to see. But he who bore the Stone tuned its shadow toward us, and we could not penetrate that darkness. It is stronger than we."*

"Two men," said Istvan to Tahion. "So, Carroll is still with him!"

"Let us hope so." Tahion remembered the gnawed human bones in the caves.

And yet—this was Calmar, who had drunk with him and sat up arguing out long nights . . .

But he remembered now—what had it been? Fifteen years? Twenty? Somewhere in between—he remembered the copies of *The Book of Anthir, The Secret Rites of the Losvik, The Book of Hidden Things,* and others, that circulated surreptitiously among the students at Elthar. He remembered the long argument in which he had maintained that the books were merely clever frauds, and Calmar had admitted that yes, certainly some of them were, but not all: some had in truth been written in Sarlow and smuggled out in the hopes of corrupting wizards to the darkness . . .

And yet he had read those books, too, and so had Arthfayel, and indeed most other Adepts of Elthar, so that was no answer. And there was a handful of Adepts—never many—who tried, with the grudging permission of the Hasturs, to do as Anthir had done and turn the Dark One's magic against them. It was often said that such men were invariably corrupted by the powers they invoked, but that was not true. Many were, but not all . . .

Yet it had been Calmar, he recalled, who had been afraid of the books . . .

His feet ached as they jarred on stone: his lungs flared and clenched. When he next saw Calmar, he would have to kill him. The walls of the dwarf tunnel raced by in a dim blur: stars shone between great banks of cloud . . .

Searing white light glared in his eyes—

—Flared and vanished as he and Istvan reeled to a stop, hands at their sword hilts . . .

"They have turned!" The swallows wheeled and hovered: high their joined voices trilled. *"They follow a passage that will take them to the edge of the hollow track of the* Tromdoel, *then back underground, under the forest floor."*

"Are men waiting for them in the forest?" Istvan asked, quickly. One of the swallows swooped away in a sudden blur.

"We see no camp of men," the silent voice trilled, *"but Komanthodel lies there, among charred and broken trees in a great, burnt area, and he seems to be waiting."*

As the swallow spoke, the two men had come up from their crouching readiness, hands dropping from hilts. Now they looked at each other with wild surmise, and with one mind they drew a deep breath and began to run again.

"Show us the corner where they turned!" Tahion gasped. A swallow blurred away, and was suddenly a tiny dot of silver wheeling far ahead.

They ran toward the dot; feet and heart and lungs all pumping, in a complex, rhythmic harmony. The bird that still circled their heads suddenly darted ahead, and at the same moment the dot ahead flew to meet them and wheeled behind them as the other turned ahead, and flashed back—and the swallows made them the centre of a slowly shrinking ellipse that showed how far that they had yet to go . . .

By the time that turning point was reached, hearts and lungs laboured, and their aching feet slowed to a walk as they hit the corner, breathing hard. Wheeling in the air, the swallows waited where two roofless corridors crossed.

"Which way?" Tahion whispered, knowing well that what the swallows heard was the mental effort of speech, rather than the sound.

"This way!" sweet voices trilled in his mind. He turned left, following.

"How far ahead?" asked Istvan.

"Closer now. Perhaps half the distance you have had to run. But the roof of shadow has gone under the earth now, and we cannot follow. But the Hasturs have asked us to tell you that the dwarves have driven off the goblins, and that Aurothror follows you with four hundred warriors."

"We should mark our trail when we get back underground," Istvan said. Tahion nodded.

"The Hasturs will be able to direct the dwarves as far as this turn. But your world is rolling out from under us: it grows harder and harder to focus our starlight within this cleft. Now we must leave you—dawn is almost here. Luck be with you!"

And the glowing, ghostly swallows dissolved into starlight.

The two men strode on, their lungs drawing deep breaths. After a while the sky began to lighten above them, and moon and star to fade.

Ahead of them now, they saw the dark cliff-face slowly colour as dim light grew. Deep gullies had washed down its side during the rain: blighted trees had fallen; great mounds of brown earth were piled on the pale bedrock.

Now fallen debris began to clutter the tunnel's floor: first a long scattering of the metallic grey dust that Tahion and Istvan both knew from long years along the Dark Border; next, a mingling of mud and broken tree roots, masses of dead, soggy, yellowed leaves; finally, masses of splintered branches that had been laboriously pushed aside by the two men whose footprints were clear in the dim, dawn light.

From the trees above came the call of a bird.

Looking up, Tahion could see the washed-out gullies where the rains had cut away the edge of the bite the *Tromdoel* had scooped out of the earth as it moved, toppling the blighted trees, dead and dying alike, into the depths below. For nearly ten feet above their heads an avalanche of wood and mud tried to hide the smoothly cut stone where the *Tromdoel* had eaten down into bedrock, and the tunnel was roofed with fallen trees. Beyond the scattered branches, a door opened into the darkness under the earth.

The light of their swords flashed down the dark corridor: Calmar and Carroll had broken through a wall of mud that had dripped down between the broken trunks. Their muddy footprints stretched down the passage as far as the light of the steel could reach.

Istvan stepped back: Tahion saw him raise his point and carve a circle in the wood of one of the fallen trees that roofed the tunnel. A single slash across the circle made a rude Sign of Hastur.

Tahion knelt to study the tracks. They were still fresh, the mud still wet. Not far ahead now . . .

From the trees at the cliff's edge came more birdcalls. Tahion stretched out his senses. The birds frightened away by the war and then by the *Tromdoel* were beginning to filter back. Through the eyes of one on the cliff, he saw the twin suns clear the horizon. He found another a little further back in the forest, digging in bark for bugs; moved to a third, joying in the working of wings . . .

The bird flew into throbbing emptiness and fire and pain. The pain of the Stone . . .

He reeled a second, then caught himself. Yes. The Stone was climbing, rising toward the trees above . . .

"What is it?" Istvan's voice asked.

"They're up there," Tahion said, breathless. "Let's move!"

They followed the footprints by swordlight, running with their steel near the floor to light their way. Suddenly, the footprints turned and climbed a flight of steps. Istvan scratched a sign in stone, and they followed, leaving their own muddy prints as an additional guide.

In the middle of the stair, the prints ended by a rough hole in the wall. Piled stone lay on the floor beside it. Istvan stooped, thrusting in with his flaming sword. By its light they saw mud scraped off on a jagged, crudely hewn floor. This was no dwarf tunnel.

"Goblin-work," said Istvan. Tahion nodded.

"I wonder if this is how he came in?" Tahion whispered.

"I don't think so." Istvan shook his head. "I think he came in through the Gates of the Singing Fountain, just before the fighting started. I *thought* I saw a man in the shadows there. I think he joined us as we were coming back."

"Came up with you and just set to treating the wounded," said Tahion. "No one was going to challenge him then. And that *was* when I first saw him."

They had to crouch double in the tunnel, their swords stretched out before them to light their way.

They came up through the floor of a dwarf tunnel: its smooth floor covered with goblin tracks, printed in fine black dust. Only a few flecks of drying mud marked the trail of the men, but a door blocked the corridor in one direction, and in the other Tahion could feel the burning of the Stone.

They ran down the long, straight passage. Suddenly, Tahion felt a change in the throbbing of the Stone: he stopped dead. Istvan ran a pace or so and came back.

"What is it?" the Seynyorean asked. Tahion shook his head, unable to say. He reached out with his nerves. Above him, could sense nothing but the Stone.

Then, groping, he began to sense living things past its edge—trees, beetles, butterflies. Then, at last, through the eyes of a bird crouching among leaves, he glimpsed distant shapes of men, and something that flashed oddly in the sunlight.

"They're—outside. The sunlight—is doing—something—something strange—to the Stone . . ."

The wildly shifting rhythm began to settle. Through the bird's eyes he saw that the flashing had disappeared, and guessed that Calmar had covered the Stone.

They went on. Great stone gates stood closed, and beside them chips of stone were piled up beside another shapeless hole. The floor was black with goblin footmarks. The smell of coal was thick.

They wriggled through the hole into a great chamber filled with tools, and carts loaded with coal, and a bewildering maze of tunnel mouths. Coal dust was everywhere. Tahion sensed the throbbing of the Stone, and running to one tunnel soon found a hole in its wall, and piles of brown earth. This tunnel was even smaller than the others, and slanted up so steeply that they had to crawl on hands and knees, bracing themselves by pressing the rough roof with their backs.

It leveled out, and they were at the centre of a maze of intersecting tunnels, floored with bedrock, but walled and roofed with earth.

The tunnel that Calmar had taken was the largest tunnel: they were able to run with their shoulders crouched and their chins tucked down against their chests. The smell of decay was everywhere, and a litter of bones. Tahion could feel nothing but the throbbing of the Stone. The tunnel twisted and turned through the earth, but its trend was upward.

Tahion felt the Stone moving away, and breathed more easily. He reached out, feeling for something beyond the blankness in which the Stone moved.

He found a bird ahead of the blankness, and it was fleeing

from something it had flown near in the forest beyond: something huge and hot that lay shrouded in smoke . . .

And now he heard the moans of burnt, dying trees . . .

"Hurry!" Tahion said. "The dragon is close!"

Sunlight glared down through a hole, and they climbed out into a clean wind under green leaves that glowed with sunlight. Tahion could feel birds and trees and living things nearby, but ahead a moving blankness cut them all away. He turned toward it, and saw a small figure moving between the trees.

A second followed. And now he felt the throbbing ache of the Stone . . .

He pointed. Istvan saw, and they both charged through the underbrush. The forest vanished from Tahion's mind, and the throbbing of the Stone pounded in his skull. He saw the gold of Carroll's hair in sunlight, and a black thatch ahead.

They burst through the bushes: Carroll and Calmar whirled. Carroll's sword splashed sunlight. Calmar's voice was too low to hear.

Carroll's eyes stared through them above his shield, and they knew that he did not see them, but some enemy of his own imagining.

"You go after Calmar." Istvan's voice was firm. "I'll keep Carroll busy." He slid his shield from his back as he spoke, and slid his arm through the straps.

"I can't—" Tahion hesitated. Together, they might have some chance, perhaps, of overpowering Carroll without killing him. But Carroll and Istvan were closely matched. And whoever won would leave the world poorer . . .

"I have a shield. You don't" The Seynyorean's voice was implacable. "You're a wizard. I'm not. You said the dragon was close! Go on, circle us while we fight, and go after the Stone! Hurry!"

Carroll sprang, sword whistling. It crashed on Istvan's steel shield. Carroll's own sounded in almost the same instant, the two sounds blending in one roar like echoes of thunder.

Tahion slipped into the bushes, barely rustling a leaf, and moved after the retreating black-haired figure, stalking his youthful friend as though he were some dangerous beast.

And how much, he wondered of his reluctance, had been concern for Carroll, or Istvan, and how much a wish not to face Calmar's treachery?

• • •

The thunder of their shields blended in a long roll: swords wheeled and dipped.

As a boy, Istvan had sought out famous swordsmen and killed them, hunting for glory.

He had had enough glory now. More than he wanted. And he had come to like Carroll.

Now he was going to have to kill him . . .

For what? So the bards could have another stupid, lying song about Istvan the Archer?

No. It was for the sunlight on the trees, for the birds that had fled from the first crash of shields; for the trees themselves, and for Sylvia's eyes; for her and their children and grandchildren, that he must fight and win. They had said that the Stone of Anthir, in the wrong hands, would destroy the Universe just as certainly as the Dark Things would . . .

The life of every living thing rode on his point. Pride and anger alike stilled. A strange serenity crept over him. His arm was the arm of the Universe, his point a part of the order of nature.

Suddenly, Carroll was giving way before him. Need-fire sparked between the blades.

Tahion rushed between small trees, drawing swiftly nearer to the man he stalked, hearing behind the echoing clamour of sword on shield.

A scent touched his nostrils, like iron in a forge, or like a stone in a campfire. He began to run, feet still hunting for the dry stick or leaf that would give him away, and alert the man he followed, striving to find the moss or grass that would make no noise . . .

Suddenly, the leaves ahead turned a sickly ashen-grey, outlined in a glare of red light.

In front of Calmar a red tower rose, and the dragon's head at the top as huge as a house. Red light streamed from its eyes.

Tahion's hands leaped to cover his ears as a roar like a thousand waterfalls drowned all sound.

But beyond that roaring was another roar: a mental thunder so loud that it drowned the crackling throb of the Stone of Anthir . . .

"STOP!" the silent voice crashed. *"Give me the Stone!"*

• • •

Istvan's hand soared on a wing of steel—shields crashed again and again. His blade shaved a long splinter of bronze and wood from the shield over which Carroll's crazed eyes glittered. Carroll's blade wheeled, sharp edge swooping for Istvan's life.

Istvan saw Carroll's arm stretching out—too far out.

His sword, still drawing back, was not yet in a position to cut, but he let his hand roll and his point met falling flesh.

Red blood flooded down the steel: the fist flew open and the sword hilt fell, the bright blade glancing from his shield edge.

Then the battered bronze fell away from the face of Carroll Mac Lir, and the eyes that blinked into Istvan's were sane.

"What? How did—" Carroll's jaw dropped. "You? How did you—why—?"

But then a roar filled ears and head; leaves all around turned black. Red light glared.

There almost seemed to be words in that roaring that shook through his bones. He staggered, seeing Carroll's whole face the colour of his gaping lips, as the red glare turned it sunset rose.

"What is the Stone to you, worm?" Calmar shouted as the deep roar died. "Another jewel for your hoard?"

"*No!*" Mental waves crashed like surf. "*With the Stone I shall rule both the Dark Masters and the Lords of Flame! None will stand against me: this world, so rich in food, will be mine, and my children's! Give it to me!*"

"*I* am Master of the Stone!" Calmar shouted, his voice tiny in the silence that followed the dragon's roar. He pulled the stone from his robe. Sunlight flared from its bright facets, and shadows formed in the air between them; once again, Tahion felt the Stone's rhythm shift. And then that strange rhythm throbbed with Calmar's voice.

"*Out of my way, worm!*" The words throbbed with pain. "*Beware, Komanthodel! I rule both Light and Darkness! Out of my way, or be destroyed!*" Power surged from the stone: black rays and light poured over red-hot stony flesh.

"*Fool!*" the dragon's mind thundered. "*That bauble has no power over me!*"

Great jaws opened like a cavern: the little hollow where the sorcerer stood was suddenly filled with flame.

Istvan ran. Behind him, Carroll threw down his shield and picked up his sword with his left hand. Sudden flame leaped at the top of the little rise. He cringed back from heat and smoke as wet trees burst loudly in the flames.

"Istvan!" A voice shouted his name. He saw Tahion crouched near the top of the rise. He ran toward him, dimly aware of Carroll at his heels.

Then he saw what was beyond the rise, and stopped, awe filling him.

Fire poured from jaws that could swallow an army: jaws that could hold a house . . .

What am I doing here? he wondered. Armies he knew, marching men, battles with the sword—but not this—not this! Until now he had only seen Komanthodel at a distance, high and far off. But that gave no idea of the ancient dragon's sheer size and power.

The vast jaws closed. Fire and smoke leaped from burnt bush and tree, and from the smouldering bones that had been Calmar Mac Tahal.

Trees crashed and fell as the dragon moved. Shoulders like red-hot mountains heaved into view, and great wings that, even folded, were vaster than the sails of a ship.

A massive foreleg came over the top of the rise where the dragon had hidden: the tower of the neck dipped.

The three watchers fell to the ground, flattening themselves in the bushes as the dragon's head stooped above the burnt bones. The foreleg reached out. Istvan stared. There was a hand at the end of the foreleg—its heel as broad as a man's body—that narrowed into long, tapering fingers.

It scattered the bones, and then a long thumb and forefinger lifted from the ashes something covered in shadow that was pierced by rays of white light: the Stone of Anthir . . .

In his mind, Istvan heard Aldamir's voice: *Komanthodel . . . of the futures I have seen, that I dread the most . . .*

The great head lifted. The monster wings unfurled, stretched out above the trees. The three men pressed themselves down into the brush.

The vast wings fell, and wind shook trees, and fanned the

flames in the hollow. The head rose up and wings drew back . . .

"We'd better run," said Tahion. "He's going to fly right over us."

Wind stripped leaves from the bushes around them, as the great wings rose and fell, lashing: it buffeted Carroll and Tahion as they tried to rise.

But Istvan crouched, mind frozen with eyes, watching the long, delicate thumb that held the Stone pressed against the fingers. He slid his arm from the heavy shield and let it lie.

The dragon drew back on its haunches and launched itself into the air. The wind of wings hurled Tahion and Carroll staggering as the dragon's massive neck passed over them, barely clearing the rim of the hill. Istvan's bent leg tensed as the vast chest passed over, long-fingered forepaws pressed tight to the muscles that moved the vast wings, with pulsing light and darkness shining between fingers as thick as a man's wrist.

The great wings rose. Tensed legs straightened. Istvan leaped into the air, stretching his body, slashing high above his head.

Heat from the dragon's flesh crisped his hair. His Hastur-blade sliced stony flesh and clove through the long, slender thumb as if it were a tree-branch.

The finger fell free, molten blood jetting and the Stone of Anthir tumbled, pulsing white and black, to the earth.

Deafening sound ached through his bones as he dived down the hillside after the falling block of flame and shadow.

Cartwheeling blackness and starlight bounced on the ground. His skilled hand swooped, and he felt the metal block in his palm. His hand vanished.

Trees splintered, and above him the glowing stone of the dragon's body fell like a burning roof. Lunging legs launched Istvan like a spear over bushes already kindling in the heat, and then a wind struck him out of the air, to crash among unburnt bushes, still holding tight to both sword and Stone. His palms burned.

Rolling up, he saw the arch of the wing like a great tent above him, and the burning wall of the dragon's breast a mere yard away. Tahion and Carroll crouched nearby. Istvan leaped to his feet.

"Run!" he shouted, but he could not hear his own voice,

only the dragon's roar throbbing through bone. He waved his sword, pointing, then sheathed it.

Tahion stared at him. The hollow above them thrashed, and trees splintered under the flailing wing. Flame spread.

They rose, ran through wind and fire, dodging from under the lashing wing, then stumbling aside as the massive breast smashed down trees. The huge neck passed over as the long body coiled and writhed, and the dragon's bellowing rang in their bones as they ran.

Now the forest was aflame around them, and the knotting coils and battering tail scythed down acres of trees.

Tahion's lips writhed as though he were shouting. He pointed, and Istvan ran in that direction.

A mound of heaped mud marked a hole in the forest floor. Tahion gestured and raced toward it, Istvan and Carroll at his heels.

Trees shattered nearby. The great red wall of the dragon's side swept toward them, snapping trees like twigs. Tahion dived down the hole; Istvan followed.

The glaring of the stone showed patches of dirt walls that bristled with broken tree roots. A smell of carrion was everywhere. They could not stand: half crouching, half crawling, they scrambled and slid down the sloping tunnel. The scent of hot stone burned away the carrion smell.

Earth shook around them: the tunnel collapsed, and they found themselves sliding in masses of earth. The tunnel grew hotter.

"*Die!*" a voice roared in Istvan's mind. "*Thief! Breathe earth! Breathe death!*"

The floor was gone: they fell, dirt pouring over them in a mound. Istvan pulled himself free—the carrion scent was overwhelming here. Pushing himself up and raising the Stone as a lantern, Istvan saw why. They had fallen into a larger burrow: it was filled with gnawed bones and half-eaten corpses of goblins, men, and beasts of many kinds.

Eyes flared, and out of a corner, with bits of rotting flesh dripping from their mouths, goblins shambled. They haltered, blinking, in the Stone's glare.

"*Back!*" Istvan shouted—but he could not hear the words: the dragon's roar had burst his eardrums.

But the goblins heard—and the goblins obeyed: they whirled and fled in panic, and vanished down a burrow's gaping maw.

"I hear you, thief!" the dragon's soundless voice boomed in his mind. *"I will find you, thief! I will kill you, thief! The Stone will not save you!"*

Tahion crawled out of the piled dirt and helped pull Carroll free. More earth fell from the low dome of the roof. Tahion tugged at Istvan's arm, and gestured toward another tunnel-mouth opposite that one down which the goblins had fled.

They followed it down into rock: a rough-hewn stone passage, too small for them. Istvan ran bent double, with rough rock scraping the cloth on his back as he ran with his head by his knees.

It twisted and wound, and suddenly they had crawled through a jagged hole into another tunnel that was planed smooth and squared, and ran straight through the stone. Dwarf-work, without a doubt.

Here again were goblin footprints stamped black with smeared coal dust, and as they went on, there was coal dust everywhere, close-spaced bootprints in coal dust. Soon they found carts of coal.

Tahion turned, waving at Istvan to stop. Istvan saw his mouth move, but there was no sound.

Deaf, he thought. He had always been proud of his hearing, proud of his ability to fight in the dark. Gone now. Deaf. He did not like the word . . .

Tahion's palm pushed at his chest. Well, he had stopped! Tahion pointed at him, and pushed the palm at him again, then, pointing a finger at his own breast, waved his hand in the air. Istvan stared at him, blinking, confused.

Tahion bit his lip. Then, teeth flashing, he brought his hands together, raised two fingers on one hand, and one finger on the other. He turned the single finger at his own chest, and then pointed at Istvan and Carroll with the other two.

The fist with single finger lifted moved away in a long curve, then returned to join the other hand, but with all five fingers spread.

"You want us to stay here while you go for help?" Istvan asked in the voice he could not hear. Tahion nodded.

Istvan did not see any sense in that, but he was too tired to argue. So he held the Stone and watched as Tahion walked away, the Sword of Kings glowing dim-red in his hands.

His ear ached in silence—horrid silence. How long, he

never knew. The silent throbbing of the Stone was constant pain.

At last, distant lights appeared in the depths of mines, and he watched suspiciously until he saw Tahion tall among a host of dwarves. Then he set the Stone down on the floor and cradled his aching head in his hands.

When he looked up again, King Aurothror and Prince Tyrin were standing before him, flanked by many others. As he sat up, they bowed.

He took the throbbing Stone from the ground between his feet and laid it in the king's hands: Aurothror bowed again as he took it, then, turning with a bow equally ceremonious, offered it to Prince Tyrin.

The Prince accepted it, then turned and trotted away, flame and shadow pulsing in his hands. Thubar and Ogar and a handful of others fell in behind him. Other dwarves crowded closer to Istvan. Cruadorn bent over him, frowning with concern, and beside his was a face that Istvan remembered as one of the healers.

He allowed the dwarf to turn his head and examine his ears. Exhaustion weighted all his limbs now; he wanted nothing so much as sleep.

Yet when he looked up and saw Tahion going off in the midst of a group of dwarves, talking busily with the king, he sprang to his feet. But the dwarf healer patted his arm gently, and motioned for him to sit down again.

Kandol and Aldamir Hastur appeared out of the air. Istvan leaped to his feet to greet them, but the Hastur-Lord waved him back, and then gently touched the tips of his fingers to Istvan's ears: his face grew sad and grave.

After a moment, a strange tickling began, deep inside the ear—almost like the tickle that led to a sneeze. Istvan struggled to hold his head still. Strange humming sounds began to reach him, and then a sharp pain that made him gasp.

The gasp was like painful thunder; he started to cry out, but Kandol Hastur-Lord laid a finger against his lips, and then, looking deep into Istvan's eyes, the Hastur-Lord spoke silently in the depths of his mind . . .

"*Make no sound! We can heal this fragile membrane, but while we weave the blood vessels together, it can easily burst again. Control yourself.*"

Pain does not hurt, Istvan reminded himself. *Fear of pain hurts!*

The sharp pains continued, but he drew his mind away from them, forcing himself to breathe slowly. He saw Aldamir standing behind Kandol, rapt with concentration, and realised that both of the Hasturs had focused their power on the healing of his ears.

At last Kandol straightened, and turning to the dwarf healer who stood nearby, made a gesture with his hand. The dwarf handed him something that might have been a lump of wax, and a moment later Istvan felt warm, soft stuff being pushed carefully into each ear.

"Now sleep, more than anything else, is what you need for healing," the Hastur-Lord whispered in his mind. *"Lean now on me."* Kandol helped him up, and threw one arm around his shoulder. Aldamir came to his other side, and the two supported his weight.

And suddenly, without transition, they were standing in the bright sunlight atop the tallest of the towers of Rath Tintallain.

"Look!" Kandol pointed out across the treetops. Far out across the forest was a great black scar, and thick smoke rose from burning wet wood.

Flame flashed within the smoke, and out of it swooped the vast wings of Komanthodel, whirling like a sword stroke as the great beast circled. Fire burst from his jaws into the smoke below.

Istvan leaned on the shoulder of the Lord of the World, watching as Komanthodel vented his anger on the land.

"He came once against the tower after you wounded him, but he could not shake my spells," Kandol murmured in Istvan's mind. *"And this time the elves were ready for him. With our help, Falmoran and Ethellin made arrows forged of ice and tipped with frozen air, so spelled that they did not melt until they met the dragon's blood. Arduiad Mac Artholon wounded the dragon sorely, until he flew out of arrowshot again and tried once more to dig you out of the tunnels. I do not think Komanthodel will trouble Rath Tintallain again. Ah! Look!"*

The dragon's circle grew, and he soared high above the smoke, spiraling outward, ever wider, widdershins around

Rath Tintallain, then away over the forest toward the waste-lands out of which he and his brood had come.

Istvan drooped in the Hastur's arms, exhaustion and pain dragging him down, closing his eyes. He was only dimly aware of the sunlight cut away, of the soft bed where the Hastur laid him down.

When he woke at last to white crystal walls, soft sheets and perfect silence, he blinked sticky eyelids for a moment, then closed them again. Another odd dream.

After lying with eyes closed for a while, he felt something soft and warm ooze out of his ear: that startled him awake, and he snapped his eyes open to meet the eyes of Kandol Hastur.

"That was the wax melting," said Kandol pleasantly. "Can you hear me speak? Let me listen with your ears just a moment: do not think that I wish to intrude." He had begun to speak in a very soft voice. Now he allowed his voice to rise as he spoke, and kept a smile on his face, although his eyes had become remote . . .

"If you are as well as you should be, come with us down the stairs. Prince Tyrin has offered to take the Anthir-Stone to his own realm and guard it there, and we have decided to accept his offer. Over the past two days, while you have slept here, he has worked with the most skilled smiths of Rath Tintallain, and with Falmoran the Sea-Elf, to create a series of chests of differing metals and minerals, which, we hope, will hold back the power of the Stone, and enable him to transport it south without throwing all the forest into confusion—or allowing the sorcerers of Sarlow to follow its course.

"Since, as Aldamir foretold, it was only your valour that stopped Komanthodel from bearing off the Stone, it is fitting that you should be there when Tyrin places the Stone in his containers. He is about to begin. Will you come?"

"Why—I—indeed, yes—but—surely—any of the men here—" Istvan blushed. Kandol laughed.

"Any could have, but only a DiVega would have! But it is just such inspired madness that has marked the DiVega name for centuries."

Istvan shook his head in confusion. An hour later, dressed in clean clothes but with muscles still aching from running bent double through goblin tunnels, Istvan walked with Kandol down the long stair.

With each floor, the Hastur-Lord's face became more drawn and haggard, his breath harsher. It was the pain of the Stone, Istvan knew, but when, toward the bottom of the stair, he muttered some half-worded expression of concern, Kandol chuckled.

"I don't practise walking enough," he said lightly. "This is the furthest these feet have traveled for centuries."

By the gates to the tunnel leading down into the dwarf-city, elves were crowded, and Aldamir Hastur. By now, Kandol was walking deeply bent, holding to the wall. His head was pulled down toward his chest, his shoulders slumped forward, and he leaned on Istvan's proffered arm, gasping with each step. Ethellin and Artholon turned as they reached the bottom of the stairs, and, rushing up, laid their hands on Kandol's shoulders. Istvan heard—but not with his ears—a climbing, beautiful chorus of soaring voices. Rain-washed air filled his lungs . . .

Kandol's voice moaned a deep sigh of relief. He straightened, head lifting, shoulders thrown back. Wrinkles faded from his face, and Istvan realised that the immortal had been aging with each step.

"Thank you," he said, his voice still weak. "Has he begun yet?"

"He should be putting it in the first chest now . . ."

"He has," said Aldamir. "Can you not feel it?"

The two elves straightened as though listening, and suddenly winced with pain . . .

"Well, indeed!" said Ethellin, "it does seem—easier."

"And that is only the first of them," Aldamir said.

"DiVega," said the Hastur-Lord, "I fear you must go on by yourself from here. We will follow when we can."

He walked quickly through the door into the corridor, and saw ahead the throbbing flame rising from the Stone. As he walked, he felt his pulse change to match the rhythmic alternation of the darkness with the light.

When he reached the tunnel's end and started down the long, steep stair, he saw that the room was crowded with men as well as dwarves.

For a moment it all seemed the same: the Anthir-Stone throbbed on its perch in the middle of the room. But as he neared the floor, something jarred. At first, he was not sure what it was.

Then he saw that the flaming thing seemed to sit in the air above its place.

He stared, then saw around it a faint, misty outline, a blurred square shape, and remembered how his hand had vanished when he had lifted the Stone.

Prince Tyrin stood beside it: he reached out, and placed his hands, not on the Stone itself, but on the misty shape around it. The flesh vanished from his hands, and with bared fingerbones he lifted the flaring, throbbing thing and set into a small chest that another dwarf—Thubar, Istvan saw—held out to him.

The chest seemed made of some dark metal—lead perhaps, or iron—but before Istvan could decide what it was, it seemed suddenly transformed into a thing of mist and glass. Prince Tyrin closed its lid, and fastened it down while the pillar of fire stabbed through. Then he set on the pillar a box that seemed carved of a single turquoise, that turned to a blue-green mist as the previous box was set into it. But this time the mist did not fade, and when Prince Tyrin fastened down the lid, the beam that stabbed through was dimmed.

Istvan heard a faint sound far down the tunnel, like raised voices rejoicing.

At the foot of the stairs, Cormac lay on a pallet with his cast stretched out and his harp beside him. Fithil sat on a bottom step, a crutch resting over his shoulder like a spear. Near him, Alphth sat elf-fashion, arms around his knees. The others stood, even Arlifayel, leaning on his staff, and, wonder of wonders, Hrivown—his chest and shoulder still swathed in bandages, his arm in a sling, but awake and unmistakably alive.

Now Tyrin took the glowing mist in his hand and lifted it. His hand did not vanish but only glowed, with black bone etched within translucent flesh. He set a box of onyx on the pillar, and lowered the turquoise cloud into it. The onyx did not fade, but turned translucent, glowing like a lamp.

Reaching the foot of the stair, Istvan stood a moment behind Alphth, then careful worked his way past him and around Fithil, while Prince Tyrin set the onyx chest into a chest of jade.

The chamber was filled with bright green light from the glowing stone box.

Thubar handed the prince a chest of gold, just big enough for a man to hold in one hand. It glowed like golden glass when the bright ray shone through it, but between each golden ray was a band of dirty-yellow fog.

Now another, larger chest of onyx was brought, that had to be carried in two hands. When the golden chest was set into it, the onyx glowed, but remained onyx.

"Well, now!" Carroll Mac Lir boomed at Istvan's side. "Here is the man himself! Can you hear now?"

"I can hear," said Istvan. "I hope you will forgive me for your wound?"

"Forgive you?" Carroll laughed. "No, indeed! I'll thank you instead! Thank you for releasing me from that sorcerer's spell." He bowed, while Istvan stood in tongue-tied embarrassment. "As for the wound," Carroll went on, "look!" He held out his arm and showed a scar that might have been months old, instead of days. "The Hasturs! If the wound is fresh enough, they can simply close it."

Meanwhile, more boxes were put into boxes, each one larger. The light in the room slowly dimmed, and now strange things began to happen. An iron chest glowed red-hot on two sides, while ice crystals formed on two others; the lid Tyrin slammed down glowed red. Two strong dwarves sweated to break the icy base from where it had frozen to the floor.

A copper chest spat sparks. The hair and beards of the dwarves who struggled with it leaped and jerked on their heads. Prince Tyrin was hurled violently across the room when he slammed down the lid.

Tahion and Arthfayel went to help. Dwarves came carrying a large wooden chest: as they walked, a strange, sloshing sound came from it. Others came pushing a wheelbarrow.

A ball of fire crackled from the chest and rolled across the room with a sharp smell that made Istvan think of the dragon. Dwarves scattered. Odd crackling sounds made Istvan look down at his scabbard. Beads of light gathered at his sword's pommel, then vanished, as though sucked into the hilt.

Eerie fires flickered up near the roof. All around the room, bits of metal acquired sudden halos, including the forge tongs that were now brought forward.

Tahion, Arthfayel, Prince Tyrin and other dwarves were

gathered close together, conferring; twice they scattered as balls of blue flame came rolling. Now another tall figure strode noiselessly past Istvan, and he saw in wonder that it was Falmoran the Sea-Elf.

Looking up the stairs, Istvan saw elves crowded together at the top, staring about them like curious children. Tuarim Mac Elathan was halfway down the stair, and Arduiad the Archer right behind. A little above he saw Brithlain, with a baby in her arms.

Falmoran joined Arthfayel and Tyrin, and they talked in low voices for a time. Then Tyrin and Falmoran took shovels and began scooping pale, soupy stuff into the oak chest. Cruadorn and Ogar Hammerhand put on heavy leather gauntlets, and then took up the long tongs.

Arthfayel stretched out his staff toward the copper chest.

Blinding lightning flared: thunder muttered and echoed in the cavern, drowning startled cries.

The thunder ended with a loud splash and Istvan, blinking, saw Ogar and Cruadorn stagger back, hair and beards floating weirdly out from their heads; Arthfayel's as well. The copper chest was sinking into the wet stuff in the wooden chest; steam rose about it.

Prince Tyrin and Falmoran began to ply their shovels. Wet mud slapped on the copper lid.

The copper chest sank. The prince leaped forward, slapped down the wooden lid: it echoed through a cavern that was suddenly dark. Then the wood began to glow.

"Quickly!" Tyrin bellowed. Dwarves rushed up with a large chest, that sounded to Istvan's renewed ears like metal as they set it down.

Yet, even as they hurried, Istvan was aware that a tension had vanished from the air, that he could breathe more easily. He heard laughter from the elves on the stair above; now they came rushing down into the chamber that they had never before been able to enter.

The darkness was lit by a dim flame from Arthfayel's staff, and now first Tahion and then others among the heroes drew their swords. Faint silvery gleams rippled on the metal chest the dwarves had brought.

But for the first time since their arrival at Rath Tintallain, the heroes' blades were dim: no evil kindled the need-fire in their steel to full flame.

The dwarves set the oaken chest gently into the new chest. The light of the swords dimmed even more. They could barely see the shadowy figures that brought in another chest, which sounded like stone or glass to Istvan's ears. The light of Arthfayel's staff made tiny night-blue gleams on the black surface.

They lifted in the metal box, and the room was suddenly filled with deep blue light.

Another metal chest was carried into the dim light. By the way the dwarves carried it, it was of considerable weight— lead, Istvan guessed. The blue light vanished inside, and they were left in total darkness. There was not even the faintest gleam of light left on Istvan's Hastur-blade, and he heard the sounds of other swords sliding, lightless, back into their scabbards.

"Could someone make a light?" roared Prince Tyrin.

A silver sun appeared, up near the vaulted roof.

"Here is light!" the voice of Kandol Hastur-Lord echoed from the dome above, and looking up, they saw him standing under the bright glow, uplifted arms bathed in silver flame.

Before Istvan or the others had time to gasp, the Hastur had stepped out into empty air, and holding the great ball of silver flame high above his head, settled as gently as a floating feather to the ground beside the metal chest.

"You can see that my Power is with me again," he said.

For a moment, all stared in silence. Then a roar of rejoicing rose, in mingled voices of elves, dwarves, and men.

Elves danced and spun around the chest. Prince Tyrin capered wildly on his hands, somersaulting with a deep-voiced bark of exaltation. Deep dwarf-voices thundered with joy.

Then, as the noise sank, Prince Tyrin called some short command, and four strong dwarves staggered in under the weight of a great chest of dark-grey stone, bound with bands of steel.

It was set on the floor, and the massive lid thrown back. Its walls were near a foot thick. Cruadron and Ogar joined Tyrin and those who had carried the chest to lift the dull lead box into the other.

The stone lid closed, and Prince Tyrin began to lock the steel bands. Ardcrillon came up beside him and tentatively reached a finger toward the chest, flinched back, then, hesitantly, touched it.

"This is wonderful!" he exclaimed. "If you had only thought of it before! All these centuries we have suffered from the pain of the Stone while we guarded it!"

"Well, soon it will be gone," Tyrin said, "and you need never think of it again."

"How will you carry such a thing?" asked Ardcrillon.

"I left orders at Dunsloc," said the prince, "for a host to gather and follow me here. In three days, they will come with wagons and beasts to draw them."

Ardcrillon stroked the chest, his face somber. Tarithwen stepped to his side, and laid a long white hand calmly upon the grey-black rock of the chest.

"Now that the Stone no longer tortures us," she said, "why should we put you to all that trouble? We have guarded the Stone for centuries. We could guard it for centuries more. . ."

"You could not," said Aldamir Hastur. "The sorcerers of Sarlow know where it is. They will mount attack after attack upon you. We barely kept the Stone from them this time. Next time they will gather greater force. And they will continue to raid Rath Tintallain until they have taken it

"Before, we dared not move the Stone for fear that dragons or sorcerers would feel it moving, and attack while it was exposed. And there was no point in moving it when anyone could recognize its power and trace it. But now that its power is sealed away, the Stone can be hidden."

"But *we* cannot," exclaimed Tarithwen. "So now they will attack us and the Stone will not even be here!"

"But *we* will be here," said Kandol. "And able to use our power."

"They will attack again, surely," said Aldamir. "This near the boundaries of Sarlow, nothing is safe from attack. But if the attacks cost them dear, and they will—and if some say the Stone is here, but others say it is there—if some say it is in Elthar and others say it is in Rath Ionuval, and still others that it is in Brannark—or Monahyard, or Mondrath, or Rathallain, or a hundred other places—then they will not know where to turn. And that will be your business, harper, to make songs of this that will be sung up and down the world—where Sarlow's spies will hear them—that will make it clear that the Stone is gone . . . none knows where. And this will baffle their councils, and confuse them, so they know not where to attack.''

''Well, it is a relief to me that I will be allowed to make songs,'' said Cormac, looking up from his bed. ''For a time I feared that, since the Anthir-Stone was so secret, you were going to ask me to vow silence before I left, so that I would have witnessed these great deeds without being free to sing of them. As it is, I can even ask for your help. Which, indeed, I should now! Tell me, Lord Hastur—or if you know, Arthfayel, or Tahion, or any of you—why is it that Calmar could pick up and carry off the Stone, when not even a Hastur can walk into a room with it without losing his power?''

''Because Calmar was a mortal,'' said Kandol.

''But there is more to it than that,'' said Tahion thoughtfully. ''Both Arthfayel and I are mortal—but we could not use our powers in the Stone's presence. Yet Calmar was able to control Carroll all the time that he was carrying the Stone.''

''Perhaps he was used to dealing with the dark and the light powers at the same time,'' Dair Mac Eykin suggested. ''I have been told that this was the method of Anthir—to use the power of Light to threaten the Darkness, and force it to your will.''

''He had read the *Book of Anthir,* I know,'' said Tahion. Istvan hesitated to speak. He could see the bitter pain this discussion caused Arthfayel, and hesitated to cause him more pain. Yet—

''Well, there is another thing that puzzles me,'' said Istvan. ''I am no wizard or seer. I have neither sensitivity nor power. Yet when I touched the Stone of Anthir—and I held it in my hands twice—I could feel that fire and darkness throbbing through my veins and my flesh, filling me—'' he hesitated, ''filling me with joy and loathing at the same time, and—it made me—sick.

''Yet the Stone did not seem to bother Anarod at all.''

He shook his head and looked around, trying to collect his thoughts. Startled, he saw that Tarithwen now held the baby in her arms. He did not know how it had gotten there; she had not had it a moment before . . .

''You remember how he stood—flipping the thing in his palm. It made me feel as though my stomach were turning with it, yet he seemed to feel it was all some joke.

''Just before he died—just before the battle started, Anarod said something to me which I did not understand. He said that—his cousin was saying that since the Stone bothered us so much, but did not bother them, that they would be helping by taking the Stone. Could Calmar have been the cousin he was talking about?''

''Yes, indeed!'' said Arthfayel. ''They were both of Clan Eamon, now that I think of it—yes, I think their grandfathers were brothers, or some such, so that they were close kin, but—'' he stroked his beard thoughtfully, ''but now that brings to mind a curious old tale about the Ua Eamon—not that I ever believed it! It always seemed to me like the kind of lie that enemies make up about you.

''Yet this much is certainly true: only a few centuries back the men and women of Clan Eamon were noted for their ugliness. I have found jokes about them in old manuscripts, and I have seen portraits of some of Anarod's ancestors . . .'' He rubbed his forehead, then went on. ''Now, the tale that—that was given to explain this, held that a woman of Clan Eamon—or, in some versions, the mother of Eamon, founder of the Clan—was captured and raped by goblins—or perhaps by the half-human Irioch who scout for Sarlow now—but that she was rescued before they could eat her. And that she bore a baby afterward—'' He paused.

''Now, the story goes on to tell that, though she was a mortal woman, she had, as so many do, a touch of elf-blood in her. Some even spoke of Hastur-blood.

''I do not know. Through the—they said it was the conflict between the darkness in the blood of the goblins, and light in the blood of the elves, that made the folk of Clan Eamon— different. Misshapen. Ugly.

''Now, over the centuries, the folk of Clan Eamon slowly came to look like other men, and the tale became merely a—'' He shrugged.

''Yet, if there were any truth to the tale—why then, both Calmar and Anarod would have inside their bodies the same conflict that exists in the Stone.''

''And the tale is true,'' said Kandol Hastur. ''I had not known that any of the Ua Eamon yet lived in the world—for in my youth, the greater number of them died in childhood because of that conflict in their very cells. It was thought that the line would die out. That was longer ago than you imagined, you see. Before the Fall of Nardis. And I have not thought of the tale for—not mere centuries, but thousands of years.''

Just then Prince Tyrin came bustling up, and strode in among them.

"Well, friends!" He smiled genially at them. "In three days the Stone goes south, and I will be honoured if any of you mortal heroes choose to accompany me. You have won the right, and we will still need to be prepared to guard the Stone, if there is some flaw in my plans."

"It is on my way home," said Garahis, "and so I will be coming with you."

"It will be upon our way home, too," said Fithil. "I think Ingulf, Karik, and I will travel with you."

"What is this?" asked Carroll, with a curious look at Ingulf.

"Fithil thinks I should go home," Ingulf said.

"Ingulf has not seen his father or his mother for near five years now," said Fithil. "It is time he went home. So we islanders may as well travel together. Is it not so, Karik?"

"Indeed!" The dark-skinned man sat up straighter.

"It matters little where I go," said Ingulf, in a dull, lifeless tone. "My life is destroyed and wasted. Airellen has been taken away from me, and I am lost and alone and hopeless in this evil—'' He stopped in the middle of a word. His face paled, but the dull pain left his eyes, and a pleading flamed there. *"Airellen?"*

He leaped to his feet and Istvan turned to follow the islander's wild eyes.

Falmoran came toward them, and at his side a slender woman in a long brown gown, and long brown-black hair flowed below her waist, and her eyes were wide and glowing. Istvan blinked. Was it Brithlain who stood there, or another who looked much like her?

"Airellen!" Ingulf ran to her, and threw himself sobbing at her feet.

And the air rippled like water in a stream in front of her face, and it was Brithlain's face.

"Look again, Ingulf," she said gently, touching his burnt face with her hand. "Look closely now! Am I Airellen?" He looked up, and shook his head, tears flowing down his cheeks. She nodded. "You see. I am not Airellen, though some have told me that I look like her. I cannot tell, for we have never

met. She has never been here. *Look* at me, Ingulf!'' His face
had dropped, wet with tears; she took it between her two
hands and lifted it until his wet mortal eyes stared into her
wide, ageless eyes.

"She has never been here,'' she said again. "It was I that
you attacked the dragon to save. Your eyes were tricked by
the light. Yet I thank you, as truly as Airellen would thank
you, had she been here. For it was a great deed, a hero's
deed, as I shall tell her if ever we meet.'' Ingulf sobbed, and
his head jerked in her hands. "I hope you're not sorry you
saved me from the dragon!'' she laughed, teasing.

"Oh, no! No!'' Ingulf shook his head violently. "No!
But—but you will not see her. I will not see her. Airellen's
father will take her away, to the Land of the Ever-Living, and
I will not see her ever again!'' His voice cracked on a sob.
Then the rich music of Falmoran's voice flowed over all.

"Say not so, Ingulf,'' said Falmoran, "for I would not
wish to leave you without hope. You are a mortal man, and
you will die very soon, as my people count these things. In
that brief time, I cannot know what pain you may cause my
daughter—or she you. Yet I cannot tell what joy you may
bring each other.'' He paused. "A few days ago, I had my
mind set that I would take Airellen away from this world —by
force, if need be. But that was hasty thought. But do not let
me give you false hope, either. I still shall seek my daughter,
and if she wishes to leave this world, my ship will take her
back to the Living Land.''

Ingulf's teeth were in his lip. He muttered some words that
none could understand.

"I do not think she will wish to go, Ingulf.'' Brithlain's
gentle fingers stroked the tears from his eyes. "I would not.''
Then Ingulf buried his face in the lap of her long brown
gown, and wept like a child.

Istvan looked away, suddenly embarrassed.

He turned to walk away, and found Prince Tyrin looking
up at him.

"And will you be joining us on our trip south?'' said the
dwarf, leaning back, beard jutting, to look into Istvan's eyes.
"It is to you, more than anyone, that we owe the safety of the
Stone, and I would be most honoured to take you to my
people.''

Istvan smiled down at him.

"I thank you for the honour you wish to do me," he said, choosing his words carefully, "but it is a long journey back to my home. I must first go to Elthar, and then wait for a ship. I would start today, if I could."

"I could take you home, DiVega," said the voice of Kandol Hastur from behind him. "I can simply take you back to the Tower of Carcosa with me, or I can put you on the ship with your men—three days out from Heyleu now, if the wind doesn't change—or I can leave you on your own doorstep, if you do not mind startling your neighbours. We can go now, if you like."

"Let me get my bag!" said Istvan, but immediately another voice broke in—

"No, *wait*, my Lord Hastur!" It was Arthfayel, and his crutch slipped and he fell to the floor. He pushed himself up. "I beg you, do not leave yet! I need your help and your justice!"

Kandol stared down at him, then helped him carefully to his feet.

"What help do you need from me?" he asked gently.

"When Anarod lay dying in my arms," said Arthfayel, "he asked—he made me promise—to care for his child. I think—I think he had remembered, despite Brithlain's spells, that Eilith was dead—it is hard to say—but he did not want the child raised by wild elves, estranged from his own kind, as if he were a Changeling, like Alphth.

"And so now it is on me to go to Tarithwen and Brithlain, and tell them that they must give me Anarod's child. That will be little to their liking, and I have sense enough to fear their anger."

Yes, Istvan thought, remembering Brithlain carrying Anarod's body to the top of Ardcrillon's tower: *I, too, would fear their anger.* "I'll get my bag!" he said to Kandol, and sprinted toward the stair.

Dwarves were lighting torches at places around the wall. The light that Kandol had brought was slowly fading. The steps were dim and gloomy. Through the jagged hole in the roof, he could see only darkness.

There was still dim light in the dwarf-fort when he climbed through the hole in the floor: but it was a twilight, and through arrow slits in the west he glimpsed a blood-bright horizon with stars pricking through above. He looked around the dusty hall, remembering how the glare of the Anthir-Stone had filled the dome with light; remembering sprouting vines, and the rainbow-winged bird . . .

He would remember Rath Tintallain well; no doubt it would haunt his dreams for years, rich in beauty.

But now he wanted to go home.

Dim though it was in the old dwarf fort, he quickly found his pack, all he owned now: his mail-shirt—which the dwarves, he found, had dried carefully, and oiled—and his other clothes, which they had cleaned and patched. That, except for a few letters and such, was all he had now: his shield was doubtless buried in the dragon-scorched soil of the forest.

And now he had no more excuse to stay away.

At the lip of the stair he heard a bell-clear voice rising, beautiful as birdsong, a sad voice he knew well: Brithlain's voice . . .

". . . and now you wish to take him from me? Is there no heart in you? To take him from my very breast, to rob him of milk, to rob me of his love? And what of him? He has already lost one mother! Now, at a stroke, you will take from him two more?"

Istvan's new ears could distinguish no words in the low mutter that answered. Ingulf's voice shouted something in anger. He went down the dim-lit stair, and heard another voice—Tarithwen's voice, richer, wilder, filled with power. . .

"*Do not dare!* Leave her be!" Again Arthfayel's words were lost. Tarithwen's voice rang up the stairs.

"And what is wrong with that, foolish man? Leave him be, it is good for him!"

The lost words of his reply crackled with anger, and Brithlain's voice soared above them as it had soared above the fire in the wood.

"And do you think yourself the only one who ever loved? Or that only mortals ever truly love? Is my love for the babe nothing? Is my milk nothing?" Istvan was halfway down the stairs now, and Arthfayel's words were still indistinct, but the elf-women's answer was a sharp bark of bitter laughter.

"Have you breasts?" cried Brithlain. "Have you milk?"

"Cruel man!" Tarithwen cried. "Do you not know what you are asking? *You* have never nursed a child!"

"True, indeed," Arthfayel's voice answered. "But is it not crueler for you to allow her to raise a child who will grow to manhood and die in what will be for her but a short time? The child is mortal, after all! And will it not be cruel to the child, also? Will he not grow like Alphth, knowing nothing of the world of men, yet not truly an elf?''

"And you an Adept of Elthar?" cried Tarithwen. "Has it been so long then, since a changeling came among you, that you do not know the original reason for changelings? Are not the greatest of your Adepts changelings?"

"No," said Arthfayel. "I know that such was true in the past, but we, and the Hasturs, have learned as we worked, and now our training methods are such that ordinary mortals may learn them—without being suckled on elf's milk, as they used to say."

"Indeed!" she cried. "And what say you to that, Kandol Shadowslayer? You have stood listening all this while, but you do not speak."

"I have been asked for justice," he said, "and if I am to take sides in your quarrel—even on such an issue—I cannot remain impartial."

"And so you will stand here silent, and judge us? Judge, then! Is my daughter to lose all that she has left of Anarod, whom she loved?"

"Grandmother," said Brithlain, "are you not the child's foster-mother also? And is not this man, by his oath to Anarod, the child's foster-father? He lives, he says, in Elthar, which he seems to think a city of men, and part of man's world! Yet it is an elf-city also, and is ruled by elves who sailed to this world with Mananan and Nuadan when the Dark Lords first returned. Why, then, should we not all live in Elthar?

"But in truth, Grandmother, this baby is not all that remains to me of Anarod. There was a piece of woman's magic that you taught me, and when I knew that Anarod was dead, but that his seed still lived in my body—''

"Brithlain!" Tarithwen whirled: a tear the unwary light showed, glittering. "But you cannot mean—not *that* spell!" Arthfayel stared.

"That spell indeed," Brithlain said calmly. "Liam shall have a sister: I am with child. But Anarod's daughter will be an elf, and not a mortal—I remembered that part of the spell, too!

"But even mortal children need mothers, Arthfayel! Or have you already chosen another mother for him?" Her eyes met his: he flinched, and looked at the floor.

"I have not," he admitted.

"And what is your judgment, Lord Hastur?" she said, turning to face the Hastur-Lord. He smiled at her.

"I think Elthar can weather your first year—wild elves have come out of the forest before, to turn the city upside down with spells." She laughed. Kandol went on. "I fear that my poor wisdom can find no more just and equal agreement. Can you, Arthfayel? Or do you have any complaint that this is unjust?"

Arthfayel looked up, stared at him a moment, then shook his head and looked down at the floor.

"Then I think I have stayed long enough," said Kandol. "Are you ready, DiVega?"

"I—almost!" he said, and stepped to the foot of the stair where the rest of the heroes were gathered.

"Tahion," he said, gripping the Forest Lord's hand. "You, I will probably meet again."

"Indeed. In a year or so, I am likely to come looking for you. The forest has been without its king too long, and so I am likely to want the service of DiVega's Company!"

"Arthfayel, Fithil, Karik, Garahis," he said, "Dair, Hrivown, Peridir, Carroll, Ingulf—" Istvan hesitated. "I do not know if I will meet any of you ever again, in life. I hope that I shall. But even if a few of us meet, it is not likely that any of us will ever fight in so fine a company as this." He leaned down to where the bard sat, tuning his harp. "And Cormac, in whatever songs you make of this, can you please find some name besides 'the Archer'? I never did like that name."

Laughter and farewells and gripping of hands all round, and kissing the hands of Tarithwen and Brithlain, somewhat to their amusement; then at last he stepped to Kandol's side.

"I am ready now," he said. "I—if I could ask a—if it is not too much trouble, if I could go to the Street of the Ancient Banners, near the crossing with the Way of Chariots—"

Kandol laughed.

"I know where you live, DiVega! Put your arms on my shoulders— no, like so, yes. . ." His own arm came around Istvan's ribs, there was a sudden dizziness, and they were standing in bright sunlight. "You are home. Fare well, Istvan DiVega."

And the Hastur-Lord was gone.

Istvan saw his own gate before him. He walked to it, pushed it open, and a few moments later a startled maid met him at the door.

"Master!" she cried, and then turning, shouted at the top of her lungs. "My Lady! He's home! The master's home!"

And then Sylvia was at the door. There was more grey in her hair than when he had left: more wrinkles in her plain, strong-boned face. But just then she was more beautiful than any of the ageless beauties and immortal queens that he had met in his travels.

And then her arms were around him, and that was enough.

Fantasy from Ace
fanciful and fantastic!

Stories

✠✠ of ✠✠

Swords and Sorcery

❧❧❧❧❧❧❧❧❧❧❧❧❧❧❧❧❧❧❧